Sergyei Mikhailovich Kravchinsky

The Career of a Nihilist

A novel

Sergyei Mikhailovich Kravchinsky

The Career of a Nihilist
A novel

ISBN/EAN: 9783337030049

Printed in Europe, USA, Canada, Australia, Japan

Cover: Foto ©Andreas Hilbeck / pixelio.de

More available books at **www.hansebooks.com**

THE CAREER
OF A NIHILIST

A NOVEL

By STEPNIAK

AUTHOR OF "UNDERGROUND RUSSIA," ETC.

SECOND EDITION

LONDON
WALTER SCOTT, 24 WARWICK LANE
NEW YORK
A. LOVELL & CO., 3 EAST 14TH STREET
1890

CONTENTS.

CONTENTS.

PART II.—UNDER FIRE.

PART III.—ALL FOR THE CAUSE.

PREFACE TO THE SECOND EDITION.

To first write on politics, and then come forward as a novelist has its inconveniences, as I had to learn at my own expense. It is like appearing in two different characters in the same play: the spectators will always have some difficulty in discarding the impression they may have received from the first whilst looking at the second.

I have nothing but thanks to offer to my English and American critics, whose reception of my novel as a novel was so cordial, whose censure was so mild, and whose praise so free and generous.

But almost all of them have persisted in viewing my novel as a sort of political pamphlet in the guise of fiction. They assumed it to be the summing up of the Nihilists' programme, both theoretical and practical, and very naturally reproached it for being exclusively negative in theory, and narrowly violent in practice.

Be it permitted to me to say a word of explanation to my future readers. If they want to know what are the Nihilists as a political party: their very modest, sensible, and practical demands, the causes which called them into existence, etc., they must seek all this elsewhere. Here they will see the Nihilists as men, and not as politicians.

Having been witness of and participator in a movement, which struck even its enemies by its spirit of boundless self-sacrifice, I wanted to show in the full light of fiction the inmost heart and soul of these humanitarian enthusiasts, with whom devotion to a cause has attained to the fervour of a religion, without being a religion.

The general interest of such a study shut out from me political aims. My sole care was to draw truthfully a certain type of modern humanity, which in our generous age is reproduced in hundreds of forms throughout the world.

If I chose the characters of my novel and laid its action among the extreme or terrorist section of Russian revolutionists, it was simply because it seemed to me better suited to my artistic purpose. Only in the whirlwind of this terrible struggle could my characters exhibit to the full what was most peculiar to them. But I was as little tempted to extol terrorism as to decry it. I only showed it, or rather let it show itself, such as it was, leaving the reader to judge it as he chooses.

It was found by most narrower than it actually was. This is partly my own fault. Working under the excusable delusion that something is known as to the general tendencies of the party which has attracted a certain amount of notice during fifteen years, I kept away from the central figures in the struggle, a picture of whose lives would be to some extent a picture of their party. They are interesting in their own way, and I hope one day to introduce some of them to my readers. But to me it was more tempting to draw the more characteristic, though less brilliant, types of the rank and file people, such as the reader will meet if he cares to follow the career of my modest hero.

I had to accept the consequences of my choice. A novelist can only tell what his characters actually do and say and feel by themselves. In dwelling upon a small retired spot of the battle-field one could not expect to show the whole battle.

But if in thus narrowing the field of my picture I have succeeded in bringing to greater prominence the human elements of Nihilist life, and making my few people more intimately known and better understood, I shall certainly not regret these unavoidable shortcomings.

PART I.

THE ENTHUSIASTS.

THE ENTHUSIASTS.

CHAPTER I.

AT LAST!

HASTILY Helen finished her frugal meal at the little Geneva *gargotte*—the favourite haunt of Russian exiles—and refused a cup of coffee. She had not denied herself this luxury since she was lucky enough to get those Russian pupils, but she was in a hurry to-day. In her pocket lay a long-expected letter from Russia. It had but now been handed to her by the old white-headed watchmaker, to whose address her foreign correspondence came. She was burning with impatience to hand over the precious missive to her friend Andrey, whom it particularly concerned, and to hear such general news as of course it contained.

Exchanging a few words with a fellow-exile, the girl went through the rows of little tables occupied by groups of men in blouses, and passed out into the street. It was only half-past seven; she was sure to find Andrey at home, he lodged close by; and in five minutes Helen was at his door, her handsome, somewhat cold, face a little flushed by her quick walk.

Andrey was alone, and at work upon a book of statistics, from which he was making extracts for his weekly article in a Russian provincial paper. He turned his head, and rose with outstretched hand to welcome his visitor.

"Here's a letter for you," said Helen, shaking hands.

"Oh," he exclaimed. "At last!"

He was a young man, of six or seven-and-twenty, with an earnest good-natured face, rather regular and firmly cut. His forehead was touched with traces of early cares, and his eyes were unusually thoughtful; but this did not impair the impression of steadiness and equanimity conveyed by his face and his strong well-shaped figure.

A slight flush rose to his brow, whilst the fingers of his thin muscular hand, with nervous haste, tore open the envelope. He unfolded a great sheet of paper, which was covered with lines wide apart, written in a minute irregular hand.

Helen, who seemed no less impatient than himself, came to his side, and laid her hand upon his shoulder, that she too might see and read.

"We had better sit down, Lena," said the young man. "you are shutting out the light with your curls."

In truth the shabby room was very scantily lighted by a single lamp, upon which was fixed a green paper shade. Only the bare boards, the legs of a few common chairs, and the lower part of a mahogany chest of drawers, the chief ornament of the place, were properly lighted up. The yellow papered walls, with a cheap lithograph of the Swiss general Dufour, a stereotype landscape, the photograph of the landlady's deceased husband, and her own school certificate framed and glazed,— all were plunged in a zone of twilight, very advantageous for them but quite unfit for reading.

Andrey brought another chair to the round dining-table, littered with books and papers, and adjusted the reflector so as to throw more light upon the corner that he used as a writing-desk. Helen sat by him, and so near, that sometimes her hair touched his. But they never heeded this in their absorption.

With a woman's quickness Helen ran over the page in a rapid glance, and was the first to offer her opinion.

"There's nothing in the letter!" she exclaimed. "Mere rubbish! We needn't waste our time in reading it."

However strange such advice might appear, it did not seem to affect Andrey, who replied quietly,—

"No, wait a bit. I recognise George's handwriting, and he generally puts in something to the purpose. It won't take long to read anyhow.

"'My dear Andrey Anempodistovitch, I hasten to inform you' . . . hm . . . hm . . . 'owing to the severe frosts' . . . hm . . . hm . . . 'sheep and the young cattle' . . . hm . . . ," murmured Andrey, skipping rapidly over the lines.

"Ah, here's something about domestic affairs. Let's see."

"'As to our domestic affairs'"—he read in the tone of a reporting clerk—"'I have to tell you . . . sister Kate married

. . . whom she met last autumn at . . . husband proved to be a man without principles or honour, who . . . and worse, . . . broken hearted. . . . I should never have thought she . . . Father is much depressed, and . . . grey hairs. Our only hope is that the all-healing balsam of time, the comforter of the afflicted. . . .' "

The pathetic passage was interrupted by a merry laugh from Helen,—or Lena, as her friend called her.

" It's easy to see," she said, " that it was written by a poet."

In no way shocked by this misplaced hilarity, Andrey went on at greater speed, muttering between his teeth the remainder of the letter.

" Yes, you were right. It was not worth reading," he said at last, showing but little sign however of his disappointment under the trying circumstances.

Presently he looked round as if searching for something.

" Here it is," he said, taking a small black phial from the mantelpiece, where it stood by a tin spirit-lamp over which he prepared his tea for breakfast.

Lena handed to him the glass brush, whilst Andrey carefully smoothed out the letter. Then dipping the brush into the bottle he passed it several times over the page before him.

The black lines, written with common ink, rapidly disappeared, as if melting in the corrosive liquid. For an instant the paper remained a blank. Then suddenly it was all movement and life. From its inmost depths, as if thrust up from below, came forth, hurrying and crowding one upon another, words, letters, phrases—here, there, everywhere ! It was a disorderly rout, as of soldiers at the call of the alarm-bugle rushing from their tents to fall into the ranks.

Then the letters stood still; the movement ceased. In some remote corner a belated word or letter still struggled to break the thin shroud under which it lay buried, slipping unobserved into its place by the side of its nimbler companions; but in the upper part of the page all was over. In place of the former mock letters, serried lines of close straight handwriting stood ready to unfold the message they had faithfully carried to the pair who now leaned over the table with flushed faces and glistening eager eyes. .

" I'll read it to you ! " exclaimed Lena. And before Andrey could say a word, or otherwise protect his property, the impatient girl snatched up the letter and began :—

"'Dear Brother,—I am charged by our friends to answer your letter, and to tell you how thoroughly we agree with you as to your return to Russia. We can assure you that the desire to see you among us has been much oftener felt than you suppose. But we always hesitated to recall you, knowing too well the dangers to which you especially will be exposed. We always postponed your recall until a moment of urgent need. That moment has now arrived. Of course you know through the papers of our recent victories. But you probably do not know how dearly they were bought. Our League has had heavy losses. Several of our best people have perished. The gendarmes believe they have crushed us altogether. Of course we shall pull through. There are more than ever ready to join us, but they have not been tried. We cannot spare your services any longer. Therefore come. We all expect you,—the old friends who have never forgotten you, and the new ones who are as anxious as ourselves to welcome you. Come as quickly as you can.'"

Lena paused. She was really glad for Andrey's sake, for they were very good friends. Raising her head, she wrapt him in a look full of sympathy.

But she could only see his close-cut black hair, stiff as a horse's mane. Andrey had drawn out his chair, and was leaning over the back of it, his chin in his hand, absorbed in contemplation of some knots in the deal floor. Whether he was shunning the glare of the lamp, or was shy of meeting her eyes, Lena did not stop to inquire. She went on with her reading.

The letter dealt with abstract matters at some length. It pointed to the considerable changes which had taken place of late in the domain of practical politics, and in the immediate objects which the party proposed to attain

"'All this,'" the writer concluded, "'will probably surprise and perhaps offend you at first, but I have no doubt that in a short time you, as a practical worker, will accept it.'"

Here Lena had to turn over the page, and was brought up short by the nonsense of the pretended letter. She had forgotten for the moment that it had to be washed away before the real one could appear. The first words she inadvertently read, affected her like the intrusion of farce into a serious drama.

She took the phial and the brush, and rapidly moistened

the remaining pages. In a few instants they underwent the same transformation. But they had a somewhat different appearance. The ordinary running hand was interrupted here and there by long passages in cipher, which evidently contained news of particular importance. The cipher was a protection if the police should conceive some special suspicion, and not satisfied with reading the letter should try chemicals to see if there were hidden contents.

The ciphering was only occasional at first, the groups of large closely-written figures rising over the even lines of the ordinary handwriting like groves and bushes upon a field of grass. But further on the clusters of ciphers became thicker, until at the middle of the third page the figures joined in a regular forest, as in tables of logarithms, without the slightest interruption of punctuation.

"Look here, Andrey, what a treat for you!" said Lena, pointing to the masses of cipher. "I am sure George put in so much of this on purpose for you!"

"A friendly service, upon my word!" rejoined the young man.

He hated the work of deciphering, and was wont to say that it was for him a sort of corporal punishment.

"Do you know," he went on, "we have at least six hours' work over this stuff?"

"Not so much as that, you lazy fellow. The two of us will get through it much quicker than that."

"But I am rather out of practice. You must write me out the key to refresh my memory."

This she did at once, and, armed each with a sheet of paper, they set themselves patiently to the task. It was by no means an easy one. George used the double cipher of the League; the original figures in the letter had to be changed by means of a key into another set of figures, and these again by the aid of a second key were finally resolved into words. This afforded an endless variety of signs for each letter of the alphabet, and made the cipher absolutely proof against discovery, even by the ablest experts of the police. But if the writing was defective it sometimes remained a mystery even to those for whom it was intended.

George, as became a poet, was by no means a model of carefulness, and at times his friends were driven to the verge of despair. Some parts of his cipher obstinately refused to yield anything but neighing, bleating, grunting, hissing syllables, from which no Christian word seemed likely to emerge. And, as if on purpose, these hitches always occurred in passages which were, or seemed to be, the most important and interesting of all. If George, who at this very moment was doing his duty in the distant capital of the Tzars, was not suddenly seized with a violent fit of hiccups, it was not because his friends failed to abuse him soundly.

Without Lena's assistance Andrey would often have come to grief. But the girl was an experienced cipher-reader, and had a knack of guessing what was amiss. When Andrey's pluck failed him, and he proposed to give up some passage as hopeless, she would take both sheets in her hand and guess by a stroke of inspiration how George must have gone wrong.

In a little more than two hours they had finished the detached pieces of cipher. These dealt with the details of Andrey's journey, giving the names and addresses of the people to whom he must apply on arriving at St Petersburg and at the Russian frontier.

Andrey carefully copied all the addresses upon a small piece of paper, which he placed in his purse, to be learned by heart before he started.

Now they had only the continuous piece to unravel. It evidently referred to a. different topic, presumably of a particularly dangerous and compromising nature, since the writer took the trouble to cipher every word.

What bloody secrets might not this forest conceal? Andrey stared at it, eager to guess. But the forest kept its secret jealously, looking provokingly mute and monotonous in its capricious variety.

After a few minutes' rest they set to work with redoubled vigour, laying bare the hidden meaning bit by bit.

Letter by letter Andrey wrote out the final results of the deciphering. When he had words enough to complete a sentence, he read it aloud to Lena. But the first words affected him so painfully, that he was unable to wait for the end of the sentence.

"Something bad has happened to Boris, I am certain!" he exclaimed. "Look here." .

Lena looked quickly at the sheet Andrey showed her and then at her own. There could be no mistake; the passage referred to Boris,—one of the ablest and most influential of

their party,—and the beginning of the sentence sounded ugly,—
more ugly than Andrey suspected, for she guessed the next two
letters that were to follow.   But she kept her own counsel, and
went on dictating.

"Five, three."

"Seven, nine;" Andrey echoed, looking at the key for the
final letter.

"Quick!" Lena exclaimed impatiently.   "Don't you see it
is an *a*."

The ill-omened *a* was put down by Andrey.

The next letter was an *r*, which was still worse.

The third, the fourth, the fifth letters were set down, and
their last doubts, if they had any, vanished.   Without another
word they went on deciphering with feverish impatience to the
end of the line, and after a few minutes' work they both saw in
black on white, "Boris has been recently arrested in Dubravnik."

They looked at each other in blank consternation.   Arrests,
like death, always appear absurd, incredible, even when they are
fully anticipated.

"In Dubravnik!   What the deuce had he to do in that
damned Dubravnik?"

"Let us go on," Lena said;   "perhaps we shall learn.
There must be some further details about his arrest."

They resumed their irritatingly slow work, unravelling in
some ten minutes, that seemed an hour, another couple of lines.
They only learned that Boris, with two other friends, had been
arrested, after a severe fight with the police.   This was little,
but it was enough to show that the case was desperate.   Whatever had been Boris's part in the struggle, he was a doomed
man.   According to a new law, all complicity in such acts was
punished with death.   And Boris was not the man to hold his
hand whilst others were fighting.

"Poor Zina!" they both sighed.

Zina was Boris's wife.

After a short pause Lena again poured forth a series of
figures, which in a few minutes yielded the name of the woman
whose lot they had been pitying.   "Zina——"

"Zina!   Is it possible?" Andrey exclaimed.

His first thought was that she also had been arrested.

But after another five minutes of painful suspense it became
clear that he was mistaken.

"Zina," the letter informed them, "has gone to Dubravnik to

survey the ground, and see what can be done towards the rescue of Boris."

"Oh, they are thinking of that! I am so glad," said Andrey. "Another reason for my hastening home."

The passage referring to Boris was followed by a list of the other victims who had recently fallen into the hands of the police. The forthcoming trials were mentioned, and the Draconian sentences foretold, according to secret information obtained from officials. The melancholy news about the friends who were in prison was briefly summarised,—all this in the calm business-like way in which reports upon the dead and wounded are drawn up after a battle.

The reverse side of the underground struggle oozed sadly out drop by drop. There was no possibility of swallowing the bitter draught at once. At the mention of some particularly sad piece of news, they could not refrain from exchanging a few words. Otherwise they went on with their work uninterruptedly, keeping their feelings to themselves.

They now got on much more rapidly than before. George's ciphering became steadier, and the unravelling went on almost without a hitch. After the dreary record of losses and sufferings, they entered upon pleasanter ground. Here George mentioned briefly, but with a faith and fervour all his own, the rapid progress of the movement in general, instancing the great fermentation of spirit which could be observed everywhere.

It was like a war-cry after a walk over a battlefield, or the look of a sunny landscape after a visit to the catacombs. The egotism of life, with its rights and its excitements, crept upon them, and they emerged from their dreary journey in much higher spirits than they could have expected.

"Yes, there will be a smash before long!" exclaimed Lena, in exultation, though she was a very orthodox "peasantist," and all the matters George alluded to were in direct opposition to the articles of her belief.

She rose to stretch her numbed limbs by walking to and fro. Presently she took the letter, carefully dried it over the lamp, and lit a match with the evident intention of setting fire to it.

"Oh, don't!" interposed Andrey, quickly.

"Why? haven't you copied the address?"

"Yes, but I want to keep the letter for a while."

"What for? that it might fall into some stranger's hands?" retorted the girl sharply.

Andrey said that these precautions were superfluous in Switzerland. But Lena was not easily persuaded; like most women engaged in conspiracies, she was a strict observer of the rules.

"But perhaps you'll accept a compromise," she said, relenting.   .

She tore off the first half of the letter containing the personal matters, and carefully erased the few pieces of cipher.

"You want to read this, don't you?" she asked.

"Never mind. I accept your bargain. I like this part certainly better, and give up my claim upon the rest," said Andrey, whilst the girl, kneeling before the fireplace, carefully burned the remainder, together with the two sheets upon which they had worked out the cipher. Her conscience at ease, she resumed her seat.

"So you are leaving us, Andrey," she said, dreamily.

There was a greater warmth than usual in the tone of her voice, and in the look of her honest bold blue eyes as she fixed them upon her companion. For those who remain, there is always something touching in the sight of a man, about to leave his place of refuge, and risk his life once more in the dominions of the Tzar.

"Will you start soon?" she asked.

"Yes," said Andrey. "The money and the passport will be here in three or four days, I hope. That is quite long enough for my preparations."

Then, after a hardly perceptible pause, he added abruptly,

"I wish I knew whether they have already found out his name."

"Whom do you mean?" inquired the girl, lifting her eyes.

"Boris. Who else?"

That great loss had not ceased gnawing at Andrey's heart all the time, notwithstanding his apparent calmness and cheerfulness.

"I do not think they could discover it so soon," Lena answered. "Boris has never been in Dubravnik before. Besides, George would have mentioned a point of such importance."

"I wish you were right," said Andrey. "The rescue would be so much easier. Anyhow I shall soon know all about it."

They talked business. The girl had evidently some

personal experience in the work of smuggling a Russian into his fatherland. She gave her friend some valuable suggestions, though he was several years her senior.

"When you are in the whirlpool, you mustn't altogether forget us here," she said, with a sigh. "You must write sometimes to me or to Vasily. I want to return also. You must manage that for me if you can."

"With pleasure. And, by-the-by, where's Vasily himself? Why haven't you brought him with you?"

"He wasn't at the café. I sent him word to come here. Probably he is out—at the opera, I think. They are playing 'Robert' to-night. Otherwise he would have been here long ago."

She put her hand into her pocket, and drew from it a large and heavy gold watch, of ancient make. It was a family possession she was very fond of, because it came to her from her father, a general of the times of Nicholas. The watch had been with her to Siberia, and now she had brought it into exile. It served occasionally as a timekeeper, but more often it lay peacefully—in her own or some friend's interest—in the pawnbroker's safe. These people lived in such close relations as practically to exclude the notion of private property. The fact that the watch was in the possession of its rightful owner was a conclusive sign that the small body of her former fellow-conspirators were for the time rather in clover.

"Oh, how late it is!" said Lena. "Past twelve. I must run home, so as to be in good time for my lesson to-morrow."

"And I, for my literary exploits," observed Andrey.

"By the way," said the girl, "you must arrange before you go for some of our people to carry on your work."

"By all means. It will do very well for Vasily. With his modest habits, eighty francs a month will be amply sufficient for all his needs."

"Certainly it will," said Lena, with unnecessary fretfulness.

"And even to spare something for taking you to concerts or the opera!"

The girl blushed, though she was prepared for some sally of this kind. Andrey always teased her about her admirer. But she had the unconquerably ready blush of fair-skinned girls.

"Vasily is a man of rigid principles, anyhow. Not a sybarite like you," she said, with a smile. "But, good-bye, I mustn't stop to quarrel with you."

He took the lamp to light her downstairs, and he watched her safely into her house, a block off across the street. Then he returned slowly to his solitary room.

The leaflet of the letter lay temptingly upon the table. Lena had guessed the truth. In asking for the letter, he intended, when alone, to feast upon those kind words from his distant friends. But he could not do it now. The girl by guessing it had spoiled his pleasure for him. He put the letter into his pocket to read next day. Now he was resolved to go to sleep.

He opened the folding-doors at the back of the room and disclosed an alcove. With this addition, his narrow and rather low room looked exactly like an empty cigar-box or a coffin.

He made the bed ready. But all was useless; he felt it impossible to sleep ; he was too excited.

Three long, long years had elapsed since Andrey Kojukhov, compromised in the first attempts at propaganda among the peasants, as well as in later struggles, had been urged by his friends to take an "airing." Since that time he had rambled over various countries, trying in vain to find some occupation for his restless spirit. Before the first year of his voluntary exile came to an end, violent home-sickness took hold of him, and he asked his friends, who held the field in St Petersburg, to allow him to return and take his place again in their ranks. It was peremptorily refused. There was a lull in the struggle ; the police had nothing in particular to run after ; and as his name was still well remembered by them, if he returned he might set all the gang in motion. Unable to do anything, he would only be a burden upon the friends, who would have to look after his safety. He ought to have understood this for himself. When there was any need of his return they would let him know. In the meantime he must keep quiet, and try to find work, either in revolutionary literature, or in the social movement abroad.

Andrey tried both, but with more zeal than success. He wrote for several Russian papers published abroad. But nature had denied him any literary talent. He felt within him an ardent enthusiastic soul ; he was far from being insensible to what was beautiful and poetical. But the channels between his sentiments and their utterance were blocked in him, and things which profoundly stirred his heart, when set down by him on paper, looked savourless and commonplace. His occasional contributions to the papers were no more than tolerably good padding.

Still less successful was he in his other attempts to procure employment during his long leave of absence. He overcame in a few months the obstacle of the language. But it was impossible for him to serve two masters at once. His heart and soul were filled with Russian cares, Russian aspirations, and Russian recollections. He felt himself a passing guest at the meetings of foreign socialists, and his home-sickness grew worse and worse. He was about to write again, when a living message from his friends arrived in the person of Helen Zubova, his companion in the conquest of the letter. Having just escaped from Siberia, she had come to St Petersburg to offer her services to the League, which at once advised her to cross the frontier and live for a while abroad. She brought, together with many greetings from his friends, an injunction to keep quiet and be reasonable. For the time there was no need of either of them in Russia. Lena's presence abroad was a material proof of this.

Nothing was left to Andrey but to make a virtue of necessity. Time had blunted the edge of his first disappointment. He had gradually made up his mind to the life of an exile, with its petty troubles and vexations, and its profound pleasures found in an unrestricted access to all the treasures of thought. Thus he passed three years of quiet uneventful existence, enlivened only by the feverish expectation of something new coming from Russia.

He did not wait in vain. After a brief pause the smouldering revolution burst out with redoubled energy, and Andrey was eager to seize the opportunity. He sent a new request, which he urged upon his friends with an energy and eloquence that unfortunately were never found in his more elaborate compositions. There were no longer any grounds for delay, and after a few more weeks of expectation, George's letter was his answer.

"Yes, at last!" he repeated, as he slowly paced up and down his coffin-like room, thinking upon his journey.

In his voice there was no exultation, but a strange calmness that had a touch of melancholy in it. The arrest of Boris?— Yes, but this was not all. The idea of the return to his country had lost something of its charm. He was surprised, and somewhat disappointed, to feel quite in a placid mood. From his former longings, he had anticipated that the summons would fill him with rapture. Now that the thing had come at last, he felt it so natural and simple, that he almost forgot the many thousand miles and the many perils of the journey which separated the expectation from the reality. The tame experiences of exile disappeared from his thoughts, and he was once more in St Petersburg, with all its well-known surroundings, as if he had left it but yesterday.

In this matter-of-fact mood he faced the important questions contained in George's letter, and felt angry with his friend for supposing that he would be persuaded so easily. No, not he. He thoroughly approved of the new acts of revolutionary terrorism, but he did not like their interpretation. The tendency of the League towards centralising all power in the hands of the Executive Committee was decidedly distasteful to him. The first thing he would try, would be to persuade his friend of the danger of such a course.

His brain began to work, and gradually he grew warm over the argument, as he strode with quickened step up and down his room.

A loud knocking suddenly interrupted his soliloquy, and recalled him to reality. It came through the floor from the lodger below, whose forbearance had been exhausted by his mad striding to and fro. With the help of a broomstick he was telegraphing an angry message to his neighbour upstairs.

"Ah," exclaimed Andrey, " it is Monsieur Cornichon. The good man wants to sleep, and does not care a fig whether the Russian revolution goes the right or the wrong way ! "

He stopped abruptly to signify his apology, and stood motionless until the knocking ceased. As he did not want to go to bed, and could not keep quiet as long as he was on his feet, he determined on taking a short walk in the beautiful spring night. He put out the lamp, and, leaving the room locked, hid the key as usual under the mat.

CHAPTER II.

IN SOLITUDE.

KNOWING the house well, Andrey groped his way down the stone staircase, and came out into the fresh air. The night was clear and bright, the full moon shone from the vault of the sky. He went down the narrow street in which his house stood, and turned to the left through a small square, shadowed by a few gigantic lime trees, under which, according to tradition, Jean Jacques Rousseau had often rested. Keeping on in the same direction, in a few minutes he found himself in an open space facing the Botanical Gardens, surrounded by gold-tipped railings, which glistened upon the dark background of exotic vegetation. A breeze so gentle, that he could hardly determine from whence it blew, fanned his face refreshingly. As he rapturously inhaled the invigorating perfumes of the night, the lake, and the gardens, he felt another man. A new sense of enjoyment took possession of him. He delighted in the world about him, in his peace of mind, in his bodily health and vigour, which imparted a peculiar elasticity to his limbs. He wanted to move, to go somewhere—but where?

The slumbering city, with its rows of shopkeepers' palaces, —the gorgeous hotels,—stretched on his left along the Rhône. He loved the powerful stream, with its blue-green or jet-black foaming waters rushing impetuously between the narrow steeps of its stony banks. On sunny suffocating days he would stand for hours watching the magical play of light upon the tremulous mosaic of the river-bed, shining amidst the dark clusters of hairy weeds.

But there were all these palaces to pass,—this congeries of prosaic and money-grubbing littlenesses, slumbering after their daily exertions. No; he could not bear this to-night, and he strode away in the opposite direction along the lake.

This favourite holiday walk of the Genevan citizens and their families was now completely deserted. Not a footstep, not one disturbing noise, broke upon the majestic quiet of the night. The lake was calm ; and the gentle rhythmical plash of the waves lulled his senses, without driving away the glorious visions which thronged his excited brain.

A new leaf of his life was to be turned. A few days hence he would be thousands of miles away in his own country, in another world, amid entirely new surroundings. How great the changes since he had left St Petersburg ! There were hardly half-a-dozen of his old companions left in the League. Only two of them were at that moment in the capital. All the rest were new people, recruited during the three years of his absence.

Would they be able to agree, and to work together without much friction? But no matter ! he had great confidence in his own power of adaptability as a practical conspirator. Of old he had been particularly fond of being thrown into entirely new places, where everything and everybody were new to him. He felt reviving in him the lust for struggle and for danger, and the cool dogged pluck, of those whom defeat renders only more obstinate and persistent

A contemptuous smile passed over his lips as he thought of the boasts of the police mentioned by George. The fools ! They supposed things to be at an end, when they were only beginning ! He knew by reputation the most prominent of the new men. Some of them he remembered having met at the meetings of the students' secret clubs. They must have grown into splendid fellows since then. It was rare luck indeed to cast in one's lot with such men. He had been pained of late by the thought that his three years' absence had reduced to the strength of a spider's thread the links which united him with his people. Now he knew that they were as closely united in common brotherhood as ever. The fulness of affection which breathed from their message found in his heart a warm response. How could he fear any possible friction or misunderstanding with men who could think of sparing him, personally a stranger to most of them, whilst they themselves were under fire ?

He did not for a moment flatter himself that there was anything in himself to merit this consideration. Though he had but just entered upon manhood, the precocity and intensity of his life had supplied him with experience which would have amply sufficed for a man ten years his senior. At twenty-seven he was a staid man, who had long outlived the

age of illusions.   The kindness of his friends did not rouse his
vanity.   Theirs was the generosity of affection, which does not
measure its gifts.   He accepted it as a good omen, with thankfulness, and bright pure joy.   Yes, this is the rock upon which
their church was built, and the gates of hell shall not prevail
against it !

He slackened his pace.   Without meaning it he had come
a long way from the town.   The moon had sunk, and was now
staring him full in the face irritatingly.   The level shore to the
right began to slope gently upwards.   He noticed a narrow
passage between the stone walls which in Switzerland are used
to fence the orchards and vineyards.   Probably it led to some
out-of-the-way place, for the grass in the crevices between the
big smooth pebbles, with which it was paved, showed it to be
but little used.

Andrey plunged into its shadows, and began to ascend the
slope.   It grew steeper as he went on.   The roof of some
building abruptly overshadowed the lane.   He looked up, and
saw a black waving line of tiles projected against the blue sky.
In the walls of the weather-beaten building were narrow perpen-
dicular slits.   It was evidently a stable.   A cow, chewing the
cud within, snorted as she smelt the approaching stranger, but
as he passed on she quietly took to her ruminating again.

A little farther vineyards began, the thick clusters of vines
overhanging the coping of the walls.   Some hundred yards
farther the lane turned short to the left, running in a broad
curve between the two long walls, which gave it the appearance
of an empty aqueduct.   A narrow flight of stone stairs built
against the hill side, marked out a shadow of exaggerated zigzags upon the rough masonry.   When Andrey had climbed
them he saw an open field dotted with hazels.   A footpath,
probably connecting the lower road with another on a higher
level, shone like a stream of water upon the emerald green
moonlit sward.

Andrey ventured into the path.   At the top of the slope
stood a clump of willows, which attracted him.   But after a short
distance the path, spreading out in a level tract of soft ground
disappeared.   Straining his eyes a little, Andrey observed in the
distance another turn of the pathway ascending a small bushy
hillock to the right.   He climbed this, and was surprised to find
himself in front of an ordinary garden-bench with arms and a
comfortable sloping back, reminding him disagreeably of man's

intrusion upon this charming solitude. The seat could not be seen from a distance : the long branches of a weeping willow under which it stood wrapped it in darkness.

Pushing aside the yielding branches, Andrey penetrated within the alluring green vault and sat down. When he raised his head and looked out, he jumped to his feet with an exclamation of wonder and delight.

What he saw was only the lake ; but from this particular spot, and at this particular moment, it looked so fantastically transfigured that he had some difficulty at first in recognising it. He stood upon a terrace, a few steps from the edge, whose height concealed all the strip of shore between it and the water. The white swollen lake was there, right under his feet, as if by some spell the ground on which he stood, trees, bench, everything, had been detached from their base and were held suspended in the air over the enormous mass of glistening water. Nay, it was too bright to be water. It seemed a gleaming sea of molten silver, without a perceptible ripple, stretching right and left far as the eye could reach, and filling all space with a flood of light reflected from its surface.

Andrey drew near the edge of the little platform that he might see better, and the illusion was at once destroyed. The tops of the houses and the trees at his feet leaped up out of the darkness, dense and murky, against the dazzling brightness of the water. The receding quay with its diminutive benches and well-trimmed plane trees, the white piers projecting into the lake like the tentacles of some strange sea-beast, the gaslit bridge and town, the low Swiss coast looming in the distance wrapped in a blue mist which made coast and sky seem one, so that the watch-fires upon the mountains appeared to be golden stars fixed in the firmament,—all this was a beautiful panorama, but it had not the magic of the other.

He returned to the bench, and was no longer angry with the people who had put it there. He was keenly alive to the beauties of nature, though he loved her fitfully and somewhat selfishly, as those absorbed in a special pursuit so often do.

This was the last time he would look upon these charming sights. It was a leave-taking before going where duty called him. There was in his heart a sense of deep unruffled peace, such as he did not remember feeling for years. The great calm of the scene spoke strongly to his soul. It seemed to him that never had his enjoyment been so full, so pure, so elevating as now.

Yet the current of thought which passed listlessly through his mind, as he sat there lost in contemplation, did not tend to harmony with the calm of the scenery.

There is a certain pleasure in thinking of afflictions when they have lost their sting and become things of the past.

Andrey passed in review his exile life, and it was exactly its darkest side which his memory sought and dwelt upon with strange persistency.

He had not shared with his kith and kin the cup of bitterness which they had been forced to drink ; and yet, somehow, he felt as if he had tasted its bitterest dregs. Thrown out of active life himself, he had only to look with folded hands— upon what? Not even upon the struggle of his friends, but upon the cold-blooded massacre of the best of them. The first onslaught of the revolution was repelled with enormous losses. A deep discouragement crept over the classes that furnished its chief contingent. The scattered remnant of once formidable forces, faithful to their banner, fought to the end. Very few of them left their country to seek refuge abroad. They were dying at their posts by scores, by hundreds, men and women, far better than he.

But why, then, was he alive?

How many times, overwhelmed with pain, had he asked himself that question !

A terrible vision rose suddenly before his memory.

It is night. A dimly lighted cell in one of the southern prisons. Its inmate—a young student—is stretched upon the straw mattress. His hands and feet are tightly bound with ropes. His head and body are covered with bruises. He has just been shamefully beaten by the gaolers, because he did not show himself sufficiently submissive. Smarting under the brutal insult, he is meditating the only revenge left him—that of a frightful suicide. Fire shall be his instrument. In the dead of the night he rises with effort from his bed. He takes off with his mouth the hot lamp glass, which scorches his lips ; he unscrews with his teeth the burner, and upsets the oil over his mattress. When it has saturated the straw, he drops upon the mattress the burning wick, and stretches himself once more upon this bed of fire. There he lies, without a groan, whilst the fire licks and burns his flesh. When the gaolers, attracted by the smoke, rush into the cell, they find him half charred and dying.

This was no nightmare. It was a frightful reality. For months the harrowing vision had persecuted Andrey, and now it rose before him as if he had seen it but yesterday.

And in the meantime, while these horrors went on there, in his own country, what was he doing? He remained in ignominious security, studying clever books, admiring the beauties of nature and the wonders of art. And his conscience, stern, implacable inquisitor, whispered in his ear insidiously: Why, is there nothing besides your friends' arguments which keeps you where you are? Are you really so anxious to give up safety and to put once more your neck into the noose, or to exchange your room for an underground cell in a ravelin of the Tzars?

In the unnatural life he led, what but empty words could he bring forward in answer to these gnawing questions? And he did not always succeed in silencing thus his terrible judge. He knew the anguish of doubt and the pangs of self-condemnation. There were moments when he deemed his former revolutionary zeal but an ebullition of youth and of love of strong sensations,—when he thought his life a failure, and himself a clod of earth aspiring to become a stone in a marble temple, a dwarf in a giant's armour, and he felt as crestfallen, crushed, and wretched as a living soul can.

Andrey completely lost control over his thoughts. He called up these memories as the German doctor called up the spirits that waited on his will—as a pastime, a kind of spiritual enjoyment. But they were too strong for him, and now they held him in their cruel clutches, and mastered him in real earnest. No sign of enjoyment could be detected in his drooped head, or in the nervous movement of the hand which swept his bowed forehead as if to brush away these crowding recollections.

But it is all over now, sunk in oblivion and nothingness, as the ugly dreams and phantasms of the night fly before the face of morning. In this solemn moment, before crossing the fatal threshold which he was certain never to recross, he could measure himself with certainty. The long years of enervating inaction had left no trace upon his soul. It was like a sword left idle in the sheath. Now he unsheathed it before him, scrutinising it with severe and experienced eye. No, there was no rust upon it; it was clean, sharp, ready for the battle as ever.

A fierce gladness flashed in his darkened eyes as he looked straight before him. He rose to his feet; he longed to get away. There was nothing to keep him here. Nature's beauties had lost the power of producing the slightest impression upon him. Mechanically he returned on his former way through the grey twilight of the grove. His face was pale, but calm and somewhat gloomy, whilst all was trembling within his heaving breast. His widely opened eyes looked wistfully into the darkness, but he scarcely saw anything. If the sharp thorns of some bush had lacerated his body, he would not have noticed it. He was almost beside himself with the violent emotions boiling from the depths of his soul and permeating his whole being.

He could not say this feeling was quite new to him. Now and then he had experienced something similar, though never had he been so wholly under its power. It was rapture, yet it was unutterably sad, as if his soul were filled with wailing, and his heart brimful of tears; but the wailings were melodious, the tears were sweet.

Out of this tumult of emotion—like the cry of an eagle soaring in the eternal calm of the skies, far above the regions of cloud and tempest—there rose in his breast the triumphant, the intoxicating consciousness of the titanic strength of the man, whom no danger, no suffering, nothing on earth, can compel to deviate one hair's-breadth from his path. He knew that he would make a good and faithful soldier of the legion which fought for the cause of their country. Because this is what gives one man power over another's heart; this is what imparts the spell of contagion to his zeal; this is what infuses into a word—a mere vibration of the air—the force to overturn and remould the human soul.

The grove through which he had passed lay far behind, and he had been walking for some time upon an open road. In his occasional rambles he had never chanced upon that side of the town. A cornfield attracted his attention. It was a mere patch, a few score yards square, so that on the vast green turf it looked like a lady's pocket-handkerchief on the carpet of a drawing-room. Yet it struck a foreigner, accustomed to see in Switzerland only mountains and vineyards, as something unexpected.

Andrey had no difficulty in guessing that the road he followed would take him back to his lodgings. But he did not feel disposed to return so soon. He wanted to sober down before reappearing among men, and he resolved to go to a little wood on the banks of the Arve commanding a view over the town from the southern side. He went thither, walking as rapidly as he could. He wanted, and expected, to be tired; but his strong young muscles, hard and tough as steel, were equal to almost any strain. To-night he seemed to be proof against fatigue; his mental excitement doubled for a time his power of endurance. But the long walk had cooled his head. He was himself again as he climbed the height of La Bâtie, his feelings running quietly in their ordinary channels, like a river after an inundation.

The moon had set. It lacked an hour or two of sunrise, but the approach of morning was already to be felt. The air was keener, the darkness was thinning, a cool wind blew from the mountains. On the western horizon huge clusters of heavy leaden-coloured clouds rapidly grew, mountain like, and stood in readiness like labourers arisen for the day's toil. The stars went out in the duller sky. The Milky Way, fading at one end, looked like the broken arch of a gigantic bridge. There the whole east was suffused with a tender transparent light, verging between pale yellow, green, and pearly white of indescribable delicacy and purity. The stars had shyly moved away to give place to the glorious apparition. One only would not dissemble her beauty. There she stood alone, wonderfully bright upon the enchanted ground, beaming and quivering like an eye that lightens and darkens under its trembling lashes. It was Venus, the poet's star. But was she not his star as well? the star of his Russia, lying yonder towards the rising sun, and even now about to awaken from the night of centuries to the glory of her morning!

Andrey resolved to go straight home. It was high time to finish his ramble. He had enjoyed himself enough, and he must waste no more time. To-morrow he would have to be up early. Lena would certainly call after her lesson. He had much to do in order to be ready for his journey without delay.

He pulled his hat over his brow, and ran down the hill. The footpath zig-zagged among the thin bushes covering the dark declivity. After a short distance the woods disappeared, and looking from the edge of the slanting footpath Andrey saw the bare declivity. It was very steep, but the ground was clayey and soft.   How delightful it would be to fling himself like a stone, bounding from one prominence to another, and then by one strong effort to stop short at the bottom!   There was a dare-devil spirit within him that urged him to the feat.   He took a few steps to the edge, and prepared himself for the first leap, which would have to be small.   But a sudden thought made him abandon this rather dangerous freak.   Suppose he should dislocate his ankle?   How then about his journey?   No, it would not do for him to be careless now.   He stepped back, and ran carefully down the pathway.

Crossing the Arve, he passed a few blocks of houses in a suburb, and emerged upon a spacious drill-ground, used for exercising recruits and for popular amusements at holiday-time. The real town began on the farther side.   Sounds of the opening day were already heard here and there.   In the middle of the street a big sorrel horse in harness, but without any cart, was walking by itself, as they often do in Switzerland; no driver was visible anywhere.   The animal's step was so steady, and it looked so amusingly self-confident and knowing, that Andrey clapped it on the neck, and asked with a smile the best way to his home.

The horse passed on without deviating an inch, with its air of a self-satisfied portly gentleman going to business.

"Oh, well!" thought Andrey, resuming his way; "you can't expect a French horse to understand Russian.   I ought to have addressed it in its native language.'   He felt sprightly and gay, as one does after a shower-bath, and was ready to amuse himself with any trifle.

In twenty minutes he was at the opposite end of the town, ascending his own staircase.   On approaching his door, he was surprised to see a line of light under it, and to find it unlocked. He thought he remembered having put out the lamp and locked up the room.   The explanation of the mystery was not far to seek.   Upon entering he saw, by the uncertain light of the flickering lamp, the body of a man lying on his bed.   The lamp stood by him.   Andrey raised it above the dark form.

"Ah, Vaska!" he exclaimed, recognising first the rosy trousers of his friend,—a perfectly unique sample of the article which Vaska, otherwise Vasily Verbitzky, had picked up by mistake in some dark shop,—then his old overcoat, and finally his good-natured swarthy face, half concealed by the abundant auburn hair.

Vasily had received Lena's message late in the night, and had come to inquire immediately about the letter. Finding Andrey absent, he had resolved to wait until he came back, and had fallen asleep. On the floor, just by the side of the bed, lay the book with which he had tried to beguile the time.

Unwilling to awaken his friend, Andrey looked round to see how to find accommodation for both. There was nothing for it but to improvise a camp bed. He spread upon the floor a large sheet of an uncut newspaper. A winter overcoat would do very well for a mattress, and the Nihilist's inevitable plaid for a blanket. But how about a pillow? Vasily had under his head both the small woollen things with which the landlady had supplied her lodger. Andrey very judiciously concluded that his guest could do very well with one of them. Slipping unceremoniously his hand under his friend's head, he removed the other. Thus disturbed, Vasily muttered in his sleep some inarticulate sounds of selfish protest. But he seemed to admit at once that he was in the wrong, for he grunted, without opening his eyes, something in a conciliatory tone, and when Andrey let his head drop again did not trouble any further.

Andrey undressed, put his watch by his side that he might be sure to rise in time, and as his head touched the pillow almost instantaneously slept the sleep of the righteous.

CHAPTER III.

SAMUEL SUSSER, called familiarly Red Shmul, chief smuggler and tavern-keeper at Ishky, a village upon the Lithuanian frontier, was serving his customers with his usual alertness. His quick eye never failed to catch the moment when one of them was thirsty, and his practised hand never poured out one drop of beer more than was necessary to show the tumbler full, while leaving as much of it as possible unfilled. But his active mind was for the moment engaged elsewhere, following the rapid train then traversing the last miles between St Petersburg and the frontier.

This morning he had received a telegram from David Stirn, a student of Jewish extraction, who had joined with the "Gois" (Christians) rebels against the authorities, and now "kept the frontier" for them. In a conventional language, agreed upon beforehand, David had announced his arrival by the evening train, with three companions, who had to be conveyed across the frontier.

Three persons at ten roubles a head is not a bad day's work. But the fact is, Red Shmul reckoned upon getting something more than that for his trouble. It was conscription time, and special precautions were taken upon the frontier to prevent the young sons of Israel from escaping military service. An honest smuggler has a right to expect some extras in a time like that. But one must be cautious with such a screw as David. Not a bad man for all that, this Mr David. A sharp head, a genuine Jewish head, who would do honour to his race anywhere. He must be a general, or something of the sort, among the "Gois." A sharp lad, who knows on which side his bread is buttered. He will get on, and an honest smuggler has nothing to fear in dealing with him. He holds his tongue well, and, once his word is given, stands to his guns. But he haggles over a penny like a gypsy at a horse fair.

Red Shmul had many opportunities for studying his strange employer. Every three or four months the young man appeared upon the frontier, bringing with him batches of "Gois," who wanted to go out of the country, or to come in. There were, moreover, books to be smuggled from abroad—a very advantageous trade, since books were paid for better than tobacco or silk. David had many connections all along the frontier, but Red Shmul was proud of being his favourite agent.

What all this meant; who the strange people were with whom David was connected; what they wanted—Red Shmul could not make up his mind about. Prompted by his Jewish curiosity, he tried to read some of the revolutionary pamphlets he had to smuggle through. With his imperfect knowledge of Russian, he could not profit much by them, and did not care to investigate further. Since so clever a fellow as David took part in it, there must be some profit to be made out of it: how else could David pay so punctually and so well those whom he employed? As the importation of these books was prohibited, like that of various other goods, it must be some high-class smuggling business, for the use of gentlemen, of which he understood little. It did not concern him to know, however, provided he was paid well. He had his own business to mind.

The whistling of the locomotive in the distance announced the arrival of the St Petersburg train.

There they are, thought Shmul, whilst, with an obsequious smile, he was serving a police-officer with a measure of brandy.

Shmul's tavern stood rather far from the station. Most of the passengers sought refreshment in nearer and better places, but some stragglers reached him. Accordingly he had to make preparations to receive his guests. He wiped the two rustic oak tables which stood on either side of the room. Then he inspected the small assortment of spirits ready for use, filling some of the glasses from the long row of bottles standing against the walls, and placed himself in waiting behind the counter.

The tavern began to fill. Several peasant farmers of the village entered the room, loudly discussing the news of the market, from which they had just returned. Two gendarmes, just relieved from guard at the station, came in for a drink, and seated themselves in the place of honour. A few ordinary customers came and went, but David did not appear. About an hour passed after the arrival of the train, and still he had not come. Shmul was too ignorant of the dangers besetting a conspirator to feel any apprehension. He concluded, therefore, that David probably had been detained somewhere, and would come on the morrow, which was Friday, the eve of the Sabbath. As it was a day of very short work, the enterprising tavern-keeper began to consider how he could profit by David's lack of punctuality, when turning to his right he saw David in person, sitting composedly at the table beside the gendarmes, paying as little attention to them as they paid to him. He was indeed the last person to be regarded with suspicion, this poorly-dressed young Jew, looking vacantly into space, with the patient air of a customer of modest means, in no hurry to leave an agreeable place and pleasant company.

He was a short broad-shouldered man, of twenty-five or so, with an attractive regular face, of marked Jewish type, and large dark-brown eyes, kind and melancholy.

Shmul served him, when his turn came, with a mug of beer, and took no further notice of him. The young man paid for his drink, and after having sipped it leisurely went away as quietly as he had come.

Once in the street, David turned the corner of the house and entered the kitchen by a back-door. In the thin light of the tallow candle he stumbled over something white and soft —a young lively kid, which jumped up from the floor and made its retreat between David's feet, raising a cloud of dust. A hen roosting upon the plate-rack, frightened in its sleep, lost its equilibrium, and with much cackling of dismay sought refuge in the opposite corner of the room.

The young man passed rapidly through the region where his presence caused so much disorder, and stepped into a dark corridor. Lighting a wax match, he ascended a flight of wooden stairs, and made his way to a small and rather dirty back room, where the Red Shmul was wont to transact his most important business.

His host was already there. Having called his wife to take his place behind the counter, he hastened to meet his visitor as soon as he noticed his intention of withdrawing.

"How do you do, Master Shmul?" said David, in the Jewish jargon. "You didn't expect me so soon?"

"I did not expect to see you at all, Mr David,—to-day, I mean. I thought you would come to-morrow."

"I had something to look after," said the young man, seating himself upon an easy-chair of doubtful colour and greasy appearance which stood against the wall.

The lean and long Shmul perched himself upon a high wooden stool with one leg wanting.

"Are your friends with you?" he inquired.

"Yes."

"All three of them?"

"All three. Two men and one lady. I left them at Foma's. We want to be on the other side early to-morrow. You have arranged everything, I hope?

"Yes, it's all right. They'll be on the other side at eight, and no mistake. But——"

Shmul stopped hesitatingly, and rubbed the left side of his nose, whilst he looked inquiringly in David's face.

"What now?" asked the other, looking up.

"Well, times are hard, you know, and the soldiers are very greedy. I had much, oh, so much, trouble to bring them round," said Shmul, pathetically raising his eyes to the ceiling, "and I had to pay them more than——"

"If so, you were wrong, Shmul, and you made a serious blunder," said David carelessly.

"Why? Is there any blunder in trying to serve you promptly?"

"Certainly not. But you must keep to fixed prices. That's the rule of the trade. The more you give, the more they'll ask. Mind that, friend, and stick to your terms. That's the rule of the trade."

"It's all very well for you to say so, Mr David!" exclaimed the smuggler spitefully, warming to his rôle of offended virtue. "But how could I help yielding? They are the masters, not I."

"A wise man must know how to make them give in," said David, imperturbably. "Suppose," he added, with a spark of humour in his large eyes, "you asked me to pay you more than is the rule. I don't say you will, but suppose you did. Well, I should answer, that the fish goes where the water is deeper, and a buyer where the ware is cheaper. Business is business. The frontier is long, and the soldiers many. If a man will not stick to the fixed price, why should you stick to him? Isn't it so?"

David smiled good-humouredly, and began to fill his small wooden pipe.

He knew of course from the first what Shmul was driving at, and he was firmly resolved to stand no nonsense. Parsimony in spending party-money was in his eyes the sacred duty of a revolutionist. But it was not his habit to deal with people harshly so long as he could help it.

"And how is your family? I forgot to ask you," he went on. "All well, I hope?"

"Quite well, thank you," answered Shmul sulkily, meditating a more resolute attack. He did not mean to lose a good opportunity.

"Nothing new in the village?" went on David, smoking his pipe unconcernedly.

"There is something new," answered the smuggler tartly, and gave his visitor some fragments of news showing the serious state of affairs on the frontier.

"Have you heard that Itzik is back?" asked David, emitting a long puff of smoke.

Shmul's heart fell. Itzik or Isaak Perlenglanz was a very shrewd smuggler of good repute in the brotherhood. Occasionally David did some business with Itzik, and Shmul always suspected the latter was anxious to oust him.

"Is he?" rejoined the smuggler, faintly. "I did not know that."

He cast an inquisitive glance at his neighbour. But David looked quite unconcerned.

"Foma told me. That's all I know," he said.

"There's no hope," thought Shmul; "he is well informed, and knows his game."

"Have your people much luggage?" asked Shmul in a matter of course tone, as if there was never any shadow of disagreement between them.

"A few bundles. Your boy can fetch it all."

"Then I'll send him to-morrow to Foma's. The money on the other side?"

"Yes. But mind, you are not to take anything from them. Only a small note on a scrap of paper to tell me that they are safe."

Shmul nodded in melancholy silence. This was another of his grudges against the young man. David was very severe, and even cruel about this. Shmul knew it only too well.

The injured smuggler shook out the long curls over his ears, and inquired hurriedly how the weather was in St Petersburg, to change the drift of his unpleasant thoughts.

But his ill-humour changed to cheerful hopefulness, when David asked whether he would be at his post in a month's time.

"I'm going to the other side," the young man explained, "and I shall have many things to pass in."

Shmul smacked his lips. This was compensation for the failure of his present expectations.

He asked no questions. David did not like it, and would let nobody know more than he chose to tell.

"You'll not forget me, I hope," said Shmul.

"No, I'll not. Only you must be on the spot. I'll write to you, to give you time to get there."

Then they entered upon a discussion of way-bills, "carriage," and so forth, and this time Shmul made no further show of objection. They parted on very friendly terms, the smuggler divided between æsthetic admiration of the other's ability and disappointment at the frustration of his own design.

"A smart fellow, there's no gainsaying that," he soliloquised as he bolted the doors and windows of the tavern. "Only our father Jacob could get over him. Still he might be a little easier with one of his own people, burdened with a large family, who finds it hard to turn an honest penny."

And he recalled with sorrow the golden times of six or seven years before, when the fare across the frontier was as much as twenty-five and even fifty roubles per head. Some fools had paid as high as a hundred. David had reduced it to a paltry ten, with no extras upon any pretext whatever. It was true enough that since David had taken things in his hands, ten times as many "Gois" were passing in and out of Russia. This was some consolation. But the good man could not help reflecting how much nicer it would be if the traffic was as brisk as now, and the fares as high as they used to be. He fell into such a dream of figures, that his heart first leaped for joy and then sank into his boots with regret.

Meanwhile David had got to Foma's house, where his company had put up for the night. The master opened to him in person, and David inquired for his friends. All was well. They had supped as he had ordered, and were now gone to bed. The men had the front room, and Foma's daughter, Marina, had taken in the lady upstairs. David thanked him, and rejoined his friends. On occasions of this sort he always stopped at Foma's, though nothing better than a trestle-bed was to be had there. Foma was the local *sotsky*,—a sort of rural policeman,—and his cabin had the advantage of perfect security.

Once inside the room, David examined everything with the attention of an officer on duty. The window-shutters were closed to prevent the passers-by from seeing the strangers within. All the luggage, his own linen sack included, was piled in a corner. His companions, worn out with their long journey, were stretched in sleep on the benches round the walls. Each had a straw pillow and such bedclothes as his host could improvise. Everything was all right. A similar bed was ready for himself; but though he was tired, he was hungry as well, and he wanted to contrive some supper. So he cut a slice of bread from the loaf on the table, took from his sack a piece of cheese, carefully wrapped up in paper, and victualled himself from his own supplies, like an old campaigner.

He was the first a-foot, as the morning sunshine slipped through the chinks of the shutters. He rapidly completed his toilet, and opened the shutters. His companions, roused by his merry voice, were soon astir with him.

Ostrogorsky, the elder, was a middle-aged man, small and bent, with the look of a withered and sickly scholar. Exiled years ago for some trifling offence in an out-of-the-way town upon the Volga, he had escaped from his place of punishment, and was going to settle permanently in foreign parts.

His companion, Sazepin, a stalwart young man of twenty-three, once a subaltern in a line regiment, was a fellow-conspirator of David's, and was so seriously compromised that he had been sent abroad by the League " for change of air."

" Make haste, boys," said David. " You must do great things to-day, and you have no time to lose. I'll go and arrange breakfast."

In the courtyard he was rejoined by the third of his company, Annie Vulitch, a girl of nineteen, implicated as a " sympathiser " in some university disturbances of a non-political character. As a foreign passport was refused her by the police, David readily consented to include her in his next batch. He was always willing to help over the frontier any one in need of it.

Annie was looking after the samovar which Foma had kindled, and David was free to busy himself about breakfast. It was as luxurious as Foma's larder could afford. This was a point of honour with David. Careless of his own comfort, he had for those under his care a solicitude that at times was very amusing. He not only watched over their safety, but took care that they should be well fed and provided for in all respects.

The dawn was past, and the first red sunbeams were shining through the tiny rough windows of the house, lighting up the room and the faces of the travellers.

David himself made tea. He always kept a good store in his travelling-sack, because it was expensive, and bad when bought at retail shops. The frugal meal was a lively one. All were in high spirits, and as merry as people are who are excited by curiosity and the expectation of danger to be met in common. They could not help thinking that crossing the frontier of the Tzar's dominions must somehow be a serious business. David assured them that it was the simplest affair in the world. Hundreds of people crossed the frontier secretly, simply to save the cost of a passport. Political offenders, provided there was nothing particular in their external appearance, could get over as easily as anybody else.

"All the same, a good many of them have been arrested at the frontier," said Annie Vulitch, with a blush.

She felt a little nervous, for she had never been in a scrape before. But she was very proud, and she was afraid her remark might be mistaken for a sign of fear.

"Yes, they have!" said David, kindling with indignation. "And by whose fault but their own? A fool can drown himself even in a pail of water by holding his head into it."

Like most men of sanguine temperament, David was prone to exaggeration. To believe him, the frontier is the best place in the world for walking about in. He was really angry with these sluggards for bringing the frontier into disrepute, and feeding the public with foolish notions as to its perils.

Their talk about the incidents of frontier life was interrupted by Ostrogorsky, who was the first to remark that their smuggler was late. This was true, and he had not appeared at ten o'clock. David had been down to the tavern, but Shmul was out. Something had gone wrong. Ostrogorsky, an irascible man, began to lose patience.

"Shall we have to spend another night here?" he asked with a wry smile.

David calmly explained that there was no danger of that. If the smuggler was not on the ground by eleven, he would go and contrive the business in another way.

Sazepin alone neither grumbled nor asked questions. He felt for David the confidence of a soldier in his commander, and it was not in his nature to doubt about anything.

When Shmul appeared in the doorway, David met him with a volley of reproaches. The smuggler excused himself: it was no fault of his, but a mere accident. The guard with whom he had made his arrangements had not been appointed for morning duty as he expected, and would not be at hand until the evening.

This was unpleasant. It was Friday. In a few hours the sacred Sabbath eve would begin, and the heaviest guerdon will not induce a smuggler of the Mosaic persuasion to break the Sabbath by lifting a finger.

A flash of anger shone in David's eyes.

"Don't be cross, Mr David," said the smuggler, "you'll not have to wait until the Sabbath is over. I have got two passports for the gentlemen, and my daughter will meet us on the way to the ferry, and give hers to the lady. We can cross at once if you like."

David explained in Russian what had occurred, and gave the two men their papers. They were not regular foreign passports, but a sort of certificate which is given to the people of the frontiers, who have business on both sides of the line, and cross and recross it continually.

Each of them opened his passport to learn the name to which he would have to answer in case of emergency. Upon Sazepin this study produced a very startling effect.

"Why! what rubbish have you brought me here?" he shouted to the smuggler; "this is a woman's!"

"So it is," said the smuggler; "and where is the harm in it?"

Interested and amazed, Sazepin's two companions approached to ascertain the truth.

There could be no doubt of it. On the passport, in large letters, and in yellowish ink, there was written, "Sarah Halper, widow of Solomon Halper, tradesman, forty years old."

They all burst into a laugh, in which Sazepin joined.

During his revolutionary career he had used many passports and played many parts, but he was for the first time a widow of forty, and objected to the experiment.

"You must change it," he said to the smuggler, "I can't pass for that widow."

Shmul raised his hands, as a cherub might his wings, and blinked.

"Why not? With God's help you will."

Sazepin, who had no such belief in Providence, insisted; but David, albeit amused at his friend's annoyance, interfered.

"It doesn't matter at all," he said, "you'll see that for yourself."

Sazepin shrugged his shoulders. How he could be taken for a widow of forty was past his comprehension; but as David was in the secret, he supposed it was all right.

The travellers prepared for their departure. They had to go empty-handed, for it is the rule on the frontier that men and goods should be smuggled separately; stuff that is saleable pays a much higher duty than mere human beings, who have no market value. Ostrogorsky, who had a small handbag with a bundle of manuscripts, was not even allowed to carry that. David took charge of everything. He was to bring it by another route, and he promised to rejoin them before long on the other side.

At the gate they met one of Shmul's offspring, who delivered his sister's passport to Vulitch.

"Now, it's all right," said David. They shook hands cordially, and parted. Sazepin and the smuggler led the way. The two others followed at some distance, so as not to attract attention. In twenty minutes they were in sight of a dirty wretched brook, such as a "hen may ford in dry weather," as the Russians have it. On both sides of it expanded a flat and dreary plain, the yellow clay showing through the fresh grass. There were groups of men and women on either shore. A flat-bottomed raft, like a large old slipper, was floating on the yellow water. A grey-haired, red-faced, stern-looking sergeant of police, his sword by his side, stood on duty.

As soon as the raft had touched the shore, and was emptied, our travellers, on a sign from their guide, jumped into it, and were followed by a dozen men and women, who crowded it so as almost to push each other overboard.

"Enough!" interposed the police officer, pushing back the crowd.

And addressing those who were in the craft, he said in a voice of command, "Your passports!"

For this was the frontier. The left hand of the dirty brook was Russia, the right Germany.

The passports were duly produced, and handed in a bundle to the pillar of law and order. His finger in the air, he hastily counted the number of heads and then the number of documents. As the two corresponded, he handed the passports back to the nearest passenger, and shouted, "All right!" With that the ferryman, who had neither rudder to steer nor pole to push with, gave Russia a kick, and the next instant the raft knocked up against Germany. The passengers leapt ashore. All was over. They were in Europe, out of the Tzar's power.

"How very simple it is!" exclaimed Vulitch, with a smile. They felt a sense of relief, and they, talking loudly, proceeded to the village, where they had to wait for David.

Had they been less absorbed in themselves they would have remarked a decently clad young man, with dark eyes and pale face, who, as he passed along the street, was struck by the agreeable and unwonted sounds of pure Russian speech.

It was Andrey, who had arrived at the place appointed in George's letter full five days before. In hourly expectation of the arrival of David, who was to meet him there, he was perishing of *ennui*.

He guessed at once that the three were Nihilists of David's band. He was tempted to address them, but checked himself. They might be strangers after all. Caution never does harm. If they were friends of David, it would not be long ere David himself appeared.

CHAPTER IV.

RETURNING to his inn, Andrey found the waiter, and did his best with his poor German to explain that in the event of visitors he would be at home all day.

His window looked upon a large green square, with several thoroughfares opening into it. He sat there watching the traffic, and about eleven o'clock his keen eyes caught sight of David's squat figure, who was advancing rapidly, swinging his arms outside the thick greatcoat he wore all the year round.

Andrey rushed downstairs. The two friends met in the hall, and embraced each other in true Russian fashion.

"Have you abused me much, old boy, for keeping you waiting?" asked David, tapping Andrey upon the shoulder.

"I did abuse you, but not very much. I was afraid something had happened you."

"What nonsense! What can happen to *me?* I was running about and making up a little batch to convey across the frontier. Two birds with one stone, as usual. It is cheaper and quicker."

"I'm sure I saw your party at the ferry an hour ago."

"Yes, those were my lot. Sazepin is among them, you know. You must certainly see him."

They were by this time alone in Andrey's rooms. David took off his overcoat, threw it upon the long horse-hair chair, and sat down.

"Now you must tell me all your news," said Andrey, standing opposite him. "How is George and all the others? What about Boris? Have you heard from Zina?"

"We have had a letter from Zina. The outlook seems rather bad, as far as we could gather from her few hints. She must soon be back in St Petersburg, and will tell you more."

"Are we not going to St Petersburg together?"

"No," said David; "I am off to Switzerland, and shall have to stay there for some time. Have you heard that the *Equilibrides* want to start a clandestine paper of their own in St Petersburg ?"

"The *Equilibrides !*" exclaimed Andrey. "Is it possible ? "

The *Equilibrides* were a secret society, so nicknamed by their rivals for their moderation and want of backbone. There was no love lost between them and the party of the Land and Liberty League to which David and Andrey belonged.

"They seem to be in earnest this time," answered David. "When they heard I was going to Switzerland, they gave me money to buy type for them."

"That looks promising," said Andrey. "I'll have a better opinion of them henceforth."

"I don't think I will," said David. "We shall see what use they make of the type. For my part, I am an unbeliever."

He looked round for a match to light his pipe. Andrey gave him a cigar.

"Then why do you take the trouble to execute their commissions ? " he asked.

"That's my business," replied David. "I am the scavenger of the revolution, and my duty is to keep the roads clear of all obstacles, and free to everybody who wants to walk in them. Whether the *Equilibrides* succeed or not, does not concern me in the least. And then," he added, " it won't be much trouble ; it will give me a few days more with my friends in Switzerland, that's all."

"I'm glad for their sake at all events. Have you written of your coming ? "

"No, I never do. It's better to drop in unexpectedly. How are they? You have told me nothing about them."

"There's nothing to tell. The life is the same, as dull as ever," answered Andrey.

David slapped his knee with his hand impatiently.

"What a feckless lot these Nihilists are !" he exclaimed. "To be living in a free country at the time of a great social movement, and to feel like fishes out of water. Is the whole world confined for you to Russia?"

With his Jewish cosmopolitanism he had often to debate such points with his Russian friends.

"You are quite right to blame us," Andrey replied, with that readiness of self-condemnation which so often conceals deep-seated satisfaction with the fault admitted. "We are the least cosmopolitan of nations, though some people say the contrary. You are the only man I know who deserves to be called a citizen of the world."

"That is flattering, but not very pleasant," said David.

Andrey did not follow the argument, asking what was exactly the feeling of the St Petersburg friends about Boris. He took the matter much to heart. Boris was his dearest friend, the man of all the world who, after George, was nearest to him.

"Nothing can be settled till Zina is back," said David. "But I am afraid we can do nothing for him just now."

"Nothing! Why?" Andrey exclaimed.

"We cannot afford it," David replied, with a sigh. "We are now in somewhat of a fix. You will see for yourself when you get there."

He went on, giving details of the losses and financial difficulties of their League.

Andrey listened, walking up and down with bowed head. It was worse than he had expected. But the idea that hope must be abandoned, aroused in him a passion of wrath which made it impossible for him to submit. His own eventual capture he was accustomed to contemplate with a good deal of equanimity. That was the fortune of war, and he was prepared for it. But to allow "those scoundrels" (as he termed the whole official body) to slaughter one's friends without a shot in their defence, was a humiliation he could not endure.

"What nonsense, our people talking about want of strength!" he exclaimed, stopping short before David. "Our strength lies round us. If we cannot find recruits, it proves that we are not worth much ourselves!"

"You cannot jump higher than your head," replied David. "We might spare a couple of men to organise the business; but what can they do if we have no money?"

"What does it matter?" Andrey said. "Nothing is so likely to replenish our coffers, and to stir men's minds, as getting up some lively business."

"Sometimes," said David. "Speak to Zina and the rest about it. We all want something done."

He rose to take his leave.

"I must go to my party," he said. "By-the-by, how shall we arrange your meeting with Sazepin? Will you go and see him, or should he come to you?"

Andrey asked who the other people were, and then proposed to go straight to their inn. He was glad to have a talk with the other two as well.

When David entered the room where his charges were assembled, he was greeted with a boisterous ovation.

Andrey was introduced to all three under an assumed name, the first that David found on his ready tongue. As strangers to the League, Ostrogorsky and Vulitch were not to be initiated into the secret of this return to Russia, and Sazepin had no difficulty in guessing who the new man was.

The party fell into two groups. Andrey and Sazepin remained seated by the table, whilst David was taken by the two others to the window at the opposite end of the room. Both Ostrogorsky and the girl were still full of wonder at the simplicity of their escape.

" One almost wants it to be more exciting," said Annie, and Ostrogorsky remarked that he expected it would have been so.

He was in a talkative mood, and told how he was assured, on good authority, that people were carried across the frontier in sacks upon men's shoulders, in the dead of night ; that they had often to spend days in close confinement, in lumber-rooms, before the smugglers could find a good opportunity. David laughed, and said that he doubted the sacks, but that for the rest his informants were probably right. In old time, when the smugglers had things all their own way, they often played some such farce on purpose to throw dust in their clients' eyes, and to show that the big sums paid to them were well earned.

Andrey in the meantime was quietly talking with Sazepin, whom he asked of various things he had seen, and about the towns where he had lived. They were left alone, with that freedom which is usual in all the social gatherings of the Nihilists, until Sazepin happened to express an opinion upon a particular body of conspirators whom he had known in a provincial town.

" A gang of babblers,—wavering between politics and socialism," he said, with his usual directness. " They try to sit upon two stools, and it won't do for these times."

This remark caught the ear of Ostrogorsky, who was a passionate debater. Slowly the little man approached the two, his hands behind his back, his heavy nose seeming to pull down his emaciated face. There had been some fencing between him and Sazepin on the journey, but he thirsted for more. With a slight sarcastic smile on his thin lips, he begged permission to inquire what, according to Sazepin, would not do for these times; whether it was sitting upon two stools, or sticking to socialism?

Sazepin retorted that he meant what he meant, and that all who call themselves revolutionists and shirk the duty of taking part in the real work of revolution, are certainly babblers, or worse!

With this Ostrogorsky agreed, but he had his own definition of the real work. The discussion attracted Vulitch, and she moved to the end of the sofa nearer to the disputants. She listened; then she struck in, and the conversation became general. David alone remained in his place, sitting upon the window-sill and dangling his feet lazily.

Once started the debate waxed warm and noisy. And no wonder,—for it soon became manifest that of the five persons present, all revolutionists and socialists, each one had some points of disagreement with all the others, and none was disposed to give way. Sazepin was an avowed terrorist, remarkable for the thoroughness and simplicity of his views upon all questions of theory and practice, and for a happy absence of any doubt or uncertainty. Annie Vulitch, too, was a terrorist,—in theory of course,—though she did not go so far as Sazepin, with whom, moreover, she disagreed completely as to the question of socialist propaganda among the working-classes. Ostrogorsky and David both leaned to the evolution-ary socialism. But these two were strongly divided upon the question of a socialistic state in the future, and upon political action in the present. As to Andrey, he could not fully agree with any of the four. But having been so long out of the current of revolutionary thought, he seemed to want system, and to be a trifle undecided. He faced now this opponent, now that; and the next moment both opponents and allies turned on him fiercely, shouting in both his ears their different arguments to prove his inconsistency. Sazepin was greatly annoyed by Andrey's conduct. A man with such antecedents ought to have sounder principles, and side at once with the good cause without idle circumlocution.

His back to the empty grate, his strong right arm just leaning upon the mantelpiece, Sazepin stood his ground firmly. He had to defend himself against all the others, who sought to impress upon him the fact that simple terrorism is decidedly too narrow a creed for a socialist.

"Then, I tell you," he roared, towering over them, " I am *not* a socialist ! "

He lingered upon every word to give it greater emphasis.

"There you are ! " exclaimed Ostrogorsky in a triumphant falsetto ; "consequently you are a *bourgeois,* an upholder of the oppression of the working-classes by the capitalists. *Quod erat demonstrandum !* "

He turned from his opponent, and began pacing up and down, humming a tune to express that there is nothing more to say about it.

"No, I am not ! " Sazepin shouted after him, in nowise disconcerted. "But socialism is not for my time. That's what I say. We have to fight the autocracy, and to win political freedom for Russia. That's all. As to socialism, I don't care a fig for it ! "

"I beg your pardon, Sazepin," interposed Andrey, "that's rather foolish. All our moral strength consists in the fact that we are socialists. Strike that away, and our strength is gone."

"And by what right," exclaimed Vulitch, jumping up from her seat, "will you ask the working-men to join you if you are not socialists ? "

"Oh, well ! " drawled Sazepin, waving his hand contemptuously. "That's all metaphysics."

Metaphysics to him meant anything that was not worth a moment's consideration.

"The issue before us," he proceeded, dominating them all with his loud voice, "is the overthrow of political despotism, and that's necessary for all. All who love Russia must join hands with us, and those who will not are traitors to the cause of the people ! " And he looked straight at Ostrogorsky, lest he should mistake to whom the words referred.

"What have the people to gain from the middle-class constitution you are fighting for ? " the undaunted little man shouted at the top of his voice, thrusting his little body at his tall opponent with the air of a bantam attacking a big mastiff. "You have forgotten all about the people, because you are a middle-class man yourself. That's what you are."

"Look here, friends," said David, pointing to the street below, "here's a fire-engine. Don't get so excited, or the innkeeper will have the hose turned on you."

Nobody paid him the least attention. His gibe was lost upon the disputants, and he relapsed into silence.

The debate went on in the same fashion, but as the disputants grew tired they grew calmer. During the discussion all of them had changed their places several times. Now Sazepin was standing near the table, with Ostrogorsky holding him by the button of the coat.

"Let me say a few words to convince you, Sazepin," he said in a sweet persuasive tone. "The history of Europe teaches us that all the great revolutions . . . ."—and he went on developing his thesis at length.

Sazepin listened, his figure bolt upright, his head a little bent, his brow slightly contracted; judging from his face, it seemed probable that the seed of Ostrogorsky's wisdom was falling in stony places.

"Friends," David interrupted, looking at his watch, "your train starts in less than two hours. It's time to think about our bodily wants; let's have some dinner. That's a point upon which you all agree, I hope."

He went downstairs to give instructions, while Ostrogorsky walked out to get change for a Russian note.

Andrey was glad of the opportunity to explain his views, which he thought had only to be understood to be universally accepted. For in the "programme" he had carefully elaborated before starting, there was room for everything and everybody. Sazepin listened attentively,

"That will never work !" he exclaimed, without a moment's hesitation, shaking his head energetically.

"Why not ?" asked Andrey.

Sazepin did not answer at once. He was collecting his thoughts, and seeking words in which to put them clearly. His controversial ardour had subsided. Andrey was a friend, and meant business. He wanted to go to the root of the matter, not merely to thrust and parry. Then his face flushed with sudden anger.

"You want us to go hand-in-hand with the liberals," he said, looking sternly upon Andrey. "But suppose they want us to keep quiet? Should we? No, by God ! We will stab and shoot and blow up, and let all cowards go to the devil !"

He thumped the table with his fist so as almost to break it.

"No, Andrey," he added more calmly, "your eclecticism won't do."

" What do *you* say to it ? " Andrey asked the girl.

" I think that we must reckon upon ourselves, and go our own way. Those who like our aims will follow," she answered, with a flush of excitement upon her face.

There was nothing in this reply which one might not have heard from hundreds of people. Yet the tone of earnestness, far deeper than mere sincerity, struck Andrey's experienced ear. Up to this moment he had been engrossed in the pleasure of this first meeting with genuine Russians. He had scarcely observed the shy girl who had taken little part in the discussion. Now that the instincts of the fisher of men were awakened, he looked upon her with closer attention. Her fresh young face was intelligent and earnest, with glistening chestnut eyes, which she kept mostly fixed on the ground. Her small yet energetic figure was clad in the plain black dress common to the hard-working Nihilist sisterhood.

At dinner he asked her about her work and her plans, and found that she was a member of a students' club secretly organised for self-education. He had no difficulty in guessing that she had been its leading spirit. Her present intention was to finish her studies somewhere in Switzerland. Andrey advised her to try Geneva, where she would readily find all she wanted ; and he gave her a note of introduction to Lena.

The start was at four o'clock. David gave his friends all necessary information, and was helpful in many ways. But his motherly solicitude had vanished. They were no longer his peculiar charges, and his whole attention and tenderness were transferred to Andrey. The pair proceeded to the latter's inn, and it was agreed that they should lodge together. They had to spend a whole Saturday in the town, and David would send word to Shmul to be ready for Sunday morning.

" Not earlier ? " inquired Andrey.

" No ; that's if we have to arrange the matter with my Jews," David explained. " But there is a man on this side whom I can see if you like."

Andrey said he would like ; and David soon returned with the good news that one Schmidt (a smuggler of German extraction) was in the town, and if they pleased would see them over the frontier that very night. Andrey jumped at the idea at once, for he was impatient to get to St Petersburg. David too was in a hurry, as he had a lot of work on hand. So a message was sent to Schmidt, and in due time the smuggler appeared.

He was a big heavy man, dressed like a farmer, with a good-natured honest German face. He greeted Andrey politely, and made a few remarks about the weather. Then he went straight to the point and told them that all was ready.

Unfortunately it appeared the young Herr had too much luggage. A revolutionist coming into the country must be well dressed, and the reverse of empty-handed, as he may be when he is leaving it. David objected to any delay, lest the young Herr should miss his train.

A brief and rapid discussion ensued between him and Schmidt in German, which Andrey was unable to follow. He understood, however, that it ended to their mutual satisfaction. The German threw Andrey's bag over his broad shoulder with one hand, and they went straight to his house.

It was a little two-storeyed cottage, with a flourishing front garden. Frau Schmidt, a portly middle-aged lady, in a white cap, was introduced, and offered refreshment.

"Where is Hans?" asked Schmidt.

Hans had just returned from his evening class, and was changing his dress.

He came downstairs at his father's call,—an apple-faced, white-headed boy of twelve, in loose trousers and short tight jacket, whose seams were nearly bursting under the pressure of his growing limbs.

"Take your hat and show these gentlemen to the grey stone which is behind the birch hill yonder. Do you understand?"

"Yes, father."

"And be quick," added Schmidt, as the boy obeyed his orders.

"Yes, father."

Schmidt bid his guests "Godspeed," accompanying them politely to the gate of the cottage, and repeating his admonition to his son and heir.

Hans was in no need of it. He was a serious boy, who understood his business, and promised to do honour to the profession followed by the long line of his forefathers. Without useless talk he took the lead of the small company, with an air of dignity and self-importance upon his round face.

The two friends followed him at a certain distance. They went out of the village and a little way along the rivulet which David's friends had crossed that afternoon. Then the stream turned off to the right, and their way lay across an open moorland, without any trace of a path. The boy, however, showed no hesitation, and went along with regular steps, slightly balancing his short thick hands, and never turning his head.

The sun had set, and the purple reflection of the skies imparted some beauty even to the dreary landscape of the Prussian lowlands. A boundless plain extended in all directions, but Andrey could already discern at a distance the miserable thatched hut of the Russian villages, which are so striking a contrast to the spacious cottages, with their roofs of red tiles, on the German side. There could be no doubt of it. Beyond these bushes lay Russia, the melancholy land after which his heart was yearning. In a few minutes he would tread this tear-sown soil, for whose sake he was so eager to place his life in jeopardy.

"I am so sorry, dear David," he said to his companion, "that we have had so little time together. There are so many things I should like to talk over with you."

"In a month or thereabout I shall be back in St Petersburg. You will not be leaving before then, I hope?"

"Oh, no! I'll hardly have time to know what I'm about. Much has changed there, I expect. But tell me, do many of our people hold the same views as Sazepin?"

"No. You need not be afraid. He is one of the few oddities. The rest have another craze, and George is their prophet. You have read his things of course?"

"Yes, I did."

"And do you like them?"

"Well, I rather do. Why not?"

"I thought so. For my part, if I had to choose, I should have preferred Sazepin."

"You will not go very far with him though," said Andrey.

"Yes. He does not see beyond his day's work, still he is the man of the day, and his is the work we are all doing. You know with him what you have and what you have not. But you Russians hate to deal with positive things that you can touch with your fingers; you must always have some fantastical nonsense to muddle your heads with. It runs in your blood, I think."

"Don't be so harsh upon us," said Andrey, smiling at his

friend's sally. "If George's belief in Russia and in our peasants' superior virtues is pushed too far, what harm is there? Are you not repeating the same things about your beloved German working-men in general, and those of Berlin in particular?"

"That's quite another thing," said David. "This isn't a belief, but a prognostication of the future, based upon the solid ground of existing facts."

"The same sauce, my dear fellow, but somewhat thinner," said Andrey. "You cannot help idealising what you are strongly attached to. With all your philosophy, you are not a bit wiser than we are; only your preferences are placed elsewhere. We are strongly attached to our people, you are not."

David did not answer for a long while. Andrey's words had touched a very sore point in his heart.

"No, I am not attached to your people," he said at last, with a slow sad voice. "Why should I be? We Jews, we love our race, which is all we have on the earth. I love it deeply and warmly. Why should I love your peasants, who hate and ill-treat my people with blind barbarity? who to-morrow will perhaps loot the house of my father, an honourable working-man, and brutally assault him, as they have done to thousands of other poor hard-working Jews? I can pity your peasants for their sufferings, as I would pity some Abyssinian or Malay slave, or any ill-used living creature; but my heart will never beat for them, and I cannot share your vain dreams and foolish admiration for them. As to so-called society, the upper classes, why! what but contempt can one feel for such wholesale cowards? No, there is nothing in your Russia worth caring for. But I knew the Nihilists, and I loved them even more than my own race. I joined and fraternised with them, and that is the only tie which binds me to your country. As soon as we have done with your Tzar's despotism, I shall expatriate myself for ever, and settle somewhere in Germany."

"But will you——" said Andrey hesitatingly, "will you find anything better there? Have you forgotten the brutality of the German mob? and was it only the mob?"

"Yes," answered David, with a look of deep sadness in his large and beautiful eyes; "we Jews, we are outcasts among the nations. Still, German working people are educated, and are in the way towards better feelings, and Germany is the only land where we are not total strangers."

He bowed his noble head, and became silent.

Andrey was deeply moved by his friend's grief. He drew nearer to him, and laid his hand softly upon his shoulder. He wanted to cheer him. He wanted to tell him that the barbarity of the Russian peasants is the fruit of mere ignorance; that they have a larger stock of human kindness and tolerance than any people in the world; that when they are half as well educated as the Germans, all medieval superstitions will disappear from among them, and leave no trace behind.

But Andrey was prevented from saying this by the apple-faced representative of the rival race, who at this very moment approached them, and said,

"Good-night, gentlemen!"

"Ah, Hans!" said David, "you want to go home?"

"Yes, sir. Mother will be anxious about me. I must make haste."

David took from his waistcoat some silver groschen for the child, patted him on his rosy cheek, and dismissed him with a kind word.

"And the frontier?" asked Andrey. "Have we to cross it by ourselves?"

"The frontier! We have already crossed it."

"But when?"

"Half-an-hour ago."

"Strange! I have seen nothing whatever, not even a guard."

"The guard was probably stopping behind that hill over there, or in some other place where he cannot be seen, nor see us."

"How very kind of him," Andrey said, with a smile.

"A very common trick of the trade," David replied. "Nobody can find fault with him for staying at a given moment at some particular point upon the line he has to watch. For a few coppers, provided he knows you, he is always glad to linger a while in any place you prefer."

"And if we were behind time, and the guard should see us as he came out?"

"He would take to his heels and run back to his place of concealment; that's all. But we must not waste time. Let's go straight to the village, lest some patrol should chance to see us. That would bring us no good; we are in the Tzar's dominions now."

In Foma's house, whither they repaired, Andrey to his great joy found his travelling-bag, which the punctual German had already brought there.

They arrived at the station just five minutes before the smoking and puffing foreign train stopped at the platform. It was a limited express, but all the safer for that, as well-to-do people are less likely to be intruded upon than the common herd.

Andrey found a compartment, in which there was only one young man, asleep in a corner, his flaxen head wrapped up in a shawl. A gendarme walking up and down the platform courteously helped him with his bag. A last friendly nod from David, the train started, and Andrey felt himself in Russia in real earnest.

CHAPTER V.

THE TWO FRIENDS.

ON, on, the black serpent with red-hot eyes is flying, now wriggling and twisting and coiling up his long glistening tail, now dashing arrow-like into the darkness, panting and wailing in its struggle with space. But more quickly still than the red-eyed serpent are flying the thoughts of the traveller whom it carries to his destiny. After the excitement of the day, Andrey is alone, and he ponders over the part he is about to take in the work he knew so well years ago, but which would be quite new to him now. His meeting with the Russians in the morning, and the uproarious chaotic discussions, had not failed to leave their mark upon him. These people brought with them a whiff of Russian air, and Andrey had scented in it something which surprised and puzzled him. There was evidently in the revolutionary sea an undercurrent, somewhat narrow and exclusive, but very impetuous and passionate. Will he, on arriving, try his utmost to bring about an alliance with the tamer though more numerous elements of society? or will he swim with the new current, in order not to throw away the precious opportunity of energetic and immediate action? About this he could be clear only when on the spot.

And here his heart ached suddenly, for his thoughts reverted to Boris. This was the man in whose cool judgment and comprehensive mind he had trusted most, and to whose advice he would have most willingly listened. The idea that he was there no longer to be spoken to, perhaps never to be heard of again, was so depressing, that it seemed to Andrey all the anticipated pleasure of seeing the St Petersburg people was gone.

"But what if George is arrested also in the meantime?" the thought crossed his mind.

This was certainly as probable as the arrest of anybody else. At that moment Andrey was in the mood to believe that misfortunes never come singly. His apprehensions grew so foolishly strong upon him, that he resolved to send George a telegram, announcing in conventional language, of course, his arrival by the morning express. This he did at the first large station, and felt relieved from his anxiety, as if the telegram could act as a preservative.

He was quite sure now that George would be at the station to meet him, and he entered freely into conversation with his travelling companion,—the same whom he had taken overnight for a curly-haired young man. When in the morning the stranger awoke, and a closer examination of him was possible, he proved to be a thin elderly gentleman of sixty, with no curls whatever upon his bald pate smooth as a billiard-ball. For fear of draughts he had covered his head for the night with a cinnamon-coloured knitted nightcap, which Andrey had mistaken in the darkness for his natural hair.

In the tedium of a long journey conversation is easily started. The old gentleman was a great talker. He could not sit face to face with a man for twelve hours without inquiring whether he was married or single, landowner, tradesman or official, or a member of some liberal profession. He was most willing, in exchange, to expound his own concerns, with a great profusion of detail. They had quite a pleasant talk together. Andrey gave himself out as a business man, returning to his affairs after a holiday trip. His companion was a head clerk in the Ministry of Domains, returning from wintering abroad. From the impressions made by foreign lands they passed to their own country, and the old gentleman appeared to Andrey to be one of the most thoroughly dissatisfied men he had ever met. He had no respect for the authorities, as he saw nothing but folly in all the acts and measures of the Government, from the emancipation downwards. He did not believe in, or wish for, the stability of existing institutions, because everything, according to him, was bad, and ought to be changed. The civil service was badly paid, the landlords were ruined, the peasants were starving and insolvent, and there was no order anywhere!

The fact that the man, to whom he poured out all these feelings and views, was a perfect stranger to him, whose name he did not ask, and who did not know his, seemed not to diminish in the least the old gentleman's expansiveness. But at the last town before St Petersburg their *tête-à-tête* was inter-

rupted by two other passengers who came into the compartment.
The old gentleman thought it wiser not to commit himself in
their presence, and he grew silent and somewhat melancholy.
When the train ran under the glass roof of the vast terminus,
he looked very severe and formal, as if he were mentally entering the lobby of his office.

Andrey leaned out of the window of the carriage to look
for George. The platform was crowded with people—men,
women, and children,—who came to meet friends or relatives.
Porters with their wheelbarrows, shouting and expostulating,
made their way between the groups. There were the inevitable
gendarmes passing up and down with dignified airs. Not seeing George, Andrey concluded that he must be waiting for him
at the outer door.

With travelling-bag in hand, Andrey was elbowing his way
through the throng, when a strong clap on the shoulder and a
well-known voice made him turn his head. It was George,
whom he had not recognised in the crowd. In the three years
of separation he had grown from a youth into a young man,
and a fair flowing beard covered his chin and cheeks. Besides,
he was dressed with an elegance which was in strong contrast
with his former nihilistic carelessness.

"What a dandy you've become," said Andrey, kissing his
friend's face with as much effusiveness as the place allowed of.
"I should not have recognised you at all."

"Can't be helped; we are serious people now, and must
keep up appearances. Any luggage?"

"No, nothing but this," answered Andrey, lifting in the
air his rather heavy bag.

In silence they passed out of the station, and took a *droshky*
for George's lodgings. They arranged themselves as best they
could upon the high and narrow seat of the open carriage.

"Now tell me how it is with you? All in good health?"
Andrey asked eagerly, as soon as the horse began to move at
slow trot.

"Yes, all our people are well," said George.

This meant, of course, that none of their friends had been
recently arrested; questions of mere health are too unimportant a matter to be inquired about amongst conspirators.

"I come in good weather, then," Andrey observed.

"Not altogether," George answered evasively; "but of
this later."

He made a movement with his eyes towards the driver, who was sitting just in front of them. A hackney-coach in St Petersburg is not the place for discussing political news.

Andrey nodded assent, and looked rapturously around upon the familiar streets.

"How nice it is to be jolting once more in this infernal vehicle!" he exclaimed. "There is nothing like it abroad, I assure you."

It made him quite happy to welcome the glorious town associated for him with so many pleasant recollections, and to know himself once more in his right place. The uncertainty of the long journey was over. He was again a unit of that mysterious body which had undermined the Tzar's power beneath his very nose, and contrived to hide itself almost under the skirts of his gendarmes and policemen. There they stood, these myrmidons of the Tzar, sword and revolver in their belts, looking at them gravely as they passed by. But Andrey knew they were more likely to arrest half of the inhabitants of the capital, than to think that there was anything suspicious in two such bright and amiable young gentlemen. The sense of the fun of the thing blunted completely the sentiment of actual danger.

George lived in Jagarinskaia Street, where he occupied a couple of rooms, with a small ante-room. There was space enough for two persons, and the friends resolved to spend a week or so together, till Andrey could find suitable lodgings for himself. It is the rule among revolutionists that two of them should not live together, unless it is necessary for "business" purposes, so that the arrest of one may not needlessly involve another in his ruin.

When Andrey had removed all traces of his long journey, George accompanied him to "headquarters," where one was sure to find a couple or so of the members of their section. They paid, always in company, a few short visits to the friends who lived near, putting off all other business until the morrow.

Thus they managed to get back home early in the afternoon. They wanted to have the day all to themselves. They had to sound each other's views and opinions on so many subjects. Andrey had so much to ask, and George so much to tell of the new men and new things with which the newcomer would have to deal. They talked long and hard, Andrey partly discussing, partly listening, trying to make the best use of his friend's information.

"Enough of politics for to-day," he said at last, when the many points which presented themselves had been thrashed out as much as they could be in a five hours' animated conversation. "You must tell me now everything about yourself, George."

George was pacing up and down the room, his hands behind him, still meditating upon graver subjects.

"Where do you want me to begin? It is a long story," he said.

"At the beginning. I know really nothing of you except what you have printed, which is very little."

"Then you know most of me," George replied, "though it certainly is very little."

"But have you not written something besides? Your other things, you know?" Andrey inquired.

He meant poetry, in which George indulged in the intervals left by his more prosaic and laborious duties as a party journalist.

"Very little," George answered; "hardly anything at all, since the publication, I mean, of my little volume, which you have seen. I have been working much of late in the young people's clubs."

"Yes? And what are your impressions? I was told by several people abroad that our rising generation is becoming very worldly-wise, and the philistines make many converts among them."

"The eternal complaint of the purblind and faint-hearted," George replied warmly, "who in the great book of life can see only the besmeared margins."

He told his own experiences, which had led him to entirely different conclusions—rather too bright than otherwise. To confirm his general statements, he mentioned several of his young friends by name.

"You must meet them some day, Andrey," he said ; "you'll agree with my opinion of them, I'm sure."

He gave in a few words some characteristics of each of them. But he did not dwell long on this matter, as a man who is in a hurry to pass to another subject of exceptional interest.

"There is one girl, whom I wish you particularly to know," he proceeded, sitting down close to Andrey on the same large settee. "Her name is Tatiana Grigorievna Repina, the daughter of the famous barrister. She is quite an extraordinary girl."

"You have a knack, my dear fellow," Andrey observed, "of discovering most extraordinary and exceptional persons, especially among girls."

"Oh, there are qualities so palpable, that it is impossible to be mistaken about them. That's just the case with Repina, who is certainly one of the most remarkable characters I ever met."

"And how old is she?" asked Andrey.

This was the weak point in George's case, and he knew it.

"She is nineteen," he said, assuming an easy tone. "But what does that matter?"

"Beautiful, I suppose?"

George did not answer. A characteristic square knot of wrinkles appeared upon his forehead, giving to his face an expression of annoyance, almost of pain.

"Don't be angry with me," Andrey hastened to apologise, taking him by the hand. "I meant no harm. The face is said to be the mirror of the soul, you know," he added, unable to altogether repress the temptation to jesting.

George's anger could not last long, and it melted away at a friendly word. He turned round with vivacity, and drew up his feet on the settee, so as to face his friend better. Then he entered into a long and very eloquent dissertation upon Tania's moral and intellectual qualities.

What struck him most in the girl was a remarkable combination of capacity for intense enthusiasm, with coolness and exactitude of practical judgment. Hers was the mind of an eventual leader, not the less powerful because endowed with feminine flexibility and grace.

All this George developed with great elegance of style and the charming candour of conviction.

Andrey listened to him with an incredulous but sympathetic smile. He was sure that nine-tenths at least of what George was saying was the work of his fecund imagination. George's heart was very affectionate, but he was singularly deficient in the middle notes in the scale of human sympathies. In his relations with his fellow-men he rapidly verged either towards a high degree of admiration or towards complete indifference. He was constantly led astray in his appreciation of people whom he met, though he pretended to know men well. He actually did know them in his way, though one could not trust his opinion. But Andrey, whose gamut of sympathetic capacities was normal, loved his friend most for that very unruliness of heart. He was delighted to find how little he had changed.

"Yes !" he exclaimed, laughing, "you must introduce me to your young friend. If one-tenth of what you say about her is true, she is certainly the flower of her generation. Where do you meet her? At your students' club, or at her parents'?"

"We meet regularly at club. But we call sometimes at the Repins—Zina and I. He is not afraid to receive ' illegal ' people. I think you had better meet Tatiana Grigorievna at her own home."

Andrey agreed with this. He was anxious to know Repin too, and expressed his satisfaction that such a big-wig as Repin was on their side.

"I am not quite sure of that," George observed. "I can't make out what his exact position is. Zina knows him better, and speaks of him very highly. The fact is, that he's been helpful to us on many difficult occasions."

George gave some instances, showing that Repin's contributions were far beyond the amounts contributed by ordinary sympathisers.

"He must be a rich man," said Andrey.

"Yes, he is very well off," George answered. "But I am not sure that all this money comes from him. Tania is rich herself. She will have a fortune when she comes of age. Some sort of maternal succession ; I don't know quite. Zina told me, but I didn't pay much attention. Certainly," he added in a soft dreamy tone, "she will be herself a much more precious acquisition for our cause than all the money she can bring with her."

Andrey turned his head rapidly towards the speaker. But he could not catch George's eyes. They were looking vacantly into space, as if in contemplation of some distant object.

Andrey uttered to himself a significant "hm !" and resolved that he would take the first opportunity to make the acquaintance of this extraordinary girl.

With the great freedom of intercourse between young people prevailing in Russia, a warm affection, and even admiration, of a young man for a girl, or *vice versa*, does not necessarily mean anything particular. They may be great friends, and nothing more. To an extravagant head like George's, the latitude of friendship was particularly wide. Still, in his tone and face, when he spoke about this girl, there was something which seemed to express rather more. Andrey desired to see them together, in order to solve doubts which were not unmixed with apprehension. He did not exactly side with those of his friends who proclaimed as a principle that a revolutionist must never love a woman. Still, he considered that it was better for them to keep aloof from such "nonsense" as long as they could. If George fell into this predicament just now, Andrey did not think he ought to be congratulated upon it, all the more since his chosen one was, as far as he could guess, a fashionable girl of a set very different from their own.

CHAPTER VI.

A MIXED PARTY.

REPIN answered his daughter's request by saying that he should be very glad to see Andrey at his house. But three weeks passed before Andrey was able to avail himself of the invitation.

Zina meanwhile had returned from her visit to Dubravnik, bringing such unfavourable news that all, herself and Andrey included, were forced to agree that, for the present at least, any attempt to rescue Boris would be hopeless. As Zina wished to talk to the Repins about the affair, in which they took a warm interest, she proposed to accompany Andrey to their house. So they expected to have a regular "illegal" tea-party under the lawyer's roof.

Andrey was living now in his own lodgings at Pesky, not far from those of Zina, so that it was convenient for both to come together. George was thus relieved from the duty of escorting his friend, which seemed to him quite a sufficient reason for going much earlier than the others. At six sharp, when he knew the family had finished their after-dinner coffee, he rang the electric bell at the outer door of the luxurious flat occupied by Repin in Konushennaia Street.

He had hardly time to inquire whether the family was at home, when rapid footsteps were heard in the adjacent room, and Tania came out to greet him with a smile and a familiar shake of the hand. She was a graceful brunette, with large black eyes beneath strongly marked eyebrows, and a well-shaped mouth, rather large. It was a lively original face, not exactly beautiful, but positively bewitching when she smiled.

"Only you!" she exclaimed, in a tone of mock disappointment.

"Yes, only I, Tatiana Grigorievna," George replied. "But you need not despair, the others are coming soon."

She led the way into the dining-room, where they found her

father—a tall grey-bearded man of about fifty-five—in company with a young gentleman of thirty, with a velvet jacket and long chestnut hair, who looked like a distinguished artist. He was Nicolas Petrovich Krivoluzky, professor at one of the St Petersburg high schools, and a great friend of Repin's.

The usual greetings over, Krivoluzky resumed his interrupted narrative about the approaching collision between the reactionary and the liberal section of the Imperial Society for the Promotion of Bee-keeping in Russia, to which he was secretary. Repin and he seemed to be deeply engrossed in the subject, and Repin laughed heartily over the tricks of the reactionists to secure a majority for the next nomination of chairman.

The young people made a polite attempt to show themselves interested in the discussion of their elders. But soon they glided into talk of their own. Tania asked George what were the questions debated at their students' club at the last meeting, at which she had been unable to be present. George answered, and then inquired in his turn whether she had prepared the summary of the book which she had to expound at the next meeting.

"Yes, I have. But I think it so abominably done, that I shall probably not read it at all. I am sorry I did not take something easier."

"Every beginning is hard," said George. "But perhaps it is not so bad as you think. Will you show it to me?"

"With pleasure. But I am sure you will think it quite as bad as I do."

She led him into her room, where upon her small neat writing-desk lay a cleanly copied, carefully sewn manuscript, written with wide margins. This she handed to him.

George took from his pocket a pencil, and set himself to read in silence, with the rapidity of a pressman accustomed to deal with copy.

Tania sat opposite, upright upon a stool, and remained silent as a fish, looking in amusing suspense at George's face. She was very anxious he should not think her a fool, yet this first effort of hers was so bad that she did not know how he could help it.

They had been acquainted only for a few months, but long enough for them to have become fast friends. The young girl never remembered leading a life so full and many-sided as since she met George. When years ago, Zina, just escaped from prison, appeared at their house, she upset Tania's tranquil thoughts by revealing to her a new world. But she was a child then, and the mysterious world in which Zina lived frightened her as much as it interested her. Now she began to see more clearly. She liked her companions, the students to whom she was introduced. At one of their meetings she had met George, who very soon became the chief figure in her intellectual life.

Listening to him, the girl felt new forces stirring in her soul. George did not flatter her, or pay her a single compliment. No self-respecting man of the generation which championed so hotly women's rights would permit himself such a vulgarity, nor would any girl of their set listen without offence. Indeed, George tried not to hurt her modesty by speaking about herself at all. Of this exquisite pleasure he took his fill at the expense of his many friends, whom he bothered with elaborate disquisitions upon the extraordinary qualities of the girl he had discovered. But he was so full of the subject, that it made its appearance somehow whatever else he said. When talking about Andrey and the pleasure of meeting him, he could not conceal from Tania how much he had spoken to Andrey about her. When there was something to say about the club to which they both belonged, it chanced, he did not know how, that this led him to illustrate, or to allude delicately to, some of the young girl's hidden qualities or revolutionary talents.

Whilst protesting and disbelieving, Tania could not help feeling elated and thankful for appreciation so high from a man who was not one of the common herd. George appeared to her with the halo of a fearless knight, fighting for a noble cause, and risking his liberty and life for it. That there was nothing but friendship between them she never doubted. Attractive as she was, and rich into the bargain, she had her ample share of courtship and admiration. Nothing resembling this could be detected in George's behaviour. He treated her like a comrade, without any sign of obsequiousness. He scolded her sometimes, and always told her the truth to her face when he thought she was in the wrong. That is why his company was so agreeable to her, and why the sweetness of his delicate half-suppressed praise was so penetrating.

She was quite relieved when, after reading her paper, George said that as far as the matter went it was not bad. With a few marks of the pencil he showed her some transpositions and abbreviations which would set it all right.

They were in the midst of their talk, when Zina and Andrey entered.

At the sight of her, the young girl forgot her paper and George and everything, in a flood of generous pity for her unfortunate friend. She knew how deeply Zina loved Boris, and it was the first time they had met since Zina's discouraging journey to Dubravnik.

With a searching frightened look in her large pathetic eyes, Tania rushed towards her friend to embrace her, and kissed her face with girlish effusiveness. But the strikingly beautiful face of the young woman was quite calm and composed. Looking at the two women at this moment, one would have supposed Tania to be the bereaved, and the other to be bent upon the charitable purpose of comforting her. Zina's deep grey eyes met Tania's distressed and sympathetic look with perfect steadiness. No cloud was visible upon the delicately modelled straight forehead, framed by a waving line of fair curls. Her bright smile showed her genuine pleasure at the welcome.

Tania felt reassured. She was so ready to be reassured, poor child. Mourning does not agree with hopeful youth.

"And where is Grigory Alexandrovitch?" Zina inquired. "At home, I suppose?"

"Yes, papa is with Krivoluzky. We fled here so as not to annoy them with our chatting," said Tania. "Now we are in such numbers, we can break in upon them safely."

George introduced Andrey to her.

"This is my chum, Tatiana Grigorievna. I beg you to like him," he said.

"I promise to try," the young girl answered, holding out to Andrey her hand, with a movement that struck him by its genuine grace.

They found that Repin and Krivoluzky had taken refuge in the study, in the midst of a cloud of smoke.

Andrey was introduced under the name of Petroff for convenience, though Repin knew of course who he was, as well as Krivoluzky, who had come on purpose to meet him.

The old barrister gave Andrey a hearty welcome. Among the older refugees there were several companions of Repin's youth, and he wanted to know how they were doing in foreign lands.

Andrey was able to satisfy his host's curiosity, as he either knew them or had heard about them all from their friends. The Russian refugees abroad form but a small body, and the oldest of them are universally known. Repin's friends were of this number. They were toiling hard, each along his own line, separated mostly from each other by political dissensions. Some were in good health, others were not. This was all the news which could be given about their rather monotonous existence.

"You will not find the life monotonous here, I am afraid," said his host. A good-natured smile parted his thick lips, but it quickly vanished, the roughly-hewn powerful face of the old lawyer assuming a serious thoughtful expression.

The conversation grew general. Repin had been to Switzerland in Herzen's time, and related his experiences and his agreeable impressions.

"What a painful contrast it must be to you," he said to Andrey, "after being accustomed for so long to complete freedom, to drop into this unfortunate country, where you cannot utter a word without being collared by a gendarme."

"The contrast is great, of course," Andrey replied. "As far as I am concerned, I do not find it so painful; certainly I am better here than I was there."

Repin shook his big head incredulously. The sight of this man, in the bloom of youth, who had come across Europe into this dreadful town, swarming with spies and police, to meet certain death for a dream, moved his heart to pity, and stung him with a sort of reproach. He looked at him and his two friends, and shook his head again.

"No, don't say that!" he resumed. "To be always in apprehension; never to have a moment of safety and peace by day; to be awakened by every unusual noise by night,—with the thought that your last moment has come! It must be dreadful!"

The good man was so much in earnest, and the pathetic picture he had drawn so distorted, that those most concerned in it burst into hearty laughter.

"I beg your pardon," said Andrey, apologetically, "but your picture is really very strong."

Repin was not in the least offended, but much interested, as an observer of human nature. The irrepressible outburst of naive and discourteous laughter was more convincing than any arguments.

"Do you mean to tell me that you do not mind the dangers besetting you?" he asked, looking round in surprise.

Zina sat at the extremity of the circle, which was formed around Repin's chair, and his eyes dwelt upon her longest, as if his general question referred to her in particular.

"It comes too often, Grigory Alexandrovitch. One soon gets accustomed to everything—unfortunately," she said, a shadow clouding for a moment her face.

It was in consequence of an unpardonable piece of carelessness that the Dubravnik tragedy, in which Boris was involved, had taken place.

But the cloud passed as naturally as it came, and her grey eyes looked as clear and firm as before.

Though the consciousness of her fresh and irreparable loss never abandoned her for a moment, it was impossible to suppose that her outward calmness was only a mask held over her face by mere effort of will. Every tone of her voice, and every line of this beautiful blonde head, breathed such sincerity, that even her stoicism must have been natural and not assumed. This, too, was the effect of long acquired habits. In the world in which Zina moved, there is at least one out of every three persons whose heart is torn to pieces by a misfortune similar to hers. Life would become impossible, and their work, admitting of not one moment's relaxation, would have stopped altogether, did they not keep their nerves in good order.

Zina was not in a talkative mood to-night, but she took part in the conversation in the same natural and simple way as she fulfilled her everyday duties. She supported Andrey when he tried to give to his host a truer idea of the life of an "illegal" man. She laughed when George undertook to prove that in Russia the "illegal" people are the only ones who, at times at least, enjoy the full protection of the laws.

"Take yourself, for example," he said to Repin, "are you sure that this very night the police will not break into your house? You have dismissed a clerk for swindling, and he might wish to take his revenge by accusing you of harbouring terrorists; you have said something against the government, and some eavesdropper will report it to the Third Section; you have written years ago in the same strain to a friend, who has been arrested, and your letter has just been discovered. Have you not actually done all this?"

Repin confessed his guilt.

"Then it is sheer carelessness on your part that you sleep with tranquillity," George went on, "because you may be arrested to-night, and to-morrow be on your way to Archangel, or to some remoter and more uncomfortable place."

The old lawyer answered with a smile that he hoped no such thing would happen to him, but of course he could not be sure of it.

"And we can!" George exclaimed, with mock triumph. "All our sins are washed away from us when we throw into the fire our old passports and reappear with a fresh one. Provided it is a good one, and we keep our eyes open, we can manage very well. I shall soon celebrate the fourth anniversary of my illegal existence."

"Then you are living twice the usual term at somebody else's expense," said Andrey. "It is calculated that the illegal people don't live more than two years on the average."

"They might prolong it at least to three years, if they were not so slow in changing their passports," George observed, chiefly for his own gratification, since nobody heard his wise remark. Tea was announced, and all rose and passed into the dining-room.

"Zinaida Petrovna," said Repin, who brought up the rear, "I have something to ask you,—please stop a moment. "Tania," he added, "send us our tea here."

He wanted to know all the particulars as to how the matter stood with her husband, for whom he had a sincere respect, and to ask whether he could be in any way useful to her.

Zina guessed what he had in his mind. There was not much to say about her own affair, which was at a deadlock, but she wanted to have a quiet talk with Repin. She had the affair of the two sisters Polivanov to arrange. The gendarmes were inclined to let them out on bail, after two years of imprisonment, as no proof against them had been yet forthcoming. It was essential to find good sureties for them at once, because the girls were said to be in bad health. Zina expected Repin would stand for one, but he had to provide another. Besides, she wanted him to obtain if possible some information from the State Attorney as to the fate of those condemned in the last political trial, who were conveyed away secretly, nobody knew where.

*   *   *

The merry voices and the laughter of the young people reached Repin and Zina from the dining-room. George fell out with Krivoluzky upon the professor's favourite hobby, that until the wholesale conversion has taken place of the Russian peasantry into landless proletarians subject to the yoke of capitalists, there is no hope for the labour movement in Russia.

The debate was led by George, the two others listening,—Tania, with the strained attention of a neophyte, trying hard to understand the learned lucubrations of the professor; Andrey, with a genuine curiosity for this new type of scientific craze. Now and then he put short questions to Krivoluzky, leaving, however, the main field to his friend. George was a brilliant debater, his enormous memory permitting him to retain all the details of his opponent's longest speeches. Andrey put in a few words, but his interest soon flagged; he had nothing or very little of that ardent passion for debate so common among the Russians, in the absence of some more substantial outlet for energy.

He was glad when Zina, having finished her conspiracy with the lawyer, to her evident satisfaction, appeared in the doorway. Repin followed her.

"Well, how stands the matter?" he asked the disputants. "Are the destinies of Russia settled already, or is there anything still left doubtful?"

The square furrow of annoyance appeared upon George's forehead before he was able to repress it. He did not like this bantering tone. Andrey, on the contrary, was delighted, and explained to Repin into what a deadlock their country was put by his learned friend.

New guests arrived; Orest Pudovikoff, a journalist, with his wife, who gave a new turn to the conversation. But Andrey did not take part in it. He joined the two ladies, who were deep in an animated discussion of their own.

"You must help me to keep her a little while with us," Tania appealed to him.

Now that Zina was going, it flashed upon the young girl that her calmness was that of self-control, not of resignation. She reproached herself with insensibility to her friend's sorrow, and wanted an opportunity to make amends, though she did not exactly know how.

"Are you really going, Zina?" asked Andrey. "It is so early."

"Yes.   I have business at Bascow Row."

"You can do your business to-morrow morning.   Do be good and stay a little," Tania insisted coaxingly, clasping Zina by the waist with the caressing grace of a kitten.

Zina laughed that short deep laugh which was one of her greatest charms.   The girl's suggestion was so incongruous. The business which called her to Bascow Row at half-past ten sharp was to meet the gaoler of the fortress, who transmitted the letters from the political prisoners detained in one of the ravelins.

"No, dear," she said, kissing the eager face turned towards her, "I can't do it to-morrow, or I should have stayed with you of my own accord.   I will look in on Saturday afternoon," she added, "but now I must run away."

She went out, giving them a parting smile from the door. It seemed as if the whole tone of their surroundings had been raised to a higher level by her presence.   The sight of great courage in bearing great misfortune, has the power of tuning souls to a higher pitch.   Tania and Andrey felt themselves drawn towards each other by their community of affection for her.

"Have you been long acquainted with Zinaida Petrovna?" Andrey asked.

"I met her when she first escaped from prison.   But it is only since she settled in St Petersburg that we have seen much of her, and I really knew what a woman she is!" Tania replied enthusiastically.

"I shall not have the same chances of seeing you often, Tatiana Grigorievna.   But I entered this house with the hope of leaving it, if possible, your friend," Andrey said, looking trustingly in her eyes.   "You are not offended at my presumption, I hope?"

"Quite the reverse," answered the girl seriously.

"Thank you.   Then let us have a good talk to begin with," said Andrey.

He looked round, and having found a retired corner invited her to take an easy-chair, and placed by it a stool for himself.

"You are far from being a stranger to me," Andrey proceeded.   "I may say you were almost an acquaintance of mine before we met.   George has spoken so much of you, and very eloquently, I assure you."

Tania blushed slightly, and felt vexed with herself, and angry with Andrey, who was the cause of the blush. Her kindly feeling for him vanished at once.

"I will repay your compliment with a vengeance," she said, "for I'm sure I have heard of you more than you can have heard of me, and from various people. So that my information has the advantage of not being one-sided."

"So much the better," said Andrey, "it gives me a claim to get compensation."

The girl's temper was not improved by seeing him so outrageously unconcerned. A delicate swelling, intended to be a frown, appeared between the long eyebrows upon the smooth and pure forehead, which no cares or sorrows had yet furrowed with wrinkles. She was accustomed to have young men show her an obsequious deference, and was not prepared to make an exception in the case of a man who was after all a perfect stranger to her. She was sorry not to have been more formal with him from the beginning.

"You regret, Tatiana Grigorievna, your former kindness, and you think I am abusing it?" Andrey said, reading her thoughts in her face.

"Well, perhaps I am," he went on, without giving her time to answer. "But you must make some allowance for us. The existence of conspirators is short, and the opportunities they have for friendly intercourse are few. We must be excused if we try to make the most of them by sometimes dropping conventional formalities. To-night our ways in life cross for a moment, and nobody can tell whether they will ever cross again. Will you permit me to speak with you quite frankly without reserve, as if we were comrades?"

The ice was broken. Under the calm tone of her strange guest the girl felt something pathetic and melancholy, which touched her generous heart, melting her superficial worldliness. She was ashamed of her suspicious reserve, which now seemed to her quite out of place with this man.

"Yes!" she exclaimed warmly, looking him in the face, "speak as you like."

Andrey was surprised at the pleasure her assent gave him. There was in the girl something which George had probably forgotten to mention, but which attracted him exceedingly, on her own account, independently of the part she might play in his friend's life.

He questioned her upon her present occupations and her intellectual pursuits, her political opinions, her doubts, and her purposes in life. His questions troubled and agitated her sometimes, but she was pleased with them, and did not try to resist the strange power this man exercised over her. After the first quarter of an hour she felt at ease with him, as if they had been long acquainted.

George joined them, unable to withstand the force of attraction, but soon withdrew. He was so anxious they should become friends, that he was ready to sacrifice himself to give them the chance to have a good talk to themselves. He contented himself with looking at the girl from a distance, hastily casting his eyes down when he met Andrey's slightly mocking glances.

At a quarter to the sacramental hour of twelve, which marks the beginning of the hours specially "unsafe," Andrey and George left, and the company broke up.

Tania retired to her bedroom full of the pleasant impressions of the evening. She took off her elegant gown—too elegant and costly for a girl of her views. George had several times hotly reproached her for her love of finery. Sitting before a large looking-glass, she arranged her black tresses for the night. She was on the whole very much satisfied with her new acquaintance. The evident desire of a man like Kojukhov to make a friend of her, flattered her youthful vanity.

"How amusingly he looked at me when he asked permission to treat me like a comrade!" she exclaimed ; and she laughed aloud, showing in the glass two brilliant rows of small white teeth, and a pair of glistening black eyes.

But as she recalled to memory the details of their unusual conversation, a strong revulsion of feeling came upon her. Kojukhov was the first conspirator of note she had met. George was really a much more prominent man, but he was an altogether exceptional one, not to be measured by the common standard. But Kojukhov, why should he care to know so much about her? Personally she could have no interest to him. He was a conspirator, and he wanted to ascertain whether she was worth enlisting or not. She was for him an eventual utility, and he had come to gauge her value. That was all. This idea made her angry with herself, and very miserable. She could not forgive herself for having been almost a party to his experiments. He had taken her by surprise ; the next time she would teach him better. The image of George sent a wave of repentance and tenderness over her heart. She began to appreciate the value of his lavish affection and delicate solicitude, by contrast with this Kojukhov.

The street-door of Repin's house had hardly closed behind them, when George seized his friend by the arm, and asked him in an excited tone,—

"Now, tell me, what do you think about Tatiana Grigorievna?"

"Well, I rather like her," was the calm reply.

George dropped his friend's arm, and turned his head aside in sulky silence. This was the reward for his self-sacrifice throughout the whole evening! He was disappointed, well-nigh offended. Was there ever such a provokingly irresponsive man as Andrey? But he soon recovered, and began to make excuses for his friend. One can't expect a man to know a person after an hour's conversation. Then, as Andrey was not prepared to talk about the girl, George, by way of consolation, undertook the task himself. His resources were great, and he could afford to give a pleasant variety to the subject.

Andrey was a very good listener, understanding quickly and objecting little. This was the primary cause of their early friendship. Now he listened to George with his usual sympathetic interest, but he seemed to agree with him about nothing.

"Strength of character!" he interrupted George; "I doubt if she has any. In the sense you mean, at all events."

George smiled at so gross a blunder on his friend's part.

"I see you do not know her at all," he said.

"Possibly. Though I think I do," Andrey replied.

"You have been probably misled by those yielding ways which fashionable girls like herself like to assume."

"Do you think her a fashionable girl? I thought her, on the contrary, very simple and natural,—a good genuine Russian girl, and nothing more."

"Nothing more! Then you did not like her at all? And you said you did."

Andrey laughed.

"You are mistaken, my dear fellow," he said good-humouredly. "And to prove that I really liked her, I tell you at once that if she falls in love with you, as you have with her, I'll give you unhesitatingly a paternal benediction."

It was the first time Andrey had spoken to George so plainly about his love affair. He wanted to see them together to be quite sure, knowing how often "this nonsense," as he called love in general, might be fanned into something inconveniently serious by friendly interference and encouragement. Now that he had seen them together no doubt was possible, and there was no reason for reticence.

The young philosopher did not suspect that this "nonsense" had already struck root in his own heart, and the only way for him to prevent the poison permeating his whole being was never to see again those black sparkling eyes, that pure forehead, and that bewitching smile.

But as there was nobody to give him that advice, and a wonderful calm reigned in his heart, Andrey did not think of flying from temptation. Indeed, he dismissed the subject from his mind altogether, because at this moment his attention was directed into an entirely different channel.

For some time past he had heard persistent and suspicious footsteps behind them. They sounded always at the same distance, and were uneven, now overbold and now overcautious, like treachery. In all probability they were followed by a spy. Andrey said nothing of his suspicions to George, fearing that, as he was a nervous man, he might turn his head in order to see the man behind them, which would put the spy on his guard and spoil their game. Taking his friend by the arm, Andrey quickened his pace as if in the heat of conversation. The man behind them quickened his pace too. Andrey repeated the experiment by slackening his speed, with the same effect. Yes, they had a spy behind them, and a foolish one into the bargain. Andrey was perfectly sure that for half a mile from Repin's door they had not been followed. The spy was probably a rambling one, attracted by some words of a suspicious nature uttered too loudly as they passed him. The thing was not serious; still they must get rid of him, especially as they were now approaching George's lodgings.

"There is a spy following us," Andrey said to his companion, "but you must not take any notice of him. At the corner of Kosoi Lane we will separate, and I will take him upon myself. It's a good bit farther to my place, you know."

"All right," said George, nodding his head.

They soon reached the point for parting. George went his way, but Andrey took a few paces, and then stopped a while to light a cigarette. Now that he saw the man's face, all doubts were dispelled. The tall post-like fellow, with big red hands and yellow hair and whiskers, bore upon his face the stamp of his profession, in the peculiar scared and strained expression, which he vainly tried to conceal by an easy and nonchalant gait.

The spy having to choose which of the two to follow, hesitated a few moments at a little distance. Andrey was the elder of the two, and he prided himself upon looking much more imposing and serious than George. He was sure the spy ought to choose him. So in all probability he would have done, but Andrey's match did not catch fire at once. He stopped a moment longer, and the spy, perplexed by his waiting, turned short to the right, plunging resolutely into the street George had taken.

This eventuality Andrey had also foreseen, and he immediately followed his man. An enemy in the front, and another in the rear, in a deserted thoroughfare, is an uncomfortable position. The pluckiest of spies will not stand it for three minutes, and in fact the wretch stopped short, as if to read a theatre bill fastened to the wall. Andrey passed him, quietly smoking his cigarette. When he was some fifteen yards away, he recognised the man's footsteps behind him once more. This was what he expected. As he walked more slowly than George, with the air of a man on the look-out for a cab, he gave his friend a considerable start, and soon saw him disappear round a corner.

Andrey's next move was to have himself followed for a while through the deserted streets, and then to take a solitary cab and, ordering it to drive to some out-of-the-way place, leave the spy on the pavement. But he was spared the expense of an unnecessary drive. The steps of his pursuer became less and less audible, and after a time were heard no more. Guessing that he was found out, the spy gave up the chase of his own accord. This confirmed Andrey's first supposition that the incident had nothing serious in it. Still, who can tell?

On returning to his rooms he carefully bolted the doors, so as not to be taken by surprise, and ascertained whether the dagger and loaded revolver he always wore in a belt under his coat were in good order.

CHAPTER VII.

TANIA WINS HER SPURS.

GEORGE'S accidental remark about the insecurity of Repin's sleep proved an ill-omened prophecy. His two dangerous guests were hardly out of sight when gendarmes appeared.

Repin was not a coward, but his blood ran cold when men, in the hated blue uniform, entered the room. His first idea was that the two young men were recognised as they left his house, and arrested in the street, and that the search in his house was only the consequence of their arrest. But the first words of the gendarmes reassured him. The unwelcome visit was due to some vague suspicions, the origin of which he could not make out. Its coincidence with the visit of the two conspirators was evidently a chance. Repin gave a sigh of relief. As for himself, he had nothing particular to fear.

The police ransacked the house, but found nothing compromising. At three in the morning they went away. In consideration of Repin's high social position he was not arrested, and had only to pay a disagreeable visit to the police office, and to answer some impertinent and foolish questions.

He was left in peace, but a watch was kept over him by the disappointed police. This was likely to have disagreeable consequences to all concerned, if the spies detected some of the rather frequent visits of Zina or George. It was necessary to inform them without the slightest delay of what had happened. Accordingly Tania was despatched the very next morning to the revolutionary camp, to warn her friends that the coast was not clear.

She started upon her errand with all the excitement of a young girl who has for the first time serious business entrusted to her. Since their house was watched, it was more than probable that each of its inmates would be followed. She was in mortal fear lest instead of a warning to her friends she might bring spies following upon her heels. How was she to escape their vigilance? With the fantastical ideas of the uninitiated as to the omnipresence and superhuman skill of the police, she was at a loss how to ascertain whether she was followed or not. She arranged her dress in a somewhat different way from her ordinary one, and she issued upon the street at the moment when the suspicious-looking man at the corner was paying one of his brief visits to the public-house. But who knows? perhaps at that window on the other side of the road there was another spy standing behind the curtains, who had seen her, and would give the signal to his companion as soon as he returned! She hastened along the street to escape the phantoms created by her own imagination, but they pursued her. What guarantee had she that this respectable old lady, going in the same direction, was not a spy? Guarantee there was certainly none. The old lady turned at the first corner and took the way to Nevsky, without so much as once looking at the girl. This was all very well, but perhaps it was a stratagem, and the would-be spy had given a wink to another to take up the pursuit! or, if this was not a spy at all, a real spy, whom she had not noticed, might be following her at a distance.

The poor girl was in a state of utter bewilderment, and was losing her head, when it occurred to her that a cousin of hers lived in a house on the Liteinaia, which communicated by a narrow passage with Mokhovaia Street. Even in the busiest time of the day few people used this thoroughfare. At the present early hour it must be quite deserted. If she passed through with nobody behind her, she might be pretty certain to escape these terrible hounds of the Third Section. The expedient was so simple, that she wondered it had not occurred to her before. She took a cab to the Liteinaia, and had the satisfaction of ascertaining that no other vehicle followed her. As to the foot passengers, she ventured to think that she need not trouble herself about them any further. She began to recover from her superstitious fears, and to consider what she should do next. Her idea was to go to George's lodgings. The active conspirators keep their private addresses very secret, communicating them as a rule only to their colleagues. But George made an exception in her case. She knew his address, and had paid one or two visits to his den. The general tone of companionship in the relations between young men and girls in Russia allows of such freedom. She would find the house, and reach his rooms without asking any questions; but would George be at home? She promised the cabman a tip, and in ten minutes was at the entrance to the wished-for passage. It was not quite deserted; two washerwomen entered it at this moment, carrying a large basket of linen. But Tania had recovered from her imaginary fears sufficiently to think it unlikely that these women would have any connection with the Third Section. The rest of the way she went on foot.

Her ring at the bell was answered almost immediately. George was at home. An exclamation of joyful surprise escaped him when he recognised his unexpected visitor.

"What good wind has blown you to my shore, Tatiana Grigorievna? My best friends have assembled under my roof to-day. You alone were missing."

With the volubility of joy he gave no time to Tania to put in a single word, and opened the door leading from the hall to the room which was his study, sitting, and dining room in one. Andrey was there, and with him a tall fair lady, whom Tania did not know.

She was Lena Zubova, who had just arrived from Switzerland.

The two girls were introduced to each other. To account for her intrusion among people whom she represented to herself as always transacting important business, Tania explained at once the cause of her visit.

The news of a domiciliary visit at the Repins' startled them all. But when they were told that nothing whatever was found, and that he was not arrested, they took the matter lightly.

"We may congratulate you upon your first political experience," Andrey said.

"It might have been the last one for us," George remarked.

He informed Lena how narrowly they had both escaped arrest the night before.

"Had we remained a few moments longer, we should have been caught, as certain as death."

"The same thing would have happened had the police walked a little faster and arrived a little earlier," Andrey observed. "Each man's destiny is written in the book of fate, and he can't escape it," he added, half seriously, half jestingly.

George said that it was always good for a man to give some help to the fates in shaping his destiny.

They both thanked Tania for having come to warn them.

Lena was the first to inquire how Tania managed to come out of a house that was probably watched.

"Are you sure you were not followed here by any one?" she asked.

Tania did not know, but she thought not.

Then she related frankly her doubts and apprehensions of the morning, and the small artifice she had used to throw off the scent any possible pursuers.

Lena clapped her hands.

"Why, you have done your part splendidly, Tatiana Grigorievna!" she exclaimed. "None of us could have managed it better."

"Indeed?" said the blushing girl. "I did not suspect it in the least."

"So much the better," observed George. "You have an inborn talent for it."

He was delighted that Tania had given this little proof of presence of mind and ability, and was quite happy to see the sympathetic regard that it won for her from his two friends.

After delivering her message, Tania rose to take her leave. Her worldly tact suggested to her not to remain longer than was necessary.

George looked at her with blank disappointment. To go almost without exchanging a word with him! This was too bad of her. Her account of the external side of the incident of the night before was all very well for the others, but he wanted to know from the dear girl ever so much about her inner impressions and feelings in that decisive experience. But Tania was shy of remaining any longer.

"You may have some business to attend to," she said to him, in a confidential whisper; "I will not stand in your way."

"Oh, no; please stay," George insisted. "This is not a business meeting. You needn't hurry away."

Andrey repeated the assurance, and joined George in pressing her to stay a little while as she was there. Her father's house was no longer safe, and they were not likely to see her for a good while.

Andrey hardly addressed her at all, leaving her to the charge of George. He paid scarcely any attention to her, and talked with Lena, whom he asked about Annie Vulitch. He seemed altogether engrossed by Lena's account of the girl, which confirmed his own favourable impression. But the consciousness of Tania's presence never left him, giving him a quiet pleasure, like what one feels in the sunlight or in the beauty of a landscape whilst one is all the time absorbed in thoughts that run in a different direction.

When half-an-hour later Tania rose, saying that her father would be uneasy if she stayed too long, Andrey felt as if the room had grown darker and something was awanting.

"What a charming face!" said Lena, when the girl was gone.

Andrey smiled.

"I don't know. Ask George's opinion on that question," he said, pointing in the direction of his friend, who had accompanied his guest downstairs. "I am not a good judge in these matters."

It was an excess of modesty on Andrey's part—on this occasion at least, because inwardly he agreed completely with Lena. In truth the girl's face was charming to-day. But what had it to do with him after all?

George returned, and they resumed the conversation which Tania's arrival had interrupted.

About twelve they were joined by Zina and Vasily Verbitzky, who had arrived from Geneva together with Lena. Andrey had fulfilled his promise given to both of them to arrange for their speedy return.

Zina was in the height of excitement. Even Vasily's imperturbable face exhibited some trace of passion.

"What's the matter?" George asked.

This Zina explained by reading them forthwith a letter from Dubravnik, full of harrowing details of the ill-treatment of the political prisoners, culminating in an unheard-of fact. By order of the attorney, a young girl, whose name was given in full, had been stripped, in the presence of gaolers and gendarmes, before being locked up, under the pretext that the prison regulations prescribed the taking of a precise personal description of every inmate.

The news was received in dead silence. The merriment of a meeting of friends had vanished. The gloomy spirit of revenge was soaring above them all, and each brooding over the same fierce thoughts.

"This cannot be left unavenged!"

"A terrible example must be made!" exclaimed Lena and George, almost simultaneously.

Andrey said nothing, because he thought it useless to speak about a thing so self-evident.

"That is exactly what the Dubravnik people seem to have resolved," Zina said. "For they ask us in their letter to lend them an experienced woman for keeping a lodging for conspirators. They say also that they require one experienced man with a cool head and a steady hand."

"I will be their man!" exclaimed Andrey hastily.

"No," Vasily interposed in his slow lazy voice; "I told Zina before we came here that I am going."

This Zina confirmed, adding that it was certainly better that Vasily should go. The question of priority was of course immaterial, but Andrey had already formed some business relations in St Petersburg, and had started upon the actual work. Vasily, on the other hand, was a new man, and as fit as one could wish for the Dubravnik business.

Her opinion settled the matter.

"Well, let it be so," said Andrey. "But if by chance you require somebody else, you have only to send me word."

There could be no divided opinion as to the choice of the woman who had to go. Zina had already been at Dubravnik; she had all the rights and qualifications on her side.

Thus both the volunteers needed were chosen. The matter had to be laid before the next meeting of the committee, with whom the actual decision rested. But this was only a formality. They knew beforehand that no objection would be made by any one.

"By-the-by," Zina asked, turning to Lena, "would you like to take my place during my absence?"

Lena answered that she would be very glad to start upon some work at once.

Zina gave her a number of details, which turned out to represent a very imposing amount of work,—propaganda among the educated youth, propaganda among workmen, and secret correspondence with the prisoners in the fortress.

"I don't know whether I shall be able to manage all this," said Lena hesitatingly; "especially with the correspondence, as I know as yet nothing of what is going on."

George promised to take this task off her hands, and offered to assist her for a time in her other work.

"You will soon strike root everywhere," he said cheerily. "To-morrow we will call on a young student friend of mine, a member of one of the clubs; through him you will get to know all the rest. In the other club you have already made an acquaintance."

"Who?"

"Tania Repina, whom you have just seen."

"Ah, that's very pleasant," Lena said.

"Has Tania been here? Anything particular?" asked Zina.

In the excitement produced by the Dubravnik news, they had all forgotten the little incident of a domiciliary visit to Repin, and had not mentioned it to the newcomers.

Zina was struck by the news, more than the matter seemed to justify.

"Does Repin know the reason for the police visit?"

"Not at all. He was told nothing, and is at a loss to guess what it came from, just as we all are," George answered.

"Then I think I know," Zina said.

"Indeed!"

"It is connected with the Dubravnik arrests. There is a vague hint in their letter the meaning of which I could not find out at first. They mention the arrest of Novakovsky, a barrister, with whom Repin was, I think, on friendly terms, and they add that I must give warning to 'Pandect number one.' I could not make out for whom this nickname was intended. Now I guess they meant Repin. It is always so with this overzeal."

"But you wouldn't have had time to forewarn him, even if you had guessed rightly," Andrey said. "The order to make a visit at Repin's was evidently given by telegraph. Besides, as no harm happened to him we needn't be much concerned."

"That is true. But, I am afraid, the affair may not end there. Novakovsky has taken part in serious affairs. This may be discovered at any moment, and Repin will be visited again, with more serious consequences. We must warn him not to be lulled into a false security."

As it was unsafe to go to Repin's house, it was agreed that one of them should call on Krivoluzky, and send word through him.

CHAPTER VIII.

ZINA and Vasily Verbitzky started in due course for Dubravnik, and a few days later a letter was received announcing their safe arrival. In ten days another letter came from Zina, reporting that the affair was in full swing, and that before long "the account would be settled." But it was not decreed that this account should be settled either sooner or later. The long and short of the story is, that the attorney who ordered the infamous act, upon receiving the news of his death sentence, was seized with such a panic that he at once left the town upon furlough, obtained under pretext of sudden illness. After a month it transpired that he had left the service of the Ministry of Justice altogether.

The Dubravnik people, furious as they were against him, had no choice but to let him alone. It is an absolute and inviolable law with the terrorists, that from the moment an official gets out of the way of his own accord, and ceases to be harmful, he is in no case to be struck down for the sake of mere revenge. Several cowards have thus escaped the fate meted out to them.

The body of people brought together for the work of revenge did not, however, disband. Since they were there, with head-quarters, a service of sentinels, everything else in readiness, it was proposed that they should undertake the more arduous enterprise of liberating the three revolutionists—Boris, and his two companions Levshin and Klein—who were awaiting trial in the Dubravnik prison.

Zina wrote to this effect to the St Petersburg people, who heartily approved the idea, and promised to support the Dubravnik branch with money and, if needful, with men.

Andrey expected to be summoned to Dubravnik every day, but he did not wonder that week after week passed and he was still at his old place. It was agreed that Zina, who was superintending the preparations, should not ask him to come until the moment for decisive action was near, and he knew by experience how difficult attempts of this kind are to organise. Thus the summer passed without bringing anything particular from Dubravnik.

In St Petersburg the season was as dull as usual. The burning heat of the short summer, which is felt the more owing to its striking contrast with the rest of the year, drives away from the suffocating and miasmic town all who have the means to get a breath of fresh air. The summer season is that in which all Russia, both labouring and intellectual, hasten to the green fields, either for work or for repose. This produces a universal lessening of tension in all branches of the intellectual and social life of the city. Rebellion, like everything else, slumbers during the hot season, its combustible elements being scattered far and wide through the land.

The summer in which occurred the events described in these pages was less inactive than usual, owing chiefly to the extension of the propaganda among workmen, of whom there are always plenty in the capital both in summer and in winter.

It was to this work that Andrey devoted himself with his whole energy, as long as his services were not required elsewhere. A considerable part of his activity in former days had been devoted to propaganda among workmen. He had many acquaintances in their ranks, some of whom were still in town, and welcomed him as an old friend. In a fortnight Andrey had grown familiar with his work and with his men. The working people liked him for his earnest simplicity and thoroughness, and listened with pleasure to his sober unadorned discourses. On his part, Andrey felt himself quite at home with them, and the propaganda among them was the work he preferred. In this he was the exact antithesis to George, who found a more congenial sphere among students and educated people, where his brilliant qualities produced their best effect.

It was a bright Sunday afternoon in the first half of August, Andrey was returning from a meeting of workmen of the Vyborg district, which was under his special charge. On reaching the Liteiny bridge he looked at his nickel watch. It was six o'clock, and he began to ponder within himself whether he should cross the Neva and return to his lodgings, or catch an omnibus which would bring him in an hour almost to the door of Repin's summer residence on the Black River. The time

and the day were convenient for a visit. Still he had some
scruples about yielding to his ardent desire to go. He had been
to Repin's twice during the last week, and it was decidedly more
prudent not to go so soon again. The cloud which seemed to
gather over Repin's head two months ago had passed away.
Novakovsky had been released, as the Dubravnik police fortunately had not discovered his compromising connections. Repin
was not troubled any further, and his house was as safe as the
house of a Russian can be.

But visits of "illegal" people constitute a danger in themselves, and must not be repeated too often.

Andrey resolved that he would be virtuous, and go home,
though his room appeared to him at this moment very lonesome
and dreary. He went towards the bridge, and even crossed the
river, thinking out carefully what he would do when he reached
home. But this was mere hypocrisy, for he knew that he was
not going home. When, on reaching the end of the bridge, he
saw the Black River omnibus coming towards him, and one free
place at the back opposite the guard's seat, he hastily secured
it, saying very judiciously to himself that as it was Sunday the
next omnibuses might be crammed full.

One must not be over-suspicious ; it spoils the temper, he
thought. In suburban districts the police are so careless, the
watch so loose, and life so easy. One visit more can't matter
much, especially on a Sunday, when guests from town are
always expected.

The meeting Andrey had just left had been a very successful one. A new section had been reported in one of the biggest
factories of the neighbourhood. The prospect was bright, and
he was disposed to look upon everything with the eyes of an
optimist.

Through the open window he could see the passengers
packed together like herrings in a barrel, the children sitting
on their elders' knees. Most of them were in their Sunday
clothes, and a certain holiday air was upon their faces. Clerks,
small tradesmen, and petty officials, unable to afford the luxury
of a summer residence out of town, were taking advantage of
the fine weather for a trip. Andrey remembered that on
Sundays there was music in the park in the evenings. Tania
would want somebody to keep her company, as her father
worked in the evenings. If Krivoluzky did not unfortunately
drop in, they would spend a delightful evening.

Since they first met two months ago, hardly a week had passed without his seeing Tania,—first by mere chance, then by combinations too happy to be entirely fortuitous. After the Repins moved to the Black River they met very frequently. The comparative freedom of the inhabitants of these summer resorts from the police, allowed of the dropping something of the rigid observances of ordinary town life. Most of his free evenings Andrey spent either at the Repins' house or at Lena Zubova's. She had taken a small room in the neighbourhood for the summer months, and Tania was frequently her guest. Thus Andrey saw a great deal of the girl.

He was so much her senior by virtue of his experience in life, that this girl of nineteen seemed to him almost a child. But there was an affinity in their tastes, in the bent of their minds, and in an almost intuitive mutual understanding, which rendered companionship with her exceedingly fascinating to him. He had no apprehension that this intimacy with a charming girl would ever imperil his peace of mind. As to her, that was out of the question; he had nothing about him to captivate the fancy. Many women "liked him very much," but they always married somebody else. This was his fate, and he cheerfully made up his mind to it. A woman's love is a great, but dangerous blessing; a conspirator had better to do without it.

As to Tania, she was loved by George,—who was to him more than a brother; and at first he believed that Tania loved George in return. This excluded all possibility of looking upon her otherwise than as a sister. Later on, he began to be in doubt about Tania's feelings towards his friend. But a bond of brotherly ease and frankness between them had become established, and grew stronger as they learned to know each other better. He liked to watch the growth and burgeoning out of a young beautiful soul with its impetuous yearnings and timid hesitations, its petulance and its despondencies.

To this and to no stronger feeling he ascribed the almost painful longing to see her, the sadness which overcame him when some untoward obstacle deprived him of this pleasure, and the constant drift of his thought to the same channel, that of late had surprised, but not alarmed him. And, strangely, it was the contemplation of the love of another that did most to keep him blind to his own. His sober appreciation of the girl contrasted so strikingly with the exaltation of his friend, that it seemed impossible that they should both be under the sway of the same feeling.

George was a rarer visitor to the Black River than Andrey. He was very busy with his writing, as most of the staff were out of the town. But Andrey expected him this Sunday, as he had not been seen anywhere during the week.

On entering Repin's pretty wooden cottage, adorned with carvings in the Russian style, Andrey found the lawyer alone. Tania was out. He was told that Lena had called after dinner, whilst George waited in the park, and had taken Tania out for a walk. They were not expected to be back till late in the evening. Sorely disappointed, Andrey was about to leave ; but his host detained him.

"Take a little rest, and smoke a cigar. I am taking my holiday now."

A freshly-published yellow magazine lay before him, an ivory paper-knife between the sheets. He cut them as he read.

"Where have you come from, and what is the news in your part of the world?" Repin asked. "Are we going to be blown up, and have you been fixing the fuse?"

"Nothing so frightful as that," Andrey replied. "I have been at our working men's meeting."

"Indeed. Are you doing much in that line?" Repin inquired.

"Yes, especially this last year."

Repin looked much interested.

"And you find that your efforts are bearing some fruit?" he asked, in a tone of doubt.

"Certainly," said Andrey ; "why should we do it otherwise?"

"Oh, people often persist most in things that are fruitless," Repin rejoined.

A nobleman by birth, educated as a member of a slave-owning caste, Repin shared with the best men of his generation the prejudice that the abyss dividing the educated people from the toiling masses is impassable. In his practice as counsel in political trials, Repin met several workmen and peasants who fraternised completely with their educated brethren. This struck him as something entirely new. But one swallow, or even half-a-dozen swallows, don't make a summer. He was as incredulous as ever, and was glad of an opportunity to hear something more upon the question from a man who presumably knew the ins and outs of it.

He listened to Andrey with grave attention, nodding his grey head in sign of assent.

"Yes, it is a good beginning," he said at the end, "and the most hopeful side of your work ; the only one, in fact, of which I unconditionally approve. I am very much obliged to you for this information."

They had often discussed various revolutionary and political matters. Of all the friends of his daughter who frequented their house, the old lawyer liked Andrey the best, and talked with him very willingly. They could never agree, of course. But they hurt each other less, and they understood each other better, than the rest, Andrey's character making up somewhat for their great disparity of age.

"Now I must be going," said Andrey, rising. "I'll take a run through the park ; perhaps I shall come across them. At all events my greeting to Tatiana Grigorievna."

He left hurriedly.

When Repin was alone, he reopened the book to resume his reading. But he could not read that night. His own thoughts and cares filled his mind, rendering him unable to follow those of the author. He was thinking about his daughter, and the tragic dilemma in which her evident leaning towards the revolution placed him.

Repin was not a partisan of the revolution as it was at that time. A man of a much earlier epoch, he was a warm adherent and active supporter of the great liberal movement of 1860 associated with the name of Herzen. He remained faithful to its traditions. When the revolutionists resolutely attacked the political despotism of their country, he could not help recognising in them the champions of his own doctrine. Though he was too old to share their hopefulness, or to approve their reckless means, he did not consider this sufficient ground for avoiding all the responsibilities and burdens of the impending struggle. He had seen too much of the horrors of despotism, not to feel that the wildest form of retaliation was natural, excusable, and even morally justifiable. He felt neither hatred nor abhorrence for those in whom considerations of political expediency did not check the impulses of temperament. Indeed, he could not help feeling a certain respect for them.

One important event which had happened three years ago did much to give consistency to his vague sympathies. Repin had been asked to appear for the defence in one of the early political trials, when political offenders were still allowed counsellors to defend them. Here he became acquainted with his client Zina Lomova, a bright accomplished girl of twenty, and with several of her companions. His theoretical leanings were strengthened by the warm personal sympathy which he felt with these good and courageous young people. When, eight months after the Draconian sentence, which he considered most iniquitous, Zina escaped, and paid him an unexpected visit at his St Petersburg residence, he received her with open arms, and offered her shelter and everything she needed. Zina in fact spent several days in his house, until with Repin's assistance she was put into communication with such of her former companions as were living in the capital as " illegal " people.

Through Zina the Repins became acquainted amongst others with Boris Maevsky, whom she married soon after. The barrister's house was the rallying-point of all that was most intellectual in society, and there was no better place where, in the absence of a free press, conspirators could gather something as to the views and feelings of those who best represented the public opinion of St Petersburg.

Some of them struck up friendship with his daughter, whom they evidently singled out as a future member of their brotherhood.

The old barrister was far-seeing enough to fear that their expectation was well founded, and that the day was approaching when his beloved child would be hurled into the bottomless abyss that swallowed up so many victims. He would have given his life to save her, but he did not see how to do it. Prohibit her from seeing the conspirators, and try to prevent any intercourse with them? But it was as morally impossible for him to force her to shun these people, as to refuse them assistance himself because this might bring him one day into trouble with the police. Besides, what was the use of prohibitions and artificial seclusion, when the contagion was in the air? Many a parent had tried this desperate course, and with what result? They saw their children rebel against their authority, and break from them in enmity and scorn. No, let the worst come to the worst, his daughter should never look upon him as an enemy. He imposed no restraint upon her freedom, relying upon the moral influence he had acquired over her to keep her from a step which he considered both reckless and hopeless. For a time he flattered himself that he was successfully keeping her within bounds, and counter-balancing the external influence upon her. But of late he had noticed a change that made him uneasy. He feared that the fatal moment he dreaded was drawing near, and now, as he sat before the open volume, his soul ached with the dull gnawing pain of helplessness.

CHAPTER IX.

A NEW CONVERT.

ANDREY changed his mind, resolving that it was better to go straight to Lena's rooms instead of rambling through the park after his friends. They would probably return home for supper, if they were not already there. He was sure that they were, and he hastened his steps, not to lose one moment of the anticipated pleasure.

But this was a day of disappointment. They were not in, and had said nothing as to the time of their return. Still he resolved to take his chance and 'wait.

Lena had a good-sized room in the upper floor, scantily furnished, but pleasantly situated. A big acacia overhung the window, its delicate leaves floating in the motionless air.

Andrey opened the window, letting in a fresh fragrance from the garden and field below. The cottage stood on the outskirts of the village. Behind it was a vast plain, sprinkled with a few bushes, and crossed by a narrow by-road leading to a cluster of houses, which made a very picturesque effect against the light green of a small birch grove. The white nights of the St Petersburg midsummer had already passed away, but the evening twilights were clear and long.

Andrey had not waited more than a quarter of an hour when the door below slammed, and he heard upon the stairs George's laughter, and then a voice which set his heart beating strongly.

Tania looked charming with her dark cheeks slightly coloured by walking and a wreath of blue-bells in her hair. She was dressed in a light blouse of yellow unbleached silk, enfolding softly and caressingly her supple figure. In her left hand she held swinging her large trimmed straw hat, which she had taken off when heated by her long walk.

Andrey rose to meet her with a happy smile. The pleasure of seeing her was doubled to him after his fear of missing her altogether.

"You've had a good walk, I see," he said, looking at her flushed face.

"Yes," she answered, throwing herself into an arm-chair, "we enjoyed it very much, and George amused us so with his stories. It is a pity you did not come earlier."

"For the sake of his stories? But perhaps I have already heard them. That's a common occurrence with old friends like us, when they often go together into society."

He turned to George.

"And how are you, old boy?" he asked. "It is such a long time since I have seen you. In a paroxysm of creation, I suppose?"

"I've been grinding at copy all the time, if you mean that," George answered.

"And now you are celebrating the crowning of the edifice, I presume?"

"Yes, I have done my work for this month," George answered, "and I celebrate my temporary release, a pleasure which only those who have to work at a literary treadmill can fully appreciate."

Tania, who was stretching her limbs lazily in the chair, turned towards the speakers, leaning both her elbows upon the arm of the chair.

"What a grumbler you are, George," she said; "I think you have less reason than anybody for complaining of your fate."

"Indeed!" the young man exclaimed, "I never suspected that. Please tell me why I am so fortunate. I promise beforehand to do the best I can to agree with you. It will be so consoling."

At this moment Lena opened the door, bringing in the tea things. She was closely followed by the housemaid with a samovar.

With the assistance of the guests the table was at once cleared of the books and papers encumbering it, the cloth was spread, and everything made ready.

"Tania, dear," said Lena, "will you preside at the tea? In my quality of mistress I shall have to entertain my guests with pleasant conversation, which is a sufficient burden in itself."

She took possession of the arm-chair which Tania had left vacant, and lighting a cigarette began to smoke in the window, paying no attention, to her guests, who, she thought, would be best amused if left to themselves.

"Well, Tatiana Grigorievna, you are keeping me in suspense. You have not yet answered my question," said George, when the household bustle was over.

"What question?" Lena inquired.

"Why I am the happiest of mortals," George explained.

"Oh, are you? I did not know that," said Lena.

"You are distorting my words, George," said Tania; "I merely said you ought not to complain against your fate."

"And why, if you please, should I be deprived of this common consolation of my fellowmen?"

"Why?" Tania drawled in a tone signifying that he must know why well enough himself.

"Because," she put in quickly, remembering something to the point, "you told me once that when you felt depressed you have only to turn it into verse, and all is well."

Tania laughed. George, she thought, had been fishing for a compliment by his assumed dulness, and she was glad to disappoint him by a little hit.

"I did not know you could be so malicious, Tatiana Grigorievna," George said. "Next time I will be more cautious, and show you only the obverse side of my trade."

He remembered very well the conversation to which Tania alluded. It was on the occasion of the publication of a small volume of his poems, which made a stir amongst his set. Tania was exceedingly moved by them, and they had a talk about artistic emotions, though, of course, he had not said exactly what she attributed to him. The girl had twisted his words on purpose to pay him out. But he was shy of speaking about these recollections, and did not correct her.

Lena, who was listening to them whilst she smoked, put down her cigarette. She was interested in the moral side of the question.

"I think," she said, "that those who are truly devoted to a great cause will be quite indifferent whether their part in it is small or great, brilliant or obscure. To aspire to play a big part is nothing but paltry ambition and egotism under another form."

Tania protested she did not mean the seeking after a prominent position, but only the enjoyment of it when it comes unbidden.

"But do you not think," Andrey said, in support of Lena's views, "you can so completely assimilate yourself with a great cause as to have no room, no desire, almost no time, for thinking about your individual self, or for pondering upon the respective share you and your friends have had in the work?"

"No," Tania answered, after a pause, shaking her head, "I am not up to that level. I am afraid I shall never be. The knowledge of my insignificance would gnaw at me, and I should envy those better endowed than myself. It must be such a delight and pride to feel that you have something valuable of your own to add to a great work."

She looked at George. It was merely a look asking for support, as he was the only one present who did not speak against her. But Andrey, who saw this look, interpreted it otherwise. He was about to insist upon the view he had expressed before, following the mechanical impulse of his habitual mode of thinking. But he could not say a word, checked by the consciousness that if he spoke he would utter a lie. At this moment he felt that he also envied in his heart those endowed for no merit of their own with the power of swaying other men's minds. The sense of his mediocrity hurt him with a bitter mortification he had never known before. He was unable to resist it, and remained silent.

The short pause in the conversation, to which the rest paid no attention, seemed to him painfully long and wearisome.

"Look, Andrey, how beautiful is the white group of houses yonder in the red light of the sunset," said Lena, from her place at the window, "it reminds me of the Alpine glow on the Swiss mountains."

Andrey was glad of this change of subject, which relieved him from perplexity, and he approached the window.

"Yes, it is very beautiful," he said, looking over the landscape with the strained attention of a boy trying to impress upon his memory the configuration of the map he will be questioned upon. The sight to which Lena drew his attention was beautiful; the blue vault of the sky, in which the pale figure of the half-grown moon was hardly perceptible, as if delicately painted upon it in faint water-colour; the cluster of white houses glowing in the rosy light against the green of the birch grove; the vanishing sunlight, tipping with gold the edges of the feathery clouds, and deepening upon the line of the horizon into a blazing purple.

But Andrey's perceptive faculties were benumbed, and he turned to look at his companions talking at the tea-table.

Tania had dropped the wreath of bluebells from her hair, and George had picked it up, entreating her to put it back again because it suited her so wonderfully. The girl laughed and blushed, but she did as she was bid, and Andrey felt exceedingly displeased both with her and with George for such foolishness.

"By-the-by," said Lena, interrupting Andrey's sullen meditations, "I have something to ask you."

She drew a chair for him, and invited him in a business-like way to sit down.

"Will you be able," she proceeded, "to spare one or two evenings a week to assist me in my work?"

"What work?" Andrey asked, rousing himself.

"At the young people's clubs. We want you to come and speak to them occasionally. I think you'll do it very well."

"I! Of what use can I be there? You know I am not fit for this work and should cut a poor figure. You should ask George, who will do ever so much better."

"I also thought he would be better," Lena said frankly, "and I have tried him already; but he says he is too busy, and has not a single evening to spare."

Perfect frankness, and even rudeness if needful, is the rule in the mutual dealings among fellow-conspirators, especially in matters connected with "business." There was nothing in Lena's remark which Andrey would not have said to her under similar circumstances; but he was decidedly out of temper to-night.

"Then you want me as padding to fill up the gap somehow?" he said, crossly.

Lena made a movement of impatience.

"Don't talk nonsense, Andrey," she exclaimed. "Answer plainly, have you time to spare or not?"

"I am very busy myself with my workmen, you know," Andrey answered, still sulkily. "But tell me," he added, trying to be more conciliatory and business-like, "why should you not go on without me, as well as you did before?"

"I wish we could," Lena answered. "But some of our people have been involved in the recent arrests, Myrtov among the rest."

"Oh, I see!" Andrey exclaimed, changing his tone.   "Was this Myrtov a member of your group?"

Lena nodded.

"I never came across him," Andrey went on, "but I have heard how he was arrested.   Judging from that he must have been a wonderfully fine fellow.   Have you any idea what is likely to happen to him?"

"Impossible to tell," said Lena.   "It will depend entirely on the gendarmes' caprice.   His is an altogether exceptional case."

Then raising a little her voice, she asked George, who was talking with Tania, whether he had heard anything fresh from the fortress concerning Myrtov's affair.

"We had a few lines from him," George answered.   "His prospects are much worse than we expected.   The police found upon his writing-desk a manuscript article intended for secret printing, and a large quantity of our papers in his room ready for distribution.   I am afraid he is a doomed man."

"Who is this Myrtov?" inquired Tania in a whisper.

"A very quiet young student," said George.   "He was arrested on Monday last by mistake instead of Taras.   You know, I suppose, who Taras is?"

"Yes, of course I do," Tania answered.

Taras Kostrov was one of the most gifted and popular among the leaders of the revolution.

"Well, Taras, under the name of Zachary Volkov, landowner of Kassimov, took lodgings in the same house in which Myrtov lived.   But when he sent his passport to the district office for registration, the police had some suspicion as to the authenticity of the supposed Zachary Volkov.   A domiciliary search was ordered.   The police came on Monday in the night, but they mistook the doors and rang the bell at Myrtov's, who lived on the fourth floor, whilst Taras's flat was one storey higher.   Myrtov was not yet in bed, as he was just writing that unfortunate article. He opened the door himself, and when asked by the police whether he was Zachary Volkov he understood in a moment what all this meant, and resolved to save Taras by sacrificing himself.   He answered in the affirmative, and the police came in, found everything, and he was forthwith arrested and taken to the fortress."

"And Taras was saved?" asked Tania in excitement.

"Yes.   All the lodgers learned in the morning, through the servants, after whom the gendarmes had inquired at the porter's lodge. Taras did not wait, of course, for the police to correct their blunder."

"But how about Myrtov?" Tania asked. "Have they found him out?"

"They have, and very soon. He took the precaution not to keep any of the letters sent to him by any one. But on examining the books seized at his room, the gendarmes found on the fly-leaf of one of them his name in full, Vladimir Myrtov. They concluded that this must be some friend of the prisoner who had lent him this book, and a new order for a domiciliary search at Vladimir Myrtov's was issued. Of course when the gendarmes came, they discovered that the man they sought had already been arrested by them two days ago in mistake for another, who had in the meantime got away."

"What did they do then?" Tania asked again.

"What had they to do," George answered, "but to vent their baffled rage upon the man they had in their clutches? They could not discover who lived under Zachary Volkov's name, but they could well guess that they had let slip from their hands somebody of importance. Myrtov knew what he had to expect, and no man would sacrifice his own life to save a nobody."

"Were they very close friends?" Tania asked.

"Who?"

"Myrtov and Taras?"

"No. Not particularly. They were merely acquaintances. Myrtov, whom I knew slightly, even disliked Taras personally for his dictatorial ways. His act of self-immolation was due to no personal feelings. That is why it is so great!" George concluded, his voice vibrating with admiration.

A solemn silence succeeded, such as expresses emotions of souls tuned to the highest pitch better than any words. Andrey, Lena, and George were all under the spell of this act of devotion, exceptional even in the annals of their party. All for a moment were overcome by the various feelings it called forth,— sorrow for the untimely loss of such a man, admiration at his deed, pride in the party which enlisted men who were equal to any sacrifice for it.

But for Tania it was something more. For her it was one of those incidents which, happening at the cross-roads of life, decide which path a man will take. Since she had made the acquaintance of Zina and then of George, Tania had been a sincere and warm sympathiser with their cause. But there is an abyss between a sympathiser willing to do something, occasionally screwing his courage up to do much for the cause he sympathises with, and an actual votary ready to go for it to any length of sacrifice because he cannot help it. This abyss had not been bridged over for Tania. Hitherto she had been on the other side of it, in the land of the Philistines. She would have remained there, had she before this day been sheltered from all further intercourse with that world in which she had lived so much of late. Her soul had not yet known for one moment those deep sweeping emotions, after which no relapse is possible into the shallow ways of the Philistines, with their timidity, half-heartedness, and sterility.

An event or a book, a living word or a stirring example, a sorrowful tale of the present or a radiant glimpse of the future— anything may be the instrument to bring about this momentous crisis. To some it may come with a violent shock, throwing into convulsions the whole of their moral nature; to others, the heart's deepest springs will be opened, as in sleep, by a delicate touch of a friendly hand. But all those who have pledged themselves for life and for death to any great cause whatsoever, must pass through such a moment of moments, for no amount of accumulated impressions can take the place of this one vivifying touch.

Such a crisis had come to Tania now. It was a moment which came and passed like a gust of wind. When George concluded his tale, and she realised it fully, she felt her heart swelling with a piercing, overwhelming pity. It was as if she had outgrown in an instant her girlhood and womanhood, her motherly instincts reaching their maturity within her maiden breast, and this young man, whom she had never seen, had been her own child, torn by cruel enemies from her arms. A flush rose to her brow, a rapid something which she had not time to analyse, but which she felt with some surprise was neither hatred nor revenge, sent a flash of light into her eyes, and all was over. The great deed was done. Here, in this out-of-the-way corner of the town, in this poor room, the echo of a noble act had riveted for ever a new heart to the same great cause.

When the girl spoke, she made no solemn vows, no emphatic declarations. She could not have done anything of the kind, even if she had not been so naturally averse from everything that had a shadow of ostentation. Neither in this hour, nor in the long years of heroic exertion and suffering which awaited her in the future, could she have told that her conversion to the cause took place at that precise moment. She did not herself realise what had passed in her heart, and the rapid emotion which filled her found an expression very strange and awkward.

"I see nothing particularly great in what Myrtov did," she said, in a low trembling voice, ashamed at her own presumption.

George cast at her a glance of questioning surprise.

"Between a man who is of great value for the cause, and another who knows himself to be of small value, the choice is clear," Tania said, without lifting her eyes from the table. "Myrtov has done only what was right. That is all."

Lena nodded approvingly. As for herself she fully agreed with Tania.

George looked at her in wonder. Never had he expected such words from Tania, he who fancied he knew her so well.

"Would you have done the same in similar circumstances?" he asked, in a faltering voice.

"If I had been ready-witted enough—yes," Tania answered unhesitatingly, looking him in the face.

She had just before answered that question to herself. That was what had called forth her first strange observation upon Myrtov's conduct. Now she merely repeated it aloud; and she relapsed into thought again, her shapely head resting upon her hand, her eyes looking dreamily out beneath her radiant brow.

Andrey, who could not turn away his eyes from her, said to himself that she was terribly beautiful at that moment; and a tremor went through him, as at the approach of some calamity. But why this sudden angry contraction of his face? It was caused by that insupportable George, who was unable to forget his courtship even at a moment so unsuitable for it.

"If moral strength has any value," George began, in an agitated voice, "the best and the greatest of our men would be a presumptuous fool if he knowingly accepted such an exchange. . . ."

He was greatly excited, and he spoke with his soul on his

lips.   But Andrey had wronged his friend in giving to his words such a frivolous interpretation.   At this moment George was quite unable to think of the girl otherwise than as a dear comrade.   It was the unveiling of a beautiful soul that he was hailing, and the things he said to her were substantially quite true, though he put them, as was his wont, in too strong words.

As to Tania, this effervescent eloquence, instead of intoxi-cating, cooled her head completely.   George's exaggerations awakened her keen sense of humour, and a joke upon the untimeliness of his oration was at the tip of her tongue.   But looking at George's face, she rebuked herself for the ungenerous thought, and felt more kindly to him.

She stretched out her hand, and gave his a frank shake.

"You are very good, George; but let us drop the subject," she said.

"What is the matter with you?" said Lena at the same moment to her neighbour.   "You look so pale."

"Do I?" Andrey stammered.   "It is probably the effect of the green reflection of the tree at the window."

But it was not the effect of the green shadow of the tree; this only helped him to conceal the ghastly paleness of his face.   It was at this very moment that a pang of jealousy tore away the scales covering his eyes.   He saw, as by a lightning flash, what had been at the bottom of his attachment to Tania since the first day of their acquaintance.   He loved this charming girl, loved her face, her blouse, the very bit of floor she was standing upon.   And at the same moment a madden-ing conviction pierced his heart like a knife : that if she should ever love anybody, it would be this glib-tongued flatterer, who at this moment was positively hateful to him.   A fit of furious irrepressible jealousy made his head swim.   It required a desperate effort to keep his seat and to maintain his self-control.   He was afraid he should betray himself if this lasted much longer.

"I must go!" he said, in a stifled voice.

The room felt suffocating.

"Is it so late?" Tania asked innocently.

She pulled out her elegant little watch, and said she would go too.

"Will you accompany me home?" she said, addressing both himself and George.

Andrey bowed in silence. Certainly he would accompany her. He wanted to be with her, and to hear her talk with George. There was within him a raging thirst for self-torture, a delight in plunging, inch by inch, the weapon into his wound. For worlds he would not have foregone this grim satisfaction. And he could not, if he would. His independence was gone. He was no longer himself. Her black eyes dragged him after them. He could not part from her so long as she would allow him to stay.

George talked with Tania all the way, but Andrey hardly opened his mouth.

Every word George said vexed him exceedingly. After the girl's rebuke, George did not openly resume his flattery. But there was flattery in his tone, in his looks, in his gestures, which was quite as distasteful to Andrey.

They shook hands with Tania at the door and turned homeward. As it was not late, George proposed they should walk in order to enjoy the splendid night.

Andrey consented. It was utterly indifferent to him.

"Was I not right when I said——" George began, driving evidently at his usual theme.

"Let it alone, please," Andrey interrupted; "I am tired of it."

He relapsed into sulky silence, answering George's questions by short monosyllables. He was angry, low-spirited, miserable. His fatal discovery placed him in a new attitude towards George, which was most painful to him.

George's conduct seemed abominable. Andrey did not believe at all in the seriousness of George's attachment to Tania. How could he love a girl whom he had not so much as taken the trouble to understand? It was all empty inflation, fireworks, begotten of his superabundant poetical imagination. George would have done much better to confine these out-pourings to pen and paper, instead of drumming them in the ear of a young and inexperienced girl.

All this Andrey would have said to his friend the day before, had he then been able to see matters clearly. But now, after the discovery of his own disgraceful entanglement, to speak in this strain was no longer possible. He had to keep his counsel, and to show a deceitful countenance. Their relations, which for so long a time had been so frank and free from any stain of deceit, were now tainted with irremovable duplicity. To keep henceforward on such terms with his intimate friend was more painful than to break altogether.

At length they had to part.

"I'll call on you to-morrow morning," said George. "Be at home. I want to read to you some new things of mine."

"A hymn in Tania's praises, I bet," was Andrey's first thought, but he answered with an effort,

"Can't you send it to the printers at once?"

This was too much. George was hurt at his most sensitive point, and the square wrinkles appeared under his felt hat.

"Of course I can't, or at least I won't," he said, in a half-offended, half-surprised tone. "I never trust my own judgment about my things."

"Well, until to-morrow then," said Andrey.

It was to some extent a business matter, which it was his duty to attend to, if George thought him necessary for it.

"What is the matter with Andrey to-night?" George asked himself, as he made his way home. "I never saw him in such a state."

Had he applied his quick mind to putting together certain signs and hints, he would probably have found out the truth; but to-night, his soul was too full of hope and ecstatical admiration for him to plunge into any analytical researches. Tania's words still rang in his ears, with the tone, the face, the pose, in which she had uttered them. Now he thoroughly understood what lay behind those words, and he was dazzled at what he saw, and penitent for having presumed that he would have to guide such a girl into the way of self-oblivion and devotion to a great cause. He, a clod of earth compared with her! It seemed to him that only to-night he knew what love for a woman is like. He was full of it, and he let himself loose, plunging into that enchanting world of dreams, beautiful as youth and fascinating as reality, above which was enthroned the black-eyed girl, leaning dreamily her radiant brow upon her bare hand.

The beloved image smiled hope to him. The hand she stretched out to him gave a warm affectionate pressure. Who knows whether, not to-day, but in good time, she may not have something deeper as answer to his devotion. Why should he any longer keep silent about his feelings? He had hesitated long enough. But was he not sure of himself now, when all his soul was one breath of love and enthusiasm to her?

He resolved to speak out when they next met.

CHAPTER X.

THE next morning George was seated in his friend's room, with a bundle of manuscript in his pocket. Andrey had slept upon, or more accurately had remained awake upon, his vexation. He looked worried, but self-possessed. He received his visitor in his usual manner, even adding certain little attentions not commonly observed in the easy and simple ways of the Russians. The unsuspecting George ascribed this to Andrey's desire to make amends for yesterday's ill-humour.

In his night's review of his inner life, caused by the new position his folly had created for him, Andrey had made up his mind upon the question of his relations with George. With this secret in his breast, he could not remain on the old footing with George ; that would be base on his part. As to making a clean breast of it, Andrey would rather have bitten off his tongue. Since it was impossible to speak out, the only alternative left him was to give up his intimacy with George, and to be with him henceforward simply on terms of comradeship. This was exceedingly unpleasant to Andrey ; but, since it could not be helped, so must it be. George was his only friend, as friendship is understood in the world in which they lived. Now he would have no friend ; that was all.

Andrey did not often swerve from his resolutions, whatever they might be, when once his mind was made up ; but it was hard to keep this one. His feelings could not at once become accustomed to the new regulations forced upon them by the superior authority of the mind. It was a relief to him when George produced his bundle of manuscript and began to read.

What he brought with him was not one of the political articles or pamphlets that he wrote "in the sweat of his brow," as he used to say, but the fruit of his hours of leisure. It was

verses, partly lyrics, partly short poems, each with a separate
subject, but so closely united by a common idea, that, taken as
a whole, the collection formed as it were disconnected cantos
of one poem.

It was the song of the dawn of the Russian revolt, as,
enthusiastic and benignant, it found its sole manifestation in
the rush of the privileged youth "among the people" to
preach the gospel of Socialism and the reign of happiness
and brotherhood.

Written at various times and in various moods, by fits and
starts, George's compositions were fragmentary and uneven.
The playful was mixed with the pathetic, short stanzas followed
cantos of longer poems. But this irregularity, and apparent
want of unity, made it easier for George to render completely
the many sides of a noble epoch that lends itself so readily to
poetic treatment.

George's verses began with a few short poems gathered
together under the title "Beneath the Paternal Roof." They
pictured the inner troubles of a young sensitive soul yearning
passionately after truth and justice, and anxiously seeking a
way out of the shameful compromises and the hateful comfort
of the life of a rich man amidst starving millions. The following section, entitled "In Green Fields," was the longest and
most varied. Here were recorded the hard toil and the pure
joys of the early propagandists. The many hardships of the
life of common labourers, which they took upon themselves,
were made light of. The tone of this part was cheerful. The
story of adventures of the propagandists, now touching, now
amusing, was interwoven with pictures of village life and scenery.

The concluding poem was the most pathetic, and, from its
artistic finish, the best of the whole. It was the swan-song of a
young propagandist about to pass from his "temporary tomb"
—the prison cell—into that which is eternal. This song was
in a minor key, mild and soft as the time of which it treated.
George's artistic feeling had prevented him from making his
hero the mouthpiece of his present views and sentiments.
His propagandist was a real man of his time,—one of those
workers, at the beginning of the day, not yet embittered by
long years of cruelty. Forgetful of the wrongs done to himself,
he neither complained nor regretted a life cut off in its bloom ;
he found his meek consolation in the thought that, prevented
from serving the people by his labours, he would still serve

them by his death. But George's sincerity and truthfulness received, as ever, their ample reward. The touching figure of his hero, slain with such wanton cruelty, spoke to the heart with more power than could any impassioned appeal to indignation and revenge.

Andrey listened enraptured, fearing to speak a word. He was under the spell of George's melodious thoughts, which soothed the evil spirit that possessed him, and he was afraid of breaking the charm.

These songs of the recent past were to him more than a work of art, they were records and reminiscences of his own life. Both he and George had been actual propagandists in their time. Before they had become terrorists, they had shared all these feelings. The young man upon his death-bed in the prison cell, personified scores of beloved and well-remembered friends who actually had met this fate, and for the same cause. Noble and pure emotions, roused by the magic of poetry, calmed Andrey's brain-fever, and moved him to better feelings towards George. They had too many common bonds between their higher moral natures,

The reading did not last more than an hour. When George had finished, Andrey burst out into frank and warm approbation; this was by far the best thing George had ever written. Andrey made some critical observations and suggestions. They talked easily and freely, and George had no longer to seek for an explanation of his friend's manner, for it was as natural and unconstrained as usual.

Andrey however refused to go for the walk which George proposed to him. He had been commissioned to write a business letter in cipher, which he had not yet started upon.

He remained standing a long time at the window, just as George had left him. He was still under the influence of the work he had just heard; it was indeed charming. George's talent had grown rapidly, and there was in him the promise of a true poet. Happy man! he had upon his brow the seal of the chosen ones. And he had a heart also; the things he did could not be the work of pure imagination. He must feel them deeply and intensely, to find for them such heart-reaching words.

The writer was receding into the background. Andrey began to think of the man, and the wound at his heart, which had closed for a moment, re-opened. But he could no longer view George's conduct in the same light as he had overnight. A man so true, sincere, and earnest could not be a coxcomb. He had wronged George in his thoughts. But George's strangely distorted views of the girl? His absurd exaggerations? Well, these were in his nature. He could not help them. It was his way of taking everything. He loved her truly all the same. Does not each man love differently, according to his nature? And she loved him too. It was only natural that a girl should find more charm in George's exalted and poetical love, than in the dull and prosaic thing which a dull and prosaic man like himself could offer her.

"Solidity, stability, durability!" Andrey bitterly said to himself.

If love were the sort of stuff of which dresses and shoes are made, he would have a fair chance. But women do not look upon love in that light, and they are quite right. Besides, why should George's love necessarily be fickle? Certainly he had scarcely any idea of the real Tania, worshipping in her stead an idol he had clad in some tinsel dresses of his own making. But if he never discovered them to be unreal, what harm was there? And suppose that in time this fantastic mantle became threadbare and fell to pieces, he would simply weave a new one instead. He is quite equal to the task, and it will be all the more diverting for both of them.

Andrey was now seated before his table. Leaning his elbow upon it, he looked dejectedly at the bare walls covered with cheap paper, and mechanically he tried to trace out the lines which would divide into two symmetrical parts the ugly green squares of the pattern. But he could make nothing of it, and turned his eyes wearily to his writing-desk.

Two months! Yes, only two months since first he met her. But he knew her just as well as if they had been acquainted for two years. He began to read her soul almost from the first day he spoke to her. Now he knew her better than she knew herself, divining qualities which she would have modestly refused to admit, and weaknesses against which in her girlish petulance she would have indignantly protested. And he would hesitate to say for which of these two she was dearer to him. He loved the whole of her, just as she was; and he could imagine nothing better, since such a one would have to be different from Tania.

He passed in review all the incidents of their brief acquaintance. He remembered almost every word she had ever said to him, every expression of her face. No, there was no hope for him. A friendship! Girls very willingly bestow that on the friends of those they love. She already loved George when he met her for the first time. In doubting this for a single moment, he was fooling himself on purpose. And if she did not love George at that time, how could she hesitate between them now? . . .

Yes; everything that life has of the choicest is for these Benjamins of nature, because they already have so much.

"Well, so let it be," Andrey said, a gloomy light kindling in his eyes. "Flowers grow upon the dreariest paths of life. Let others pluck and enjoy them in peace. We, the obscure workers, will keep for ourselves the thorns, and we shall make no complaint."

He sighed, and then resolutely set to work. For several hours he lived in the world of figures, whispering numbers, consulting the key, making calculations, writing with strained angry application, hardly lifting his head. He wanted to get his letter to headquarters in good time, because the man who was going to Dubravnik would start in the afternoon.

At headquarters he found Lena, whose day of service it was.

"There's something that concerns you from Dubravnik," she said.

She produced from the drawer a letter from Zina, still wet from the application of the chemicals.

" Here it is, and there's your name," she said, pointing with her finger to an isolated group of figures on the last page.

Andrey read the passage, which ran thus :—

" As for the business I am about, there are complications, and "—here stood the group of figures—" will do well to come here if he can manage it."

Few things could have been so welcome to Andrey as this invitation, and he resolved at once to accept it.

"Well, what do you say?" Lena asked, rather coldly. " Shall you go ?"

" Most certainly I shall," Andrey answered.

" I expected that you would," said the girl, with a frown.

Andrey knew that Lena would dislike the step he was taking, and he knew why.

" I must go," he said, apologetically. " Though Zina's

summons is not a peremptory one, I know she would not send it at all if it was not important that I should come."

"And you'll throw to the dogs the propaganda among the workmen you have started so well, and everything else?" Lena went on angrily, without listening to him. "It's always the way with our revolutionists of noble extraction, who only await the first opportunity to throw themselves into exciting terrorist business!"

Lena was a "peasantist" by conviction, or, more exactly, a "propagandist" pure and simple. The socialist propaganda among peasants and working-men was, according to her, the only form of activity to which the revolutionists ought to devote their energies. They ought to pay no attention whatever to the fierce persecutions of the Government, which only tended to divert them into political action.

She valued Andrey very much as a successful propagandist, and she was especially vexed with him for giving up the work, perhaps for ever. There was nothing easier than to break one's neck in an enterprise of the Dubravnik kind. She attacked him vehemently, accusing him of want of perseverance.

Andrey protested good-naturedly.

"I should be very glad to persevere in my work," he said. "but it would be disgraceful for our party not to make some effort to rescue our friend."

"There's no disgrace for the party, or for a man devoted to his cause, in spending his life and his energies where they can be of the greatest use," Lena retorted.

"Do you consider, then, Boris and the other two so value-less for the cause that they are not worth the trouble of a rescue?" Andrey asked sharply.

"They are of as much value as the best among us," Lena rejoined, "but we shall do nothing but hang about our prisons if we try to release all who are worth delivering."

"The best course, therefore," Andrey replied ironically, "is to let them all rot there? Isn't it?"

"Those who are alive have something better to do than to break their necks in trying to disinter their dead," Lena said, without flinching.

"Then you would probably advise the miners, whose companions have been buried by the crumbling of a shaft, to proceed with their work, and not to make any attempt at rescue, if it involved some risk to themselves," Andrey suggested.

"Let your miners alone, for goodness' sake, for they prove nothing," exclaimed Lena. "A simile is not an argument. We have no faith in our work; that's the fact. If we had faith, we would have pluck enough to stick to it."

"No, thanks!" Andrey said, with a sneer. "I don't envy such sheepish pluck, and don't pretend to have it."

He was very angry with what he termed Lena's obtuse doctrinarianism. The girl was very cross too. Sinces he had read Zina's letter in the morning, she had been boiling over with indignation at Andrey's anticipated desertion. They almost quarrelled, but they made peace at the end.

"It's useless for us to waste time in quarrelling," Andrey said. "You know well enough that I shall go to Dubravnik whatever you say or do not say to me. As I shall probably not see you before starting, I had better say good-bye to you at once."

They kissed each other, as is the custom among Russian men and women of their set, though the girl still bore a grudge to Andrey for his want of seriousness. But he tried to soothe her, by telling her that it would be only a short furlough. He would return in a month or so, with his three companions, all of whom he promised to induce to join her propagandist circle.

Before leaving the town Andrey put all his business matters in good order, handing over his acquaintances among the workmen to good substitutes for himself. He worked so well that in two days he started for Dubravnik, in much better spirits than he had been for some time.

PART II.

UNDER FIRE.

UNDER FIRE.

CHAPTER I.

DAVID AGAIN.

NOBODY in St Petersburg knew the address of the Dubravnik headquarters. Andrey was accordingly directed to call on two sisters, Mary and Catherine Dudorov, and to inquire of them as to Zina's whereabouts.

Not without difficulty Andrey discovered the obscure lane in which they lived, and found their grim unplastered hungry-looking red brick house.

At the very top of an endless stone staircase with worn-out steps, Andrey stopped before a yellow-painted door.

They must be here, for there was nothing but the garret above.

His ring at the bell was answered by a tall very poorly clad girl, with a sickly complexion, who might have been thirty as easily as twenty.

"What do you want, please?" she asked coldly, raising her eyes only as far as the visitor's breast.

"Do the Miss Dudorovs live here?" Andrey inquired.

"Step in," the girl said curtly.

Andrey was led by her into a room, where the signs of poverty struck even the eyes of a Nihilist, who is not likely to be very exacting about material comfort. The whole of the furniture, if sold by auction, would not have fetched more than a few roubles.

The room was divided by a curtain of cheap chintz into two compartments. The front part, in which Andrey was received, served as a sitting-room, the back part was reserved as a bedroom.

"What is it you want, please?" the girl repeated, in the same chilling tone.

"I want to see Miss Dudorov," Andrey answered drily.

"Me or Masha?" the girl inquired.

"You are Catherine Dudorov, then?" Andrey said. "I come with a message to both of you from Lena Zubova, and my name is Kojukhov."

The girl's sickly face brightened up in a moment.

"I am so glad!" she exclaimed. "Take a seat. I'll call my sister at once."

She went out hurriedly, and Andrey seated himself by the bare deal table. Bundles of manuscript, differing in size and handwriting, were scattered over it. At one of the corners was an orderly pile of freshly-written foolscap.

Andrey knew from Lena, to whom the two sisters were distantly related, that they had inherited from their father a small fortune. But they gave it up to the last penny for the cause. Now they were evidently earning their livelihood by copying, and by any other work they could get. Upon one of the stools Andrey saw a piece of embroidery in brilliant silk, too luxurious and useless to be intended for the personal use of the dwellers in that more than modest room.

In a moment Masha rushed in, informed by her sister of the arrival of their interesting visitor from St Petersburg. She was the elder of the two, but she looked the younger, thanks to her lively face, with its small turned-up nose and bright hazel eyes.

"We didn't expect you so soon," she said. "Zina told us that you would hardly be able to come for three days. You want to see her at once, I suppose?"

"Yes, if it is not inconvenient to you."

"Not in the least. I will be ready in a moment, and will show you the way. It isn't very far."

She dived behind the curtain, and Andrey heard her bustling about before the toilet-table.

The sisters were very anxious to keep their guest for a while. They wanted to ask him many questions about St Petersburg. But they did not want to detain him.

"How is Lena?" asked the younger sister, who had stayed with him.

Andrey told in a few words what he knew about her.

"Listen, Kojukhov," Masha's voice rang out from behind

the curtain. "We know David's address too. I can take you to him, if you like."

"David is in Dubravnik, then!" Andrey exclaimed, casting on the curtain a look of glad surprise. "I did not know this. But come out, please, that we may cease talking in this ghostly fashion."

"In a minute," Masha answered, still behind the curtain.

She came out of her hiding-place, in another dress, holding still in her mouth a few hair-pins.

"David has been to the Roumanian frontier to arrange with his Jews about smuggling our books from abroad," Masha said, whilst she fastened with her hair-pins the tresses upon her bowed head. "He stopped here on his way. . . . I do not really know whither."

"Now I'm quite ready," she said at last, putting on her hat. "To whom do you want to go, to Zina or to David?"

Between two such offers the choice was difficult.

"Let us go to the nearer of the two," Andrey said.

Neither was far off, but David's place happened to be nearer.

"Shall you make a long stay at Dubravnik?" Masha inquired as they walked along.

"I don't know. . . . It will depend, . . ." Andrey answered, evasively.

He did not know whether the girl was a regular member of the section, and was initiated into the secret of the affair for which he had come.

"Are you staying permanently in the town?" he asked, in order to change the conversation.

"No. We live in the country, and shall return to it before long. We came to Dubravnik to get certificates as teachers. We have been promised places as schoolmistresses in some village if we pass our examinations here."

"It must be hard for you to study for your examinations and go on with all this copying and embroidery."

Masha smiled.

"It was much harder for us, I assure you," she said, cheerfully, "before we got all this work. Now we get on pretty well, and in a few months we shall be settled in the country."

"I see you are 'peasantists,' like Lena," Andrey remarked.

"Yes, we are. Are not you? From what Lena told us, I thought you were."

"Oh no," Andrey replied; "I don't go to such extremes."

He began to argue his point with the girl, whom he wished to convert to sounder views. Their discussion was animated, but not bitter or vehement. The fierce dissensions between the "terrorists" and the "peasantists" were as yet in a latent state. The two factions had occasional skirmishes, but they worked side by side in the same societies without much friction.

They found David at home, playing with a dirty little urchin with big blue eyes and a forest of yellow curls, who ran away hastily on seeing the strangers. It was the inn-keeper's daughter. David was fond of children, like all genuine Jews, notwithstanding all his objections to family life.

He was making a temporary stay in a Jewish inn, where he seemed to be quite at home. He stopped there always when he came to Dubravnik, and was on the best of terms with the landlord. Nobody asked any passport from him, and he was known simply as David.

He was as happy to see Andrey as Andrey was to see him.

"You come just in the nick of time, my good friend," said he. "Had you been one day later, I should have missed you altogether, for I leave town to-morrow."

Masha made a move to go home.

"Now, good-bye," she said to Andrey. "I hope you'll not forget the road to our house."

Having fulfilled her mission, she wanted to leave them free "to conspire."

David stopped her.

"Wait a moment. I want to ask you which of your Odessa friends remained at their old places after the recent arrests, so that I may find them."

"Are you going to Odessa?" Andrey asked, with some surprise.

"Yes, to Odessa."

"But you were there only three weeks ago! Never in my life have I seen a man with such a lust for travelling," he added, turning to the girl.

"Lust for travelling!" David protested. "It drives me mad to think what a lot of money I have thrown away in these three weeks, to say nothing of the waste of time. It's all the work of these foolish peasantists, for whom our friend feels such tenderness," and he nodded at Masha.

"These poor peasantists," the girl sighed; "they are your scapegoats in everything."

"Listen one minute," David insisted, taking Andrey by the coat sleeve. "I told them again and again I would pass over the frontier as many of their books as they liked; it was no trouble to me—it only extends my business. They had only to defray their share of the expense, and to keep a man to receive their parcels on this side of the frontier. This they never did," he added, throwing a reproachful glance at Masha, "so that I had to bring the books up to town. Still I went on doing the frontier business for them, and all went well for a time. But a few weeks ago they had the misfortune to enlist as a member of their section Abrumka Blum, who, though a Jew, is a born fool. You have had some experience with him, I suppose?"

Andrey nodded, smiling.

"Well, I don't know whether these peasantists thought Abrumka clever enough for them, or for some other reason, but the fact is that since they have got a Jew of their own, they resolved they would have a frontier of their own too."

"Oh, David!" Masha tried to expostulate.

"No, no; let me finish, you shall have your say afterwards. Well, Abrumka was sent to Kishenev with a lot of money, and he arranged a frontier for them, agreeing to pay for books . . . "—here David made a pause to prepare a dramatic effect—"eighteen roubles per pood."

He looked in silence at Andrey, then at Masha, and then at Andrey again.

Masha seemed to him sufficiently confounded, but Andrey was not in the least impressed, as he had not the slightest idea what was a reasonable price.

"Eighteen roubles a pood! It is unheard of. I never pay more than six," David exclaimed. "It's a shame to pay such prices. It spoils the frontier for all of us! It makes the smugglers intractable."

He warmed to his subject, accompanying his peroration with strange Jewish gesticulation, which came back to him when he was much excited.

"Naturally," he went on in a calmer voice, "as soon as I learned this I made a row. We returned to our previous arrangement, and I had to start to the frontier in order to make everything straight."

"You succeeded, I hope?" said Andrey.

"Yes ; but for how long I don't know. I am not certain they will not play me the same trick again, if they get hold of let us say another Jew a bit cleverer than Abrumka."

"You ought to be ashamed to speak so, David," Masha interposed. "I heard about that frontier business from the Odessa people."

"Well, wasn't it as I said?"

"Certainly not. Your frontier is the German one, which is very distant, and where there are none of their people ; whilst the Roumanian frontier is quite near Odessa, and they have an affiliated branch at Kamenetz, close to it. That's why they sent Abrumka to try his luck. There was neither want of confidence in you, nor anything like a desire to boast of the possession of their own frontier."

David waved his hand ironically.

"Well, well," he said, "you can't catch an old bird with chaff. I know what I know. Tell me rather where I can find your Abrumka, to whom I have to communicate the results of my journey."

Masha gave him the desired address.

"Now I must get ready," David said ; "I have an appointment with Zina this morning."

He fetched from the corner his faithful linen sack, and plunged his hand into it, groping about to find something. But as he was not able to find it, he began to turn out on the sofa its varied contents. A shirt, a washing glove, a hair brush, a small feather cushion, one volume of a German novel, a pair of socks, several round tin boxes with various contents, and many other things followed in rapid succession. It was a complete outfit for a man whose life is spent mostly in a railway carriage.

"This sack of mine is a very queer one ; what you want is always at the bottom," David said, catching hold of a palm-tree barrel of Swiss workmanship, which rolled out at last upon the sofa.

He unscrewed the barrel, which contained an assortment of buttons, white and black thread, a needle-case, a thimble, and a pair of scissors. Then he took off his overcoat, and set to work tailoring.

"Give it me," said Masha, "I'll mend it for you."

"No, I can do it much better. Woman's work does not last," David replied.

. In order to be useful in some way Andrey began to put back David's things into the sack. There was among the rest a small green bag six or seven inches long. When Andrey took it up a strange object fell out. At first he mistook it for a child's toy, such as David might have bought for one of his favourites. It was a small wooden cube, an inch in height, upon a diminutive pedestal. But long and heavy strips of leather were fastened to it, showing that it was an object of use. Through the opening of the small sack Andrey saw that it contained something woollen, with alternate black and white stripes, which he recognised at once as the Jewish praying implements. He had gone one day into a Jewish synagogue, and could not be mistaken. The cube was the diminutive altar they fix to their forehead whilst reciting their prayers; the striped towel was the sacred *talith* for covering the head and shoulders.

"Look here, see what he's got!" Andrey said to Masha, showing her the cube and the striped towel.

Both burst out laughing. It was so amusing to see these things in the possession of David, a freethinker like all the rest.

"That's my passport; and what's more," said David, "I never travel without it. It works like magic to drive away spies and police, when they take it in their head to suspect me of being a Nihilist."

He smiled, cutting the thread with his white teeth.

"Now let us go to Zina," he said. "I am ready to appear before our leader."

Masha begged them to give her best wishes to Zina, and to Annie as well.

"Who is this Annie?" Andrey inquired, when they were alone.

"Annie Vulitch, an old acquaintance of yours. You met her at the frontier, don't you recollect? She says she remembers you very well. She came back from Switzerland, and now is playing the part of housemaid at headquarters."

"Yes," Andrey said, "I remember her well. But was it prudent to entrust so young a girl with so important a post?"

"I was inclined to think so myself at first," David said. "But she plays her part splendidly. She was chosen by Zina, who has the same gift for knowing the people as she has for attaching them to herself."

CHAPTER II.

THAT afternoon there was an informal council of war in Zina's little house in one of the suburbs of Dubravnik. Only four persons were present,—the two women, Andrey, and David.

Vulitch took little part in the conversation. Buried in a deep arm-chair, so that her tiny feet were dangling in mid-air, she listened, moving her brisk blackberry eyes from one speaker to another.

Zina explained to Andrey all the details of their plan of rescue, and asked for his opinion.

"You are a newcomer, and your head is fresh. You can judge better than any of us."

Andrey continued to look in silence at the rough map of the prison Zina had traced for him.

"Speak out, for goodness sake!" Zina said. "Are you struck dumb?"

"Well," Andrey at last replied, "to tell you the truth I don't like your plan at all. Too many things have to work into each other. Such plans never turn out well. It's too complicated; a slight hitch at one point will ruin the whole affair. Besides, the very base of it is not solid. That is my opinion."

The whole enterprise was based upon the co-operation of the common criminals, with whom the political prisoners had succeeded in establishing secret relations. Two of these, one formerly a highway robber nicknamed Berkut, and another a pickpocket named Kunitzin, volunteered to help Boris and his friends to escape. Their offer was accepted. The subterranean passage by which the escape had to be made was fairly forward, and ought to be finished in a week or so. It was all dug by Berkut and Kunizin. Their cell was on the ground floor, whilst the political offenders, watched much more vigorously, were locked up in the cells of the upper storey of the prison.

When everything was ready, on the night chosen, the political prisoners were to open the doors of their cells with skeleton keys, descend to the cell of the common prisoners, and thence to the subterranean passage.

The great danger was not in the fact that two common criminals played in it so conspicuous a part. In this there was nothing very extraordinary. Political prisoners, when kept in the same gaols with the common offenders, very often acquire a strong and beneficial influence over them, awakening their moral nature, and converting them sometimes into devoted friends. Both Kunitzin and Berkut were said to be devoted to Boris body and soul, and they had proved on many occasions that they could be trusted. But they were locked up in a cell with fifteen other prisoners, who as a matter of course, were in the secret of the subterranean work. None of them knew that the passage was intended for political prisoners. Berkut and Kunitzin only said they intended to escape themselves, and the brotherhood of outcasts kept their secrets well. But it would be enough if one of the lot got drunk on the smuggled brandy for some fatal word to be let fall in the hearing of the guards. Finally, there was the passing from one storey to another through corridors watched day and night.

"It is very risky, all this," Andrey summed up. "They'll be caught for certain during these wanderings, if not before."

"What escape isn't very risky, Andrey?" Zina rejoined. "But look here, I'll show you that what you call wanderings are not so dangerous as you think."

She took a fresh sheet of paper and made an additional plan of the interior of the prison, which she knew to the minutest detail.

There were nine political prisoners just now in the Dubravnik gaol. Their cells were in two contiguous corridors that ran at right angles in the north-western corner of the building. Boris and his two companions were fortunately all in the same corridor. After the midnight round, Zalessky, one of the prisoners in the other gallery, was to call to his door and engage in talk with the special guard appointed to watch the political prisoners. Zalessky had done it several times already, in order that the guard should see nothing suspicious in this proceeding. Zina showed on the plan that from Zalessky's door the guard would be unable to see anything in the other gallery; it was equally likely that he would also hear nothing. The hinges of the door, as well as the locks of the cells, were carefully oiled beforehand, and the fugitives were to walk in their socks.

Once outside their cells, the fugitives would have to open with a skeleton key the door at the top of the stairs leading to the ground floor, and descend into the gallery of the common offenders. There was only one guard for all the four blocks on the ground floor, who had to walk all round the gallery. The fugitives would have only to wait a while upon the stairs to catch the moment when the guard would be out of sight. Then they were to slip into the cell of Berkut and Kunitzin, who would be expecting them, and who would show them to the mouth of the subterranean passage.

"And where does the passage open outside?" Andrey asked.

"Here," said Zina, marking upon her first map a spot outside the outer wall.

"And the sentinel?"

"Here."

She marked another spot upon the line of the wall very near the former.

"You see!" Andrey said. "The men must climb out of the passage under the very nose of the sentinel."

He invited Vulitch and David to look, as if calling them as witnesses.

"If you were charged with placing the sentinels, you would certainly have disposed them so as to smooth all difficulties for those who wanted to escape," Zina exclaimed, losing her patience. "But since it is not so, we must make the best of it, and accept what can't be helped."

Zina had as keen a perception of details as Andrey. But there was the difference of their temper. Andrey could be bold to madness when he was in real earnest in a matter; but he wanted time to warm himself up to any affair in which he was embarked. Obstacles were the first thing that struck him. Zina, on the contrary, with her more excitable nature, launched into full swing on the spot, maintaining the same pace up to the end. When they happened to be partners in the same affair they always quarrelled.

"Well, let's take our chance," Andrey said. "We must do the best we can. As to the sentinel, I have an idea. . . . But I must see the place myself. Tell me, what's the part you propose to give me?"

Zina explained it. A carriage was to wait outside near the opening of the passage, to take the fugitives to a place of safety. Vasily, who was a good driver and knew the town well, was to be the coachman. But it was thought useful to have another reliable man on the spot, his hands free, capable of helping the fugitives to get in, and of defending them in case of emergency.

Andrey nodded in sign of assent.

"You were quite right," he said; "there's no saying what may happen."

It was decided that to-morrow afternoon Andrey should examine the spot under Vasily's direction. Then the council was closed.

"Where can I see you to-morrow?" David asked Andrey before leaving.

"I have no idea. Ask Zina. I am under her orders."

"Come to Rokhalsky's in the morning," Zina said. "We shall all be there to-morrow. You will learn there how Andrey and Vasily will arrange between themselves about the lodging. They will live together at Vasily's inn."

Vasily occupied a room in the inn where his horse was stalled. He gave himself out as the coachman and footman of a small merchant, who had been detained at Romny fair but was to arrive shortly.

Andrey would have to play the part of this imaginary master, and he had therefore to provide himself with clothes suitable to his new passport and new position,—a long national kaftan, a pair of long boots, a cap and waistcoat of the common pattern, and so on. In the meantime, Vasily was to announce to the innkeeper the arrival of his master.

David was charged to inform Vasily at once of Andrey's arrival. To-morrow, at Rokhalsky's, they were to make definite arrangements for the next day, when Andrey was to be installed at the inn.

Vasily himself never came to Zina's house, and the two lodgings were kept as completely isolated as possible. The inn was only a temporary refuge. The police would have no difficulty in finding it out, as soon as the rescue was attempted. The inn had, therefore, to be abandoned, horse and carriage included, the same night that the attempt took place, and Vasily and Andrey would take refuge in another place. As to the fugitives, they would be secreted at Zina's house, where they would have to remain in close confinement whilst the police were turning the town upside down in order to catch them. It was therefore essential that Zina's place should be kept free from all connection with the inn, and in general as clear as possible from anything likely to excite suspicion. The two women lived almost completely secluded. The people engaged in the undertaking met outside, in public gardens or squares, for brief communications; or when they all had to discuss anything together, they met at some friend's house, such as Rokhalsky's.

"Where will you put me for to-night?" Andrey asked when David left.

"I think you may as well stop here for one day," Zina said.

Andrey would have been very glad of this opportunity to be in Zina's company, but he thought it not advisable from the business point of view. To-morrow morning was the meeting at Rokhalsky's, which he wished to attend. He would have to go out and return in the day-time. He might be seen, and some one might suspect that strangers were harboured in the house.

"Then I'll escort you to Rokhalsky's directly," Zina said. "He'll be glad to give you shelter for the night, and you'll be on the spot for to-morrow's meeting."

At dusk they left and went into the town.

Rokhalsky was a good-natured man, of independent means and liberal views, on friendly terms with the conspirators. He received many guests of all sorts, never had any quarrel with the police, and his house was considered one of the safest refuges in Dubravnik.

On approaching a newly built mansion in one of the quiet streets of the aristocratic quarter, Zina pointed out to Andrey a row of lighted windows on the third storey.

"We shall find him at home," she said. "Most likely they have a party to-night."

"You are early people in Dubravnik, then," Andrey observed, "and exceedingly parsimonious too, for there is not a single cab in the street."

"The poorer sort have probably come first on foot," Zina said, carelessly.

When they came nearer, Andrey saw in a window on the first floor of the house opposite two old ladies, who turned their heads up, it seemed to him, in the direction of Rokhalsky's lodging, as if they were pointing it out to each other. Both looked somewhat excited.

A suspicion crossed Andrey's mind.

"Wait a moment," he said to Zina. "Instead of going in together, let me go first. There's something about the place I don't like."

"Oh no! Rokhalsky is perfectly safe," Zina exclaimed, moving towards the entrance.

The double-panelled entrance door was open. Upon the paved hall and the white stone stairs Andrey observed footprints that seemed to him too large and too many.

As Zina was turning to enter the door, Andrey took her gloved hand, and putting it under his strong arm drew her past the door.

"It's very likely that Rokhalsky is safe," he said. "No doubt he is safe, since you say so. But what harm is there, if you wait two minutes in the street, whilst I run in to inquire?"

A strange obstinacy took possession of him. These insignificant signs, caught by the senses, but too feeble to be formulated distinctly in the mind, produced in Andrey what superstitious people would call a presentiment. But Zina did not share this. She was accustomed to the place, and but yesterday had paid a visit to Rokhalsky.

"Nonsense!" she said, freeing her hand.

"If you won't let me go alone, I'll not go at all," Andrey said bluntly.

Zina shrugged her shoulders and looked him in the face, impressed in spite of herself with his persistency.

"If you think the case worth suspicion," she said, "we had better not go at all, but wait a while in the street, walking up and down until something turns up."

It was certainly the wisest course to follow. But men can't be expected to be always wise. A toper who has valiantly passed the door of one public-house, runs a greater risk of entering the next. A man who can congratulate himself upon a prudent first step, feels often disposed to make the next one so much the more foolish.

Zina and Andrey's respective positions were now reversed.

"There's no need to make such a fuss about every trifle," Andrey said. "We might spend hours in the street without seeing anything. Wait for me at this corner; I'll return in a minute."

He entered the hall. There was not a soul in it. A dead silence reigned through the house. When he ascended the first flight of stairs, the door of one of the flats upon the landing opened. A wrinkled beardless face—Andrey could not see whether of an old man or an old woman—peeped out, gave him a sharp inquisitive glance, and instantly disappeared. He heard the door slammed behind him and hastily bolted from inside.

"Strange!"

Andrey ascended the stairs with as cautious a step as was consistent with the necessity of not betraying any want of confidence. It was absolutely necessary to ascertain how things stood with Rokhalsky, for their meeting was to be held there the next morning.

He quickly made his plan of action. He would pass the third floor, where Rokhalsky lived, and go up to the fourth. He would see the name of the people who lodge there. Then he would descend, and ring the bell at Rokhalsky's. If the police opened the door, he would inquire after the people upstairs, as if by mistake. In any case it was well to get ready his arms, which he never took off.

He unbuttoned the holster of his revolver, and shifted forward the dagger hanging by his side so as to have it ready under his hand in case of need.

Reaching the floor, where Rokhalsky's small brass plate was visible, he stopped awhile. He could not make up his mind whether to go higher or not. His plan was a good one in principle; but there was an unpleasant risk in having his retreat cut off. He inwardly reproached himself for not having asked the upper lodger's name of Zina, who might know it. The noise of a door rapidly unbolted, and the characteristic tinkling of spurs and swords, rendered all hesitation superfluous. The police were in Rokhalsky's flat. Four gendarmes were posted in the lobby, with orders to apprehend every one who came.

They heard Andrey's cautious steps, and were only waiting for him to touch the bell to open the door and fly upon him. As he did not ring, they were afraid he might go away without giving them the chance of catching him, and resolved to make a sortie.

But before they had time to open the door, Andrey had already turned the corner downstairs, flinging himself downwards like a ball. He did not see the gendarmes, but only heard their shouting, the trampling of their feet, the clash of their swords, as they rushed after him. It was a mad chase, neither of the parties seeing, both of them only hearing, each other. But the match was unequal between the clumsy soldiers, encumbered with their long cavalry swords, and an agile young man like Andrey, whose experience of mountain excursions proved on this occasion of great use. Jumping down six or seven steps at once, he distanced the gendarmes at the first storey. Running past the gas burner within reach of his hand, an inspiration seized him. He extinguished the gas. At the next landing he did the same ; and, by a rapid movement, threw across the passage the long wooden bench which stood near the wall. It was now quite dark on the stairs. His pursuers slackened speed, as Andrey ascertained by the lessening of the noise. Then he had the pleasure of hearing some one stumbling over his improvised barricade, and falling heavily with a curse. The noise ceased almost completely; the gendarmes had to grope their way cautiously down, fearing more mischief. Andrey turned out the gas in the hall too, and came out upon the street, closing the entrance door behind him, so as to make the darkness more complete.

Zina, who was standing a hundred yards from the house, had heard nothing of the noise on the stairs. Andrey returned she thought rather too quickly. But on seeing him approach with a composed, though accelerated step, his eyes glistening, but with no outward sign of excitement upon his face, she moved towards him.

Andrey stopped her with a gesture.

"The gendarmes!" he whispered when he was near her.

Then he offered her, in the most gallant fashion, his arm, and led her toward Rokhalsky's entrance. As the gendarmes would pour forth from it in a moment, it was better they should see their faces and not their backs.

Zina made no objection. She was experienced enough in things of this kind to understand at once Andrey's stratagem, and she thought it sensible.

They had not taken ten steps when the door was flung open

violently, and the four dishevelled and shattered gendarmes rushed out, one of them covering with a handkerchief his bleeding nose. They looked round bewildered, and seeing nobody but a well-dressed gentleman and a lady approaching they ran towards them.

"Your honour," shouted hurriedly the first of them, "have you seen a man running?"

"Out of this door?" Andrey inquired, pointing to that of Rokhalsky's house.

"Yes, yes!"

"With a red beard and a grey hat?"

"Yes, no . . . no matter! which way has he gone?"

"That way." Andrey pointed up the lane behind them. "He has just run by us, and must have turned into the first block to the right. You will catch him yet . . . but run quickly . . ."

They did run quickly, and were soon out of sight.

Zina and Andrey proceeded arm in arm calmly and respectably. They turned into the first street, and Zina took a passing carriage, giving the driver the first direction that occurred to her, in a natural desire to get as quickly as possible from a dangerous place.

The incident was over. They were safe as before.

"An 'unexpected reprimand,'" Andrey said, using the popular expression borrowed from a well-known comedy.

He was unwilling to speak more clearly in the cab.

"Yes," Zina answered; "that's a punishment for your refusal to stop with us for the night."

"Punishment! what are you thinking of, Zina?" Andrey could not help exclaiming. "It's a reward for my good behaviour. Just think what would have happened at the same place to-morrow at ten, if I hadn't gone there."

"Dear me, yes!" Zina exclaimed. "I had quite forgotten about to-morrow. My head's been like a pumpkin lately."

What Andrey meant was, that the police would certainly place an ambush at Rokhalsky's lodging, and most of their friends would have fallen into the trap.

Zina stood up, grasped the iron frame of the coach-box, and raising her voice so as to dominate the rumble of the wheels, gave a new direction to the cabman.

They soon alighted at the corner of a street, and Zina dismissed the cab.

"Now tell me all about it," she said, taking Andrey's arm again.

Andrey in a few words told his adventure,—his suspicions, his discovery, and his escape.

"It's indeed a bit of good luck for us that we went there," said the young woman, thoughtfully. " To think on what trifles our fate depends! Now we must send David, or somebody else, to make the round of our people and warn them. We are near David's inn. Do you recognise the place?"

"Not in the least."

"We are approaching it from another side."

She left his arm, and stepped into a dark gateway. Here she took off her elegant hat, and tied it up in her white pocket-handkerchief. She gave Andrey her umbrella, took off her gloves, and covered her head with her shawl, tying it under her chin in the fashion of a Russian peasant.

Thus attired, with the white parcel in her hand, she might well be taken for a young and pretty seamstress carrying a parcel to a customer.

"Wait for me here," she said; "in a quarter of an hour I'll be back. Show me your watch."

She compared it with hers.

"At three minutes to eight; neither before nor after, at this very spot."

"You have kept your St Petersburg ways," said Andrey, approvingly.

"Yes. Nothing so trying as to wait indefinitely."

She plunged into the darkness.

Andrey watched a while the white spot of the parcel in her hand. Then that disappeared also.

He observed the house carefully, and choosing the straightest direction he could find, walked along, looking now and then at his watch. When a little less than half his time was over he turned back, retracing his steps and trying to keep to the same regular pace. He was only one minute before his time.

The white spot reappeared in the distance; it seemed to Andrey at the same place and of the same size, though now it was not the parcel. Zina wore her hat again, holding her handkerchief in her hand. A black figure was by her side. It was David, who wanted to congratulate Andrey upon his narrow escape.

"These small towns are confoundedly hot places at times," he said, laughing. "It's well you have scalded your fingers at the outset."

Zina repeated to David some final instructions, and he left at once on his errand.

"I feel nervous," she said, when they were alone. "David told me of another quite unexpected arrest of a man in a good social position. I won't trust your safety to big-wigs any longer. You shall stop with us."

"Very well. Let us go home."

"Yes, only we had better go in after ten o'clock. The street will be all asleep at that hour, and nobody will see you.

They had two hours before them, which they had to spend somehow.

Andrey proposed they should take a walk to the river. They could talk and enjoy the splendid southern night.

"No," Zina said, "we can spend our evening more usefully. Let us pass by the prison; this will save you the necessity of going to it with Vasily. It's good you should examine the place by night, as the escape will take place then."

They went straight to the prison. It was a big square two-storeyed building, towering above a high wall which shut it out from the rest of the world. A large dreary square, without any trace of vegetation, surrounded it, joining at one corner the open fields.

Zina and Andrey made a circuit of the square by the adjacent streets, and emerged at the mouth of the street where the carriage had to stand. The whole position could be viewed from here.

"Just observe the general aspect," Zina said. "You needn't count the steps, or measure any distance; Vasily has already done that several times. He will tell you everything."

The position for Vasily's carriage was satisfactory, or, more exactly, the least objectionable that could be found. It was rather too far away from the opening of the subterranean passage, but it was protected by houses from sight, and possibly fire from the prison wall. The street was a good one. Even at this comparatively early hour there was not a soul in it.

Andrey communicated his impressions to Zina.

"The weak point is here," she said, pointing to a shabby wine-shop some two hundred yards off. "The neighbourhood is a desert at midnight. But drinking goes on till two o'clock in that infernal shop.   In case of alarm the waiters or some foolish customers may come out and cause some difficulty."

"Oh, as to that, you needn't be uneasy," said Andrey. "It'll be my business to keep them in order, or settle their account if they persist in mixing in what does not concern them.   I should even propose that Vasily should stand nearer to the public-house, it'll seem more natural.   I'll stand on the look-out at the end of the street, and will give Vasily a signal to move a little farther off when the fugitives are coming out from the passage."

They plunged once more into by-streets, and presently came out on another part of the prison square.   Zina led her companion across it, parallel to the prison wall.

"These are the cells of the politicals," she said, pointing to a row of windows in the upper storey, some of which were dark, others dimly lighted from within.

"Can you show me Boris's window?" Andrey asked, in an agitated voice.

"The seventh from the angle.   It is lighted; he must be reading now.   Lévshin is in the fifth, Klein in the third cell from the angle.   Both their windows are dark; they must be asleep. But you needn't stare so indecently at a prison window," she added, pushing his arm; "the sentinel is looking at you."

Andrey had not expected that he was going to be brought so close to Boris that night.   The thought that his friend was there, behind this thin window glass, within reach of his voice, if not of his hand, agitated him exceedingly.   For a moment a mad idea crossed his brain, to shout Boris's name, in order that he might by chance recognise them.   Zina had to drag him by the arm to make him move on.

They walked along in silence.   When the prison square was fairly behind them, Andrey asked,

"Could he see us if we passed in the daytime?"

"No," Zina answered.   "The windows are cut very high in the wall, and are covered with white paint through which nothing can be seen.   But I'll write to him that we have passed by his window to-night, and have seen the light in his cell.   He'll be pleased."

"I'll write to him also.   Can I?" Andrey asked.

"Oh, yes; as often as you like.   I can pass anything to him; we are in active correspondence now.   But it was a very difficult matter to win over his guards.   Do you know,

I have been twice within a hairsbreadth of being arrested myself. I always had the bad luck to hit on the wrong men."

They talked about Boris all the way back. When at home Zina showed Andrey the photograph of her little son Boria, which she had received only a few days ago.

"Is he not charming!" she exclaimed, with a mother's pride, holding before Andrey, without letting it go, the portrait of a baby with chubby hands, round wondering eyes, and open mouth.

"A nice baby," he said. "Do you not think your boy is very like Boris?"

"Exactly the same face," Zina exclaimed, glad to hear this from an outsider; "and he will be in time as good a conspirator as his father. He is only a year and four months old, but he has already helped the revolution to the measure of his power."

Zina told how she took the child, then nine months old, to Kharkoff, when she had to keep the headquarters for the conspirators.

"There is nothing," she smiled, "that makes your house look so peaceful and innocent, and keeps off suspicions so well, as the presence of a child. My Boria was very useful to us on that occasion. Now tell me, has any one of us started on the revolutionary work so early as he? You see there's fair hope that he'll do well when he comes of age."

Andrey expressed his hope that when the child came of age their country would be in no need of conspirators.

"And what have you done with it now?" he asked.

A momentary cloud passed over the young woman's face.

"I couldn't keep him with me, lest in case of my arrest the child also should have to try the experience of the jail. It would be rather too early. The boy is now with Boris's mother in the country. They are very fond of him, and send me all the news about him. I hope to see him, if I can manage it, after our business here is over. . . ."

They talked far into the night in the dining-room, where a bed was improvised for Andrey, Vulitch having retired to sleep. Zina asked him about George, Tania, and Repin. Noticing something strange in the tone of his answers about the girl, she asked what was the matter. They were on terms which justified such a question. But Andrey avoided making any confidence. He could not speak lightly of his heart's troubles; but he would have been ashamed to speak of them as something serious to a woman in Zina's position.

CHAPTER III.

ANDREY and Vasily, during the next few days, went through all the necessary operations, and got themselves satisfactorily settled at their inn. They lived there a whole month, and still the affair of the escape was just at the same point.

A few days after Andrey's arrival at Dubravnik a very untoward hitch in their enterprise occurred. The common offenders of Berkut and Kunitzin's cell were blessed with the company of a certain Zuckat, a coiner, who they had reason to suspect was a spy for the prison authorities. It was resolved, at the council of the inmates of the cell, that the digging of the subterranean passage must be suspended until they had got rid of the unwelcome companion. For three weeks the whole company exerted themselves adroitly in rendering life unsupportable to the newcomer. They succeeded at last in compelling the man to implore the prison authorities to transfer him to another cell. The work of excavation had now been resumed for a few days.

These delays were exceedingly disagreeable, exhausting to the funds, and irritating to the nerves. The chief actors in the coming attempt had to spend their time in complete idleness. It would be folly for them to risk compromising themselves by taking part in the regular work of propaganda, which was going on in Dubravnik as elsewhere. They had to keep aloof from it, as well as from everything else. A most careful study of the field of their future action, and of the surrounding streets, was completed in a few days. This done, there was nothing for them but to sit down and wait.

In his quality of business man, Andrey could not stay always at home ; this would look suspicious. Besides, he had to keep up relations with Zina, who was the centre for all information. Every morning he left the inn, and went either to the public gardens, or to some other place agreed upon the previous day, where—if there was anything worth telling—he was met at eleven o'clock exactly, sometimes by Zina, but more often by Vulitch. The girl seemed to find great pleasure in his company, and Zina willingly yielded to her this little distraction.

The remainder of the day Andrey spent in his room. Vasily, when he had fulfilled his coachman's and footman's duties, came to keep him company. It cannot be said they enjoyed the time much. Their outward calm notwithstanding, they were too excited by the expectation of what was coming, to find pleasure in study or in reading of any kind. Even novels could scarcely fix their attention. Occasionally they talked,—the various sides and aspects of the revolution, their common acquaintances, current literature, Gambetta and Bismarck, all were laid under requisition. But neither of the two was very fond of talking, and most of their time they spent in silence, sitting or lying, each in his corner, smoking their pipes.

Vasily bore this kind of life with remarkable ease. He minded his horse, greased the harness, and looked in the windows for hours, his pipe in his mouth, with imperturbable dreamy calmness, as if he had never done anything else. Andrey tried to face it as best he could,—a fighting man must know how to wait. Patience in preparation is as essential for the success of an enterprise, as courage and pluck in its execution. But Andrey was bored to death by this monotonous existence, especially at first, when the habits of his very active life in St Petersburg were still fresh upon him. After a time he grew more accustomed to his new conditions, and the acute form of *ennui* subsided. Still he expected the day of decisive action with burning impatience,—a day of deliverance for himself, as well as for his imprisoned friends.

The sun was already setting. The two friends were at home just as usual. Andrey was lazily stretched upon a long chair, an open volume by his side, which he was not reading; Vasily was sitting by the window smoking his pipe,—when somebody knocked.

Vasily jumped up, and ran into the ante-room, where he slept and where he was supposed to live. It would be improper for him, footman and coachman, to sit in his master's presence.

With an alacrity one could hardly have expected from so

clumsy a fellow, Vasily seized a brush, put his left hand in one of his supposed master's boots, and began to clean it with the innocent-minded mien of a thorough footman.

"Come in," Andrey said, from the front room.

It was Vulitch who entered. Vasily's performance was unnecessary this time. Replacing the boot and the brush, he followed the girl to the front room.

Vulitch called at the inn at long intervals, always asking after Vasily, the coachman. There was no indiscretion in that. She was dressed like a smart· housemaid, and it was natural that Vasily, an unmarried fellow, should have a sweetheart.

To-day, having met nobody in the hall, the girl walked upstairs and knocked at the door.

"Would you like to join in a little open-air picnic?" she asked. "The elder Dudorov has passed her examination successfully. Only a few friends are coming, but it's sure to be a merry gathering."

Both Andrey and Vasily accepted very willingly.

"Will Zina be one of the party?" Andrey asked.

"No, *they* will not come. But they have given me permission to go," said the girl, playfully, using the plural form to denote her mistress, as servants are wont to do in Russia as a sign of respect.

She walked to the sofa, from which Andrey rose, lifting her skirt a little as women do when crossing the street in muddy weather. As she sat down, she took care that her dress should not rest upon the floor.

The rooms in which the two friends lived were indeed by no means a model of cleanliness. The square table constantly rubbed by their sleeves was comparatively clean ; it was only covered at the corners with dust and bread-crumbs. But on the floor, the grey blue layer of soft downy dust spread like the first thin snow on an even courtyard. Pieces of white, yellow, brown, and blue wrapping paper were scattered about in picturesque disorder, like so many coloured pebbles. Some of them were already covered with a thin veil of dust, which dulled their original colour, showing that this was not the first day they had lain there. The many coloured mosaic of the floor was completed by bits of eggshell, ends of cigarettes, dried up crusts of bread, which cracked under foot, and when moved drew with them dense masses of dust, like a strong magnet plunged into iron filings.

The fact is that the room was engaged by Andrey "without attendance." Everything, the sweeping included, devolved upon his supposed footman. Vasily ran the errands, cleaned Andrey's boots, and lit the samovar for him with praiseworthy punctuality. But he considered sweeping the room a waste fo time and energy. He saw no philosophical reason why the dust upon which we tread in the streets should be so much objected to on the floor. As Andrey did not much mind either, the room was swept about once a month.

The proposed picnic was to take place in a small wood a mile from the town. It was a long walk to the place. The supper, which had to be cooked on the spot, was to be late in the evening. Vasily, a practical man, resolved that it was wise to fortify themselves with something before starting. He had everything necessary at hand, and would get something ready in no time.

They did not care to have a dinner every day at a restaurant, because it was expensive, and not very safe to go to a place frequented by all sorts of people. They therefore ate at home, improvising dinners which cost little money and no trouble,— a piece of ham, half-a-dozen eggs, a couple of herrings, with the inevitable tea, sufficed very well for their simple tastes.

Vasily opened the cupboard in which he kept the tea-tray, the bread, and provisions. There was a big loaf, tea, sugar, and plenty of milk. This would have sufficed for an ordinary meal. But he wanted to have something better on this occasion. He ran to a shop near, and in a minute or two returned with a piece of cheese and a bulgy packet of hot sausages wrapped up in paper.

The samovar was ready by this time, boiling and puffing. Vasily put it on the table, and made tea. Their household chattels were scanty,—two plates and two forks for the whole company. Vulitch as the guest, and Andrey as the master, were offered one each. Vasily, in his quality of servant, had to content himself with a saucer and his pocket-knife, which he wore attached to his belt by a string.

"But, for goodness' sake, I can't eat on such a table as this. You could plant potatoes on it," said Vulitch, while, with the end of her finger, she drew some figures in the accumulated dust.

"Oh, is that all!" Vasily said. "I'll make it right in a minute."

He looked round for a duster, and his eyes fell upon his rose-coloured trousers, hanging conspicuously upon the wall. Vasily was a thrifty housekeeper, who was much pained at the thought of getting rid of anything. He had brought the whole of his wardrobe from Switzerland, expecting that it might come in useful in some way or other. But as he was peremptorily forbidden by Zina to wear his extraordinary trousers, which everywhere attracted attention, he kept them hanging up in his room, to give it, as he said, "the air of an inhabited place." But now he forgot thrift in his ardent desire to oblige a lady. Snatching from the nail his long-preserved trousers, he tore a great piece out of them, and gallantly cleaned the table therewith, before the laughing girl could interfere.

"You are a regular savage, Vasily!" she exclaimed.

"Why?" Vasily asked, in innocent surprise. "Woollen dusters clean much better than linen."

"Possibly. But it's a pity you use neither woollen nor linen dusters, nor brooms of any kind, as far as I can see," she said, pointing to the floor. "You ought to be ashamed to keep your master's room in such a state."

Vasily only shrugged his shoulders.

"Oh, the room? that's nothing," Andrey interrupted. "Ask us rather if we haven't relapsed into a state of savagery altogether."

He told how Vasily, since he had become a coachman, only washed his face on Sundays, and had got into the habit of never using a towel, wiping his face against the pillow, and letting his hands dry of themselves.

"It makes one's hands and face coarser," Vasily explained in a matter-of-fact tone.

He paid no further attention to his friend's jokes, but sipped his tea with pensive imperturbability, as if they were laughing at somebody else.

The tea over, Vasily and Vulitch left, Andrey remaining behind for a time. It was not wise for them to be seen all going out together. Andrey rejoined them in one of the squares, just out of sight of the inn.

It was already growing dark when they approached the oak wood upon the eastern side of the town. The wood was empty, as it was a week-day. The fresh evening breeze brought to them the sound of a distant melody, sung in an agreeable though not very strong baritone.

"I recognise the voice," Vulitch exclaimed. "It's Vatajko who is singing."

She seized Andrey's arm in order to make him walk more quickly. She was passionately fond of music, this daughter of the south, and was a singer herself.

Following the direction of the voice, they soon came upon a little green patch of field on the border of the wood, encircled upon three sides by a thick wall of trees. On the fourth side it .was bordered with bushes, screening it from view without shutting out of sight the suburbs of Dubravnik and the meadows which stretched to the right and left.

The singer was sitting under a tree. He was a very young man, who looked twice his age, thanks to the luxuriant growth which covered his cheeks and chin. He was a fellow-student of Vulitch.

A lady in a dark-blue dress stood by listening. She was of middle height, and rather slim. The very delicate white skin, the fair hair half circling with short curls her mild lovely face, and her eyes of the purest blue, made her look something between an angel and a pet-lamb.

She introduced herself as Voinova.

"Varia? Oh, I beg your pardon for the familiarity! Varvara Alexevna?" Andrey said, interrogatively.

"Yes, Varvara Alexevna, or Varia, which I like better," the young woman said kindly.

She was a well-known woman, this Varia Voinova. Her friends were justified in naming her the mother of the afflicted. Wife of a surgeon of liberal views, she had made the looking after of political prisoners the chief object of her life, doing all that she could to alleviate their sufferings, as if they had all been members of her own family.

"It is well that I have met you both," she said, with a smile, to Andrey and Vasily, whom she saw also for the first time. "When your turn comes, I shall take care of you with the more heart."

They thanked her for her promise, protesting that they did not intend to give her the opportunity just yet.

The sisters Dudorov were in the wood collecting dry wood for the fire that was to be lighted. Attracted by the sound of new voices, they came out, followed by a young man in a grey blouse, with pale eyes, pale yellow hair, and a button-like nose set in a comical face. He held in his arms a big bundle of wood, which he threw on the grass.

"Ah, Botcharov!" Vulitch exclaimed. "Come here, I want to introduce you to my friends."

Botcharov was one of the members of the Dubravnik branch of the League. He was a "legal" man, that is, a man who lived under his real name, with a genuine passport. But he had recently got into some trouble with the police.

They sat down on the grass, and Andrey expressed surprise at seeing Botcharov moving about so freely. He had been told he was strictly watched by the police.

"So I am," Botcharov answered, with a serious air. "But I made an arrangement with the spy appointed to watch me, and we get on very well together. He comes once a week to my rooms, I give him my instructions as to the places I choose to say that I have visited, and he doesn't bother me with his presence any further."

Vulitch thought it must be very expensive to obtain such immunity.

"Oh, no!" Botcharov exclaimed, "I'm not such a fool as that. It won't cost me a penny. I compelled my man to surrender at discretion. One day, a fortnight ago, when I was quite tired of having him constantly at my heels, I came out in the morning, a piece of bread and sausage in my pocket, and began to walk from one place to another, never stopping for a moment. So I walked and walked, until the evening came, my spy dragging himself always at my heels. I was exceedingly tired, but I knew he must be more tired still, for he had not eaten since the early morning. And I shouted to him now and then, 'Ah you blackguard, I'll make you put your tongue out! I'll make you walk until the dawn, and you dare not leave me, for I forewarn you that I am going to make a visit to a great revolutionist.' My man followed me sullenly, without answering, until he could hold no more, and burst forth indignantly, 'I am also a man, sir, and not a dog. You ought to be ashamed to treat me as you are doing. I have a wife and children to feed, sir.'

"Who would suppose that these scoundrels had wives and children? Well, I relented, and proposed to my man the agreement, which he at once accepted, to our mutual satisfaction, and I am a free man again."

A new guest, who was late, joined them at this moment, apologising for being detained from the pleasant company by his many occupations. It was a certain Mironov, formerly a clerk to a village community. The sisters Dudorov and the Dubravnik people in general thought much of him on account of his close connections with the peasants, so that to some extent he was the lion of the season.

He had been invited on purpose to meet Andrey and Vasily, with whom he at once entered into conversation, with the peculiar ease of manner of a man who knows himself to be a celebrity, and is quite sure of being interesting to everybody.

"Mironov! here is Voinova, who is burning with impatience to make your acquaintance!" the elder Dudorov shouted, laughing.

"No, not at all!" Voinova protested.

"Yes, yes! come here!"

Mironov smiled at Andrey apologetically, as if to say, "I can't help it! I wish I could remain with you, but every position has its inconveniences."

"What a disgusting man," Vulitch whispered to Andrey, when he was gone. "I should not have come if I had known he would be here."

"Why? What have you against him?" Andrey asked. "They say he is a remarkable propagandist among the peasants."

"He says it himself, so we must believe him. Perhaps he is. But he is hateful to me all the same."

The pile in the meantime had been lighted, and the black iron kettle hung over the fire. Vasily undertook to superintend the cooking of the maize porridge and bacon for their supper.

It was now quite dark outside the circle lit by the fire. The sky hung heavy over the wood, a few stars sending their pale rays through the opening made by the lofty trees. The lights were kindled in the town, which seemed to have expanded, and at the same time receded to a greater distance, looking like a huge island separated from them by a vast sea of darkness.

All sat down in the red light of the fire, looking silently at the puffing kettle. Vasily was minding the fire, and stirring the porridge now and then with a long spoon. His shadow, as he moved round, now stretched enormously upon the level ground, now crept up the stem of some old tree, now broke in pieces and melted away upon the irregular wall of projecting branches fantastically lighted from below. The beetles were humming in the air, piercing for an instant the sphere of light and then disappearing into the darkness. The crackling of the fire made the silence around seem absolute.

"Just the time for telling ghost stories," said Vulitch.

"Why not for singing something?" said Masha Dudorov. "Vatajko, Vulitch," she proceeded, "why shouldn't you manage a chorus for us?"

Some Russian songs were tried, but with little success. Vatajko and Vulitch were the only singers, and Botcharov sang out of tune on purpose to make fun.

Vulitch was saving her voice, and sang second. She knew her turn was coming, and she wanted to sing to-day with all her soul and power.

The southern element was strongly represented in the company, and soon clamoured for a genuine Ukrainian song.

Vulitch consented.

"What shall I sing?" she asked Andrey, who was sitting next her.

"The one which you'll feel most," he answered, deferentially.

Vulitch gave a knowing nod.

She took off her jacket, that it should not be in her way, and rose to take her place at some distance from the rest. For a moment she stood thoughtful, her face serious and almost stern, and then she began to sing. Her half-closed eyes were looking far away, and she seemed engrossed by the song. Yet she felt that Andrey's eyes were riveted upon her, and that he was admiring and wondering. This excited and stimulated her, and gave to her song a peculiar charm for herself. It was one of those many records of the epoch when the Ukrainian Cossacks carried into the south-east the war of the cross against the Mahomedans,—a ballad about a young Cossack who left his home and his sweetheart, and went to the land of the infidels to liberate from chains and slavery his comrades pining in the Turkish prisons.

Vulitch was not a professional singer, though she might have become one had she cared for it. Hers was a voice that could fill space. Within the four walls of a sitting-room it hurt the ear by excess of strength. She would have done much had she gone through a regular training. But no training would have taught her to sing better than she sang the songs of her country. She was born in the bosom of the people, amidst the wide steppes out of which these broad and thrilling melodies have grown. She sang them as only the natives can sing, and her voice was soft and tender under the sky vault, in the calmness of the night, as she sent forth wave on wave of melody across the sleeping steppes.

She was not applauded or in any audible way encouraged by her audience. Only Masha whispered to Botcharov that she had never heard Annie sing so well as that day. Vasily frowned at the fire, leaning his cheek on his hand, and nodding his head now and then. Andrey had moved away a little to hear better, and to be quite alone.

The girl did not see him, but she felt where he was. When she had finished her song, she turned towards him at once, her face flushed with artistic excitement, and with the consciousness of success. With a light bound she was by his side, and dropped upon the grass without giving him time to spread out anything for her. She looked exceedingly pretty in that charming dress for a girl, the national Ukrainian costume. Instead of a bodice she wore a loose white chemise, open at the throat, and richly embroidered in red and blue. A broad scarlet ribbon tied round her slender waist fell over a short dark-blue skirt. Her long brown tresses were plaited in with ribbon, and several rows of corals were fastened round her bare throat.

"One would willingly go and fight the Turks," Andrey said to her, "only to be sung about afterwards as you have sung to-night."

"You liked my song? I am so glad. I sang it for you," she whispered, "and it's all about you. I am sure you will succeed in breaking our friends' chains, as my Cossack did."

"It will be your success too, Annie," Andrey answered, "for you have as great a share in it as I."

"No, we women can take no part in Cossack deeds, and we have no share in the Cossack's glory," she said, in a tone of regret. "We can only hold your horses, and bring you the sword and the rifle. But we are not going to grumble; we are glad enough to do even that," she added cheerfully.

Under the action of some inner fire, her eyes glistened more brightly, her cheeks glowed with intensity of life and joy. Ordinarily silent, she was all gaiety that night, animating every one with her frolicsome dare-devil spirit.

The supper was very merry and very bad, because Vasily, most careful when there was no particular need for it, forgot to stir just at the critical moment, and allowed the porridge to get burnt. Then Vulitch proposed they should all jump across the fire, as the peasant girls and lads are wont to do in the midsummer nights. She jumped herself with Andrey, with Vatajko, and Andrey again. Then she sang them "The Moon," an Ukrainian love song, with such sweetness and melancholy that Vasily was on the point of bursting into tears. And when he implored her to sing it again, she burst forth with the merriest song she knew, brimful of the pure sparkling fun of the Ukrainians, which to the impassioned vehement merriment of the Great Russians is as the song of the skylark hovering in the morning sky to the cry of the sea-gull playing with the storm.

She delighted in her power of swaying at will the feelings and emotions of others. She liked to see how Vasily's face brightened on · a sudden, how he made a gesture with his hands as if throwing something to the ground, and how his heavy shoulders moved as if he were on the point of jumping to his feet and dancing.

But her own heart did not share in the gaiety she was rousing in the hearts of the others. It grew sadder and sadder as she went on with her merry song. At the end her strength failed her; a rising sob contracted her throat, and her last joyful note broke down pitiably. She had to make an effort to keep back her tears.

She sat down at a distance, alone, and nothing could induce her to sing any more. She hardly spoke for the rest of the evening; her only wish was now, that the party should break up and she might be alone.

Of all those present, Andrey was the only one to whom that broken note said something, nay, everything. He was already to some extent prepared for the revelation. The girl was too careless in keeping the secret which was burning in her heart.

He could doubt no longer. She loved him. And he— what had he to give in exchange for this greatest of treasures —a woman's soul? Mere gratitude and friendship, which she would not know what to do with.

He tried to tell himself that he felt sorry for this discovery. But he knew he was not. There are men of exceptionally delicate nature, in whom an unhappy love produces a peculiar kindness and tenderness for women in general. Andrey was not of their number. Disappointed in his love for Tania, he could not help feeling revengeful against women in general. His first feeling now was that of cruel satisfaction. The humiliation to his man's pride was wiped away. The idea that this did not make him a whit happier only came later. Now he felt proud and elated.

They had to walk back to the town together. At the gates the party broke up. Andrey and Vasily proposed that they should accompany the girl to her house. But she declined energetically; she was in no need of an escort, and could find her way easily alone. When Andrey wanted to insist she grew angry.

Andrey and Vasily went to their inn. Here a surprise awaited them; upon the hall table lay a letter directed to Andrey. The waiter on duty was sleeping on the bench. They awakened him, and were informed that the errand boy from the "office," to which Andrey was supposed to go every morning, had called in his absence and left this message. It was an open note, containing a few words, roughly scrawled and badly spelled, requesting Andrey to be at the office to-morrow morning at ten instead of eleven.

The message could only be from Zina, and it meant that something had happened. Without some great necessity Zina would not have interrupted the regularity of their proceedings.

CHAPTER IV.

A NEW PLAN.

THEY were to meet that morning in the public gardens. Half-an-hour before the time Andrey was on the bench at the bottom of a secluded walk. He saw between the trees Zina's light-brown dress, and went to meet her half way.

"What's the matter?" he asked.

She did not answer at once. A gentleman taking his morning stroll happened to pass by at the moment. For some time they walked in silence. Zina's face was grave and pre-occupied; something had evidently happened, though Andrey was unable to guess of what nature.

"Well?" he asked, when they were out of anybody's hearing.

"All is ruined again," Zina answered, looking him in the face. "The passage has been discovered by the gaolers."

Andrey stopped, aghast.

"Discovered!" he exclaimed.

"Last night. But let's go to that bench. I'll tell you everything."

They sat upon Zina's favourite bench. It was secluded, and at the same time allowed any person approaching from a distance to be seen.

Here the young woman related briefly how the thing happened. Kunitzin had just descended into the passage to dig out the last few feet of earth, when a row occurred among his fellow-prisoners. They were playing at cards. One of the players had cheated, and another flew at him with a knife and wounded him in the shoulder. The guards ran in at the noise. Kunitzin had hardly time to jump into his bed; but he had not time to put back properly the board that covered the opening of the passage. One of the guards stumbled against its projecting edge, and in a moment had discovered the passage.

Andrey looked at Zina attentively whilst she was speaking, but he hardly listened to what she said. Their plan was ruined, that was the only thing he realised clearly.

"That's the fruit of our procrastination!" he exclaimed reproachfully.

He was so aggrieved that he did not think how unjust and cruel was his remark.

"We might have fared much worse if we hadn't been cautious," Zina replied calmly. "If the gaolers had got wind of the thing beforehand through Zuckat, a trap would have been laid and all our people caught. Now we have only to begin the thing over again."

"For the third time, I suppose!" Andrey put in peevishly.

"No, for the fifth. We have tried and abandoned three different plans before we started this one."

"What will be our next move, then? Have we anything left us?" Andrey asked, trying to be calm.

"Something will turn up, I hope. We must see. . . . Boris may suggest something. . . . Our money is running short—that is the worst of it."

A long pause ensued, both keeping to their own thoughts.

Zina broke the silence.

"I am informed that the attorney has received from St Petersburg the order to push on Boris's trial."

She had learned this from the wife of one of the officials connected with the prosecution. It was her habit to communicate to Andrey all her news.

"What does it amount to?" Andrey inquired.

"To nothing particular. They'll have to undergo some new interrogations; that is all."

"Are the interrogations made in the precincts of the gaol, or are the prisoners moved elsewhere?" Andrey asked, an idea flashing into his mind.

"The interrogations are made in the city," Zina replied. "The examining commission thinks it derogatory to their dignity to go after their victims. The prisoners are brought under escort to the court where the commission holds its sittings."

"What if we tried an attempt at rescue on the way?" Andrey asked, turning on the bench towards Zina.

She looked astonished.

"In the street of a big town? In open daylight? Are you in your senses?"

"I don't positively propose such a plan. It's only a suggestion which is worth thinking about at all events. Could you tell me how large the escort would be?"

"They were escorted by four gendarmes last time."

"Only four! It isn't so bad as one might have expected."

He began now to defend his plan more seriously, urging that the danger of attacking a police force by daylight in a public thoroughfare was not so great as seemed at first sight. If the attempt were actually made, the thing would be decided one way or another in half a minute. A crowd would have no time to assemble. In all probability at the first shots strangers will run away to get out of the scuffle. Moreover, it would be easy to choose for the attack a place little frequented by the public. The prison stood upon the outskirts of the town, and the streets near it were almost empty at the busiest time of the day.

"But you forget one essential," Zina interposed. "There is the escort. Four men must be tackled by at least four men on our side, admitting as you say the advantage to us of a surprise. With the three prisoners, there will be seven. Two additional carriages, with two additional coachmen, are necessary to carry them all off. Only think what a confusion it will be. . . ."

"With a little energy on our part we could find money and men for it all the same," Andrey said.

"Possibly. But it will be a regular battle, and not a surprise. It isn't what we are aiming at. What is the use of rescuing the prisoners, if we lose some of their rescuers in exchange?"

Andrey uttered a meditative "Yes," and moved restlessly in his place. His plan was too complicated; there was no denying that.

He did not insist upon it any longer, looking fixedly at the gravel beneath his feet.

He tried in his mind to cut it down here and there; one carriage and one assailant might be struck off perhaps; . . . still it was too big a business. . . .

"But what would you say," Zina asked, with a sudden inspiration, "if the prisoners could be armed?"

"That would be capital! But is it possible?"

"I think it is. The warder passes them anything. Once before he let them have a bundle of saws and a bunch of keys.

He can contrive to pass in three small revolvers just as well. I'll inquire at all events."

"Yes, as soon as you can. It will simplify the whole thing enormously."

The next morning when they met again, Zina was able to tell Andrey, to his great delight, that the warder thought the thing was perfectly feasible.

Thus amended the scheme became workable. At the meeting of the group it was accepted at once. It was resolved that, with the prisoners armed, two assailants would be sufficient, with two carriages, to carry them all off. Vasily was commissioned to buy a new horse and a new carriage, whilst Zina was to enter into communication with the Dubravnik people for the two additional men, one as coachman and one to fight.

But now a new turn of affairs compelled them to hasten their preparations, so as to be ready for almost immediate action.

Zina was informed that the prisoners would be summoned to the interrogation within a fortnight, if not sooner. It was impossible to prepare in so short a time all that was necessary for the new attempt. Yet it was impossible to lose perhaps their last chance of trying a rescue.

To cut short all difficulties, Andrey proposed that no new man should be engaged. Provided he had a decent animal to ride, he would undertake to rout the escort alone by a cavalry charge, if the prisoners joined attack from their side at the same moment. Boris and his two companions were all three resolute men. They would have the advantage of two, perhaps three, shots. If they succeeded in disabling one man of their escort,—which was not supposing too much, —the numerical advantage would be on their side. Four of them could rout the rest of the escort. Vasily's part was to be the same. He had only to buy cabman's clothes, and brighten up his carriage in order to make it presentable in daylight. The three prisoners could be carried off without much difficulty in one carriage. Being on horseback, Andrey would be able to take care of himself, and even to cover, if needful, Vasily's retreat.

The plan was a very risky one; for, after all, the prisoners were prisoners. Andrey alone would be free to make the assault. Vasily could hardly be of much use, as he had to look after the carriage. But Andrey had an unshakable faith in his plan, and he succeeded in imparting that faith to his companions. What recommended his proposal to all, was its simplicity and also its cheapness. The long delays had exhausted the funds obtained for the enterprise. Zina, who had extraordinary talent for finding money, succeeded in borrowing, through Botcharov, two hundred pounds from a Dubravnik gentleman, to be returned by the St Petersburg friends within three months. But this was all the money they could reckon upon for the present.

The strictest economy was necessary. Andrey's plan reduced the additional expense to the acquisition of a horse and saddle, which was not much.

"You needn't get me a racehorse," he said to Zina, who as cashier was more than anybody else open to arguments of this nature. "A common beast will do very well to impede pursuers in cabs, if there should be any. But if there chances to be a horseman among them,—a cossack or cavalry man,—racer or no racer, it's all over."

Andrey's amended plan was finally accepted unanimously. A feverish activity succeeded the somnolent condition of expectation. In a few hours Vasily and Andrey had made the round of the second-rate horsedealers. They found a tolerably good little mare from the steppes with small head and straight back. The owner guaranteed that the horse was well trained for the saddle. They returned in the afternoon with a saddle Vasily bought secondhand. They tried the horse carefully, and after hard bargaining brought their new purchase to the inn. The next few days Andrey spent on horseback getting to know his nag. It proved to be a high-spirited animal, of tolerable speed, and not very skittish. This last point was of great importance, as during the coming affray shots would certainly be exchanged. He had some trouble in accustoming his Rosinante, as he playfully called the mare, to the noise of fire-arms. When in a secluded glade he fired off the first shot by the horse's ear, she jumped under him as if she were mad. But at the second and third shots the mare behaved better. After a week's practice, both rider and horse were quite ready for action. A shot between the ears made her shiver, but that was all. The rest of the day Andrey spent studying the new field of action and the lines of retreat.

Zina in the meantime was busily engaged instructing

the company of sentinels, watchmen, and errand-bearers. They were eight in number, and had by a series of skilful and delicate operations to bring together the assailants and the escort at the right place and at the right moment.

The time when the prisoners would be summoned to the hall was known only approximately. The choice of day and hour depended entirely on the attorney's convenience. It was therefore necessary that all through the time that the summons was probable, everything should be in readiness for action at a moment's notice.

The signal to set the whole machine in motion had to be given from the prison itself. Before they were consigned to the escort of gendarmes the prisoners had to change their dresses, and were searched to the skin in the prison office. As soon as they were ordered downstairs, Klein, for whom it was most convenient, was to place a piece of blue paper in a corner of his window, which he could reach by standing upon his stool.

Every day, from nine in the morning until three in the afternoon, when there was a sitting in the hall, this window was watched with an opera-glass from the row of houses opposite the prison. Two friends had taken a room there. When one was tired, the other took his place so as not to lose sight of the window for a moment.

On the appearance of the signal in Klein's window, one of the watchmen was to run downstairs into a public-house where Vatajko, who was the errand-bearer, would be sitting in company with one of the sentinels. The latter was to give notice to his companions, waiting in another public-house, that they should move to their posts; whilst Vatajko was to take the cab he had in readiness, and go at full speed to give the signal to Vasily at his inn. Here everything—men, horses, carriage—was kept in readiness for immediate departure.

Taking into account the time occupied by changing dresses, searching, and going through the formalities usual before prisoners are handed over to an escort, Andrey and Vasily would have ample time to receive Vatajko's message, and to reach the place where they had to wait, before the prisoners left the gaol.

The journey from the prison to the hall ought to take about forty minutes. After crossing the prison square—an affair of two or three minutes—the escort would enter a lane, about a quarter of a mile long, leading to a newly opened avenue, which crossed the suburbs a little to the east of the prison. It was wide, and not completely built up. Two rows of freshly-planted lime trees, which would not impede the movement of a carriage or a horse, ran on both sides of it. There was no police station the whole length of the avenue, and only a few shops towards the city end. The escort would be in this avenue for about twelve minutes. It was resolved that the attack should be made here. The spot chosen was some four or five minutes' distance from the corner of the lane. A line of five sentinels, each one of them in sight of another, was to stretch from the prison square to the avenue, in order to communicate instantly by special signals everything of importance to the assailants, who were to keep out of sight till the decisive moment.

Everything considered, it was thought better by far to make the attempt on the way to the hall. But if this should be impossible, from some impediment,—a detachment of soldiers or policemen, a funeral or wedding procession, or anything of the kind, passing along the street at the critical moment,—the attempt was to be postponed until the prisoners were returning to the gaol. In this case a change of front had to be executed. The attack was to be made at the same spot, for there was no better all along the route; but Andrey and Vasily would have to wait at another place. All the men of the staff—the sentinels and the rest—would move toward the hall to form a new line, in order to watch the rather uncertain route that the escort might take back to the prison, and to send the signals to Andrey. As some confusion might easily arise at this place, Zina was to be on the spot in person to keep everything in good order.

The whole arrangement was complicated and delicate. All had to work with the smoothness and precision of clockwork. The slightest hitch or delay might ruin everything.

To be sure that the whole machine worked well, on Sunday morning, when everything was ready, an actual rehearsal was gone through. The part of the escorted prisoners was played by Masha Dudorov and Botcharov, the latter carrying for fun a big coil of rope on his left shoulder, to make himself more like a gendarme with his shoulder-knots. In due time the two went solemnly from the prison square to the hall, and an hour after back again, the sentinels making their signals as they passed, errand-bearers and assailants going through all their respective movements as at the real attempt.

On the whole all went very well. The time and the distance were calculated correctly. The men knew their parts thoroughly. Some signals were changed, as they proved to be not sufficiently clear at a distance.

It was high time that all should be ready. There was reason to expect that the prisoners would be summoned in the next week—either on Monday or Wednesday. As Monday passed quietly, and there was no sitting of the commission on Tuesday or Thursday, it was pretty certain that Wednesday would be the day.

Vasily was up before six. He examined for the hundredth time every screw in the carriage, every nail in his horses' shoes, every buckle in the harness. Everything was in perfect order, cleaned and greased as if for a parade.

He gave an extra feed of oats to the horses, and rubbed them down with particular care. Then he went upstairs, washed his face, combed his hair, and brushed his clothes. When the clock struck eight he awakened Andrey, who was sleeping soundly, having been at work late on the previous evening.

Vasily lighted the samovar for their tea, and was going to the stables to harness the horses, when the door opened and Zina entered.

She had her market-basket in her hand, her grey shawl wrapped round her head, and falling over her shoulders.

She may have dropped in by chance to suggest something new. Often things were thought of at the last moment. So at least Andrey said to himself, to remove his misgivings at the unexpected visit. But when the young woman took off the shawl, which covered her mouth and chin, and Andrey saw her pale agitated face, his heart sank within him.

"Another misfortune!" he exclaimed.

"No. But read that," Zina said, handing him a telegram from St Petersburg, which he read at a glance.

It was from Taras Kostrov, and was couched in the terms of an innocent commercial message. But its meaning was only too grave. Taras, speaking evidently at the bidding of the committee, requested that their attempt should be post-poned for three days.

It was evident that something very important, which

had to take place at St Petersburg the next day or the day after, would be frustrated in some way if the telegram about the Dubravnik attempt reached the police beforehand.

Andrey, as well as Zina, had sufficient experience to know that such untoward coincidences were very possible. But they knew also—Andrey at all events knew—that as the matter stood now, to accede to such a request might mean sacrificing their scheme altogether.

"How do you like that?" Andrey said sarcastically, passing the telegram to Vasily.

For answer Vasily crumpled the telegram in his fist and threw it upon the table with a long whistle.

"And I had greased the carriage and cleaned the horses so well for to-day!" flashed across his mind, amidst his deep regret.

Andrey wanted to make short work of this new hindrance.

"It's too late for us to put it off," he said.

"Certainly not," Zina answered. "Since it is not yet done, it can easily be postponed."

"But this will mean giving it up altogether. It may be our last chance."

"Perhaps," Zina said.

"Well," retorted Andrey, growing obstinate; "I don't think they have the right to ask such a thing; and if they do, we are fully justified in carrying out our plan to the end. It has been decided upon, mind that. We work at it for months, we are on the point of bringing it to a happy conclusion, and now, for the sake of some new scheme, perhaps a mere fancy project, we are asked to give up an affair in which the lives of three persons are involved! No, that is too much. Nothing will ever be done if our party adopts such tactics as this."

Zina fired up, as if these words were meant as an offence to her.

"Don't talk nonsense, Andrey!" she exclaimed. "They know very well how the matter stands with us. Do you suppose they are unable to weigh just as well as we can here what is risked by a delay? If they send us such a telegram, their affair must be more important than ours. You know yourself that we must give way."

These were her words. And the look in her large grey eyes said to him at the same time:—"Why do you torment me to no purpose?   Do you think I am less concerned in the matter than you? or that I have not had over and over again all these thoughts myself?"

Andrey bit his lips nervously, and did not insist any further.

" Are they "—he meant the prisoners—" forewarned that nothing will be done to-day?" he asked.

" I had no time to do that," Zina answered.   " The telegram came yesterday night long after my meeting with the gaoler. They'll see nothing and nobody in the streets, and will easily guess that nothing can be done."

" No, this must not be.   They will simply conclude that we have not had time to come to our posts, and will expect that the attempt will be made on their return.   They must be forewarned at once.   Perhaps they will be able so to manage as to necessitate a second examination."

" That's true ; but how can we warn them now?"

" Why should we not go to meet them in the street? Seeing me on foot with you, they will understand that we came simply to see them, and that nothing can be done to-day."

Zina was much pleased at the proposal.   But she feared the men of the escort might notice Andrey's face, and have some suspicions if they recognised him on another occasion on horseback in another dress.

" Confound these precautions !" Andrey exclaimed.   " They will not remember my face more than any of the hundreds of people they will meet on the way."

Vasily sided with Andrey, as he usually did, and Zina yielded.   They left at once.

When they had gone a few hundred steps from the inn they saw a cab coming toward them at full speed.   Vatajko's hairy face peeped from behind the shoulder of the driver, to whom he was saying something.

" Hallo ! stop !" Andrey shouted.

Vatajko jumped from the cab.   He was bringing the message that in Klein's window the signal had appeared. The prisoners were summoned to the court.   The sentinels were all at their posts.

" Run back and dismiss them," Zina said.   " They mustn't be seen in the street.   There's nothing to be done to-day."

Seeing his troubled face, she added, " It's nothing particular ; only a delay of three days."

Vatajko hastened back to fulfil his new mission.   Zina and

Andrey went to the avenue, where they expected to meet the prisoners.

It was a cold autumnal morning, such as a sudden north wind brings over the warm damp country. A fine cold rain began to fall, cutting face and hands with its oblique drops. As they walked on the rain increased, making the passengers in the streets run plunging their shivering necks into their coat collars. Zina opened her umbrella. Andrey had none, as he belonged for the time being to a class which is not much in the habit of umbrella carrying. But he did not mind the inclemency of the skies.

"What beautiful weather," he observed, with a sigh, pointing to the street.

Zina smiled, and nodded assent.

It was splendid weather for an affair like theirs, and it was a pity to lose such an opportunity. Even the most frequented thoroughfares were almost empty.

When they turned into the lime-tree avenue, whose whole length they could see from end to end, both started.

"There they are!" they said together, in a subdued voice without moving their heads.

Through the veil of the thick rain they saw their friends advancing up the middle of the street. Two gendarmes marched in front, two in the rear. The three prisoners were in the middle. Soon they could be seen clearly, and could see their friends in their turn.

Of the three Boris alone looked strong and healthy. He marched in the middle, his long chestnut beard flying in the wind. His face expressed the pleasure he felt at the unexpected meeting, without a shade of concern as to its significance. Levshin and Klein were pale, perhaps from ill-health, perhaps from emotion.

The two groups of friends advanced towards each other, all maintaining the appearance of complete indifference. The nearer they came, the more urgent it was to suppress every sign of caring for, or even so much as noticing, each other. Yet they saw and felt each other without looking.

Zina slackened her pace. They advanced now as slowly as possible, but the distance between the two groups diminished with extreme rapidity. To prolong for a few moments the intense pleasure and the intense pain of this mute interview, Zina stepped beneath the porch of a house, as if seeking protection from the rain.   Here a very ingenious idea crossed her mind, which she immediately put into execution.

Raising her umbrella handle above her head, she glanced at Boris, and began to knock at the door of the house with the air of a mistress who knows she is expected and does not wish to ring.

Andrey was somewhat surprised that Zina should knock at the door of a strange house, but he at once guessed that there must be something behind it.   In fact, Zina was telegraphing to her husband a message in the prison knock alphabet, in which each letter is represented by a small number of differently modulated knocks.   Both Zina and Boris had spent several years of their youth in prison, and could read the knock language by sight as well as by the ear, just as experienced officials can read a telegram as it is tapped out by the receiving apparatus.

The words Zina communicated to Boris were : "Get another examination."   She knocked out her message so quickly, that she finished before the prisoners had passed.   A slight, hardly perceptible nod of Boris told her that he understood, and would act accordingly.

At this moment the door at which Zina was knocking opened, and a housemaid appeared to inquire what the lady wanted.

Zina asked whether Colonel Ivan Petrovitch Krutikoff— the first name that came into her head—was at home.   Being told that this was the Protopop Sakharov's house, and no Colonel Krutikoff was known in the place, Zina apologised for her mistake and went off.

The prisoners were already at a distance.

Zina and Andrey returned to their quarters in the best spirits.   They were sure now that the delay would have no evil consequences.

CHAPTER V.

LETTERS were exchanged between Boris and Zina the same evening. Zina explained to the prisoners the cause and the extent of the delay. Boris informed his friends that he had acted in accordance with the hint given him; a new examination was sure to take place at the next sitting of the commission. This would be on Saturday, as there was no sitting earlier.

On the Friday the affair which caused the delay came off in St Petersburg, and Andrey and Vasily both congratulated themselves that they had followed Zina's advice. Nevertheless, as he said good-bye at their last interview, Andrey warned her:

"If you have to-night another telegram like the last, don't bring it to our place to-morrow. We'll on no account stop now, and it will only disturb our peace of mind to no purpose."

"You needn't be afraid of that," Zina answered; "such things don't happen every other day."

They sat once again—for the last time—upon the same bench, where three weeks before Andrey learned the failure of the old plan of escape, and where they laid the basis of the new one.

They thought, but did not speak of the morrow. There was nothing to say; all was settled, and nothing could be altered. They had provided all that they could, and taken all measures which the most careful consideration suggested. Now the course of events was out of their control. The issue depended upon a hundred accidents, which they must be prepared to meet boldly and skilfully, but which they could neither estimate nor foresee.

Zina looked at her watch.

"It's time for me to go home," she said, rising.

"Good-bye," Andrey said, shaking hurriedly both the hands she stretched out to him.

They took leave of each other in their simple undemonstrative way, as they were wont to do every day. They might be watched by somebody, and they avoided instinctively anything unusual in their manner for fear of raising suspicion. Too much was at stake in to-morrow's affair for them to omit the slightest precaution.

Next morning, from nine onwards, Vasily, attired in his cabman's dress, sat outside the gate of the inn, watching anxiously the corner of the street.

At half-past ten Vatajko's cab turned the corner and drove by the inn without stopping. The young man held in his hand a white pocket handkerchief—the signal. He even waved it slightly in the air, the better to emphasise his errand.

This was quite superfluous; but Vatajko was excited, and too young to appreciate the excessive sobriety which an old conspirator would have maintained under similar circumstances.

Vasily rushed upstairs to inform Andrey, and met him on the stairs. He had seen the signal from the window, and descended composedly into the courtyard, fully equipped for the day.

His horse was already saddled, eating at the manger. He put the bit into its mouth and tightened the girths. Vasily had in the meantime turned the carriage toward the gates, and, mounting the box, drove rapidly away. With one bound Andrey leapt into the saddle, and followed close behind the carriage.

When outside the gate they gave each other a hasty nod of farewell, without so much as exchanging a glance. They knew not whether they would ever meet again. But each was at this moment absorbed in the business he had in hand. They went in different directions, as they had to stand at different points before joining in the common action.

In ten minutes Andrey reached a little out-of-the-way square, formerly a market-place, a short distance from the city end of the fateful avenue. Vatajko, appointed his special sentinel, was already there. He had just dismissed the cab in which he came, and had plunged into a narrow crooked lane connecting the square and the avenue. Standing in the middle of the lane, Vatajko could see and be seen from both ends of it, and thus transmit all signals from the avenue to Andrey.

Passing the mouth of the lane, Andrey saw his sentinel

at his post, signalling to him that the prisoners were not yet out of the prison gates. Vasily, whom Andrey could not see, was already at his post at the opposite end of the lane, receiving signals from the line of sentinels that stretched up to the prison square.

Andrey dismounted, and led his horse by the bridle round the place as if to give it an airing. A horseman motionless in the middle of a square, would have been a sight so unusual as to attract attention. He was dressed in a short national *armiak*, under the skirt of which his arms could be easily hidden. Passing the lane leading to the avenue, he saw Vatajko at his post. His felt hat was on his head; this meant that the prisoners were still within the walls of the gaol. But at this very moment Vatajko took off his hat, and stood uncovered, picking a straw off it. Andrey's heart gave a bound; the prisoners had come out of the gaol; they were approaching.

He did not mount, however, his horse. Holding it by the bridle, he quietly went on his way: he had another most important signal to receive.

The prisoners were to be armed with short revolvers, which the gaoler had undertaken to convey to them. As prisoners before leaving the gaol are closely searched, it was a difficult matter to arm them. The gaoler who was helping in the escape proposed putting their weapons in the pockets of their overcoats, which he would throw over their shoulders in the hall when all formalities were over.

Everything depended upon the success of this ruse. The prisoners, on passing the first of the sentinels, were to make a sign to say whether they had the arms. This would decide whether the rescue could be attempted that day at all.

Vatajko, who until then had been playing the part of a loiterer looking at the pictures in a stationer's windows, abandoned all attempts at keeping up appearances. He stood, his legs apart, in the middle of the lane, watching with breathless attention Vasily's movements. When the desired signal was given, he turned round, and ran to communicate the good news to Andrey.

His work as sentinel was over. There was no longer any signal for him to watch for, because Vasily had rapidly moved forward so as to be at the place of the coming fight. He had to get to his place beforehand, in order that the escort might see him there.

Andrey, on the contrary, was bound to keep moving all the time. He had to arrange so as to meet the escort at the right place. It was too early for him to appear as yet upon the avenue; he had to wait some five or six minutes longer. He made the round of his small square once again, still leading his horse by the bridle, and trying to keep at his ordinary pace.

Vatajko walked by his side upon the pavement.

"Don't move far from the mouth of the lane,"—Andrey was repeating to him his last instructions,—"and don't be excited. If nothing happens, you'll hasten to tell Zina. You remember the place where she'll be waiting? The boulevard, third bench from the entrance."

"Yes; I remember very well."

This referred to the possibility of the affair being postponed until the return journey to the gaol. But Andrey sincerely hoped there would be no necessity for such an undesirable delay.

"Now it's time!" he exclaimed.

He jumped lightly into the saddle, Vatajko holding the horse's head for him.

"Farewell," the boy said, "the day depends on you."

"And on my Rosinante," Andrey said, smiling, patting the horse's neck.

With a friendly nod, he rode at a trot into the lane where Vatajko had been standing.

When he turned the corner of the avenue he checked his horse, and looked before him. The street was all safe. His eyes, as if by magnetic attraction, were drawn to a small column, which at the great distance seemed motionless, though it was advancing at a regular military pace.

"There they are, and no mistake!" Andrey said to himself. "Whatever happens, the day will not pass in vain."

With his longsighted eyes he could make out each of the three prisoners, and he noticed that Boris wore a short jacket, without his overcoat. He was probably unarmed. That was a pity. But Levshin and Klein were all right. They would be enough. The prisoners evidently thought so, since they gave the signal that they were armed.

On the left side of the street Andrey saw Vasily's carriage, and upon the box Vasily himself. Of him he could only see the broad indolently-curved back, in the blue cabman's coat, and the glistening hat. His pose was exactly that of an overworked cabman, waiting indifferently for a passenger.

'There was no other vehicle in the street. It was the duty of the sentinels, now relieved from their posts, to prevent any cab stopping in the street, lest it should be requisitioned by the gendarmes for the pursuit. The sentinels had to take off every cab to some distant place, and then to repair to the boulevard, where Zina was sitting, and wait further instruc·tions from her.

The two parties advanced slowly towards each other, Andrey keeping his horse always at a walk. The avenue was not crowded ; only a few passers-by were seen here and there. But the street was living its merry life in the bright morning sun. A stout woman, in an apron fastened very high under the breast, pushed along a coster's barrow, filling the air with shrill praises of her wares. Two dirty boys, with their mouths open, looked in ecstatical admiration at her tempting treasures, wondering why the grown-up people, who can do everything they choose, passed by so carelessly. The windows of the houses were open. Merry faces were peeping out enjoying the fine weather. Loud talk and laughter was heard from one balcony.

To Andrey with just so much knowledge of the future as he possessed, there was something strange and wonderful in this innocent carelessness of the street, which in a few moments was to be the scene of a fierce struggle of tumult and bloodshed.

The fight had to take place some twenty yards behind Vasily's carriage, so as not to impede the flight. At the moment when the prisoners fired, Andrey was to be already in the rear of the escort. He was to turn suddenly round at the first shot, charging the escort whilst they were engaged in the scuffle with their prisoners. He therefore regulated his movements so as to pass the escort when they were near Vasily's carriage. With a slight pressure of his leg he directed his docile horse into the space between the carriage and the escort. He did not look at the prisoners, nor did the prisoners look at him, but they were watching each other anxiously. Levshin was the nearest to him. Andrey felt almost physically his eager inquiring look, and he gave an imperceptible nod of encouragement. It was merely a kind of welcome, by which he meant nothing particular. But the excited prisoner took it probably for a signal. In one flash Andrey saw him draw a revolver from his pocket, and point it at the gendarme walking behind him. Then a shot, and a fierce imprecation sounding from the midst of a cloud of smoke which for an instant prevented Andrey from seeing anything further.

The affair had begun. Wheeling the horse round, Andrey drew his revolver and waited, his finger on the trigger. Through the dispersing smoke he saw the gendarme, who was not hurt, throw himself upon his assailant, and catch him by the throat. The next moment Andrey's revolver was smoking in his hand, and the gendarme had fallen to the ground. A scene of undescribable confusion ensued.

The gendarmes' shouts, the women's screams, the shrieks of the passers-by running away in all directions, the clash together of the hurriedly closed windows, mingled with the noise of the quick random shots.

Seeing the action taking place too near his carriage, Vasily moved forward, stopping at a distance of some thirty yards. With his reins in one hand, his revolver in the other, he watched the fight and the street, turning fiercely his head right and left, his small eyes glistening like those of a wild boar. Levshin, freed from his foe, ran towards the carriage and jumped into it unmolested. Klein was about to follow his example. But the sergeant, a tall strong fellow, who brought up the rear, had time to seize his hand and snatch his revolver from him. Andrey rushed to his help. The sergeant fired at him but missed, pulled to and fro by Klein, whom he still held in his grip. In a minute Andrey was upon him, and putting his horse on its haunches threatened to trample the sergeant down.

Compelled to protect himself against the horse's hoofs, the sergeant loosed his hold on Klein, who twisted himself out of his hands and ran towards the carriage. The sergeant jumped on to the right, with the object of turning Andrey's horse round and recapturing his prisoner. But, quick as thought, Andrey pushed his horse between them.

"You're in too much of a hurry, my friend!" he cried, levelling his revolver.

Two shots were fired at one moment. Andrey hit the sergeant in the arm, which fell powerless, dropping the revolver. The sergeant's bullet pierced the skirt of Andrey's armiak, without hurting him; but it struck Vasily's horse, which made a bound, and at once ran away, in spite of all Vasily's efforts. Two of the prisoners were safe. Boris was left behind. But two men of the escort were no longer able to fight. There were now two against two. Boris could be carried off on the croup of the horse.

"One more effort and the day is ours!" Andrey said, jubilantly to himself, preparing for a new charge.

Boris was some twenty yards off, struggling vigorously with two gendarmes trying to bind him with the ropes of their shoulder-knots. He had run away from them, as he was unarmed, with the view of escaping by himself in the tumult, if he was unable to reach Vasily's carriage. But he was seized, and was now in a very evil plight.

"Hold out, friend!" Andrey shouted to him, "I'll be with you in a minute."

He rushed to Boris's assistance. But here he made a grave mistake. Andrey was a good shot, and it was for him to make the best use of this. But when he saw a red-whiskered gendarme putting a slip-knot on Boris's elbow, he forgot everything, and giving spur to his horse he flew upon them. The sergeant, who was wounded but not disabled, ran to join his comrades. Andrey charged him full tilt, carrying as it were upon his horse's breast the sergeant's bulky body, which struck like a living battering-ram the red-whiskered gendarme. The man fell to the ground, but Boris was dragged down with him; and the horse, following the impulse of the first rush, carried its rider some distance behind the field of the fight.

Thus a few priceless moments were wasted, and the chances were turning rapidly against Andrey. When he pulled the horse round, he saw Boris standing motionless between the two gendarmes. He struggled no more; his face was distorted with anger, and his eyes were fixed on something threatening from a distance.

"Save yourself! the police!" Andrey heard him shout, in a voice which he would never forget as long as he lived.

He looked back, and an imprecation of despair escaped him. Two policemen, attracted by the noise of the shots, were running along the avenue. A third had just emerged upon the street a little farther off.

Boris was lost! . . .

But they were far away yet; one more attempt could be made. With rage and despair struggling in his breast,

Andrey rushed with clenched teeth upon the bullets of the gendarmes, with the mad hope of killing all three before the police reached the place. But he was in too great a hurry. He fired almost without taking aim, careless of the thought that he might as likely as not hit Boris himself. What harm if he did kill him? Better to be shot by a friend than to be strangled by the hangman! Andrey's four bullets missed most shamefully, whilst one of the gendarmes hit him in the leg. He threw furiously to the ground his empty revolver, and seized a second one he had in reserve.

"Fly! the deuce! they'll catch you!" the voice of Boris rang out from the smoke, more imperatively than before.

The two policemen were upon Andrey. One of them seized him by the skirt of his coat to drag him from the horse. Andrey turned right round in the saddle, and dealt the man a blow with his heavy revolver on the head that sent him rolling on the ground. But there was no longer any hope; the day was lost. He set spurs to his horse, gathering up the bridle that it might not be seized by any one, and in no time he was out of the affray. Some parting bullets whistled round his ears. He heard behind him the frantic shouts of the gendarmes.

But woe to the man who should have tried to stop him at this moment! Fortunately nobody did try. His mare, which seemed to be as anxious as he was to get out of the unpleasant place, carried him off at a speed that did honour to her devotion. In half a minute he was at the end of the avenue, the open fields lying before him. But he did not choose to gallop that way. Turning to the left, he plunged into a labyrinth of small streets of the old working-class suburb. Slackening his speed to a trot, Andrey turned several times to the right and to the left, so as to confuse his pursuers when they inquired after the direction he had taken. Finally, he chose a narrow dark passage, in which only two small children were to be seen, and came out through it upon an open road. Here once again he put his horse to full speed, flying like an arrow over the soft unpaved ground.

At the south-eastern gate he saw a policeman on duty looking at him as he passed.

Andrey turned into the street that led into the town, knowing that the policeman would report this when questioned. A few blocks on he turned once more to the right, and emerged again upon the open space, resuming his former route.

When he saw the wooden crosses of the ancient cemetery he checked his horse. This was the end of his journey. There was no need to go farther; he was now at the opposite end of the town, three miles away from the place of the encounter. The police would spend two hours at least in tracing him. He was practically out of danger, but there was no need to lose time.

Looking round to ascertain that nobody saw him, Andrey dismounted, and, leading his horse behind him, got down into the deep ditch of the old cemetery.

Here for the first time he thought about his wound. It was nothing, a mere scratch, which did not impede his movements. But the blood oozing from it must be stopped, lest it should serve as a guide to his pursuers. He improvised a bandage. This done, he unfastened a small sack that was behind his saddle. It contained a long military overcoat of light grey linen stuff, such as poor retired officers wear, and a military hat. Andrey put his own hat in the pocket and donned his new coat, which gave him an altogether different appearance. The horse had to be left behind, to become the meagre trophy of the police. In its quality of irresponsible creature, it ran no risk of ill-treatment for its participation in a political crime. The idea of leaving on the animal a note to this effect crossed Andrey's mind as he unsaddled and unbridled it.

But he was in no mood for joking. Now that the excitement of the personal danger was over, the poorness of their success appeared in full to his mind.

"What a disappointment! what a fearful blow to Zina!" he repeatedly bitterly to himself.

He left the cemetery, and, sad and heavy at heart, entered the town, directing his steps to the new refuge prepared for them by Vasily.

CHAPTER VI.

THE new refuge to which Andrey repaired was in the city. Quite a fortnight before Vasily had engaged a room in a lodging-house. It was necessary that the landlady, if asked to give information about her lodgers, should say that Onesime Pavluk—Vasily's new name—had lived in her house many days before the affair of the lime-tree avenue. To say the truth, Vasily had another personal object in securing a new lodging beforehand,—he wanted a place where he could bestow as much of their property as could easily be removed. Unless this were done everything would be lost at the inn, which they of course had to abandon immediately after the attempt. But of these personal considerations Vasily kept the secret to himself, so as not to give his improvident comrades another pretext for chaffing him.

As Vasily was disengaged in the evenings, and did not mind the trouble of taking a run of a few miles, he contrived to live nominally in two places at once. Every evening at dusk he appeared at his new lodgings, a parcel of his belongings under his arm, saying that he had just come from his day's work. About midnight, when all the house was asleep, he went back, after having disordered his bed so as to make the landlady believe that he slept there and left early in the morning.

Vasily persuaded Andrey to make his appearance at the lodgings a few days before the attempt, so as to make their new place quite safe. He introduced his friend to the landlady as his lodger to whom he had underlet one-half of his room with board. Andrey was said to be a clerk by profession, having often pressing work to do at home. Thus after the attempt Andrey was able to stop all day long in the house without exciting suspicion. It would be dangerous for him to appear in the street during these first days. The town was all upside down. The gendarmes seemed to be more anxious to lay hold on him than even to recapture the two escaped prisoners, against whom they had no personal grudge. A detailed and very accurate description of figure, face, hair, eyes, and so on, was given to hundreds of spies and policemen, who were on the look-out for him everywhere. Andrey's real name had, moreover, transpired somehow, probably in consequence of some indiscretion of those who knew it. This of course only increased the zest of his pursuers. He had many old accounts unsettled with the police, which were now recalled to their memory.

Vasily's position was a much better one. Though the order to apprehend the coachman was as peremptory, the spies and agents did not know in this case whom to seek. Andrey had engrossed so much of the gendarmes' attention that they had not noticed the face of his companion. The description the excited gendarmes gave of Vasily were in conflict with those of the ostlers and waiters of the inn where his carriage was found ; so much so, that the police came to the conclusion that the man who attended to the horses in the inn, and the man who drove the carriage at the attempt, were probably two different persons.

Vasily at all events considered himself as safe in Dubravnik now as he was before. He appeared freely in the streets. He did all the errands, purchased the food, brought Andrey newspapers and the news of their friends, which he received through Vulitch, whom he met now every two days in the public gardens. He did all he could to distract his friend, and to dispel the despondency which he saw clearly gnawed at Andrey's heart, though he said little about it.

In fact, the week Andrey spent in this new hiding-place after the attempt was one of the saddest in his life. That two of the prisoners had been torn out of the enemy's hands seemed not to console him in the least for the loss of Boris. Levshin and Klein were friends for whose sake he would not have hesitated one moment to strike a blow and risk his life. Had these two been the only ones concerned, he would have been the happiest of men. But now he could not bring himself to look upon the attempt otherwise than as a failure. The loss of Boris spoilt everything.

It was not exactly pity for Boris which tormented him most. At this moment Andrey did not dwell much upon the fate awaiting Boris. What made his heart ache was rather self-pity not to have Boris there and then, and pity for Zina, mingled with a kind of shame that he had disappointed her expectations and inflicted such pain on her. But for a few blunders of his the day would have ended so differently. Boris would be with Zina, and, the quarantine over, he would have been with them too. The picture was so enchanting, so vivid, and had been so nearly within his grasp, that now he wanted to shriek with pain and anger at the thought that it was an empty dream, a cruel play of the imagination.

He did not for one moment admit that Boris should be given up altogether. A new attempt must be made. A fresh charge would be brought against Boris—that of attempting escape. The authorities would try to find out how the plot was contrived. This would cause no end of delay, which must be made use of for a rescue. Andrey planned one or two in his imagination. But these were vague far-off dreams,—castles in the air rather than actual projects. The recent events were, on the contrary, burning in his memory. Why did he give that foolish nod to Levshin, which made him fire at the wrong moment without allowing Klein time to get ready? Why had he lost his head when he saw Boris struggling with the two gendarmes? Had he but regulated the speed of his horse better, or even charged in an oblique direction, he would have trampled down one of the gendarmes, instead of throwing Boris to the ground. Andrey invented hundreds of combinations, all better than those he actually had made, and that would have undoubtedly led to another issue. The idea that each of these second thoughts might have turned out ill in its own way, escaped his mind altogether. He saw only one side of his fancies. Success appeared to him so easy, simple, natural, that the harsh reality upon which he fell back after these day-dreams seemed something monstrous and incredible.

In the solitude of his temporary seclusion, Andrey's dark mood only grew worse instead of better as the days went by. Vasily was much pained to see this. He made some clumsy efforts at cheering Andrey. But he was shy and irresolute, little accustomed to influence others, disbelieving his powers of persuasion, and fearing that he might hurt Andrey's feelings instead of doing him any good.

He wisely resolved that the best course to follow was to let Andrey alone. He would become himself again when he was able once more to mix freely with his friends and take part in the common work. It would not be long to wait. The paroxysm of police activity had already considerably subsided; finding nobody, they came to the conclusion that all those connected with the attempt had already left the town. It was time for Andrey to relax his quarantine; he would no longer run much risk by appearing in the streets.

All this Vasily communicated to Andrey, who agreed with him in an absent sort of way, but seemed in no hurry to profit by what he said.

"There's an illumination and fireworks in the town to-day," Vasily added. "Vulitch wants to go to see them, and she said she would call to take you with her."

Andrey only shrugged his shoulders. He said he was not interested in the least in the illumination or the fireworks.

"I'll keep watch over the room. But there's no reason why you should deny yourself this innocent pleasure," he added. "Go, and you shall tell me what I have lost by staying at home."

This was not what Vasily wanted.

"I can't go with Vulitch," he replied, "for I have an appointment with Zina to-night."

He left at once, though he knew that he would get to the place of meeting a good hour before the time. The girl was to come soon, and he thought he had better go and leave them alone. He hoped that she would be better able than himself to dispel Andrey's gloomy state of mind.

Vasily's kindness and modesty were indeed the best advisers. In fits of moral sickness, such as that under which Andrey was prostrated, a woman's friendship is the best of physicians. For a man will never show to another man the heart-wounds that he will confess to a woman.

After the discovery he had made at the picnic, Andrey did not seek Annie's company, but he did nothing to avoid her. They had something more serious to think about, both of them, than their hearts' troubles, and the girl would have felt offended had he acted otherwise. They saw each other frequently, and became very intimate.

When the girl came, and had told the news of the day, Andrey was the first to lead the conversation to personal grounds.

"You see, Annie," he said, "you were mistaken the other night in predicting for me a success."

He alluded to the words she said at the Dudarovs' picnic in the wood.

"I wasn't mistaken as to one part of it, at all events," the girl observed discreetly. "But how is your wound? Vasily said it was nothing, but you look very ill."

Andrey, with a wave of the hand, assured her that the wound was not worth speaking of. He would be as blithe as a lark with a dozen wounds like this one, if the affair had ended as it ought.

He spoke of what was troubling him in a strain in which he never spoke to Vasily. He made a clean breast of his tardy regrets and bitter self-accusations.

The girl's warm and vehement protests did not change his opinion. But he was pleased, nevertheless, that she should think as she did, although she was wrong.

"Are our fugitives still at your house?" he asked.

"No, they left Dubravnik last night for Odessa. The town has already settled down again. There's nothing exceptional in the streets. You needn't stop any longer always in your room, it might look suspicious."

She asked him to accompany her to the illuminations, and to her delight Andrey consented.

"I have quite forgotten to give you Zina's message, to bring which I came," Vulitch said, taking Andrey's arm when they were in the street. "Your St Petersburg friends write that a girl of your acquaintance has been proposed by George as a new member. George asks whether Zina and you will vouch for her."

"What's the girl's name?" Andrey asked, a sudden flush rising to his face.

He knew only too well who that girl was. There was only one girl with whom they all three were acquainted, and whom George was very likely indeed to propose.

"Tania Repina," Vulitch answered, looking at him suspiciously.

"Ah, Repina! and it's George who proposes her?" Andrey said, more and more confused.

The girl's hand resting upon his arm quivered, and then grew stiff as if it were benumbed.

"Who is this Tania Repina?" she asked, in a stifled voice.

"A friend of ours ; the daughter of Repin the barrister," Andrey answered, looking straight in front of him.

The small hand tightened on his arm nervously, and the girl slowly drew herself away as if to examine him better.

"A friend, you say ? "

"Of course, a friend," Andrey answered, meeting the girl's glance for a moment.

Annie's face darkened. Her glistening eyes assumed an expression of hostility, almost of hatred.

"It's not true, you love her ! " she almost cried, throwing his arm away from her.

Andrey turned to her angrily. What right, he thought, has this girl to pry into the secrets he had never disclosed to any one ? For a moment their looks crossed like two glittering swords in a duel. But Andrey, from whom the first thrust had to come, turned his head away.

They went a few steps in silence. When he looked at her again, his face was no longer angry, but sad.

"Well, . . . yes, I love her," he said. "Are you satisfied now ? "

"And she, she loves you ? " the girl whispered, bending her head.

"No, she does not love me, if you wish to know."

The girl bent her head still lower, and began to remove with the point of her umbrella something from the varnished toe of her shoe.

"But why ? " she asked, drawing herself up.

There was such naïve self-betraying wonder in her tone, that Andrey smiled.

"That can hardly be interesting to you," he said softly. "But there is one thing I wish you to know and remember, Annie," he went on ; "it is that I haven't said what I have told you to a living soul."

"Not even to her ? "

"She is the last person to whom I would say it. . . . But let's speak about it no more. You got me out not for cross-examination, but for recreation, and you must keep to that."

"Oh, I will," the girl exclaimed, joyfully, taking his arm again, and raising to him her smiling face. "I wish I could——" she added, lowering her voice.

"You'll tell Zina that I give my vote for the admission," Andrey concluded, in a business-like tone.

They were scarcely out of sight when Vasily returned home. He felt exceedingly pleased to find that Andrey was out. The visit to the illuminations was suggested by himself, and he was sure that it would do Andrey much good; Vulitch was just the pleasant companion to cheer him up. This Vasily said to himself with inward satisfaction, not quite free from a touch of envy. He realised so vividly the pleasure he would have himself felt in Andrey's place !

Clumsy and rough in appearance as he was, Vasily was yet very tender hearted. He had fallen in love a number of times, but he seemed to have a singular preference for the hopeless and silent sort of love, setting his heart always upon the wrong persons—women with whom he had not the slightest chance of success. It was by her cold inaccessibility that Lena had fascinated him. He was still faithful to her in his inmost heart. But of late he seemed to have discovered somehow, that he might love Vulitch quite as hopelessly as he loved Lena. He was not yet in love with the girl, but he had begun to indulge in dreaming about her, and in paying her certain little attentions which she never noticed.

Now he gave himself up to the pleasant anticipations of her coming. She will probably step up, he thought, and have a cup of tea after the long walk. Sitting by the table Vasily waited, listening dreamily to the soft noise of the samovar, which he kept ready for his friends, when he heard the front door slam, and soon after the sound of footsteps approaching his room. He rose and opened the door. But instead of those whom he expected, he found himself face to face with the police. The frightened figure of the landlady was seen behind.

" There you have it ! " Vasily exclaimed to himself in amazement. " It must be all on account of that damned passport of mine."

Thus far he had guessed right.

Vasily's head was a very queer one. When he acted without one moment's forethought, he showed in the most difficult circumstances a surprising ability and fecundity of resource. But when he wanted to be particularly clever, and set himself to ponder deeply upon something, it often happened that "his mind muddled his reason," as the Russians have it, and he committed blunders outrageously gross and comical.

One of these curious slips of logic he made whilst preparing their last refuge. The false passport he got from the Dubravnik people did not meet with his complete approbation. It certified to the right of the fictitious young man Onesime Pavluk, who had completed his studies in a secondary school, to be admitted to a higher one. This was rather a gentle-man's passport, and Vasily very judiciously preferred to play the part of a common man—an artisan or a pedlar. Taking counsel with his superior wisdom, he resolved to improve the passport, and to make it unobjectionable by a little scraping. Vasily was very skilful in "healing" passports as well as in manual operations generally. He washed off the obnoxious "higher," and put in its stead the humble "primary," in exactly the same handwriting as that in which the remainder of the document was written. The operation succeeded to his complete satisfaction.

When he imparted his achievement to his companion, Andrey laughed at him outright. The passport, according to him, was quite spoiled by the correction. It was sheer nonsense that the completion of studies in a school of a superior sort should entitle a man to admittance to an inferior school.

Vasily was struck by the truth of this observation, which strangely had not occurred to him before. But the friends consoled themselves with the consideration that the thing was done and could not be helped. The passport was already handed to the police for registration. Besides, the officials never read the heaps of passports presented for registration, examining only the seals, the signatures, and the outward appearance.

"And if they read it by chance," Andrey suggested, laughing, "they'll tax your correction for a slip of the pen, for no man in his senses would put such a thing in a false passport on purpose."

It occurred just as Andrey conjectured. The *kvartalny*, or police inspector, happened to read the strange passage. But as the passport was perfect in all other respects, and had on its back the marks of several police registrations at several other police-offices, he did not think the matter worth the trouble of a regular arrest. He registered the passport, and laid it on one side, intending to bring it in person on the earliest opportunity to the owner, to make inquiries, and take further action if necessary.

The appearance of the police surprised Vasily, but did not disconcert him. He answered readily the kvartalny's questions, giving himself out as a locksmith of Poltava railway station, who came to Dubravnik in search of work, but was about to return to his old place.   With his rough face, hard hands, and plain dress, Vasily looked exactly like a common workman or an artisan of the town.   He played his part of simpleton so well, counterfeiting with such ability the people's language, their ingenuousness, and even their timidity before the police, that the kvartalny dismissed at once all suspicions as to Vasily himself.

But the landlady informed him that there lived with Vasily another lodger, whose passport was not as yet presented for registration, and whose description was such as to justify curiosity.

Vasily explained, with the candour and volubility of innocence, how by a mere chance he made the acquaintance of this Ivan Zalupalov—which was Andrey's passport name—and accepted him as a lodger for so much a week.

"Have you asked for his passport?" the kvartalny inquired.

"Certainly, your honour," was Vasily's ready answer ; "and I took it from him, lest he should run away without paying his rent.   One must be careful with strangers, your honour."

Vasily produced from his bootleg the important document, wrapped in a rag.

"But why have you not presented it at once for registration?" asked the kvartalny severely.

Vasily's heart went instantly into his boots.   His face at all events showed it unmistakably.

"For want of time, your honour," he stammered.   "I beg you to excuse me."

The kvartalny made no answer, but looked displeased. Vasily scratched his neck, kneaded the floor with his feet, and plunged his hand into his pocket.   Producing a small silver coin, he laid it timidly on the corner of the table before the kvartalny.

"Don't despise my offering, your honour," he said, bowing low.   "It's little, but it's from a pure heart."

"Put it away, you fool!" the kvartalny said, declining the modest bribe.

But he did not think the worse of Vasily for this manifestation of loyalty.

"When will your lodger come back?" he asked.

"I can't tell your honour," Vasily answered, resuming his cheerful tone.   "He has a partiality for drinking, this man—if

I dare mention this before your honour. He comes home very late sometimes. One night he didn't return at all."

"Well, I'll wait anyhow," said the kvartalny, taking a stool resolutely. "And you, what's your name?"

"Onesime, your honour."

"Well, Onesime, you go downstairs and tell the sergeant who waits in the street to step up. And you come with him too."

Vasily's heart fell. All his comedy was to no purpose.

But he had no choice other than to play his part to the end. He executed the errand, and returned accompanied by the sergeant.

Suspecting nothing of the dangers awaiting him at home, Andrey in the meantime wandered about with Vulitch. They went to the illuminations, and spent a quarter of an hour in the public garden. Andrey found no pleasure in what he saw. Everything seemed to him irritatingly stupid that night,—the fireworks, the illuminations, and above all the childish merriment of the crowd of grown-up people who found amusement in such nonsense.

They returned early. Andrey wanted to see the girl home, but Vulitch objected. Their house was recently "tarnished" by the stay of the two fugitives. It was better he should not come near it. She proposed therefore to accompany him to his own lodgings.

A few houses from his door they stopped.

"Won't you step up? it is not late," said Andrey.

"No, I must hurry home; I promised to be back at ten."

They shook hands, and Andrey went in.

On ascending the dimly-lighted, rather dirty stairs, Andrey saw Vasily standing at the top of them. He was barefooted, hatless, and in his shirt sleeves. His cheeks were pale. He gesticulated violently and strangely. As far as Andrey could guess, his friend wished him to keep silent, and not to move. He stopped short accordingly. Walking noiselessly with his bare feet, Vasily rapidly descended toward Andrey, and putting his mouth to his ear whispered:

"The police are in our room. Be off as quickly as you can."

"The police! then let's go together," Andrey whispered in return.

Vasily shook his head energetically in sign of refusal, and, without any further explanation, he ran rapidly upstairs and disappeared, to Andrey's surprise not into their room, but into a small unoccupied lumber-room opposite.

When the grey tape of Vasily's waistcoat, projecting at his back after the fashion of a short pigtail, had plunged into the dark room,—no hope of explanation being left,—Andrey descended on tiptoe into the street.

Vulitch had not yet turned the corner.

"An-nie!" Andrey called, in a distinct though subdued voice, which went far in the silence of the night.

The girl turned her head, and moved to meet him. She thought that Andrey had forgotten to tell her something of importance.

"It was decreed that I should accompany you to your house to-night," he said; "the police are in mine."

The girl started.

"The police! Vasily arrested?"

"No, he's certainly not arrested, or they wouldn't let him wait in the stairs to forewarn me."

He related their strange interview.

"What puzzles me most," he said, "is that Vasily has remained in the house, whilst he could so easily have left it with me."

"Yes, it's very strange," said Vulitch.

It was a strange adventure indeed, one of those which happen only to men like Vasily.

Having executed the kvartalny's errand, and ushered the enemy into his own room, Vasily sat quietly upon the end of a stool in the corner. He looked as innocent and unconcerned as one might wish, but he was very uneasy in his mind. The time went on. Andrey might return any minute, probably accompanied by the girl.

The two policemen began to talk, the tall sergeant standing by the side of his superior and leaning to whisper in his ear. Vasily saw clearly how the kvartalny, and after him the sergeant, looked at a place by the door, which would be hidden when Andrey opened it.

They were planning how to attack Andrey from the front and from the rear at once, the blackguards!

But how to prevent it? The windows of their room looked into the court-yard, so that he could not give Andrey any signal of danger. He would hardly be of much use in the coming fight, for he happened to be unarmed, his revolver was in the breast pocket of his jacket, which he had taken off before the police came, and which he could not possibly reach now without exciting suspicions. Vasily was at a loss how to find some expedient, when the distant cracking of a rocket suggested a good idea to him.

"Your honour!" he exclaimed, in a most innocent tone; "may I go to look at the fireworks from the window? There's a lumber-room opposite from which all the garden can be seen."

The kvartalny was anxious to be alone with his sergeant.

"Yes, go if you like," he said; "but don't go far. You'll be wanted directly."

Thus Vasily succeeded in escaping to the lumber-room, where he spent a very bad quarter of an hour, standing at the door and listening with palpitating heart to every noise from below.

When he had forewarned Andrey, he returned to the lumber-room relieved and happy, and this time fully enjoyed his well-merited amusement.

He was a peaceful, inoffensive, and rather lazy fellow, this Vasily. He disliked trouble of any kind, taking life as easily as it was possible for him, and preferring always to smooth over or cautiously circumvent all obstacles instead of violently breaking through them.

CHAPTER VII.

THERE was considerable uneasiness as to Vasily's fate in Zina's house, where Andrey took temporary refuge. They all guessed something of the nature of his troubles. The police had probably dropped in at his lodgings by chance ; Vasily had got entangled somehow or other. They knew him, and expected him to get clear of his difficulties and rejoin them—at the latest the next morning. But the morning passed, and Vasily gave no sign.

They grew uneasy. Zina went to the abode of her friend the gaoler, and sent to him through his wife a request to find out immediately the names of all the people recently arrested. When they met at the usual time, the gaoler was able to assure Zina that Vasily was not among them. Vulitch was in the meantime despatched into the town to make reconnoitres among the Dubravnik people. She returned with the strange but comforting news that Vatajko had met Vasily in the streets, free, as no escort or policeman was seen at his side. But Vasily was evidently in some fix, for he passed rapidly, making to Vatajko the sign not to approach or to speak to him.

This was a confirmation of their early supposition. Vasily had got entangled with the police by some accident, and now was playing a game to befool them.

"We may be easy about him now," Andrey said. "I'm sure he'll do them, and will be with us before long."

Zina hoped so too.

Their new fears having subsided, their old cares and anxieties came once more to the front.

In the evening when tea was finished, and all three were assembled in Zina's sitting-room, no household duties diverting the ladies from conversation, Andrey entered upon the matter by asking Zina what were now her views and intentions as to Boris.

He was walking up and down the small room, his hands behind his back, not looking at Zina whilst he put the question.

"I'll show you a letter on the subject from Boris," Zina said. "I got it the day after the attempt. I was so upset then, that I forgot to send it over to your place; but I have kept it for you."

She went to fetch from a hiding-place two pieces of paper, —one long and narrow, as if cut from a newspaper margin; another, a square piece a few inches in area, a fly-leaf from some book. Both pieces were covered with closely-packed writing in pencil.

In this letter, written the night following the disaster, Boris thanked the friends who had risked their lives for his sake— Andrey in particular—in terms so warm and affectionate that tears filled Andrey's eyes. But as matters stood now, Boris considered all further attempts at his rescue to be hopeless, and likely to involve his friends in ruin. He concluded by requesting Andrey to return to St Petersburg at once, and the others to disband without useless delay.

"You don't think, I hope, this conclusion in any way binding for us?" Andrey said, trying to keep calm and matter-of-fact.

"No, I don't!" Zina exclaimed, vehemently.

"I am glad you're not discouraged," Andrey went on. "In affairs like this, pluck is everything. People have failed four times, and escaped on the fifth; we shall be luckier next time."

"Yes; but on one point Boris is quite right," Zina proceeded. "You mustn't take part in this affair any longer. You have done all a man could. To remain here longer, would be to court your own ruin."

"The same might be said about yourself."

"No, it isn't the same. The police don't know me, whilst they have found out your name, and are mad against you. Besides," she added, "there are considerations of a personal nature why I must go on with the work myself."

Andrey stopped in front of her.

"Considerations of a personal nature?" he said with surprise. "I don't understand you, Zina; or, if I understand what you mean, I emphatically protest against your putting the matter on the paltry grounds of personal affection. We undertook it, because Boris is a man of high value for our cause, not because he is personally dear to some of us. Our feelings have nothing to do with it."

"I would never allow any one to risk himself for Boris, if I thought his rescue was only a personal affair of my own," Zina said.

"Well, what does it matter then who of us does it?" Andrey said. "You contradict yourself."

"No," she replied. "I spoke of the past. But now things have changed for the worse, and this makes all the difference. If Boris was a stranger to me, I should have probably said that the affair must be given up. But I can't. . . . That's why I must do it myself. . . ."

She frowned, and bent her head over the table, which stood in front of the sofa on which she sat.

"You understand now, I suppose," she added, in a calmer tone, raising her head again, "that considerations of a personal nature must also be taken into account sometimes."

He sat down on a stool opposite her, and taking her hand raised it gently to his lips.

Zina's reluctant confession only confirmed what he had said to himself long ago. She was consumed by a slow fire. The constant suspense, the brooding over an affair on which depended Boris's life, was more than flesh could bear. A sudden bereavement was easier to support than this. And now her pain had reached a point when reason ceased to control her feelings. If she remained in Dubravnik, she would do something desperate, and only ruin herself to no purpose. She must be dragged away at any price.

"Listen to me, Zina; and you, Annie, listen too, for you must help me to persuade her," Andrey said, still keeping Zina's hand in his. "You are quite right in saying that, hunted down as I am now, I could not be of much use here. But this can be easily set right. What I propose is this: I'll start to-morrow for St Petersburg, and will remain there, let us say, a fortnight. I'll frequent the students' clubs, and the drawing-room parties, and mix in everything to make as much noise as I can. Thus I shall attract to myself as much of the attention of the police as possible. And then, when they are quite sure that I am in St Petersburg for good, I'll quietly return to Dubravnik. But you must entrust things to me entirely, and leave the town altogether. Personal feelings must be taken into consideration sometimes, as you said. You are killing yourself staying here, and this must not be. Take it as a prompting of my personal friendship for you, if you'll not take it for something better—but don't be obstinate. Accept my proposal, and let us change places! Will you? Why do you not answer?"

Zina sat thinking, her head bowed down upon her breast. It pained her to hurt Andrey by rejecting a proposal made in such terms. But she couldn't help it.

"No, I cannot," she said, shaking her head slowly.

He rose from his stool, and paced twice up and down the room. . . .

Vulitch, crouched in the corner, dared not interfere. What could she say after Andrey's appeal?

Andrey was silent too. It was useless to argue the point further. Zina had made up her mind to perish, and perish she would. . . . He could not stop her, and he had no heart to be angry with her obstinacy. She could not act otherwise in her particular circumstances, and her motives were good. But nobody would be happier for that. . . .

"Don't marry, young man, follow my advice——" Andrey burst out, reciting the two lines of a song to give vent to his inmost feelings

He addressed his edifying remark to nobody in particular, least of all to Zina, who was past benefiting by the good advice.

But it was Zina who caught the ball he had thrown into the air. She was glad of an opening which promised to divert the conversation from a subject too painful to her.

Leaning pensively over the table, she drew with her finger some figures upon the cloth.

"That's the moral you draw from the fable, is it?" she said.

Andrey did not answer at once. Zina, leaning back, caressed demurely the yellow Vaska, her favourite cat, who sprang upon her knees, anxious to make one of the company. With her expectant look she followed Andrey.

"Certainly I do. How can I help it?" Andrey said at last.

He had tried to accept Zina's decision with as much inward submissiveness and humility as he could muster. What came from so good a woman, inspired by such good motives, must needs be the right. He did not hope to see her again, and his only wish now was not to spoil the few hours they had to spend together.

He sat down by her side on the sofa.

"Those who have to fight such a hard battle as ours, ought to steel their breasts against feelings too tender for us," he said in an absent way.

He felt downhearted, and was not in the least disposed to start upon a new debate. But Zina took the offensive this time. The point which Andrey's remark brought out, was one on which she had thought much of late. She did not wish Andrey to leave her with the impression that she had come to disavow what she had valued so highly before.

"Why, then," she asked, with a touch of irony, "do you not accept at once Netchaiev's view, that the more a revolutionist resembles a wooden log the nearer he is to perfection? All strong human affections are ties and trammels. Only, what would be the use of people who are incapable of having any?"

"You confuse two very different orders of feelings," Andrey said, evasively.

Zina wanted to reply. But just then something occurred that interrupted their talk altogether.

"Stop a minute. I heard knocking somewhere," Andrey said.

They listened. No knocking was heard, but a strange noise as if a handful of gravel had been thrown against the window panes.

"Some street boy's prank!" Zina said.

They saw nobody in the street. But Vulitch opened the window, and looking out of it, exclaimed joyfully in a loud voice—

"It's Vasily!"

She rushed downstairs to let him in.

In a minute Vasily's big figure and beaming face appeared in the doorway, a trunk in one hand, a bundle of linen in the other.

Andrey and Zina rose to meet, to embrace, and to cheer him, as if he had returned from a long journey.

"I told you he would get off clear!" Andrey exclaimed, giving his friend a slap on the shoulder which made him totter. "Now, tell us what have you been at all this time."

"Oh, it was a troublesome business!" Vasily exclaimed, throwing himself on a chair. "I can hardly believe I am out of it."

"Have you been arrested?" Vulitch asked.

"Worse!" Vasily said, waving his hand.

"What? tortured perhaps?" Zina asked, with a smile.

"Worse than that, I assure you!" Vasily repeated.

"But what on earth has befallen to you, old fellow?" Andrey asked. "Tell us all in good order."

Vasily then related how the police came, how they inquired after Andrey, how he played the simpleton, and obtained permission to go and look at the fireworks from the lumber-room.

"But why did you not make off with me at once after you had warned me?" Andrey asked.

"Well," Vasily said, scratching his neck, "it would have been the best thing to do, if I only knew what was going to happen afterwards. But I thought that the police would get out of the way of themselves, and leave me in peace. So I resolved to remain for a while."

"Well, what happened next? Did they stay waiting for me long?"

"Till past midnight," Vasily said, indignantly. "They called me in half an hour after I saw you, and I had to keep them company. And the most curious thing is," he added, in another tone, "that it was I who detained them, giving them hope that perhaps you might come!"

A wondering uncertain smile played upon Vasily's lips, but disappeared immediately, and his face became serious again.

"Well," he proceeded, "at half-past twelve the policemen rose and put their hats on. They were going to the devil at last, I thought. Before leaving, the kvartalny instructed me not to tell you when you came back a word about his visit, adding that he would call again the next day at eight. This was an additional bother; but I didn't want to spoil my passport by running away, and resolved to wait for him quietly.

"He came.

"'Has your lodger returned?'

"'No, your honour.'

"'Where can he be?'

"'Don't know, your honour.'

"I made sure he would go away for good now. But he stuck to me like a limpet.

"'Look here, Onesime,' he said to me, very kindly, 'I see you are an honest fellow, and I'll give you three roubles if you behave properly. Leave your things here, and make a round of the public-houses and coffee-rooms in the neighbourhood; perhaps you'll find your lodger somewhere.'

"'Yes, your honour,' I said, 'but I must start for Poltava to-day.'

"'Never mind, you have plenty of time before you. You'll earn three roubles if you catch your lodger, mind that.' And he gave me instructions :—'When you meet him, don't frighten him. Tell him that his passport has been duly registered, and returned to you safely. He'll be glad to hear that, and will come along with you freely. Then, when you pass the first policeman, catch him by the collar, and give him into custody. Do you understand?'

"'Yes, your honour,' I said.

"'Will you do all just as I tell you?'

"'Certainly, your honour,' I said."

Vasily, in relating the story of his adventure, had entered into the spirit of his recent performance. Amidst the hearty laughter of his friends he recited his part, exactly as he had improvised it before the kvartalny. He bent his head on one side, stretched his neck, and twitched his lips, as a man paying close attention, and nodded his head in sign of assent with tremendous energy.

"We left the house together," he proceeded, "and I went to make my round of the taverns and public-houses. I couldn't help it, for I might be followed and watched by a spy. It was then that I met Vatajko in the street, but I preferred not to speak to him. At four in the afternoon I returned to my house. The Poltava train would start in an hour and a half. I might fairly consider my tribulations well over.

"I settled my accounts, packed my things, and came down into the street, thinking what was the best way to join you, when, lo and behold! my kvartalny in plain clothes watching me, and trying to hide himself behind a corner. The damned villain! he was after me again. I had no choice but to go to the railway station instead of coming to you. I took a cab, the kvartalny followed at some distance in another. We reached the station long before the time for the train to start. The booking-office was not yet open. The kvartalny took refuge near the bookstall. I walked up and down, looking at the ceiling, the windows, the doors, at everything but my kvartalny, whom I am supposed not to see. Yet I did not lose sight of him for a moment. I expected that he would be satisfied at last on seeing me safe at the station, and would leave me alone. But no; he was always there, watching.

The booking-office was opened. People began to put themselves in line to get their tickets. He was still there, the villain! I strolled across the hall, and took my place by the railing. This would be enough for him, I hoped.

"The kvartalny rose indeed, but only to come nearer, and saunter by the booking-office.

"I was greatly perplexed what to do. To take a ticket for Poltava, and to get out at the first station? But I had only two roubles in my pocket—not half enough to pay my fare. To ask for a ticket for the next station, not for Poltava? I could not do it, because the kvartalny would hear me, and suspect I had deceived him in everything else, and probably arrest me.

"The people passed on one by one. I came nearer and nearer to the window of the booking-office, and still I had no idea whatever what to do, and how the thing would end for me.

"Finally, I was face to face with the clerk. The kvartalny was at my back, behind the railings.

"'A ticket for Poltava, third!' I say, in a resolute, loud voice, and I began to unbutton the top of my waistcoat to take the money from my bosom.

"'Be quick; you are keeping people waiting,' the clerk shouts.

"'In a moment,' I answer, firmly.

"I pull out from my bosom the cross, I look at it, and then I thrust my hands into my hair.

"'Brethren orthodox! I am robbed!' I cry at the top of my voice, and I run from the booking-office like a madman.

"A crowd gathers round me, and I begin to tell that I had a twenty-five rouble note, all my savings, tied with a string to the cross in my bosom, but that a scoundrel of a lodger, whom I picked up from the street, has robbed me of the money in the night and run away. And I wipe away with my coat sleeve the tears, the real tears, flowing from my eyes at the tale of my misfortune!"

Vasily's rough face lit up for an instant with his half wondering smile, which disappeared as rapidly as it came, as he resumed his story.

"When I thought my audience sufficiently moved, I dried my tears, seized my trunk, and was off as quick as I could, jumping into the first cab I met at the gate."

"And the kvartalny," Vulitch asked, "did he not follow you any longer?"

"No, he did not.   I was so upset with the loss of all my property, that I lost sight of him for a moment.   But when we were fairly off, I turned back and saw nobody behind me.   I spent the remainder of the evening in moving from one place to another, to be sure that I wasn't followed.   He has left me alone this time for good."

"He has probably gone home," Zina said, laughing, "to write to his chief a report upon the wicked tricks the revolutionists play upon simpletons whom they have ensnared."

"But, for goodness' sake," Andrey asked, "why did you return to the house in the afternoon when once you were let alone?   That's what I can't understand.   You could have easily got rid of any possible spy following you without all that trouble."

Vasily shrugged his shoulders, surprised in his turn by the question.

"And my luggage which was left there?" he said.

Andrey burst into a heartier laugh than he had laughed during all Vasily's story.

"Now, you must certainly see what treasures our Vaska went to rescue from the dragon's claws," he said to the ladies.

He moved towards the trunk, with the evident intention of exhibiting its contents to the admiration of the company.   But Vasily snatched it from his hands, and sat upon it resolutely. He would not permit such things to be exhibited before the ladies.

The next day, Andrey took leave of his friends, and started back to St Petersburg, charged by Zina to raise money for the continuation of their enterprise.   Vasily remained in Dubravnik.   He very truly observed, that, thanks to his happy exterior, he was equally safe anywhere, and he was resolved to preserve his allegiance to Zina to the last.   There was something truly chivalrous at the bottom of Vasily's character, which was seen at its best in his bearing towards women.   He had always a lady of his heart after whom he was sighing; but, as a true knight, he was ready to serve any lady who might be in need of him, and to no one else was he so deeply devoted as to Zina.

CHAPTER VIII.

AN UNEXPECTED COMPLICATION.

ST PETERSBURG was in its holiday dress when Andrey set foot upon its pavement again. The first snow had just fallen, and that is a grand holiday time for every Northerner.

Streets, footpaths, benches, roofs, the decks of the numerous craft huddled all along the narrow canal which stretched upon Andrey's left,—all was covered with a neat, sparkling sheet of virgin snow. The black motionless trees looked fantastically transformed under that thick deposit of white down, covering even the thinnest twig. The sun was lost in the enormous depth of slowly falling snow. But it was exceedingly clear below. The bright shadowless ground shone with a soft light, which rejoiced the eye and the heart after the dreary dulness of the autumnal brown. The air was fresh and bracing, filled with the exhilarating smells of the snow and of the winter. The passers-by, bestrewn with big white flakes all over their hats, coats, beards and hair, looked oddly as if at a carnival. The faces were merry, the horses trotted briskly. Some sleighs glided here and there, their owners proud of being the first to welcome beautiful queen winter.

Yielding involuntarily to the general gaiety, Andrey walked rapidly along the Ligovsky canal, hastening towards Lena's house. He had not announced his arrival to anybody this time; but he knew that Lena lived now at the canal, very near the railway station, and he might easily catch her.

The girl was just coming out of the gate, a small fur cap upon her head, fresh and bright as the day, when Andrey called her by her name.

She stared at him, surprised. Then her face brightened with a smile of hearty welcome.

"There you are once more!" she exclaimed. "I feared that after what happened in Dubravnik you would stick there faster than ever. But have you returned for good?" she asked.

"Yes, for good," said Andrey.

Lena was going out on some business of her own, but for Andrey's sake she resolved to make a circuit and accompany him to headquarters. She questioned him about the Dubravnik attempt, which had made a considerable impression in the revolutionary world. Andrey satisfied her curiosity, without eagerness, but without reluctance. The change of place and of surroundings had blunted the painfulness of his recollections. He could now speak of the affair calmly, as of a thing past, which must be accepted just as it was.

"And what is the news in your parts?" he asked the girl in his turn.

"In the section you mean?"

"Yes."

"Well, nothing particular. Tania has been elected a member. She had her five guarantors, and nobody opposed. She has already accepted. I hope we have made a good acquisition in her."

"I am sure of it," Andrey said.

"She has been working for some time in the Narva district, and she does well enough for a beginner," Lena went on. "It is a pity she will have to leave the town."

"Will she?" Andrey asked, with sudden sadness.

"She goes to Moscow," Lena replied. "It was resolved to strengthen our section there, which is rather weak. George has been commissioned to go on a propaganda trip to Moscow, and Tania volunteered to accompany him. She has got good connections in the town, who might prove available."

"I see now . . ." Andrey stammered, turning his face aside to conceal his trouble.

The news did not surprise him. He was prepared to hear something of the kind. But the keen chilling pain he felt at Lena's words, showed him how much hidden hope still lingered in his foolish heart.

"You know, people say that they will probably marry soon," Lena went on, innocently, roasting him on a slow fire. "They are said to have been in love with each other for a long time. But I do not believe it ; I have not noticed it, anyhow. It is probably mere gossip."

"Why not? George is a very good fellow," Andrey said, in an honest attempt to be impartial.

Lena did not suspect in the least that this conversation

might have any special significance for Andrey. She did not
notice his trouble, little observant as she was by nature and
habit. Love had not yet spoken in her own heart, and love
affairs in general were matters of the smallest possible interest
to her. The rumours about Tania and George were for her
simply a bit of news, and she passed on easily and unconcernedly to other topics.

At headquarters Andrey met several friends, George among
them. He threw himself on Andrey's neck with an exclamation of joy. He had also shared Lena's apprehensions that
Andrey would remain in Dubravnik. His return was therefore
a double pleasure to him.

George inquired anxiously about Zina. Andrey told him
frankly everything, without concealing his fears as to her position. They talked together easily and cordially. But when
the others went away, and Andrey remained alone with George,
both felt a sort of uneasiness. Andrey was burning with impatience to know something about Tania, but he could not
screw up his courage to ask. And George, as if on purpose,
did not even so much as mention the girl's name.

This was so contrary to George's usual habit of talking
about Tania, in season and out of season, that Andrey at once
concluded that he did it on purpose. George had evidently
guessed his secret, and abstained from speaking of Tania so as
not to hurt him. It was very good of him, and Andrey resolved to take the hint. He talked on indifferent topics as
best he could. Finally, unable to hold out any longer, he
asked whether Tania lived still at her father's house.

"Oh no," George answered. "It was quite impossible,
because she would have involved him in no end of troubles.
She lives by herself in lodgings in the district where she
works."

George added nothing more, but he fixed upon his friend a
look of mingled kindness and melancholy, which stung Andrey
to the quick. He turned his head aside, and asked abruptly
about George's paper. After this he carefully avoided mentioning Tania's name again. This doleful look of George was
gall and wormwood to him.

Andrey resumed his favourite work of propaganda, seclud-
ing himself almost entirely in his Wyborg district. He seemed
to hunger for work, taking upon himself all he could get.
Even the exacting fault-finding Lena was delighted with him

saying that he seemed in a fair way to making up in no time for his short leave of absence.

At the same time, Andrey's former unwillingness to appear as propagandist among educated people grew into a positive aversion. He refused peremptorily to go to any of the students' meetings, or parties outside their business meetings. He seldom saw even his friends and fellow-conspirators. What for? It would be merely self-indulgence and waste of time. He was in the sternest mood, trying to purge his life of all that was not strictly duty.

George was the only person to whom he paid any visits. Probably because at present it was for him rather a penance than otherwise ; he was so anxious to prove to himself that his fit of vulgar jealousy was well over, and that he felt as friendly with George as ever. He would have kept his resolution but for that unbearable look of doleful compassion which he noticed now and then in George's expressive eyes. He called twice in the first week after his arrival, and then stopped his visits, alleging as pretext want of time.

Tania he would as lief not see at all. He was glad that the fulfilment of the mission entrusted to him by Zina did not require a personal interview with her. Since the day Tania had become a member of their society, all her fortune belonged to the cause, and she, as a matter of course, had no more voice in disposing of her money than any other member of their brotherhood. Andrey easily obtained from the League half of the sum needed, which Zina required immediately. The other half was promised to him within a month by Repin, whom he went to see a few days after his return from Dubravnik.

He met Tania a fortnight later, at a meeting of the group to which they both belonged. It was a small special meeting, composed of about a dozen men and women engaged in the propaganda among workmen. The famous Taras Kostrov was among those present. He was one of the pioneers of this form of propaganda. Stress of business had compelled him long ago to give up actual work, but he dropped in occasionally at these meetings when time permitted. To-day he came for a short time to meet a friend, Shepelev, one of the permanent members of the group, with whom he had special business to talk over.

Though the room was full of people, it was Taras Kostrov alone whom one saw at first, for it was impossible not to be attracted by his proud, powerful face, of remarkable manly beauty, breathing intelligence, and boundless courage.

Andrey exchanged a friendly nod with Kostrov, and went to shake hands with Tania, whom he saw in the farthest corner of the room absorbed in reading a freshly issued popular pamphlet.

It was not without misgivings that Andrey went to this meeting, at which he knew he should see Tania. But now that they were face to face he felt nothing but a calm pleasure. The girl received him in a friendly way, but soon resumed her reading, in which she seemed to be greatly interested. Andrey did not want to disturb her. He stretched out his hand over several heads to Lena, who was not far off, and took a seat.

The company was not yet complete, though the appointed time had already passed. The room was filled with the buzz of subdued voices of people talking to beguile the time. Taras and Shepelev went on assiduously with their business. Shepelev —a pale-faced young man, with long hair and a yellow beard, in long boots and a high waistcoat buttoned up to the collar, such as the Russian artisans are wont to wear—was explaining something to his companion. Taras listened, looking absently before him. He could follow a speech very closely, and yet be thinking about another subject—he understood everything so well at a hint. At this moment his restless mind was far away : he was thinking of a proposal he meant to make at a meeting of a very different nature, to which he had to go in half-an-hour. He knew very well that his motion would provoke a tempest. This made him feel exceedingly soft and tender by anticipation. That was why his dark glistening eyes were so unusually kind when he turned them upon his interlocutor, and the tone of his occasional remarks was so gentle and sweet.

Taras Kostrov was known as one of the strongest men of the party, as he was certainly the most domineering. But he wore a velvet glove upon his iron hand. His manners were soft and winning, and his speeches, when his passion was at its highest, became "sweeter than honey," as his adversaries used to say.

When all were assembled, the discussion was opened in an informal way. Shepelev, who had finished his affair with Taras, looked round, and seeing there was nobody wanting, plunged into business. He began to say, without any kind of exordium, what had been done in his district since the last meeting, and what was in preparation. He was freely interrupted by questions, suggestions, and criticisms from the audience. The discussion resembled more a free talk between friends than a formal debate.

Lena had to speak after Shepelev. But she did not want to make any report to-day. There was no change worth speaking of in her district.

"Let us rather hear what Tania has to tell. She has new ground to work upon, and fruitful ground, I hope."

"Not very, up to the present, I am bound to confess," Tania said.

The prospect for the future was, however, not so bad, as was elicited by the questions of several friends, among whom Taras and Andrey were prominent.

It was evident that the district, if well managed, might become in time an important centre.

"Would it not be well," suggested Taras, "that an experienced man should be transferred—for a time at least—to the Narva district?"

He could not wait to hear the result of his proposal. The inexorable watch warned him that he must be off. He shook hands with Shepelev, and left hurriedly.

"I am just of Taras's opinion," Lena said. "We have nobody free, but some of us can leave an old place where the propaganda has struck root well. For starting, a man will be better, I think, than a woman."

She looked at Andrey, who felt with trouble and mortification that he was beginning to blush under this significant glance. His resolution not to see Tania outside business meetings like this, vanished away at Lena's glance, as if it had never been. Now he knew that in reality he had come to this very meeting with the hope that something would turn up to bring him nearer to the girl.

"Shepelev can leave his place," one voice said.

Andrey felt very unhappy. It seemed to him that his chance was gone. Shepelev was one of the best and most experienced of the propagandists.

"Yes, let Shepelev go to the Narva district," several voices repeated.

The question seemed settled, but Lena interposed. "I think," she said, "Andrey will do much better than Shepelev."

She proceeded to give her reasons, reviewing with perfect frankness and equanimity the respective qualifications of the two men. Shepelev, she admitted, was very good as lecturer and debater. The workmen understood him well, and were easily converted by him. But he was not the fittest person to work up a new field and pick out new men; he was neither active nor enterprising enough for that. Besides, he was slow in making acquaintance with the people. Andrey in both respects was the better man of the two.

Lena made her speech in a uniform business-like tone, without raising her voice a single note. Her blue eyes, which she moved as she spoke from one candidate to the other, rested upon them with the same placid calmness when she made a compliment as when she put forward a cutting criticism.

Shepelev listened to the discursive examination of himself very attentively, his elbow on the arm of his chair, twisting his yellow beard between his fingers. He smiled now and then at Lena's sharpest remarks, enjoying quietly the girl's straight-forwardness.

"Yes, I think you will do better here than I," he said to Andrey, when Lena had finished. "Can you leave your district without inconvenience?"

Now that the thing which he so ardently wished a minute before depended upon one word of his, he was taken with a sudden fear, as if an abyss had opened before his eyes.

"Of course he can!" said Lena, who knew Andrey's district as well as he did.

Andrey looked timidly at Tania, who was next him. The girl seemed troubled and perplexed at the unlooked-for proposal. This hurt Andrey profoundly. Why should they both be so much concerned about him? It was odd enough on George's part; but from her he certainly did not expect this. Love or no love, he was not a milksop; and he would prove to them that in all matters connected with the cause, he would never be influenced by considerations touching his personal feelings.

His mind was made up at once, and he gave his full and unreserved consent to the new arrangement.

When the discussion on current affairs was over, he begged Tania, in a rather formal way, to tell him some more particulars about her work, which was now their common concern.

She explained what she could, adding that her workmen

would meet at her house that evening. The best thing would be for Andrey to go with her at once, to see them all, and find out for himself.

Andrey was disengaged for the rest of the day. There was no reason why he should not accept a proposal which was so agreeable to him. They left at once, Andrey feeling considerably softened toward the girl.

On the way he asked her how her father took their separation, and whether she saw him often. This topic brought them at once to the close terms of their earlier acquaintance. Andrey had a sincere regard for the old barrister. Tania knew this, and it gave her particular pleasure to remember it now. With George she could hardly speak of her family drama. All his sensitiveness and delicacy notwithstanding, he was dull as wood upon certain points; it exasperated her sometimes to feel that this side of her life was almost incomprehensible to him. With Andrey it was different, and it did her good to unbosom herself upon a question that pained her so much.

Tania did not live alone. The conspirators had at their disposal several elderly women, mostly former servants in the families of revolutionists. They were employed as housekeepers, when no particular skill was required for the office. Few of them understood anything of the revolution, but they were all faithful and trustworthy as old family servants. One of these women, formerly Zina's nurse, was lent to Tania, as her housekeeper and supposed landlady.

Tania gaily showed Andrey her new apartment, which was not very prepossessing and much unlike her old dwelling-place. The lodgings—the best she could find in a convenient street—were rather too spacious for her. They consisted of five rooms on a flat, of which only three could be filled by Tania's scanty stock of furniture. The two others were quite empty, giving to the place an uncomfortable desolate appearance. The girl pretended that it made it look like an old castle.

The largest room, provided with a long deal table and a number of rough stools and benches, was the one where the meetings were held.

The workmen soon came in. They were seven in number, arriving, for the sake of precaution, in two batches.

Andrey was introduced by Tania as a friend, intending to settle in the neighbourhood and take part in their common work. All were glad to hear it, and he was at once treated as one of the family. He did not want, however, to interfere in the work, preferring to see how Tania acquitted herself in her new duties.

He prepared himself for a good deal of indulgence. But he recognised very soon that condescension would be out of place. Tania, this delicate, high bred girl, who had spent all her life in drawing-rooms, seemed to be quite at home among these children of toil. Without any effort and with no other teacher than her ardent desire to be understood, she used a language and a style which they had no difficulty in grasping. She put so much of her soul in the work that she became almost one with her audience.

All this was very promising, though she was not without her shortcomings. She was afraid to give full play to her own impulses. Once or twice Andrey caught in the girl's words a warm, contagious thrill of deep feeling. But just when her own emotion began to tell upon the audience, she checked herself, like a timid rider, who dares not take advantage of the generous fire of his steed.

A little experience and practice would teach her to do better. She had very good stuff in her anyhow. If at the beginning Andrey tried not to be too exacting, at the end he had to be careful not to overlook her deficiencies.

The reading finished, they began to talk. Andrey joined in the conversation, bringing forward topics upon which each could say his word. He wanted to get an idea of his new companions.

They parted on the best terms, the workmen having obtained from Andrey a promise to come again, as soon as he had moved into their district.

Tania detained Andrey for another hour or so; she was so anxious to have a talk with him.

The girl was in the honeymoon of her revolutionary activity. Everything connected with it was fresh and engrossing. Habit had not yet entered as a sedative into her ardour, nor had experience taught her to be cautious. She brought all the warmth of a woman and of a neophyte into her relations with her workmen.

Her first question to Andrey when they were alone was, how he liked her pupils. According to her each of them had something promising or sympathetic about him. Andrey did not exactly share her views.   But he was in high spirits to-night, ready to see the best in everything.

"I am sure, anyhow," he said, "that in a few months we shall have a good organisation in this district."

Tania was much elated at such brilliant prospects.

"We must divide the work to be more successful," she suggested.   "I will take upon myself the teaching and the preliminary work.   You shall give them the final polish."

"If division of labour there must be," Andrey said, " I think that it will be rather for you to give our men the final polish, and for me to pick them up from the crowd.   I always held the opinion that in awakening souls, we men must give the palm to women.   I do not think that our case is an exception to that general rule."

The girl looked at him in surprise.   It was difficult for her to believe that he meant what he said.

"But I am hardly able to speak to them, and I know so little," she said.

"Of course you will have to work hard yourself," Andrey said.   "But I assure you that erudition is not the chief quality in a good propagandist.   It is nothing compared with . . ."

"With what?" the girl said, eagerly.

"With the power to move hearts and to infuse into them your own devotion.   Perhaps you wish me to tell you the secret of doing that?"

"By all means!" Tania exclaimed.   "You must not keep such knowledge for your own benefit."

"It is to feel all this yourself."

Tania burst into laughter.   She expected something extraordinary and at the same time very practical.   And it was only that. . . .

"Why, then, should women have any advantage over men?" she asked.   "Are our men unfeeling or not devoted?"

"No.   But there are degrees and a world of difference between them, you know.   I cannot help becoming Pindaric when I think of our women, and that does not suit a man like me.   I really think they are too good for our Mother Russia—for the time we live in at all events."

He stopped, pensively.

"You will succeed too in the work you have chosen," he added, looking at her earnestly.   "You have the very precious qualities required to achieve great success in that line. Trust to my prophecy, for I know something about it."

He spoke soberly, but the eyes that he lifted on the girl glowed with admiration. He was so happy to be able to sincerely pay her that modest homage.

Tania blushed with the intense surprise and pleasure these words gave her.

"I would give much for your prophecy to prove true," she said, and then asked, "When shall you be able to move to our district?"

"In a few days. But I may as well begin my work from to-morrow. Two hours' distance is not much."

"Very well. I will expect you then to-morrow evening," the girl said, giving to Andrey a strong and warm shake of the hand.

Andrey returned home a happy man. He was feasting upon the recollections of the evening, and the certainty of seeing the girl again to-morrow. In this new and higher phase of her life, Tania appeared to him as if transfigured and glorified. Her best qualities which he had formerly only anticipated, were now in full bloom. And what a rapidity of growth! Such wonders, he thought, happen only with girls. He left her a child. Now she was a woman, but as free from self-consciousness as a child. He felt that he loved her now more deeply than ever, but his apprehensions of the morning had entirely vanished. His former resolution to avoid the girl seemed to him now utterly absurd. He did not expect, and did not seek, any return for his love. Why, then, should he avoid the girl, with whom he had so much in common? They had worked very well that night together, and they would work in the same way in the future, no matter whether he loved her much or little or not at all. The old romancers might well consider love-making the chief interest in life. He knew better than that.

CHAPTER IX.

AT THE SAME WORK.

ANDREY had many opportunities for congratulating himself upon his courageous resolution to take the bull by the horns. During the month which followed his removal to the Narva district he knew that happiness which is second only to the raptures of a returned love: the companionship of the woman one loves in a work into which both of them put the best of their souls.

The trifling, dull, everyday details had for him a new significance and charm. The little successes he achieved in his work, were now actual triumphs, that filled him with keen joy. He was exceptionally successful in his propaganda all this time. He became more perceptive and eloquent, the warmth of his own affection making him feel kindlier to other men.

Most of his time he spent out of doors. The twenty-four hours hardly sufficed for him to do all the work he had on hand. Thanks to the introductions he received from Tania's workmen, the circle of his connections extended rapidly. Out of his many new friends and sympathisers he had to choose men whom it was safe to invite to Tania's evenings. As the workmen who were present at those meetings ran as much risk as if they were parties to a wilful murder or arson, it was the custom that no candidate for one of their small clubs should be invited without the consent and approbation of all the members. Andrey and Tania adhered to this wise rule; but Andrey soon acquired such popularity, that practically all abided by his advice. A clever educated man is a giant intellectually in a crowd of illiterate peasants and mechanics —provided that he knows how to win their confidence.

The number of their adherents grew rapidly. Another centre, in which two young men lived, was founded in the district. It was risky to receive too many people at the same house. The original stock began to give forth shoots. Still, numerically, it was a very small affair. The propagandists assembled around them only the picked men, and addressed small gatherings, such as can meet safely in private lodgings.

But it is in small gatherings that true zealots can be best educated. It is when spoken from man to man, face to face, that the human word produces its greatest effect. Their propaganda, its small extent notwithstanding, was very fruitful. They not merely imparted to their men certain doctrines, they educated them in the same high feelings that animated themselves.

In this common work, Tania's part was certainly not smaller than that of her elder companion and guide. In his ardour to push forward the girl, Andrey kept to his idea of division of labour between them—perhaps too closely. He took upon himself the task of establishing new connections, opening new fields, and getting hold of new men. But when they met in the evenings in Tania's room, he was wont to leave the best part of the work to her.

Thanks to his constant encouragement, Tania got rid of what makes women so weak when they have to do intellectual work in company with men—the consciousness of inferiority. Her mind and speech, once freed from the trammels of a depressing apprehension, grew and strengthened visibly. Her mornings she spent mostly at home, reading and studying diligently to fit herself better for her favourite work. In the evenings, if they had no meeting of their own, she was often invited to attend a meeting of some of their companions, amongst whom she began to acquire a reputation.

Andrey was delighted with the girl's success, more than he ever had been with his own. He did not notice how his feeling towards the girl, which was never merely a fancy, acquired an ever-increasing depth. Every day he discovered new attractions in her. It seemed to him that into all that Tania did she threw something of her own, which made it fresh and exquisitely fine. Her love to the people seemed to him so warm and sincere; her calmness and simplicity in accepting the dangers which surrounded her, and her indifference to the fate which was in store for her, seemed to him so touching and beautiful. All that he had known and seen so many times done by other girls, now acquired for him a new meaning and a new charm. It is thus that a picture by a great master, when we stand before it in rapt contemplation, reveals to us endless beauties unsuspected at a cursory glance.

At some moments a secret dread crept over Andrey's heart; he felt that he was beginning to love terribly in earnest. But such moments were few and brief. Usually he was possessed by a delightful inward calm, in which even his jealousy was lulled to sleep.

He saw George occasionally, though not very often. The young poet was again very busy, and Andrey went rarely to town. George had ceased for some time to persecute Andrey with that exasperating doleful look of his. Their relations were improved by this, but they were not the same as before. A certain constraint remained between them. Andrey laid the fault of it entirely upon his friend. If George cared for their friendship, he ought to be the first to speak frankly. Andrey felt quite ready on his part not to grudge him the girl's love. Their common work had established between himself and Tania a strong link, which, as he thought, nothing could break. Tania's tastes were modest and homely like his own. He doubted whether she would feel any particular attraction for the domain of high politics in which George moved, whilst he was sure that, marriage or no marriage, she would never give up her present kind of work. Whatever happened, he was certain that his own share in Tania's spiritual life would always be the greater. This made him inclined to be generous.

Every time he happened to be alone with George he expected an explanation. But George evidently avoided approaching the burning subject, and kept his friend in a painful suspense.

Andrey knew that he could easily clear up everything by speaking to Tania directly; they were friends enough for that. But every time he was on the point of putting his question, an insuperable dread detained him,—the dread, as he thought, of offending her by an indiscretion. He preferred not to think about her love to George. The present was so delightful, that there was no need to spoil it by anticipating the unpleasant eventualities of the future. When thoughts of this kind crossed his mind, he simply drove them away as one drives obnoxious birds from a cornfield.

The only thing which caused him real pain for the present, was the impossibility of spending as much time with the girl as he wished. It pained him to leave her even for an hour. But this privation was imposed on both of them by the exigencies of their work, and he bore it with resignation, requiting himself by taking good care not to waste any of his opportunities of seeing her. He certainly could not be jealous of their common cause.

He was satisfied, and happy on the whole. It was a calm and refined sort of happiness, which did not turn his head; but Andrey consoled himself with the idea, that what had to last long must naturally be calm. He firmly believed that their present relations would be prolonged indefinitely, until a little circumstance showed him that the edifice he supposed to be built of stone, was rather a house of cards that a touch of the finger would overturn.

CHAPTER X.

ONE evening Tania and Andrey were sitting alone in their workroom. It was very late, and the whole house was plunged in the first deep sleep. The young people had returned half an hour before from a meeting at the house of one of their companions. The evening had been an exceptionally successful and agreeable one. Tania had chosen for to-night's reading a very touching story of popular life and suffering. She was excited by it herself, and spoke unusually well. She went home in her happiest mood. Andrey accompanied her, as usual, to her house. He was in good spirits also, and could not withstand the desire to step up to her room for another half-hour, under the pretext that after so much talking it was right to have a cup of tea.

Tania brought him in, opening the door with her latch-key. The housekeeper had already gone to bed. They did not want to disturb her, preferring to provide for their needs themselves. With much bustling and laughing they lighted their samovar, and ransacked the cupboards, Tania having cautiously stolen the keys from under the housekeeper's pillow, where the good woman was wont to put them for the night.

When the things were upon the table, both discovered that they were quite hungry. They had the pleasantest supper, and talked gaily.

Andrey mentioned the story which had been read.

"We must recommend it to our friends," he said. "I don't remember any other story so stirring to our workmen as this one. It must be made, I think, a permanent addition to our stock."

Tania agreed, and promised that she would take it to Lena at her first visit.

"But perhaps it is not the horse, but the rider, who won the prize," Andrey said, smiling. "I hope that after to-night's experience you have no longer any doubt as to your capacities and brilliant future as propagandist among workmen."

"Yes, I hope I shall do something in that way," Tania said, happy as a skylark trying its young wings and taking its first flight. "Now I am beginning to be afraid that I have got so used to speaking to workmen, that I shall lose altogether the capacity for addressing people of our own set."

"Would it be such a great loss to you?" Andrey asked, good-humouredly.

"Of course it would, especially now!" Tania exclaimed, with youthful warmth.

"Why?" Andrey inquired.

The girl's words jarred somewhat unpleasantly upon his ear.

"Because I am about to try my strength on that field," she said, "and I am so anxious to carry havoc amidst my old friends there. You know, George said to me yesterday we are to start for our Moscow trip in a week or so."

A chill came over Andrey's heart. The girl had said nothing new to him. He had never forgotten Tania's projected trip with George. He could not forget it, if he would. This was one of the most obnoxious birds that visited his cornfield, which he had the greatest difficulty in scaring away. He was prepared for the fact, but he never thought that she would be so exultant at the prospect of leaving him and the work to which he had believed her to be so strongly attached. It was the girl's way of speaking of it which made his heart ache so painfully.

He fixed a dismal look upon the beautiful happy face, trying in vain to discover upon it something more in harmony with his own feelings.

"Are you so impatient to go to Moscow?" he asked, dejectedly.

Tania gave no answer to Andrey's question. Her eyes closed, a bright smile on her lips, she only made a number of small affirmative nods.

Her flushed face said the rest. She left him without a regret, without a thought. He was nothing to her, whilst she was everything to him. She was satisfied with his company, only for want of something better. As soon as he was out of her sight, she would forget his very existence.

Andrey's lips turned pale.

"I quite realise that you should be delighted at going to

Moscow," he said, in a calm slow voice, whilst inwardly he was boiling with rage. "It's such dull drudgery to repeat always the same thing to a handful of common workmen. It's much more exciting to score a success among an educated set, who will sing your praises and will publish your achievements far and wide."

The girl started at this outrageous accusation. She could hardly believe her ears. She lifted upon him her wide open bewildered eyes, but she could not recognise that cold stern face, which she was accustomed to see so kind and so friendly.

"Do you consider me so frivolous?" she stammered.

Her voice trembled. Tears shone in her eyes.

The sight filled him with burning remorse. He was ready to throw himself at her feet, and implore forgiveness for the first pain he had caused her. But some evil spirit, stronger than himself, took possession of him, filling his words with gall and poison.

"How can I help being disappointed in you," he burst forth vehemently, "if you tell me yourself that you burn with impatience to give up a work which you said you liked; when the hope of shining among philistines and high-class puppets turns your head; when——"

He was unable to proceed. He seized his hat and ran out of the house, without taking leave of the girl.

Everything grew gloomy from that evening. They patched up their first quarrel on the morrow, but that did not improve the matter. The base of their friendship was shaken. Andrey believed no longer in the existence of those solid moral ties between them, in which hitherto he had had such a trust.

He recognised, of course, when the heat of passion was over, that he had exaggerated when he supposed the girl utterly indifferent to his very existence. She might no doubt retain a bit of lukewarm friendship for him. But this was worse than nothing. He thirsted for all; and the little he had served only to show how much was kept back. Of jealousy of George he did not think any longer. George or another, or nobody at all, what did it matter to him? He was jealous of every moment, every thought, she did not share with him. His new jealousy destroyed the old one, as a strong pain makes us forget a lesser ache. In the charming and dangerous intimacy in which they had lived, Andrey's feelings had grown upon him imperceptibly. Now they burst forth fiercely, filling his heart, kindling his blood. He could not exist without her, for in her absence he did nothing but torment himself about her. To run away was now out of the question. He calculated the hours and the minutes he had to wait before he could decently see her again. But as soon as he had secured for himself this happiness, the remembrance of his wrongs surged out of the depths of his heart, overwhelming all that was good and benevolent in his feelings toward the girl. The very enjoyment of her presence turned to poison for him. The deep, the penetrating pleasure of yielding and submitting to the beautiful child was gone. He felt humiliated at being so much at her mercy, revolting against her power of making him happy or wretched at pleasure. This inward struggle kept him in constant irritation. He became peevish and captious, trying to find fault with her, wrangling about everything; and he was not ashamed to use the advantages of his superior dialectical skill and experience to torment her the more effectively.

Tania received his first rebukes without defending herself; they hurt her too much for that. But soon she lost confidence in his fairness, and began to resent his unjustifiable ill-temper. The mutual understanding established by many months of friendly intercourse was destroyed in a few days. When alone, free from these galling influences, Andrey saw with horror how rapidly their estrangement was growing. He tried to regain the lost ground by offering her apologies. And the next moment he began all over again.

Tania was no less miserable than Andrey. One morning, coming unexpectedly, he saw by her eyes that she had been crying. He accused himself of being the greatest of villains, and was about to confess everything. But the girl received his first words so badly, that they fell out worse than ever.

They were rolling down a steep declivity, and had to hurl themselves to the bottom without any possibility of stopping. A complete and irrevocable rupture was certain to occur before long. Andrey wished that it would come soon; this would put an end to an intolerable position. He would be compelled by force of circumstances to leave her, a thing which he had not strength to do on his own initiative. Yet he dreaded the blow, and made awkward efforts to put the fatal moment off.

He took the extreme resolution of not seeing her outside the hours of their work. On Friday he kept to his room stoically.   Friday was Andrey's best day; they had no meeting to attend, and were wont either to go on some visit to town, or to spend it in Tania's rooms reading something together or talking.   Now he resolved not to call on her at all.   But it cost him so much to keep to his resolution, that the next day he came much before the usual time, under the pretext that he wanted to speak with her upon the choice of the subject to discuss at the coming meeting.

This they settled in a few minutes, and he had nothing more to say.   For the first time he could not find a subject for conversation with Tania.   He repented that he had broken his resolution, and had come so early to make a fool of himself. This put him at once in a bad humour.

"How long is it since you have seen Lisa?" he asked, to fill up the disagreeable gap.

He had not done it on purpose, but he certainly could not have chosen a subject more unpleasant for himself.

Lisa was a very fashionable cousin of Tania's.   Andrey knew her a little, and there was no love lost between them. Besides, her name reminded him of the unfortunate Moscow trip.   It was at Lisa's house that Tania intended to stop on her arrival in the town.

"Not since last winter, when she paid a visit to St Petersburg," she answered, curtly and seriously.

Tania had some needlework in her hand, and was sewing assiduously, her head turned in profile to Andrey.

The silence returned,—a strained, painful silence, filling the nerves with uneasiness, like the stifling calm before the outburst of a tempest.

To break the insufferable tension, Tania tried to bring forward something connected with their common work, which formerly afforded them such an inexhaustible source for exchange of thoughts and feelings.

But Andrey did not take the bait; it was not for this that he had come.   Then, as the girl renewed nervously her efforts, he grew vexed that she should try to bring the conversation to matters which after all were of such small interest to her.

He abruptly changed the subject, turning to topics which would be much more appropriate to the occasion,—her Moscow plans and acquaintances, in whom he exhibited now a keen, though not benevolent interest.

Tania answered without lifting her eyes from the needlework. But her fingers trembled, and her stitches often went wrong. She knew well that this time Andrey had broached the subject on purpose to hurt her. But she had made her resolution not to be provoked, and not to quarrel with Andrey, as long as she could help it. In three days she would start with George for Moscow, and on returning she would settle in some other district. She did not want to part with Andrey in enmity.

But, instead of soothing, her calmness drove Andrey to the extreme verge of irritation and despair. It proved to him that he had become so utterly indifferent to her, that no opinion of his would in the least affect her. He had nothing left but the cruel pleasure of ascertaining whether that indifference had any limits. He scoffed at her most cherished plans, ran down her Moscow friends, and finished by saying that, according to his experience, people who came over into their ranks from the midst of the fashionable world, were able only for a time to don the garb of democrats; in one way or in another the old Adam will reappear in them, and the sooner the better.

This was too much for Tania to bear. She rose from her seat, exasperated, indignant.

"Listen, Andrey! . . ." she began, in a voice quivering with anger.

Andrey rose also, his face pale, his right hand resting upon the table. The spirit of mischief which hitherto had possessed him vanished at once. The moment he had expected, had provoked, and yet dreaded, had come, and he was ready to receive the blow. The small oil reflector fixed to the wall lit up his bowed forehead and knitted brows. He looked gloomy and suffering.

"Andrey," the girl exclaimed, softening suddenly, "tell me why you have so changed towards me for some days past? If you find something bad in me, why do you not tell me frankly and in a brotherly fashion as you used to? And if you can't, why should we harass each other as we do? Is it not better we should separate, and go each our own way?"

She was no longer angry, but sad. Her voice was soft and kind. But Andrey became a shade paler still.

"I wish I could leave you, Tania. I wish I had never met you at all," he said, in a hardly audible voice.

"Why? Have I caused you—— ?"

She was checked by a sudden foreboding of something immense which flashed across her mind.

"Are you blind, then?" Andrey said, almost rudely. "Do you not see that I love you to madness!"

He lifted his eyes upon her, and his whole frame was shaken with a momentary wonder, which passed into a rapturous breath-suspending joy. Had he seen aright? Her face brightened. She had stretched both her hands toward him, she made a step forward, and all was done. She threw herself upon his neck, bursting into happy tears.

"Tania, dear, my own! Is it possible? You love me?" he asked, in a tremulous voice.

She only pressed closer to him.

"You made me suffer so much," she whispered.

"Forgive me. I have suffered horribly myself; but it is all over now. We shall be happy!" he exclaimed triumphantly. "The gods themselves will envy our happiness!"

He led her to a chair, and knelt down at her side. He covered with kisses her cold hands, and her flushed, bashful face. He made her the avowal of his absorbing passion, and asked how she came to love him. He wanted facts, confirmations, to be quite sure of that happiness which had fallen upon him as from the skies.

"I thought you loved George," he said, with a smile of mixed confusion and pride.

"George is the best of men—much better than you are," she said, pressing her finger strongly against his forehead. "But since the night you spoke to me at our house—do you remember? —you have possessed my heart. It all grew upon me stronger and stronger. . . . I don't know why. I suppose for some sin of my ancestors," she said, with a smile, bestowing upon the young man a long look of love.

The sound of the bell at the entrance door recalled them to reality. It was the first batch of workmen arriving.

Andrey went to let them in. The girl received them, and betook herself to her work as usual. She looked only uncommonly beautiful, as if glorified with the calm solemnity of a great happiness. But Andrey could not curb the tempestuous exultation of his heart. Even Tania's presence was not sufficient to enable him to attend to anything except his own feelings. He took leave of them, and left hurriedly.

Outside it was a bitter frost; the winter, at its onset, covering with the shroud of death, earth, trees, and houses. But Andrey was unconscious of the cold, as of all his surroundings. There was in his heart a boiling spring of life, which made his cheeks glow and sent the blood coursing rapidly through his veins, as he walked through the darkness of the early northern night.

He was not dreaming; it was true, she loved him! Her hands had rested there, around his neck; he felt their touch still. Her first shy kiss burned upon his lips. That dazzling beauty, that harmonious spirit, the treasures of which he alone knew—were his, all his, solely and for ever! The world around him, other men and himself—all seemed changed and renewed, and in the depth of his soul, stirred as it had never been before, an exultant voice was singing a hymn of praise to the abstract impersonal thing above, the object of their common devotion, which now appeared to him as a living being, one that could be spoken to and hear his ardent vows. He knew that the girl he loved would never have cast a glance upon him, but for his faithfulness to the great cause in which they were both engaged.

His thoughts reverted to George, and a repentant tenderness filled his heart. How rudely he had behaved towards him; how churlishly he had received his unwavering kindness. Yes, he must go straight to him, he must make a clean breast of it, and tell him, Brother, I have sinned before heaven and against you.

George was at home, buried amidst his books and manuscripts. The moment he saw Andrey's face, he understood on what errand he had come. It seemed that he was prepared long ago for what Andrey wanted to tell him.

He stopped Andrey's clumsy and confused confessions at the first words, and shook his hand, wishing him happiness. Not a shadow of jealousy could be detected in his large blue eyes, as he looked upon his happy rival. This did not surprise Andrey at all, for he knew that it would be thus. But it seemed very strange to him that George should accept it all as a matter of course.

"I knew months ago that she loved you," George said, calmly.

"Did you? But how could you?" Andrey asked.

"In the simplest way possible; she told me herself on one occasion. . . ."

He paused for a moment, as if drifting off into some recollections.

"That's why," he proceeded, "I was compelled to keep dumb as a fish. Otherwise I should have spoken."

"Spoken ? To whom ? "

" To you, of course. To whom else ? "

" George, pray don't tell me all that at once, if you don't want to crush me altogether with your surpassing virtues," Andrey said, trying to conceal his confusion under a playful tone.

George shrugged his shoulders.

" What are you saying of virtues. It would be only consistent with my love to both of you. Would you not have done it yourself if you had been in my position ? " he said, fixing on his friend a sly look of assumed simplicity.

Andrey blushed crimson with the painful blush of shame. He knew that he would have been unable to act in that way. It pained him to confess his coarser nature.

Seeing how well he had hit the mark, George burst into a hearty laugh, so completely devoid of malice that Andrey felt relieved, and finished by laughing too.

Then George stopped, and said seriously—

" I hope you will not be jealous of me because I shall accompany Tania to Moscow ? "

" No, I have not fallen as low as that kind of jealousy, and I hope I never shall," Andrey exclaimed, smiling. " You need not think me worse than I am."

CHAPTER XI.

TANIA promised to return soon, and she kept her word. In a fortnight Andrey was at the railway station again to take his bride in his arms. They were married soon after. No priest or policeman was requested to interfere in the matter. The union was completed by giving publicity to their intentions, as is the rule in the world in which they lived.

The marriage changed in no way the external part of their life. They resumed the same work as before, though they had to settle at the opposite end of the capital, as the old district became too hot for them. In one of the bye-streets near the Cronversky they found small lodgings, consisting of two rooms, with a kitchen in which Tania cooked their meals.

The rooms were small, and shabbily furnished. The floor was bare, the ceiling not very lofty. The windows were small, and for the most part covered with an opaque deposit of hoar frost, as hard winter was outside, though spring was already drawing near. On a sunny day they could enjoy the view of a block of ugly monotonous houses on the opposite side of the street. There was nothing picturesque or poetical in the dwelling, which was almost dreary in its bareness. Yet this was their paradise,—if this expression can be allowed in the sober language of modern humanity.

The first, all-absorbing, rapturous happiness soon passed; it was too incompatible with the life they lived and saw around them. But it gave place to a calmer and higher happiness, of community of thoughts and feelings, of the never-ending charm of mutual knowledge, which for lovers begins only after marriage.

They were as fully and completely happy as they ever dreamed of being.

True, an important element of complete happiness did not exist for them. They had not even any illusion as to its longevity. Theirs was only a short respite, and they knew it. The sword of Damocles hung constantly over their heads. Any day and hour might be their last. Some of the many dangers besetting the everyday life of conspirators approached them closely, as if to whisper a *memento mori*, now to Andrey, now to Tania, now to both of them together.

But they did not complain of this. The dangers which surrounded their path were the torch-bearers of their love. What they valued and loved in each other most, was precisely this unlimited devotion to their country, this readiness to give up for its sake everything and at any moment. If they were able to love each other without doubt, division, or restraint, with all the powers of their young enthusiasm, this was because they each found in the other the embodiment of that lofty ideal of heroism after which each of them aspired. Since faithfulness to themselves, to their ideas, to their love, imposed upon them this life of constant danger, they did not shrink. Let the unavoidable come; they would not cast down their eyes before it.

They did not court the ghastly goddess of self-immolation; they were both too full of vigorous physical health for that, and life had too many charms for them now. But they did not fear. The gloom of the future did not mar the beauty of their present. It only gave a value to every hour, every moment, they had to spend together.

One morning, it was at the beginning of spring, Andrey asked Tania to read him aloud from a new magazine they had brought yesterday from her father, with whom they had spent the evening.

They both enjoyed immensely reading together, and talking on what they had read. But to-day Tania replied that she was in no mood to read anything. A cloud hung over her brow; the first, perhaps, in the four months of their marriage.

"What's the matter with you, dear?" Andrey asked, anxiously. "You look so appallingly serious and solemn."

Tania could not tell exactly what was the matter. Nothing particular; only a strange depression of spirit.

She was sitting in the chair near her desk. Andrey sat upon the floor at her feet, which was his favourite pose when they could enjoy a free talk.

"Come, tell me what you are thinking about, and I'll try to find out for myself what ails you."

"You needn't mind about it," she said ; "a mere depression of mind, which will pass of its own accord."

"But I want to know what you are depressed about. Is it about me, perhaps? If so, you are quite wrong, for you couldn't find with a lantern a better husband than I am."

"Don't joke, Andrey," Tania said, letting her vague melancholy run that way. "We are happy now, but who. can tell whether it is for good or for evil that we married."

"Every priest, if we had asked any to meddle in our affairs, would have told you that it is for good and for evil," Andrey said. "But whence these strange doubts? I never heard you speak in that way before? Do you regret that you married me?"

"No, I don't regret, on my own account," she said, putting her hand upon Andrey's thick hair, and looking him in the face. "But perhaps you would regret it some day. I have been often told how revolutionists grow worse when they get married."

"Then it is the fear of spoiling my spotless self that troubles your peace of mind?"

He could not proceed in the same strain, her deep dark eyes were so earnestly, pathetically sad.

A warm wave of thankfulness and love surged up in his breast as he looked from below into those dear eyes, drinking in their caressing light.

"My darling, you have made another and better man of me! You have opened in my heart such springs of enthusiasm, devotion, and faith in men, as I never thought to possess. Is it for you to speak thus?"

"Have I?" she said, incredulously, caressing his hair.

"Oh, I wish I could tell you all! Do you know I was very religious when a boy, and afterwards I was told that it is in religion that man's spirit soars highest. But when I am with you, and your hand resting upon my head ; or when in solitude I begin to think of you and of myself,—I feel the same sweetness of humility, the same thrill of adoration, the same ardent yearning after moral purity and sacrifice, which overwhelmed my heart in the days of my childhood. I'm glad to own my defects and weaknesses, because it is before you that I have to bow my head, and I long to be cleansed of them that I may come without fear into your presence. . . ."

Transfigured with the glow of enthusiasm he was beautiful, he was eloquent. Tania listened, serious, wondering, almost carried away by his passionate outburst. But at his last words she stretched her hands forwards, as if his utterances were actual incense that she wanted to keep off.

"Andrey, I pray you, don't speak to me in that way if you love me. I'll disbelieve in your love if you try to exalt me so out of all proportion. I know that I have nothing extraordinary about me, and I wish that you would take me for what I am."

Andrey listened to this little sermon with a calm smile. He took her hand deliberately, and kissed one by one each of her fingers in turn.

"Child," he said at last, "who told you that I consider you to be so much of an exception to our common nature? No, dear, I'm not a boy any longer. I know that we are both of us ordinary people. I weave no day-dreams about you; I love you. But do you think that only the rare and the extraordinary can be loved? How miserable our world would be if that were so! I know that among our fellow-conspirators there are women as good and pure-minded and devoted as you. But what does it matter to me? I see the sun, and I feel its warmth basking in its rays, and I proceed calmly to my day's work or to my rest. But to-morrow I see the same sun, perhaps even less brilliant and beautiful than yesterday, only the clouds gathered round him in a somewhat different way, the colours grouped in another manner, which so affects my eyes that I stop rapturous and ecstatic before him. I don't know, and I don't care to know, why I love you. . . ."

"Oh, I know now," Tania interposed, laughing, "and I'll tell you at once. Your tastes are exceedingly modest. I am sure you become ecstatic before the sun when it is so thoroughly clouded as to resemble a big round oil-spot upon a paper lantern. There's no wrangling about tastes, and I consent to be your sun on such condition."

She was merry; she smiled gaily. But her eyes were serious, answering to a deeper feeling, which gradually absorbed everything else, streaming forth unchecked in one long, long look. How he loved those dark changeful eyes, of a brown topaz with their deep and transparent purity! How he loved that look of hers, which always made his heart throb and sink in happiness as on the first day when she bestowed it upon him!

"My joy!" he exclaimed, in a quivering voice, drawing his face near to hers, "tell me why should I be so happy? What right have I to be so overwhelmingly happy, when such gloom and sorrow is around us? I feel crushed down when I ask myself, What have I done to merit all you have given me, and how shall I ever repay it?"

She closed his mouth with her hand. Her wondrous eyes changed; their mysterious depths closed as with a veil, and the tremulous fires which glared somewhere at their bottom were spent. They looked grave and serious.

"You mustn't rave in this way," she said, earnestly. "A woman's love is not a prize; it's a free gift on both sides."

The rebuke cooled Andrey, but only for a moment, as fresh fuel thrown into an oven cools the fire.

"You are right; you are always right, dear. But I must only be the more grateful to you on that account. I should have sung hymns in praise of you, like the old troubadour, if I only knew how to make them."

"My troubadour," she said, with a relenting smile, "what would our fellow-conspirators say, I wonder, if they knew that Andrey Kojukhov, the stern, the unflinching, sings rhapsodies like this?"

"They would only put greater confidence in me, if they are wise," Andrey retorted promptly. "For there is nothing I would not do or endure to be worthy of your love. Believe me, only a born coward fears that in the moment of his supreme danger love to a woman will check his devotion to his country. They will find me ready when my hour comes. And you, my beautiful sun, you will say to me, like the Circassian maid arming her lover to the battle,

"'My dearest, be bold in facing your fate.'"

"I'll try," she said, with a faint smile, casting her admiring eyes upon the bold smiling face uplifted towards her.

Never had she loved him so dearly, never was she so proud and happy to be so beloved by such a man. But at the same moment, the possibility of losing him, which she had admitted hitherto without believing it, dawned upon her mind with the keen anguish of reality.

With a nervous impulsiveness, in strong contrast with her words, she threw her hands round his neck, and pressed vehemently to her breast that head, so fearless, so careless of danger, which at this moment was dearer to her than all the world.

A loud ring of the bell, followed by two feebler ones, filled with its discordant din the whole of their small lodgings.

This was a friend's ring.   Yet both started, and looked into each other's face.

Andrey rose hastily and went to open the door.

Tania, who remained at her place, heard first Andrey's joyful exclamation upon the recognition of an unexpected friend.   But the welcome fell deadened as a stone falls when thrown into a quagmire.   She heard the stifled rapid whisper of several voices, and then an ominous silence.

Andrey returned to the room, followed by George, and a young man whom she did not know.   Andrey was pale.   The two others looked sad and very serious.

"What has happened?" she exclaimed, with anxiety, rising to meet them all.

"A terrible disaster," Andrey said.   "Zina and Vasily have been arrested after a hot fight.   Both will be sentenced to death in a few weeks, for certain.   Vulitch has been shot in the affray."

He threw himself upon a chair, and passed his hand over his forehead.   The two guests sat down also.   The stranger happened to be opposite Tania, and their eyes met.

"Vatajko," he said, introducing himself, as the others did not do it.   "I have just come from Dubravnik with the news, and with a special message to your husband."

"When did it all happen?" she asked.

"Three days ago," Vatajko answered.   "The police tried to keep it secret, but they cannot.   To-morrow it will appear in all the newspapers.   The whole town is full of it."

He began to relate in a slow suppressed voice the details of the disaster.   But as he went on he gradually warmed to his subject.   When he came to the story of the fight, he was quite ecstatic.   It was indeed a good feat.   In the dead of the night the police had tried to penetrate into the lodgings which Zina and Vasily occupied.   They unscrewed the hinges of the outer door, so as to enter unheard and surprise every one in bed.   They would certainly have succeeded in their object, but it chanced that Vulitch was reading late in her room.   She heard the suspicious noise, and as she saw the gendarmes unfastening the doors, she fired at them when they least expected it.   She drove them back upon the stairs by repeated shots, and alone kept them at bay for a few minutes, until she was struck by a bullet in the head. She died as Vasily rushed to her assistance.

"What a lioness she was, that little girl! And what a good death!" Andrey could not help exclaiming.

"The other two," Vatajko proceeded, "made an attempt to force a passage with their revolvers, but it was impossible. Then they retreated to the inner rooms, and barricaded the entrance. They burned all the compromising documents, and they kept the police at bay for half-an-hour, until, having spent all their cartridges, they gave themselves up as prisoners."

Vatajko added, that according to their information they would be tried in a few weeks together with Boris. Zina had been implicated in the same affairs as Boris, and the police were very glad to have laid hands on her at last. Vasily would be tried for armed resistance. There could be no doubt that all three would be condemned to death.

"But this must not be!" Vatajko exclaimed passionately. "We'll deliver them by main force!"

He rose from his seat in the heat of his excitement. Now moving, now stopping before one or the other, and gesticulating vehemently, he told them that the Dubravnik section had decided to attempt a rescue with all their force. The whole body of revolutionists is in warm sympathy with the affair. Volunteers could be enrolled to any number among the young people of the educated classes and the artisans of the town. If the secret of the enterprise is rigorously kept, they might succeed. At all events they were resolved to try it.

"We have decided," he concluded, addressing Andrey, "that for an affair of such importance an *ataman* must be nominated, and we have unanimously elected you. I have been sent to explain to you everything, and to ask whether you will join with us in the affair."

Ataman means head man, or leader. As a rule, the undertakings of all kinds are managed on a democratic principle; every detail of importance is discussed and settled by the votes of all those who take part in the affair. But in the enterprises of a military character, requiring special rapidity and energy of action, the direction is often entrusted to one man called *ataman*, to whom all the rest give implicit obedience.

Andrey lifted his head and looked at the bearer of a proposal of such gravity.

"Have you well weighed your choice?" he asked. "I

have never been ataman in any affair before, and this will be a particularly serious one."

"We could not have a better man than you, if we had ordered one to be made on purpose," Vatajko said warmly.

He explained the reasons which had determined Andrey's nomination. All the members of the section knew him personally, and had full confidence in him. Besides, he was very popular with the bulk of the revolutionists of the town, who knew him by reputation, and would follow him better than any other man.

"Let it be, then, as you wish," Andrey said; "I am ready to serve in any capacity in an affair like this."

"So I told them—so I told them!" Vatajko repeated, shaking Andrey's hand effusively. "We all think," he added, "that you need not come to Dubravnik at once. If the police get wind that you are there, they'll be put on their guard. You had better remain here till the time draws near. We shall be in constant communication, and will consult you upon everything."

Thus it was that once again Andrey was taken from his quiet work and his happy uneventful life to be thrown into the very vortex of the revolutionary storm.

He paid a short visit to Dubravnik merely for the purpose of trying the ground. Here he learned that Botcharov, on whom he had reckoned for the coming affair, and the sisters Dudorov, all three had been arrested a few days before. This was very unpleasant. But at first he did not ascribe much importance to the fact of their arrest; he thought they would be released after a short time. But soon after his arrival Varia Voinova called on him. She had been on her usual visit to the prison, where she had learned something that had made her cry with grief and indignation. Mironov, whom Andrey and Vasily had met at the picnic with the sisters Dudorov, had been arrested three months ago. From the very first he had shown the white feather. Now, in order to exculpate himself and get out of prison, the wretch was beginning to confess all that he knew, or that he surmised, bringing numbers of people into trouble.

It was in consequence of his revelations that Botcharov and the Dudorovs had been arrested. He had spoken, among other things, of that unfortunate picnic in the wood, mentioning the names of all who were present. The accident, however insignificant in itself, established the fact of an acquaintance between the Dudorovs and Botcharov and the active conspirators like Andrey and Vasily. They were all three to be tried with Boris, Zina, and Vasily,—a companionship which boded them no good.

For the rest, Andrey's impressions were rather favourable. As far as the projected rescue was concerned, matters in Dubravnik were much better than he had expected. There was the best fighting material at hand, and he had formed a splendid plan of action. They had a fair chance of success; and how glorious such a success would be! His fighting instincts were awakened. As to dangers—he did not think of them, and, in the bottom of his heart, did not believe in them.

He returned to Tania high-spirited and happy. But for her the days of peace were gone. She fully recognised that Andrey was right to go,—that it was absolutely impossible that on such occasions her Andrey should remain behind. But this was a poor consolation. It did not dispel her fears and anxieties about him.

PART III.

———†———

ALL FOR THE CAUSE.

ALL FOR THE CAUSE.

CHAPTER I.

THE STUTTERER.

ONE of the districts of the good town of Dubravnik is called "The Mounds,"—a name that sounds strangely nowadays, for not a single mound can be discovered either in its sandy streets or amongst the large orchards and uncared-for gardens. Probably the name was more appropriate in times gone by, when the place was first reclaimed from the wilderness, for the most part by the nobles of the province who wanted residences in the town. Many of the houses still bear traces of their origin. The spacious courts are surrounded by numerous offices, for the accommodation of the scores of servants that always accompanied the nobles in their periodical migration into the towns. Stables, coach-houses, bath-houses, testify to our fathers' attempts to preserve as much as possible the country mode of life. The houses themselves,—those which are not yet pulled down to give place to new ones,—built mostly of wood, are not without architectural pretensions. Here and there one could see balconies with ornamental cornices and balustrades, diminutive turrets surmounted by spires, festooned doors and windows, bearing witness to the whims and fancies of people who had some kind of artistic proclivities.

After the emancipation, these spired and turreted houses of the former slave-owners passed into the hands of the middle men that so often succeeded the nobles in the possession of their landed estates. The merchants and speculators of all sorts who ousted the ruined nobles, did not remain long in possession of places unsuitable for business purposes, and little attractive to them in other ways. They stayed there simply as conquerors in a city taken by storm—just long enough to strip the estates of all that could be converted into ready money.

Once again the "Mounds" changed their aspect and their population. Houses, offices, and belongings were now rented for the most part by small citizens of the working class. For them the chief value of the estates was in the land that adjoined them—gardens and orchards, which were cultivated for vegetables. As to the houses—those they relet to gentlefolk, their own families huddled together in some one or other of the outbuildings. This arrangement seemed to be permanent. The proprietors were able to raise the rent rapidly, and the tenants were able to scrape the rent together somehow. The town supplied a good market for vegetables, turning out an always increasing number of people to whom the words "nature" and "fresh air" had some significance, and who were willing to pay a moderate price for enjoying both.

In one of these houses, at the beginning of the spring, two lodgers were sitting before an open window. One of them was looking eagerly into the dark street, examining with care every new figure that appeared under the dim light of the oil lantern.

It was Vatajko. The other was Andrey, who had come over to Dubravnik a fortnight before, and had settled with his friend in that quiet place.

"Nobody coming?" he asked.

"Nobody," was the answer.

"Very strange," Andrey resumed, after a pause. "The sitting of the tribunal must have been ended at least three hours ago. The Stutterer had ample time to see his cousin and to come on here."

"Perhaps she hasn't got an admission ticket," Vatajko suggested.

"Nonsense!" Andrey exclaimed. "How can they refuse a ticket to a girl in her station?"

"Then we must assume the Stutterer has blown himself up. He is such a punctual man," Vatajko said, jestingly.

"It's possible," Andrey answered, seriously; "he is so careless with his stuff that it might happen to him at any moment."

"Hadn't I better run over to his place and ask?" said Vatajko.

"What about? Whether he's blown up or not?"

"No. Whether he has seen his cousin, and what she told him."

"If he's blown up, he won't be able to tell you anything; and if he's not, he will come here in the meantime, and you'll miss him. We'd better wait."

A long pause followed.

"But it's so tiresome!" Vatajko broke out. "When the Stutterer comes I'll make it hot for him, take my word for it!"

He was casting a last hopeless look in one direction down the empty street, when he heard the noise of a carriage approaching from the other.

"Ah, here he is at last!" Vatajko exclaimed, at once forgetting his grudge.

Andrey also went to the window, and saw the Stutterer driving rapidly towards them in an open carriage. He was a middle-aged man, with long dark beard reaching almost to his belt, and in figure he looked like a Hercules. Touching with his long hand the driver's shoulder, he ordered him to stop at the gate.

This was a transgression of the rules, but he was in too great a hurry to pull up at a distance from the house.

In another minute he entered the room, bowing his head so as not to strike it against the lintel of the door. Vatajko had already carefully closed the window, let down the blinds, and lit a pair of candles.

"Now, what's your news?" Andrey asked. "Speak out quick."

"In a minute; give me time to take my coat off. Nothing particular, I warn you beforehand," the visitor answered, stuttering slightly.

On closer examination he did not appear to be a Hercules at all. He was lean, and stooped somewhat. His beard was not dark but light chestnut, descending in two long wisps downwards. But his meagre long face was remarkable for a pair of grey eyes, glistening and restless.

"Have you seen your cousin?" Andrey asked.

"Yes, I have."

"Then sit down and tell us everything in the right order."

The Stutterer took a seat, and began his tale.

The trial they were expecting had actually begun before

the military tribunal. Little had been done in the first sitting, but some inferences could already be drawn by experts as to the drift of future proceedings. Most of the members of the bench had been appointed for this special trial by the governor, presumably because they offered special pledges of servility.

Though no military tribunal—ordinary or exceptional—offers much guarantee of justice for political offenders, this was a bad sign. These precautions showed that the government had some especially evil design. The speech of the imperial prosecutor, opening the proceedings, was very important from this point of view, because in all trials of this kind the bench is ruled by the prosecutor.

As to the three chief prisoners, only one charge could be expected. Not so for the other three, Botcharov and the two Dudorovs, who were innocent of any real offence beyond mere acquaintance with conspirators. It was a very bad sign that the prosecutor accused them all of having formed one secret society, intended for the overthrow of the throne, and so forth. Such an interpretation of their mutual relations—if accepted by the court—meant death to all six, for death is the penalty for conspirators against " the throne."

" But is it possible ? " Vatajko broke in. " What proofs of a conspiracy has the blackguard "—he meant the prosecutor— "brought ? "

" The famous picnic in the wood, at which Mironov was present," the Stutterer answered. "The Dudorovs and Botcharov have admitted that they took part in it. From Vasily they got no answer whatever, for he remained dumb all through his detention. But there again is Mironov, who testifies that Vasily was at the picnic with Andrey and Vulitch. Besides, the porter in the Dudorovs' house has recognised the photograph of Vulitch, and has testified that she called several times on the Dudorovs."

The Stutterer closed his mouth, considering the matter fully explained.

Botcharov was a friend of the Dudorovs, the Dudorovs were friends of Vulitch, Vulitch was a friend of Zina, Andrey, and Vasily.

All the six prisoners were in the same gang. Since some of them had admittedly conspired " against the throne," the rest must have been of one mind with them.

All this the Stutterer had no need to explain to his friends, for they had not come from the moon. They were Russians, and they knew the old trick only too well.

"And how are the accused?" Andrey asked, passing on to more interesting topics.

"My informant said that they were so absorbed in talking with each other after so many months of separation, that they paid hardly any attention to the proceedings; but at one point they made a fearful commotion."

Then the Stutterer related the peculiar feature of the trial which caused that vehement outburst; the foul calumnies which the prosecutor—with the permission of the judges— thought fit to pour forth upon the accused, the three women amongst them especially.

The Stutterer could not tell all, for he had not been in the court himself, and his informant omitted much. But what he said was enough to throw Vatajko into a fit of passion.

"The scoundrels!" he exclaimed, putting both his hands to his throbbing temples. "I wish I had them a couple of yards away, to prove on them the effect of one of our bombs."

But not a muscle in the face of his elder companion moved.

"Why, friend! Did you expect them to behave like decent persons?"

"No, but it's provoking all the same," he replied. "Even butchers, when they lead beasts to the slaughter-house, don't throw dirt on their heads."

"How could you expect the Emperor's trusted hound to have the delicacy of a butcher?" Andrey said. "Besides, who cares what fellows of that stamp say or don't say? They would charge their own mothers with adultery, if they were well enough paid for it."

"But I can't believe that all the six will be sentenced to death. Three of them have really done nothing!" Vatajko exclaimed, clinging to his hope.

"You are very naïve, my boy, I see," the Stutterer said, ironically.

He fixed for a moment his restless glistening eyes upon the young man, and then turned them away scornfully. His wife—who also had done nothing—had been torn away from him and kept in prison for years, until she went mad, and in a fit of suicidal mania had cut her throat with a piece of a broken tumbler. Vatajko's faint-hearted desire to attribute something human to the police excited in him a feeling of indignation mitigated only by contempt.

"As for the sentence," Andrey said, "I am pretty sure it will be that. It will give the governor an opportunity to make a show of humanity by commuting the penalty for the sisters Dudorov, and probably for Botcharov also. Perhaps the tribunal will take something off the prosecutor's exorbitant demands, to make a show of their independence. They always arrange comedies of this sort among themselves. I don't think that more than three of the sentences will be confirmed— Boris and Vasily for certain, and then either Zina or Botcharov," Andrey concluded, in a somewhat unsteady voice. "But why do we speculate upon these matters?" he added, after a pause. "Tell us rather how your work is going on, Stutterer."

"Everything is ready. I have prepared bombs for fifty men, and two dozen more than were ordered. I have only to fit the touch holes. That I can do at a few hours' notice."

They talked of their project, and half-an-hour later the Stutterer departed, with somewhat greater precautions than he had taken on his arrival.

CHAPTER II.

THE trial of the six revolutionists lasted five days. It ought to have lasted at least three times as long, had the tribunal followed the usual forms of procedure prescribed by the military code, which certainly does not err on the side of slowness. But the town was too much excited by the sight of the judicial tragedy which was going on in its midst. The general public was excluded from the court. The admission tickets were distributed with the utmost care among the officials, their wives, and a small number of private citizens of unexceptional loyalty. To prevent any possible manifestation of sympathy outside, strong patrols of police and gendarmes watched all the streets, dispersing those who assembled near the court, and taking into custody the obstinate and persistent.

Yet a swarm of sympathisers and of simple curiosity seekers was continually hovering round the place. Whenever any gentlemen or ladies came out, they were instantly surrounded by a dozen people, perfect strangers to them, who emerged nobody knew whence, to question them upon the trial within. On returning home from the sittings, the people who had got in by ticket were sure to find some acquaintance or friend waiting for them, who had been unable to gain admittance, but who was, as a rule, much more anxious than the privileged ones to know about the case.

From husband to wife, from friend to friend, the sensational news spread over the town with surprising rapidity. Though the newspaper accounts were exceedingly meagre, and often distorted, all those who felt any interest in the matter were tolerably well informed as to what was going on. The sympathy of the general public was as usual with the weaker. The daily and hourly reports of the behaviour of the two parties were certainly calculated to strengthen these sympathies. The town was in a fever of excitement. The contagion spread even to those usually indifferent to politics. Alarmed by the symptoms of a growing ferment, which might possibly culminate in "disturbances," the governor of the province privately ordered the presiding judge and the imperial prosecutor to hasten matters, and to bring on the final act speedily. Formalities were hurried through, the proceedings pushed on post haste. The comedy grew rapidly towards its tragic end.

It was known in town that the sentence would be pronounced on Thursday, the fifth day of the trial. The excitement of the public, especially a certain section of it, was such that the authorities took measures against a possible outbreak. The interior of the court was crammed with soldiers and police. A battalion of infantry and two squadrons of Cossacks were kept under arms in the yard of the Patent Office close by. The police patrols were doubled.

But the number of those who now thronged the place had quadrupled. In the evening, after the closing of the factories, crowds of workmen joined them. The police were not strong enough to keep these back without recourse to firearms. These they did not wish to use so soon.

In the court itself the appearance of the public had considerably changed within these five days. By dint of entreating and pestering their high-class friends and relatives, as well as by occasionally bribing some warder, many of those whom it was particularly intended to keep out had succeeded in gaining admittance. Both prisoners and judges, when they looked at the audience, were surprised to see that it was no longer so uniformly "respectable" as at first. By the side of tchinovniks,— some fat, some lean, all clean shaven (as officers in the civil service),—and amongst decorated colonels and generals, representing the unimpeachably loyal element, one might discover people whose aspect was more neutral, and here and there a sprinkling of individuals, both men and women, whose loyalty was in all probability of the wrong colour.

In the second row of chairs, the wife of the president of the Board of Control—an undoubtedly loyal lady—was displaying a new rustling silk gown, her showy jewellery, and her own chubby beaming face. She was dreadfully afraid of these Nihilists, and only came because she was told by a friend that it would be so awfully interesting. Her great fear was that the women prisoners might scream and fall into hysterics, which would shock her very delicate nerves. But at this good lady's elbow one might see a girl, in whom, by the bold and serious expression of her face, it was easy to recognise a Nihilist, though she wore her hair long, and had on a tolerably fine blue silk dress—borrowed for the occasion. In the back rows one could discover unmistakable Nihilist faces, students and short-haired unconventionally-dressed girls. The curly head and lovely agitated face of Varia Voinova was conspicuous among them. She had obtained her ticket from the wife of one of the prison officials. To prevail upon the timid lady, she had promised that in case of detection she would say that she had spirited it away from the table during a visit.

The bench retired at eleven at night to decide in their quality of judges and jury upon the question both of guilt and punishment.

They did not return until half-past two in the morning. But very few of the public thought of leaving. The verdict had to be given at any price. They knew that their expectations would not be disappointed, and the longer they waited the less was their inclination to leave. The tribunal might return at any moment,—and the public waited and waited. The time dragged slowly on. The hall, crammed to its full capacity, was suffocating, as the windows were carefully closed to prevent any possible communication between the public within and the crowd outside. This added to the general exhaustion and weariness. In the grey dull light of the approaching morning the court-room looked strangely oppressive. Six candles, in silver candlesticks, glimmering upon the judges' table, gave it a lugubrious, funereal aspect. The closely packed people were almost silent. Few cared to discuss the probable issue of the debates which were evidently going on in the consultation room.

From the prisoners' box a hum of suppressed voices came, uninterruptedly audible throughout the hushed assembly. The prisoners knew that after the sentence was read they would be separated, and not allowed to see each other until the day of execution. They tried to profit by the short time they were to be together. Judging by their unbroken rapid talk they were in good spirits, and not in the least broken down by the fate they anticipated. But the public could not see any of them, as they sat all six upon wooden benches, surrounded by twelve gendarmes with their drawn swords on their shoulders.

The crowd outside the building, which the sleepy and exhausted policemen now left to take care of itself, was neither so patient nor so calm. They were excited by their victory over the police, and, moreover, represented the most turbulent section of the population. The Nihilist, or, to speak more exactly, the liberal and advanced elements, were in strong force. As a part of the loiterers, tired by the long waiting, withdrew, these were brought into closer contact, and began to form in the front an almost compact body. Many happened to be acquainted, and they talked, giving vent to their feelings freely, thereby showing clearly that they were not yet conspirators.

A handkerchief was raised at one of the windows.

"The verdict!" shouted a voice in the crowd. Instantly all noise ceased, and the crowd pressed towards the windows with upturned faces.

Within, the voice of the usher was announcing the last scene of the shameless farce. The tribunal was about to enter to read the sentence.

Rising to their feet as one man, the people stood in breathless expectation. A silence as of death fell upon the many-headed crowd. One could almost hear the beating of so many hearts,—some in agony of fear for those near to them, some in the excitement of the dramatic tension of the moment.

One by one the six members of the tribunal appeared upon the platform, behind the long green table lit by the six lugubrious candles. Their appearance was not exactly what might be expected in judges administering justice. Their troubled worn-out looks were suggestive rather of a great villainy just committed, with full knowledge, than of a stern though painful duty fulfilled. The six prisoners who faced them were certainly the calmer and more dignified of the two groups. They also rose from their seats when the tribunal was announced, and now stood in full view of the public. But at first few looked at them. All eyes were riveted upon the presiding judge, who, a white sheet of paper in his hands, was about to utter the fatal words.

In a voice raised to an unusually high pitch he read the preamble, which seemed to last an eternity. At last the first words of the sentence were uttered, sending an electric thrill throughout the audience. The name of Boris came first, followed by a long mumbling to which nobody paid attention,—

it was the enumeration of his offences. Then a short pause, and
the sentence—death ! Though no one expected him to be
spared, the word fell upon strained nerves like the blow of a
hammer. Vasily's name followed, with a mumbling less irk-
some, for it was shorter, and then another blow of the hammer
—death ! The nerves shiver, but hold good. The third in the
roll is Zina, whose fate had been the most discussed, because
the most uncertain. The silence seemed to have deepened.
Life or death ? life or death ? all asked in their hearts, whilst
the long mumbling went on. Offences are heaped upon
offences. The threatening hammer rises higher and higher,
then a short suspense, and again it falls with a crash—death !

A sigh, gathering into a groan, ran through the hall. All,
even the most prejudiced, turned their eyes with unmixed
sympathy and awe upon that young, noble, beautiful woman,
standing so calmly and modestly in front of her companions.
Most had expected that, as a woman, she would be spared.
The sentence was a tremendous shock; but there was a sense
of relief in the assembly,—the worst was over. The three
remaining prisoners were so little compromised, or were rather
not compromised at all, they would be let off with a nominal
punishment.

The mumbling affixed to Botcharov's name, which came
next, was such as to lull the inattentive audience to complete
tranquillity. The list was composed of such trifling offences.
Most people ceased to listen altogether, when suddenly a suspicious quivering in the judge's voice, a short pause, and the
sentence—death !—resounded amidst universal stupefaction.
A wondering "ha !" escaped from all lips. Men looked at
their neighbours to ascertain whether they had not misheard
the word.

"Many thanks, gentlemen judges !" the voice of the condemned man resounds sneeringly.

No ; there was no mistake. He was condemned to die.
But what for? How? The intense curiosity to hear what
would follow kept as yet the people's indignant protest within
bounds.

The judge had not the courage to call the prisoner to
order, and pretended not to hear the interruption, glad that it
was not something worse, and he hastened on to the following
name. It was that of the elder Dudorov. This time the
public followed with strained attention all the circumlocutions

and windings of the clumsy summing-up of offences. The
mumbling seemed interminable. It was all about trifles again.
Impossible that the extreme penalty should be inflicted. But
the public was on its guard now. There was the same
treacherous prolixity, and abstruseness in the statement of
motives. Some phrases sounded ugly,—doubts, alternated
with hopes, irritating men's nerves to the extremity. The
hammer was hanging in the air,—now rising, now sinking, and
then rising again. Then the blow was struck at last, it was—
death !

The suppressed passion burst forth on a sudden. Shrieks,
hysterical cries of women, groans, and curses, filled the air.
People jump upon their seats, shouting and gesticulating wildly,
as if they had gone mad on a sudden. It was a scene of disorder such as had never been witnessed within those walls.

The good lady in the second row—the wife of the chairman of the Board of Control—fainted from her own excitement, without waiting for the female prisoners to scream. The
officer commanding the escort, who was personally acquainted
with her, rushed to her with a decanter of water. But the girl
in blue silk who sat next her suddenly barred his way.

"Don't touch her !" she cried in his face, stretching her
hand over the reclining body of the lady.

And such was the intensity of execration in her voice, her
gesture, and flashing eyes, that the gallant young man fell back,
and retreated like a beaten dog ; whilst the girl took a glass of
water from the council table, and gave the senseless woman
sisterly help. She saw her for the first time, and did not even
know her name. But she supposed her to be a sympathiser
and friend (as she was perhaps at the moment when she fainted),
and this was sufficient. She must protect her from the hateful
touch of a gendarme.

Upon the bench the disorder and confusion were hardly
less than among the public.

The presiding judge, the paleness of shame in his face,
strove to face the storm. He failed completely, but he did not
order the court to be cleared. He wished, on the contrary,
that the public should remain and listen to the end of his
paper, which trembled in his hand. The sixth of the prisoners,
the younger of the sisters Dudorov, in consideration of her
youth, was condemned—not to death, as the prosecutor had
asked—but to fifteen years' penal servitude. They had offered

this sop to their slavish consciences, and they wished their act of courage to be made known. But in the general uproar nobody could catch one word of what was read. A young man —the same who had waved the handkerchief—opened the window, and, leaning out, shouted to the people in the street,—

"To death! All sentenced to death!"

He affirmed afterwards that he had heard this distinctly read by the presiding judge, though he certainly could not have done so.

A threatening yell was heard in answer from the crowd below, adding to the consternation in the court. Some among the representatives of the "loyal" elements thought that the crowd was about to storm the place, and that they would be massacred wholesale. In a fit of panic they began to shriek and yell on their own account. The police officer appointed to watch outside rushed to the judge. They confabulated for a moment, and the policeman ran out by the back way. The president had ordered troops to be called out, and the street to be cleared at any price. The judges slipped out of sight, hiding themselves in the inner rooms, whilst the policemen began to clear the hall.

A bloody encounter seemed imminent. But it did not take place. The extreme section—the organised body of revolutionists—were not favourable to provoking a fight with the police. They were all under the direct or indirect influence of the men who formed part of Andrey's conspiracy. Now the conspirators had every reason to avoid any armed encounter, which would only imperil the more serious work of rescue.

The manifestation was quite spontaneous, made chiefly by outsiders, acting under the impulse of the moment. It was good so far as it went, but not further.

Restraining influences coming from the more extreme to the more moderate never fail to produce their effect. When a squadron of Cossacks, followed by infantry, appeared at the end of the street, the crowd dispersed, with nothing worse than much noise and a few stones thrown at the soldiers.

CHAPTER III.

THE carrying out of the death sentence in Russia is rarely deferred for more than for a few days. Two days after the verdict,—that is, on the Saturday,—the papers announced that the governor-general had commuted the death penalty for the elder Dudorov into twelve years' hard labour, and reduced to six years the term of penal servitude for her younger sister. This was a very liberal reduction, and excited the most sanguine hopes among a large section of the public, always glad to dismiss an unpleasant idea on the first plausible pretext. It was confidentially expected that the other four would be dealt with as mercifully, though nothing was settled yet as to their fate. The governor hesitated, or probably waited for instructions from St Petersburg. He was said, however, personally to be in favour of leniency. Words to this effect were reported by people who either said they had heard them themselves, or got them from "most trustworthy sources."

As to Andrey and his fellow-conspirators, they did not share in these illusions, because they had authentic information about everything that went on in the enemy's camp.

They knew that the governor had settled nothing as yet, so that the words attributed to him were either fiction or deliberate lies. There could be no hope for Vasily or Boris. But it was possible that Zina or Botcharov, or perhaps both, would have their sentence commuted,—Zina as a woman, Botcharov because innocent of any real offence. The only charge against him was that he had advanced money for the revolution. But nothing could be said for certain as to their fate. All depended on the mood for the moment of the St Petersburg authorities.

The work of conspiracy became distressingly difficult under these circumstances. Any imprudence that might lead to its discovery would be fatal. All four prisoners would be executed by way of retaliation. The concentration of the direction of affairs in the hands of one man proved a great help in this case; the danger of many meetings and consultations was avoided. But even for one man it was difficult to act boldly and energetically under such depressing apprehensions.

Only seven men were in the secret of the plot up to the present moment, although the number of people considered necessary for carrying it into effect was about seven times seven. It was certainly impossible to attempt anything against the armed escort with a small number, notwithstanding the virtue of their extraordinary missiles. The main body of the conspirators had to be recruited a day or two before the time of action. This was the safest means of keeping the secret of an enterprise that required so many accomplices. The seven men forming the backbone of the plot were chosen out of those revolutionists of the town who had the largest connections in the brotherhood. They had to keep an eye upon from five to ten men each, to whom they could make the offer of joining the conspiracy with little chance of refusal and no danger of betrayal. It rested with Andrey to give the signal for the formation of this body.

This plan combined caution with speed. But as the time advanced, it seemed to Andrey more and more urgent to make a choice, sacrificing either caution or speed for the sake of the other.

Saturday and Sunday brought nothing new. On Monday the rumour spread through the town that a batch of ordinary offenders had been seen digging under escort in the Push-karsky field. It was there that the gallows would be erected. But for how many was it intended? It was far too large to be meant for one. For two—three—or for all four? The town was again agitated with rumours, this time of the gloomiest nature. The same people who three days before had spoken with confidence of a respite, now asserted the very opposite.

Andrey knew that these rumours were as baseless as their predecessors. The governor kept his own counsel, speaking to nobody about the affair. But the delay was in itself suspicious. Political offenders have been executed almost by stealth within a few hours of the signing of the sentence, to avoid any possible agitation of the public mind. Suppose that the governor intended to do this now? Between the fear of having no time to get ready for action, and the danger of having their secret divulged by setting the plot on foot too early, it was difficult to choose.

Andrey resolved to stick to his earlier plan, and to wait until the last. He had been fortunate enough to establish, through the medium of a girl, a cousin of the Stutterer, excellent communications with the very headquarters of the enemy. He would know all about the impending execution within two hours after the orders issued from the governor's study. Thus, if the worst came to the worst, he would still have seven or eight hours available. All the fifty men could not be assembled on so short a notice, but they would have thirty or forty for certain. It was better to run the risk of having smaller numbers, than of giving warning to the police. It was unlikely, however, that the governor would be so forgetful to keep up the appearance of dignity as to order a very hasty execution.

Andrey never left his room for a minute, as the girl he expected might come at any time.

On the night between Monday and Tuesday, Andrey was sleeping with the light uncertain sleep of expectation, when a slight knock at the window made him start up wide awake.

He opened the window, and, looking out, saw in the shadow of the wall the dark form of a woman, too small for Xenia, the girl whom he expected.

" Who are you? " Andrey asked, in a whisper.

" I am Xenia Dmitrievna's maid. She could not come herself, and she sends this letter," whispered the voice from below.

" Give it me !" Andrey exclaimed, stretching out his hand.

" I don't know you," the girl said, stepping back ; " I am ordered to deliver the message into Alexander Ilitch's own hands."

Andrey turned to wake Vatajko, but he was already at the window. He exchanged greetings with the girl, whom probably he had seen before, for Andrey noticed a smile of recognition upon the face below. Then a white envelope glistened rapidly in the faint light as it passed from hand to hand. The girl departed, as if seized with sudden fear, without giving time for thanks.

A small night-light was burning in the corner of their bedroom. In times of exceptional danger, when the police might intrude at any moment, Andrey was wont always to have a light burning at night. With the precious and awful message in his hand, he sat down upon the floor beside the light, bending over it so that the glimmer might fall upon the sheet, and ran his eyes over the following words, traced in pencil :—

"The sentence confirmed by the governor for all four. Execution fixed for Wednesday next, at ten in the morning, at Pushkarsky field."

It was signed "X." That meant Xenia.

For a moment he remained sitting on the floor, collecting his thoughts. The news struck him more than he cared to confess. He had entertained no hope as to Boris or Vasily. But Zina, Botcharov—Botcharov especially.

It is only just and fair that good and benevolent people should pity most the innocent victims of Russian despotism. The revolutionists themselves, who hold their own views upon the question of "guilt" and "innocence" in these matters, also pity most their innocent companions, for these are the truly unfortunate among them. They have done nothing, and they are not prepared beforehand to meet their hard fate. They die with regret, perhaps with remorse, that they have been too cautious, too slow in the past, and all to no purpose. This Botcharov was no longer a stranger to Andrey, who had learned to appreciate and to love him during the trial, in which the gallant and ready-witted young man had played so brilliant a part. Through all these days of anxiety perhaps nobody's fate weighed on him so much as Botcharov's. And now he was to be hanged, and Zina also.

"Read it aloud !" Vatajko urged.

Andrey rose, and handed the letter to him. He could not read it himself, and he absolutely did not hear the exclamation which escaped from his friend. This brutal cynical insult threw him into one of those fits of rage, when the resentment and indignation of a civilised man change into the unbridled fury of the primitive savage. The wild, the unreasoning thirst for revenge, for returning pain for pain, outweighed everything else within him. Pale of face, his teeth clenched, he trampled rapidly up and down the small room, as a hungry animal paces up and down its cage.

Vatajko sat on the bed, his back bent, the letter still in his hand, following his friend with his eyes.

"Well," Andrey said, regaining mastery over himself; "perhaps it'll turn out for our good. Our men will fight better, and strike without sparing. Now I must go to head-quarters."

Vatajko had at once to make the round of their fellow-conspirators in order to summon them to an early meeting.

"As soon as it is day," Andrey said, "you will go to the Stutterer and tell him to be ready with the bombs and everything for the afternoon. At six you will go with a car to fetch them, and carry them—you know where."

"Yes, I know."

"Good-bye, then. I must be off at once."

It was about four in the morning when Andrey came out into the street. He had thirty hours before him, quite enough to do everything thoroughly and without haste ; but he wished the first meeting of his fellow-conspirators to take place before the news of the confirmation of the sentence was made public.

Quickening his pace, he reached headquarters in half-an-hour. He entered with the help of a latch-key, unnoticed, unheard. All in the house were asleep. His companions would not begin to assemble for an hour yet. Whilst waiting for them, he made his own preparations.

With a map of the town before him, he traced the road which the procession must take. Thanks to the practical knowledge of the town he possessed, he could easily and at once choose the best place for action. He fixed his mind upon a short street, between two turnings of the road, not very far from the place of execution. It might be thickly crowded on account of its position, but this disadvantage was compensated by an exceptionally good retreat,—first, through a series of narrow lanes, where the troops could be easily kept back by bombs ; second, through the public garden, which stood on the bank of the river. In the garden, the high iron gates could be closed, and locked with two or three big locks that it would be easy to buy during the day. Moreover, some torpedoes, which the Stutterer had invented, and which he recommended very highly, could be placed there to impede yet more the pursuing troops.

The conspirators had a boat, already fitted up, for it was intended from the first to make use of the river. Now the boat could be moved to the wharf of the garden, and could take on board the four rescued prisoners, and such as were wounded. The rest of the assailants were to issue from the farthest end of the garden, protected by the bushes, and mix

quietly with the crowd waiting for the execution in the Push-
karsky field.

Andrey's colleagues flocked in rapidly from various sides.
At a quarter to six all seven were there, and a small council
of war was held.   It was very short.

"You have heard?" Andrey asked them as they came in.

"We have heard," they answered, and they plunged at
once into the matter.

Andrey laid down in a few words his plan, which was approved without discussion.   He was told the place and time
of the three meetings at which the rest of the recruits were to
be assembled.   It was decided beforehand that they should
have several small meetings instead of one big one.   Andrey
had to come, if only for a short time, to each of these three
meetings.   This was thought useful, and was not difficult to
manage.

All was settled in little more than half-an-hour, and the
seven men started to their different quarters.

In the meantime the news, which had awaked the conspirators, had been quietly set up by the compositors, and was
about to be offered to the peaceful citizens of Dubravnik as a
morning greeting.

Few were the readers whose heart did not ache at the
announcement that four persons, of whom one was a woman,
were to be executed.   Russians are not accustomed to capital
punishment.   The penalty of death has been abolished for more
than a century for all except political offences.   Long terms of
penal servitude are considered a sufficient punishment for all
other crimes, however heinous.   This distinction the public
conscience has never been able to endorse.   No amount of
persuasion will induce the simple unsophisticated people to
believe that political offenders, whoever they be, are worse than
murderers or incendiaries, or highway robbers.   The educated
and thinking people felt only pity, indignation, or rage, according to their individual temperaments and opinions.

The chosen men were certainly not among the lukewarm.
Most of them had received their summons, and had given their
promise to come for the discussion of public business of importance, before they had read in the papers the news of the
impending execution.   But after reading it, all guessed and
hoped that this was to be the object of the mysterious meeting
to which they were called.   When they were told that every-

thing was already prepared, and when they heard the outlines of the plan and the name of the man who was to be their leader, there was everywhere a unanimous adhesion, everywhere confidence in success. Andrey appeared at the three meetings, with all his usual coolness of head, and with the fierce indignation of that especial day. In his present mood he was exactly the man for the occasion.

On returning to his headquarters from the last of them, Andrey had a very pleasant surprise. David had been waiting for him there for some time. He was on the other side of the frontier, on an errand of his, when a letter from St Petersburg informed him of what was going on in Dubravnik. He left immediately for Mother Russia, travelling day and night, and reached Dubravnik just in the nick of time.

"I came to put myself under your orders, Andrey," he said. "You'll give me something to do, I suppose."

"As much as you like, old boy," was the cheerful reply.

Andrey had improved greatly since the morning. Contact with his new comrades had cheered him. He was satisfied with the men whom he had to lead in the morrow's fight, at least as thoroughly as they were satisfied with him.

"We may fairly hope to carry the day," he said to David. "With missiles like ours fifty men can do much, if they're determined to fight in earnest. And they are determined, take my word for it. You'll see some samples presently. We have our last council of war here at seven, to get everything in order."

At the appointed time the men began to come, one by one. David knew some of them, and was introduced to the others as their new companion.

The council was brighter, noisier, and more thorough-going than that held in the morning. The work of organisation, which then they had contemplated as possible, was now actually carried out. Like Andrey, all felt that it could not have been managed better. They were hopeful, and they did not regard the danger which they had to encounter for so good a cause.

The business was entered upon as soon as all were assembled. Discussion there was none; the time was too precious. But many were the suggestions given by all, which Andrey either accepted at once or rejected, giving his decision as final, and not to be questioned. The general plan was very simple. To-morrow, at seven in the morning, Andrey with ten men would be on the spot to secure the position beforehand. The other forty were to keep out of sight at several places in the neighbourhood. He would send them word to come up in batches as the crowd of spectators gathered in the street. It would be dangerous to have all of them crowded together at one point, if the rest of the road was thinly occupied. In case the crowd should be dense, they would have to place themselves in front of it, in two half platoons facing each other. This was to prevent their being overthrown and scattered by the rush of panic-stricken people. The crowd would then run away behind, without interfering with them.

If, on the other hand, the place was thinly occupied, the conspirators would have to be scattered about. In that case, Andrey with his ten men would form a sort of vanguard, to stop the procession, and give time for the rest to rush up from all points. All this, and many other things, could be settled at the decisive moment.

"Now," said Andrey, looking at his watch, "it's time to go for our arms."

It was half-past seven. The bombs must have been brought by this time from the Stutterer's house by Vatajko. They had to be taken by the seven men and carried to places of safety, so that they might be distributed to their people early on the morrow. It was considered dangerous to let the fifty conspirators have the missiles by themselves during the night. Haphazard domiciliary visits might be made by the police on the eve of the execution. A bomb discovered somewhere by chance, would put them on their guard at once.

The more usual arms, such as revolvers, could be distributed at once.

The council ended, and the men rose to depart. They had to meet next day on the battle-field.

From what Andrey remembered of classical history, he knew that it is the duty of captains on similar occasions to address his companions. But he was not a man of many words, and he was afraid that it would appear foolish if he began exhorting these men.

"Until to-morrow, then!" he said simply, as he exchanged a hearty shake of the hand with each of them.

The first party was about to leave, when David called Andrey's attention to a suspicious-looking individual hanging about their house.

"I have seen him for the last ten minutes," David said,

He seems to pay particular attention to our windows, although he tries not to show it."

Andrey looked into the street.

"Oh, it's a friend!" he said, reassuringly, recognising a menial clerk of the police, who for a small fee kept him well informed upon all he could learn in his official capacity.

"The man is looking for a signal in the windows that the coast is clear, and that he may come to see Vatajko or me."

He asked his friends not to go yet. The clerk's communication might be of interest to all of them.

"Don't come near the windows," he admonished some of the curious. "The man is very timid, and may be easily scared away."

The windows were deserted, and Andrey was able to have his few minutes' talk with the clerk undisturbed.

When he returned, his face was far from calm, though he looked much more angry than troubled.

"The police have already got wind of our affair," he said sternly. "Some one has blabbed. It's disgraceful!"

"How? what? Impossible! Are you sure of what you say?" were the simultaneous outcries of protest.

"There is no doubt. The man told me, that shortly before the closing of the offices a police inspector rushed in, asking for the head of the police. Five minutes later, they both went hurriedly to the governor. They were much excited, and talked in a subdued voice as they passed the office. The clerk affirms positively that he heard the words 'dynamite bombs' muttered. Invent or dream them he could not, for he had no idea of our plans himself. The story tells its own tale, I suppose."

The assembly was dumbfounded. The fact was there, undeniable, unmistakable, yet past all comprehension. Conspirators are not always discreet, as they should be. Some of the newly enlisted men might have talked to a sister, a sweetheart, or an intimate friend. This was within human possibilities. That is why the majority had to be enlisted at the last moment. But the secret could not have been spread so far in that way. Only downright treason could account for so rapid a discovery.

The same offensive, degrading thought was to be read in the eyes of all the seven, as they looked in each other's faces.

Hurriedly the seven heads were put together. Hasty questions were passed, and answered in whispers,—questions too shocking to be said aloud, especially in presence of Andrey and David, who were for the moment two "strangers."

"No, it was impossible. They had asked no one but reliable people!" all of the seven protested energetically, vouching for their men. "The police, in hourly expectation of some plot, had probably got frightened by some phantom of their own imagining. The real facts could not have leaked out; the incident would have no ill consequences, because the error must needs be soon discovered, and the suspicions would be allayed."

A loud ring of the bell at the entrance, accompanied by a peremptory knock at the door, relieved Andrey from the necessity of answering. He only ironically nodded his head at the door, and drew his revolver.

All understood the signal, and drew their arms also, resolved to sell their lives dearly. David alone, though an "illegal" man, was unarmed. But he did not want to be behind the rest, and he took a beautiful bright American "five-shooter" from a friend who was very fond of firearms, and had a spare one with him.

With his back against the wall, his big revolver in his right hand, Andrey gloomily unbolted the door with his left.

When it was flung open, the friends within heard—not a shot, but an angry exclamation from Andrey.

"What the deuce! Why couldn't you announce yourself in a more sensible fashion?"

"I was in such a hurry," Vatajko apologised, for it was he.

"The bombs are already delivered, I suppose?" Andrey asked, relenting.

"No," Vatajko answered; "the bombs could not be delivered."

"How! not delivered yet? What have you been doing all this time, then?" Andrey flew at him again.

They were in the room, with the eight other men looking at them anxiously.

"A great misfortune!" Vatajko burst forth. "The Stutterer is wounded; perhaps dead by this time. There was an explosion in his room about mid-day. As we passed the house with our hand-cart, we saw that all the windows in his floor were blown out, some completely torn away. It must have been something terrible!"

"But the bombs? How about the bombs?" Andrey asked. "Have you been in the house?"

"No, we haven't been in. We saw the police inspector enter it at that very moment. Men, whom I took for detectives, were busy in the courtyard. We could see that the house was invested by the police."

That was bad indeed; terribly bad!

"What did you do then?" Andrey asked. "Have you ascertained whether this was the case?"

"Yes. We passed on, and then I left the cart in charge of the other fellow, and returned to the house from the river side. The gardener's daughter was working in the orchard; I went up and spoke to her. She told me that there had been an explosion, that the Stutterer was lying unconscious upstairs, and that the police were in the house. I told her not to tell any one that she had spoken to me, and hid myself in some bushes behind the palings. Through a chink I could see the gates and a part of the courtyard. I saw two prison carriages come in. Immediately the Stutterer was carried out upon a litter, and locked up into one of them. Then the men brought from the house, with the utmost caution, various things, which they put in the second carriage. Some big boxes first, then a lot of jars, and then the bombs, which they carried out one by one, the police inspector keeping at a distance.

"I did not wait any longer, but hastened here to tell you everything. There was nothing to wait for."

He ended, amidst a general silence.

Yes, there was nothing more to wait for, nothing to hope for any longer! Andrey knew it too well. Had they but been in possession of the missiles, he would have defied everything and attempted the rescue on the morrow, no matter if the enemy were forewarned. But now all was at an end, everything had collapsed! In fourteen hours, Zina, Boris, Botcharov, and Vasily would be hanged. There was no chance for one of them. And they were so hopeful, so certain, that their march to the scaffold would be their march to freedom. . . . He pressed his forehead against his clenched fist in an agony of despair. It would have been better that nothing had ever been tried, than to have such hopes wrecked at the last moment.

Nobody was inclined to break the silence. It was one of these moments when everybody congratulates himself that he is not the leader, and that not upon him devolves the duty of finding some issue out of the pathless maze.

"What's to be done now?" David asked Andrey, giving utterance to what each of those present was thinking.

As Andrey raised his head, he saw all eyes fixed upon him with the same question. This surprised him greatly.

"What's to be done!" he exclaimed. "Don't you see that the one thing we can do for our condemned friends now, is to warn them that no hope is left, so that they may have some time to prepare themselves for meeting their fate!"

A groan sounded through the room. The advice seemed so strange and unexpected from Andrey. Through their very reliance upon him some of them were slow in coming to a conclusion. The decision to which Andrey had been hurried, within the last few moments, was a surprise to them.

Objection and protest were raised, and grew louder and louder. They urged that the attempt must be made, even without the bombs. They were fifty men, resolved to fight to the last. There was still time to increase their number, and to find arms for as many, or perhaps more. Why should they give up everything?

Vatajko was among the most ardent partisans of fight-at-any-price, dwelling on the shame of withdrawal, with all the bluntness of expression common to Russians on similar occasions. To Andrey's surprise, David seemed to approve of the same line of conduct. But it was useless; he had quite made up his mind. What could a handful of men, armed with daggers and revolvers, do against rifles and serried lines of bayonets, especially now that the authorities were forewarned? It would be a wholesale and useless slaughter, that would dishearten the people, instead of inspiring them as a good example.

"Then you need not take part in it!" Vatajko exclaimed, losing all self-control. "If you refuse, we'll go by ourselves. But we will not look on with folded hands while a woman is hanged!"

Andrey was at this moment as incapable of reproving the breach of discipline as of feeling personal offence.

"My friend," he said, putting his hand on Vatajko's shoulder, "why do you want to sadden the last moments of our condemned friends? We can't possibly rescue any of them; we shall be all slaughtered before their eyes. Why should we aggravate with such a sight a trial in itself hard enough?"

The young man bowed his head, and was silent. Nobody spoke again. The meeting dispersed mournfully, to undo what they had done; and Andrey hastened to fulfil his last duty to his friends, to let them know everything, that they might have no vain hope. They must go to meet their fate, with eyes open as became people such as they.

He took the letter to the prison warder who carried his correspondence for him. He learned afterwards that his letter reached its destination that very evening. It was even answered by Zina, in the name of her companions. Her letter was not a sad one; if anything, it was rather cheerful. But the reading of it tore Andrey's heart, and made him, the man of iron nerve, cry like a child, because, delayed in transmission, it reached him two days after all was over, and the hand that wrote those touching lines was cold and stiff, and the heart that inspired them had ceased to beat.

CHAPTER IV.

ANDREY awoke with a start, as if some one had given him a thrust in the side. At the same moment the bell at the neighbouring belfry was striking the hour. He looked at his watch, which lay upon the stool by his bedside with his revolver and dagger. It was five o'clock. Then he understood. On the previous day, whilst still in the full swing of preparations for the coming fight, he had fixed in his mind that he must wake up at five, to be on the spot in time. Andrey possessed that power of waking up at will at a fixed hour. He had not thought of it, and now he woke up mechanically, though there was no longer anything to be in a hurry about.

The night before, he had come home late, thoroughly exhausted by the ungrateful task of preventing any mad outburst of the hot-headed,—a task he was unwilling to shift entirely to his companion's shoulders. But the few hours of rest did not restore him, because even in sleep a dim sense of the reality never altogether left him. He woke with the full consciousness of what the coming day would bring with it.

Vatajko slept in the same room, with the happy soundness of twenty. Andrey thought of waking him before going out, but on second thoughts he abstained. The young man's good-natured hairy face looked so calm and contented in sleep, it was a pity to call him before it was necessary to the miseries of reality.

Andrey dressed, and forced himself to eat a crust of bread. Then he left the room noiselessly and went downstairs.

The sun had by this time already risen, though hidden by a thin mist which covered the sky and promised rain. The town was still asleep; the shutters were closed everywhere. Dustmen, woodcarriers, night cabmen, returning to their inns, broke the silence of the empty streets. Here and there a porter was sweeping the footpath before a house. The passengers were few, and for the most part hurried along. But among them Andrey met several men with slow walk, haggard eyes, and sad worn faces, whom he guessed at once to be his fellow-sufferers,—friends or acquaintances of the condemned, or more probably simple sympathisers, whom that night of agony had driven, like him, from their roofs into the open air. To judge by appearances, they must have wandered long, perhaps all through the gloomy night, trying to wear out by bodily fatigue their mental distress.

Without any thought or distinct feeling, save a dull gnawing pain, Andrey walked whither his feet carried him, until he found himself unexpectedly at a place he well remembered. He stopped to look round. The street was flanked by two rows of tall white houses. A slanting lane opened into it on his left, and down it could be seen the projecting corner of another street. The public garden was farther on. This was the place where they had intended to strike their blow. He came to it he knew not how. Yesterday he had been there, full of hope, to verify with his own eyes the details of the map before he led his men to the fight.

That was only a few hours ago, but now it all seemed no more than a vague and distant dream. Yet it was not a dream, but a thing within the reach of their hands, if ever anything was.

He sat down on a curbstone, thinking despondently. How different would have been his feelings here and now but for an unfortunate accident! What could have been the cause of that explosion which ruined everything? Accident or imprudence? Probably imprudence. The man had grown accustomed to deal with his precious stuff as if it were nothing more than dough. In the haste of the last hours he had probably been more heedless than ever. But Andrey could not think harshly of the Stutterer at this moment. He was too sad to feel anything but pity towards him. Poor man! he wished him dead. It must be so horrible for him to know he was the involuntary cause of such a tremendous collapse. Yet he might have the ill fortune to survive, and then he would be hanged a month hence. Victims! victims! no end of them. The scoundrels have not time to kill off one batch, before another is filled up from among the best, the noblest.

At this juncture a pair of the "scoundrels" of whom he was thinking appeared at some distance patrolling the street. One was an officer, another an underling of the police service. Both were insignificant, utterly despicable, samples of their species. But what did it matter? They were two of that species still, and they were within reach of his hand. As he saw them approach, a wild hunger for revenge set his blood boiling. All the reckless words and proposals of his hot-headed friends of the Vatajko type, which he had so vigorously rejected the night before, seemed to have been merely stored up, and were repeated now in his mind with the self-same tones and words that he had heard yesterday. But this time they were convincing. The holster of his revolver moved forward of itself; the handle of his dagger pressed caressingly the palm of his hand. A well-combined plan of assault achieved itself instantly in his head, without his will taking any part. Fortunately his reason was as yet not altogether swamped. He jumped up from the curbstone, and, without turning his head, went away swiftly, fearing that he might yield to the foolish temptation when the men were within arm's length.

No, he had presumed too much upon his nerves. If the sight of these two poor wretches excited him to such a degree, what would it be when he saw the execution? He would certainly betray himself in some way. Better not go at all than risk that. And what for? He would have an opportunity of seeing closely enough the details of at least one execution—his own to wit, when his turn came. But he was certainly not prepared voluntarily to lose a single one of the days allotted for his share of the struggle.

He resolved to walk, and walk without stopping, until the time fixed for the execution had passed, and then to return to headquarters.

He plunged into a maze of small streets leading to the centre of the town, intending to cross straight through it. But the more he advanced, the more his movements were impeded by the crowds of people moving in the opposite direction. The streets were blocked with them. There were hundreds, thousands, walking, riding, running towards the same point, hurrying to secure the best places.

Were they thinking of what they were about to stare at? Did any of them understand it? With whom were they in sympathy? With those to be killed, or with those who were to kill them? Nothing could be guessed from these wooden faces, which kept their secret well, if they had one to keep.

Would they wear that mask to the last, or presently drop it, showing love or hatred—anything human—behind it?

The wooden faces, the jackets, the coats,—long and short, blue, grey, black,—the women's gowns and men's hats, grew thicker and thicker. They now blocked the way altogether with a compact mass, through which one had to force a passage by dint of hard elbowing. What for? Was there anything he wanted to reach beyond? Andrey ceased to struggle. His face also became wooden, as by contagion; and he abandoned himself to the hurrying stream of human beings, taking automatically the direction in which he was carried by it. They walked tolerably quickly at first, then more slowly and slowly. How long the time was Andrey could not tell. He only knew that it was very long. Now and then they had to stop, the passage being impeded by other crowds moving in from other streets. As the people were pressed closer together, the buzz of their voices became louder. Andrey heard the talking, wooden as the faces, jarring upon his ears with its flatness and vulgarity. But for his life he could not have remembered a single word he heard.

Then there was a longer pause, as that of many streams converging upon the one narrow entrance into a broad sea. When the obstruction ceased, and the crowd hurried forward again, Andrey found himself suddenly free in an open square, and he shuddered from head to foot. High before him, against the clear sky, rose four black gallows,—angular, motionless, horrible! He looked instinctively at his neighbours right and left: the extremes of mirth and the extremes of horror must be shared with fellow-men. All eyes were fixed on the same black angular things, and the wooden faces wore now an expression of fear and consternation. The crowd pressed onwards nevertheless, and Andrey with it.

The four black gallows stood upon a black platform with a black balustrade, and black steps in the middle by which the condemned would ascend to the platform. Andrey could see from his place the ropes and the blocks and the rings. The ropes oscillated slowly, slowly, in the air, and seemed as heavy as if they were about to break away from the cross-beams. A merry-looking square-built man, with a small flaxen beard, dressed in a red shirt and velvet Russian coat, his hat set dashingly on one side, walked up and down the black platform. This was the hangman, waiting to get to work. At the foot of the black steps was a motley group of men in military uniforms, with serious faces. Several of them were on horseback. All this—the black platform, and the group of figures and the horsemen—was clasped in on all sides by a thick ring of infantry, their bayonets glistening in their hands. Death alone could pass these walls of flesh and iron, cold and hard as stone. At some distance from that first living wall stood another, formed of squadrons of cavalry. They were not very far from the spectators, so that their faces could be seen, and it would be hard to determine which looked more indifferent, the horses, or the men upon them. Another space, narrower than the former, was kept clear behind the horses' haunches; and then came a thin line of policemen on foot, to keep the crowd from intruding upon it.

Fresh torrents of people continually poured forth upon the square, occupying every corner of ground left for their use, all staring in patient expectation at the high black platform on which the monster they all so dreaded—death—was to burst forth in person,—awful, yet for them innocuous,—and begin its ghastly dance, on which they would look horror-stricken and fascinated, as monkeys are by the eyes of a serpent.

It was not for this disgraceful show that Andrey had come. He wanted to see for the last time the faces of his friends, perhaps to exchange a look of silent farewell with them. Through the double row of soldiers between them it was impossible to obtain that in this position.

He extricated himself from the throng, and passing before a line of mounted gendarmes, who watched the crowd from behind, he made his way to the street by which the condemned would enter the square. Two rows of police kept the middle clear for the passage of the car and the escort, but the footpaths were so completely blocked by spectators that it was impossible to find room there. Andrey made a short circuit, coming out on the street farther on, where it was not thronged so densely.

He took his stand and waited. The spectators here were genuine representatives of the " masses," all others having presumably secured better places. It was interesting to observe them. The people seemed to have been waiting here for a long while, for they had time to become acquainted with one another, and to get tired of the long wait. They seemed to have entirely forgotten the object which called them from their homes. Andrey listened attentively, trying to catch what they were talking about. Very few spoke of anything connected with the coming execution.

An old woman who stood in front of him scolded a girl for having forgotten to put the porridge in the oven before she left, an omission which meant a row when the men came home to dinner. A tall slim lad, with sloping shoulders, and long neck clasped closely by a chintz shirt, was biting off the husks of sunflower seed with an air of perfect content, caring only as it seemed about spitting the husks as far as possible towards the middle of the street. A buxom young woman, a baby on her bosom, pushed herself to the front beyond the prescribed line. The young policeman standing on duty near came to remind her of this trespass, making some coarse joke on the trouble she would have in getting another baby if the one she now had was trampled to death by the horses. The woman retorted sharply, and the crowd laughed good-humouredly. But at Andrey's back a voice was now raised, continuing some discussion, evidently upon politics.

"Oh, no! Not against the Tzar. Gentlemen against gentlemen, I tell you. Nobody can lift his hand against the Tzar, because no weapon can touch him."

Andrey turned his head. The speaker was a middle-aged man, in the blue national overcoat, probably a small shopkeeper. His companion, who looked like a sexton or an undertaker's assistant, answered something in a low voice, which Andrey could not catch.

Upon his right a genuine peasant, in a grey overcoat, with a thin sunburnt face and small grizzly beard on a protruding chin, was also talking politics to another peasant, though these "politics" were somewhat of a curious nature.

"So they laid hold on the four ; those who will be executed to-day. But the fifth, who was their chief, was not caught, because he transformed himself into a yellow cat, and escaped up the chimney. But he returned always in the shape of a cat to visit the old place. Then they caught him for good, and now the bishop is reading from the holy books over him, to break the spell and compel him to resume the shape of a man again."

"Really !" the other exclaimed, wonderingly.

"Of course. People say it was in all the newspapers."

Andrey remembered then that the " penny-a-liners " of the press had made much fuss about Zina's yellow cat, found in her lodging mewing for food the day after the arrest. Of the whole catastrophe, it was this incident that struck most the popular fancy, and gave rise to the curious tale.

At this moment an indistinct murmur ran all along the crowd, which swayed and rustled like the underwood of a forest shaken by a gust of wind.

"They are coming! they are coming!" whispered thousands of voices.

Instantly all talk was interrupted in the middle of a word. In the dead silence a distant rumble of drums was heard.

An orderly galloped along the road towards the place of execution. A detachment of Cossacks followed at a trot on their spirited horses. The people looked at them as they passed, but not one head turned to follow them. They waited, all eyes fixed in the same direction, with the same expression of awe and expectation. The solemn procession they looked for appeared at last, sending a nervous tremor through the crowd, which at this moment formed but one body.

Upon the white background of the sky, Andrey saw a waving line of black glistening helmets surmounted by a cluster of lances, through which he discerned four vague outlines resembling human heads and shoulders. These outlines, and the steel-tipped lances swaying above the black waving line of helmets, seemed to form one body with the living mass below, advancing slowly, slowly as a tortoise.

As they came nearer, he could see the car, the horses, the driver, and the driver's face, but the faces of the four human figures towering above them all he could not see. At last he discerned why.

They are turned backwards, each sitting on a high stool, the shoulders tied to it by large strips of black leather. They are dressed all in something grey, formless, clumsy, so that they all looked alike, as if they were wrapped in blankets. Nearer they come, formless as before, but he sees the colour of their hair, and recognises the dark-brown of Vasily, the lighter hair of Boris, and the flaxen of Botcharov. But he still cannot make out that the fourth figure on Boris's right hand is Zina. With the short abundant flaxen curls on her uncovered head, which the wind played with, she looked like a young boy.

"They have cut her hair to hang her more easily," Andrey guessed at last.

A bird—whether a dove, or a raven, or a buzzard, he could

not see—flew over the heads of the condemned. It must have seen the faces of these four towering figures, and also the four black angular things that stood awaiting them not far off upon the black platform, and, as if stricken with panic, it flew away as swiftly as its strong wings could carry it. How he envied this creature, which could fly far, far from this sinful bloodstained earth! Even had he wings, he could not move from the spot now. Horror has its attractive power, like beauty. Shivering as in a fit of fever, his heart beating violently, his eyes did not so much as wink, lest he should lose the one instant when he might exchange glances with them. Yet he dreaded that moment, foreseeing that something awful might come out of it. He would have run away, if his feet had not been nailed to the ground, as his eyes were to the four towering figures.

Boris made a twist on his seat, straining with his strong shoulders the straps which held him, and turned his face towards the crowd on his left. Andrey, who saw him in profile, guessed by the movement of his lips that he was shouting something to the people below. He had tried to do this several times on the way. But the roll of the drums became so deafening, that not a word could be heard. He gave up the attempt, throwing himself angrily back. Another few turns of the wheels, and Andrey saw all of them in full face.

They sat close to each other, resting their feet upon the same board. Boris looked angry and defiant,—a valiant champion, overcome by numbers, chained, but unsubdued to the last. Vasily was speaking to Botcharov, who was last in the line, saying evidently something cheering, for a faint smile appeared upon the young man's lips. On that commanding eminence Vasily's features lost their roughness. Calm, self-possessed, grave, he appeared to Andrey a different man from the one he had known before.

But upon a platform of any kind it is the woman that reigns over the crowd. The eyes of the multitude were fixed upon that one face next to Boris. Beautiful as woman ever was, her head encircled by her hair as by a halo, her face bashfully blushing under the gaze of so many eyes, she cast a kind pitying look over the people below, who at this moment had but one feeling for her. She was looking for somebody there. In her farewell letter, which Andrey had not yet received at this time, she had said that all of them would be glad if one of their friends would take his stand in some conspicuous place on the way to the scaffold, so that they might see each other. She expected that Andrey would come, and was seeking him in the crowd. She discovered him at once. There he stood, directly under her feet, with head raised towards her. Their eyes met.

Neither then nor afterwards could Andrey understand how it came to pass, but in that moment everything was changed in him, as if in that kind pitying look there was some spell. Anxieties and fears, nay, even indignation, regrets, revenge— all were forgotten, submerged by something thrilling, vehement, undescribable. It was more than enthusiasm, more than readiness to bear everything. It was a positive thirst for martyrdom —a feeling he always deprecated in others, and never suspected himself to possess—which burst forth within him now. To be there, among them, upon that black car of infamy, his shoulders fastened to the wood like those of that woman, bending her radiant brow above the crowd,—this was not punishment, this was not horror, it was the fulfilment of an ardent desire, of a dream of supreme happiness ! Forgetting the place, the crowd, the dangers, everything,—conscious only of an irresistible impulse,—he made a step forward, stretching both his hands towards her. He did not cry aloud words which would have ruined him irrevocably, only because his voice forsook him ; or perhaps his words were lost in the noise of the drums, as his movement was in the rush of the crowd which closed in on both sides, swelling the enormous following of the advancing procession.

When he could see anything through the mist that suffused his eyes, there was some kind of disorder or scuffle in the middle of the road. A man had been seized by two policemen, who were dragging him to the nearest station, holding him under the armpits, as the deacons hold the bishop when leading him into the church. To his considerable surprise, Andrey recognised in the arrested man the same peasant who had been talking all the stuff about the yellow cat and the exorcism. The man, impressed in his own way by the sight of the condemned, had knelt as they passed, and bowed to the ground, reciting some kind of prayer on their behalf.

The car, and the crowd which followed it, had already passed along. Andrey had no desire to follow them. What for? He had got his message from them. What more could he wish for? He stood watching as the car and the crowd disappeared behind a corner, leaving the street almost empty. Then he went away quietly. He crossed the suburb, which was a desert, and passed the eastern gates, hardly noticing that he was walking for some time upon an unpaved road bordered by open fields and orchards. He was absorbed in his thoughts, but no longer stunned, for he could now think connectedly. His meditations were exceedingly sad, it is true, but in quite another way and for other reasons than those of the morning.

Thin bushes stretched before him. A little farther on was a leafless grove, through which the grey sky gleamed. The form of the branches and the stems showed them to be oak trees. Andrey turned his head to look at the town, and recognised that this was the same grove where, six months ago, they had their picnic with the sisters Dudorov. His walk had now an object; he wished to see the place again, as one may wish to pay a visit to the cemetery where one's family lies buried.

He found the place. Here was the tree under which Vulitch sang. Here the spot where the fire was lit, Vasily stirring the porridge, Botcharov and the two Dudorovs sitting round. How full of hope, of energy, of devotion, they were then—and what was the upshot of it all !

The place was barren and dreary under the dull leaden sky. The very trees, lifting to heaven their black knotty branches like contorted hands, seemed aching and in pain. But a ray of sunlight broke through the cloud, and the whole scene was transfigured. Fresh buds, not seen before, appeared all over the branches, harbingers of new life to come. The tender new grass under the trees and over the vast expanse of fields below, the white town yonder—all smiled cheerfully in return to the smile of heaven.

How out of place and out of harmony this joyfulness seemed now to Andrey. But on a sudden his heart ached and beat violently, and something contracted his throat convulsively. It flashed upon him, not as a supposition, but as a firm, unshakable conviction, that just now all must be over there—on the black platform. He sank down upon a mound of earth, covering his eyes. But immediately he rose again. Such griefs as this are sacred trust. They must be stored up in the depth of heart and memory, and kept there whole,—not to be idly wasted by outpouring.

He went rapidly back to the town, almost running, not to

be alone. Face to face with men indifferent, perhaps hostile, he would show nothing,—he was certain of that.

The town resumed its usual aspect. The life suspended for a brief while hastened to flow back into its ordinary channels. The suburb was empty still; the crowd, ebbing back, had not yet reached' it. But a little farther on he met its vanguard, and then more and more folk. They had had their fill of breathless horror and feverish shivering, and of that stunned amazement and sadness which follows upon such sights. All this was left behind. Now they talked loudly, and moved briskly, as soldiers disbanded after a long drill, at which they have been forcibly kept silent.

The show was over, and the spectators hastened home. How many of the crowd were bringing back any idea or feeling to be remembered for life? and how many nothing more than a better appetite for the coming dinner?

At the headquarters a certain number of revolutionists had assembled spontaneously. But the women were conspicuous by their absence. Many of the men did not appear until late in the evening. Among those present Andrey saw George—the last man he would have expected to meet that day.

The St Petersburg section had learned of the explosion in the Stutterer's house, and of the subsequent discoveries made by the Dubravnik police, a little earlier than Andrey himself, for the news had been immediately telegraphed to the central police office, and thence secretly conveyed to them. They learned at the same time that Andrey's presence in Dubravnik was no longer a secret, and that a number of spies, knowing him by sight, were on the point of being sent to hunt him down. Alarmed by the imminent danger to Andrey, Tania easily persuaded George to start immediately for Dubravnik with the news, so as to gain upon a letter half a day, and one full day at least upon the spies who were coming to chase him.

But George was in no hurry to speak to Andrey of his errand, and Andrey did not care to ask what brought him. They shook hands hurriedly, George making a little room on the sofa where he was crouching. Andrey sat down by his side, and both listened.

It was "the Uncle"—a middle-aged gentleman, with clean shaven face—who engrossed the attention of his companions. In consideration of the post he filled in the civil service, he had the right of admission to the black platform, and he had availed himself of this privilege in order that the condemned should see one friendly face at least among their enemies. He had witnessed the whole proceeding, and he related it now in an even, hollow voice, and a simple matter-of-fact way, without a digression, or one word of comment.

Two men stood near the speaker. The rest, six or seven in number, were scattered over the room, sitting upon stools and sofas or in the window seats, stiffened in various attitudes, and not moving or looking at each other. All listened. Nobody asked questions, nobody made remarks.

When the final act drew near, Andrey felt that George was shaken throughout with a nervous shiver. He pressed his arm strongly, and drew it down to bid him keep quiet, and not interrupt the narration with any outburst. George mastered himself, and listened to the ghastly details of wanton brutality to the end. But here his nerves got the better of him. He burst into hysterics.

Andrey seized him by the shoulder, shaking him violently.

"You whining woman!" he said, furiously. "It's with blood, not with tears, that such things must be answered."

A great and terrible idea took shape in his mind in that moment. But he gave no utterance to it. It must be thought over and over again before it was spoken. For there are words which it is a crime to throw upon the wind, and a shame to retreat from when once uttered.

George calmed himself after a while, and they joined the circle of friends talking together. Nothing was heard but vehement appeals for prompt revenge. The governor-general, the imperial prosecutor, the head of the gendarmes, were put forward as "candidates" upon whose heads the blow had to fall.

Andrey alone said nothing. It would not be bad, all this, he thought, but is the game worth the candle? What is the use of these petty attempts against officials, big or little, who are all and each menials and dependants, with no will, no power of their own? The odious edifice of despotism will not be so much as shaken. The government can always return ten blows for one, and the revolution will be simply transformed into a private contest between police and conspirators. If the blow is to tell, it must be aimed higher,—at the man who is the keystone, and the head of the system.

He listened indifferently to the excited talk, which had lost all interest for him, and soon, taking George by the arm, he withdrew.

They went for a long stroll, so as to be quite alone. George told his errand, insisting, on his side, that Andrey should start that very night for St Petersburg. Thus he would escape the net spread for him. Andrey acceded to this advice. There was nothing to detain him in Dubravnik any longer.

They spent the day in the city, and had a long talk together. George had time to recover from the nervous shock caused him by the "Uncle's" account of the execution. Now it was he that was the firmer of the two.

"We need not be dispirited at defeats," he said, with his usual faith. "Our victory depends upon our capacity for bearing defeat after defeat."

"Possibly," said Andrey, "but in that case we must aim our blows, so that our very defeats should make an epoch."

"What do you mean?" George asked, his quick eye catching something peculiar in Andrey's face.

"You will know in time," Andrey said evasively, unwilling to be more explicit.

CHAPTER V

THE FAREWELL LETTER.

WHEN they returned, they found Vatajko waiting for them anxiously. David was there, more wearied and downcast than Andrey had ever seen him.

"What a pity you did not come earlier!" were the first words of Vatajko to the newcomers. "Uncle has been here to see you, Andrey."

"What for?"

"There is a letter for you from Zina, about which he wanted to speak."

"A letter from Zina!" Andrey exclaimed. "Where is it? Hasn't he left it in your hands?"

"No. He could not get hold of it without a word from you. That is why he came. The gaoler was at the tavern as usual with the letter. But you did not come."

This was true; Andrey had thought there was nothing more to come for.

"Then I will go and see the man myself at once," he said, anxious to make amends.

"It is too late," Vatajko replied. "You have barely time to catch your train."

"Confound the train! I'll see the man to-morrow, if I can't to-night."

They prevailed upon him, however, to meet the man in some popular tea-room. This was safer than paying him a visit at his house.

Early next morning Vatajko went to the gaoler's house, in order to arrange a meeting at mid-day. He returned without having been able to arrange anything. The man was on duty in the prison, and would not be back till late at night.

"He hasn't taken Zina's letter with him to the prison, I presume," Andrey said. "Could not his wife give it you?"

"I asked her," Vatajko answered. "But she said that he

keeps these letters secreted in some hiding-place, which she herself does not know."

This was vexatious in the extreme. It meant the delay of another day at least,—a delay longer than Andrey could possibly afford, if he wanted to avoid the spies.

"Then I'll go and see him in the prison," he said, amidst a general stupefaction. ·

"In the prison ! Are you in your senses?" Vatajko exclaimed.

"Why not," said Andrey. "To-day the politicals are allowed their weekly visits. I will go to Varia's lodgings, and will accompany her in her regular visit to the sisters Dudorov."

"But you will be recognised and arrested on the spot!" George exclaimed.

"No fear of that," said Andrey. "Who on earth will ever dream of looking for me in the reception-room of a prison? It only seems to be dangerous. Besides," he added in a calm, absent tone, "I should have gone all the same even if it was really dangerous. I must get that letter before I start."

The thing had to be done. That message from his dead friends had for him more than a sentimental interest. He had an unshaken belief that it contained something that would give him some clue to the issue from his present intolerable perplexity, and he was resolved to see it at all costs.

David was silent. He was troubled in mind and hesitating, for he seemed as anxious as Andrey to see Zina's letter. But he joined with George in dissuading Andrey from wantonly risking himself within the lion's jaws. He offered to remain a couple of days more in Dubravnik and take the letter with him to St Petersburg.

But Andrey could not be brought to listen to reason. During these last days he had lived in an atmosphere saturated with death and all sorts of horrors, so that his perception of danger was quite benumbed.

"There's no need to make such a fuss !" he said impatiently. "I will go myself, and shall be back in time to catch the train. We will meet there."

Without waiting for further objection Andrey left hurriedly to catch Varia at home.

The political prisoners were allowed visitors between two and four in the afternoon. It was about half-past one when Andrey, with a bag containing food and a few books from a

lending library in his hand, approached the grim square building, connected with so many of his recollections.   Varia
Voinova walked by his side.   She knew how simple were the
proceedings in connection with the visiting of prisoners, and she
acceded readily enough to Andrey's request.   It seemed to
her such good fun.   But as she came within sight of that awful
building, a few hundred paces from the massive iron gate, by
which stood an armed sentinel, she was seized with a sudden
fear and remorse.   Once within, would her companion ever be
free to come out again?

"Listen, Kojukhov," she said.   "Give me the bag, and go
home.   I fear that your joke will end badly."

Andrey raised his sunken head, as one suddenly awakened.

"What must be, must be "—he quoted absently a fatalistic
Russian saying.

In fact he was not thinking at all of what might await him,
and paid no attention to the young woman's warning.   The
idea preying upon his mind as he caught sight of the prison
gate was that two days ago from that same gate his four dead
friends had passed on their way to the scaffold.

The sentinel unbolted and opened the wicket at their
approach.   He bolted it again noisily as soon as they had
crossed the high threshold.   Andrey was within the lion's
jaws.

Upon hearing himself thus secured, he felt for a moment
the surprise and helplessness of a man suddenly thrown into a
dungeon.   He looked and listened.   A subdued hum of
voices was heard, but all around was complete darkness.   The
scanty light penetrated only through the chinks in the two
massive gates closing both ends of the arched passage in which
they stood.   The prison was a quadrilateral building, enclosing
a small courtyard.   The passage that led to it served also as a
kind of waiting-room for visitors on reception days.

When Andrey's eyes had grown accustomed to the semi-
obscurity, he saw a crowd of people—men, women, and here
and there children, huddled together behind iron railings on
both sides of the narrow passage.   The majority of them were
visitors for the common offenders.   But in a corner on the
right side of the entrance one could see a group of people—
men and women, whose dress showed them to belong to the
"privileged" classes.   They were distinguished too from the
rest of the visitors by the abundance of flowers and the parcels

of books that many held in their hands. Those were the visitors for the "politicals."

Varia made her way towards them, followed at some distance by Andrey. The habitual surroundings and familiar faces had completely restored her equanimity. She forgot to think of the dangers of a place where she was herself quite at home. All the visitors were her acquaintances and friends. They shook hands, asking questions and exchanging news. A pale-faced dark lady holding by the hand a boy of ten detained Varia a little longer than the rest. She had a big nosegay in her basket.

"What beautiful flowers you have brought," Varia said. "Give me some for my prisoners. I have not brought them any to-day."

The lady handed her all the flowers, which Varia untied, taking unceremoniously half of them. Of this she kept one part for herself and gave the other to a tall grey-haired gentleman standing a few paces off.

"Take these for your daughter," she said. "There is nothing prisoners like so much as flowers."

Then she went to an aged peasant woman, in a plain village dress, her head wrapped in a brown chintz kerchief.

"Has your son any money to his account?" she asked.

"Yes, little mother, he has two roubles left," the woman answered.

"That is too little for a month," Varia said. "I will bring you another couple of roubles for him next Sunday."

She took from her pocket a worn, rather thick, note-book, in which she wrote down something. In her quality of revolutionary sister of charity, she had the control of the prison fund, and took care that all the prisoners, rich and poor, should have their share of money, books, linen, and the like.

"Who is that lady with the child?" Andrey asked, when she came to him again.

"The wife of Palizin, the judge," Varia answered. "He is to be transported to the Siberian mines. She will follow him. It will be hard upon the poor soul, for she is leaving the boy with her relations."

Varia told him about the other visitors without waiting to be asked. The old gentleman was a merchant of the town, and came to take leave of his youngest daughter, who was to follow her two elder sisters to Eastern Siberia. The peasant woman was the mother of a promising self-taught young scholar. Others were men and women of all classes and stations whom the community of grief had united.

The clattering of the chains and bolts at the inner gate interrupted them. The gate was flung open, lighting up the arched passage for a brief space. The opening was filled up again by the huge prison van that rolled in. It was a batch of common offenders, who were leaving the prison.

The inner gate was closed again, and carefully locked. The outer was then opened. The van moved on and was gone, and the arched passage was plunged once again into gloom.

They waited in silence. Now and then at the door leading to the offices a guard appeared, shouting the names of those who were to be visited.

"Have we long to wait?" Andrey asked his guide.

"No," she said. "The forgers have already had their interview; that of the thieves and burglars will be soon over. We follow next on the list," she added, with a smile.

The outer wicket slammed once again, admitting an old man in the worn-out greatcoat of an official. He looked round disconcertedly, blinking his small eyes, and trying to recover his breath. Apparently he had hurried, so as to be in time. As he took off his hat to wipe, with a pocket handkerchief, his forehead and bald skull, his face appeared to Andrey not altogether unknown.

"Ah, here is Mikael Evgrafich at last!" Varia broke off.

A stout police inspector appeared at the office door, at the bottom of the recess behind the railing.

"Visitors for the politicals!" he shouted.

Varia ascended the few stone steps leading to the office door, and was by his side directly.

"Mikael Evgrafich," she addressed the officer, whom she knew familiarly, "here is the brother of the Dudorovs, whom I have brought with me. He came from Moscow on purpose, and goes back to-morrow. He had no time to get a permit, but I am sure——"

The officer threw a scrutinising glance at the pretended brother, who came forward and bowed politely.

"Write his name down in the office," he said, turning to Varia. "But don't let this occur again. You know the rules."

The old bald-headed gentleman had also approached in

the meantime. On hearing the name of Dudorov he gave a
start, and bestowed a look of the utmost surprise upon the
young man who was said to be the brother of the two prisoners.
He uttered a wondering " 'hm !" but apparently made up his
mind to keep his own counsel.

"I beg your pardon, sir," he said, calmly enough, to the
officer, "but I also came on purpose to see the Dudorovs. I
am Timothy Dudorov, their uncle."

"I can't grant you an interview," the officer said peremptorily. "There are already two persons to visit the prisoners."

"But I have a special permit, and they are my nieces.
Since you admit strangers," the old man said, throwing a sus
picious glance at Andrey.

"Impossible. Come some other day," the official said,
without listening to him.

He gave in a loud voice some orders to his underlings, and
turned back into the office. But the old man would not hold
his peace. He was quite exasperated at the want of respect
shown to him.

"It is unheard of! I will lodge a complaint with the
director himself!" he exclaimed, angrily, moving towards the
office.

Varia's blood ran cold. She foresaw a catastrophe. Rushing to the troublesome old man, she caught him by the hand.

"What are you doing!" she whispered, drawing him aside.
"He is Masha's sweetheart. They love each other to distraction. He wants to marry her as soon as her fate is made
known. He comes to-day on purpose to settle the matter with
her. You will ruin their prospects of happiness if you make a
scandal. Just keep quiet. I will arrange everything for you."

"Oh, I understand!" the old man said, complacently.
"You ought to have told me that at once."

Varia slipped into the office to fulfil her promise, and the
old man went to shake hands with his future relative.

"I know your secret, young man, and wish you joy and
happiness," he began, but checked himself suddenly, staring at
the young man.

Andrey lifted his eyes at him, wondering what he meant,
and stared too. They recognised each other. The old man
was Andrey's fellow-traveller on the journey to St Petersburg.

"I think we have met somewhere," the old man lisped out,
in a faltering voice.

His anger and his complacency were all gone on a sudden. He remembered what he had said in that railway carriage, and was seized with a fright that paralysed all his faculties.

"Perhaps," Andrey said discreetly, "but I cannot exactly remember on what occasion."

The old gentleman did not choose to refresh his memory. But he felt at once very friendly towards the young man, whom he had no reason any longer to fear.

"I will not stand in your way as to seeing Masha," he said. "You will carry her my greetings, if I cannot manage to see her. We old people must give a chance to the young."

He went on in his garrulous fashion talking about the girls, praising both of them, Masha in particular, and expatiating on his great wonder when he learned that they were entangled in these conspiracies.

"It is an epidemic, sir, a real epidemic," he repeated.

Varia found them talking friendly to each other. She had arranged everything to their mutual satisfaction. The two sisters would be summoned separately. The old man would see his younger niece. She and Andrey would see the elder afterwards.

In a few minutes old Dudorov was summoned. He was in the first batch of visitors. A quarter of an hour later he returned, apparently very much satisfied with himself. On passing them he whispered to Andrey, confidentially:

"I dropped a word about your coming! Masha will be glad to hear of it beforehand."

Other batches of visitors to the politicals were admitted,— fathers, mothers, wives. They went in file by file, hurrying and expectant, carrying their parcels and flowers. When they returned, there were no flowers in their hands, and no light on their faces. The short dive into the gloomy pit seemed to have bereft them of both. Some of them were quite shaken, though they did their best to keep a brave countenance. They passed one by one, like so many ghosts, into the twilight of the arched vestibule. To Andrey the spectacle was depressing in the extreme. Not very sensitive as a rule, his nerves, shaken by the events of the last days, had acquired a peculiar subtlety. He read the silent tragedies hidden behind these faces as if they were written on them, and it seemed to him that in all his life he had not seen so much suffering as in the short two hours he spent in the prison vestibule.

Their turn came at last. The name of Maria Dudorov was shouted among those of the last batch of the prisoners who were to be visited.

"Come!" Varia said to him.

She led him rapidly through dark corridors, where they rubbed elbows with several people going in the opposite direction, whose faces they could not see. They were ushered into a very lofty bright place, more like a corridor than a room. All along, on both sides of the entrance, ran what looked like two enormous cupboards, in which the glass panels were replaced by thick wire grating. A little examination showed that these partitions were double. Behind each of them, three or four yards away, was another quite similar, and a guard walked up and down in the space between. At the end of the room sat two other guards, looking very sleepy. They had to watch the visitors.

"But where are the prisoners?" Andrey asked, seeing none.

"They will be brought in directly. We had to be secured first," Varia answered.

The chief guard rose and said that all who had brought anything for the prisoners must give it to the guard on duty.

Andrey took the parcel from Varia and went to the wicket, behind which stood the guard who was on duty. It was their friend, the very man whom Andrey wanted so much to see. He allowed the other visitors to get through their business first, and then pushed through the wicket his own rather large parcel.

"For the sisters Dudorov," he said aloud.

Whilst the guard approached, throwing on the bearer a lazy, indifferent glance, Andrey whispered :

"I must have the letter to-day. Tell me where you keep it."

The man seemed to have heard nothing. He opened the parcel slowly, examining, one by one, everything it contained.

"In the back room, under the old box," he said, without raising his eyes from the roast fowl he was cutting in four to see that no letter was hidden in its flesh.

Varia was already talking with Masha Dudorov, who was leaning against the grating on the other side of the passage, her face looking like a pale patch under her thick iron veil.

"Then it was you that are my sweetheart!" she exclaimed, merrily, when he came to her. "I was quite at a loss to guess what it meant when Katia brought me the message from uncle. How did you like the old fellow?"

"I have already met him once," Andrey answered. "But how are you? How is your sister?"

The girl said they were both well, and expecting to be sent to Siberia without much delay. She even knew to which mine they would be sent.

Andrey had several friends there, to whom he asked her to carry his greetings.

They spoke in a hushed voice, not to be heard outside, but they were in no way restrained in their talking, as the guard, their friend, pretended not to hear.

The girl promised to fulfil faithfully Andrey's errand. In her turn she sent him, from behind the gratings, her warm wish that he might be free for long, and be able to do more than they had done.

"I will do my best!" Andrey answered, earnestly.

The unusual conversation caught the ear of Masha's neighbour, the prisoner who was having his interview on her left. They exchanged a few words in a whisper.

"My neighbour, Palizin, wants to make your acquaintance, Andrey," the girl said.

The short energetic man, of about forty, with a square chin and a square head, was really the well-known conspirator, formerly a justice, Palizin. Andrey might have guessed it earlier from the fact of his wife standing with her boy against his compartment.

It was a strange mode of making acquaintance, yet Andrey was glad of the opportunity. He said how sorry he was that they could not meet on this side of the grating.

"Never mind. Who knows that we shall not meet there some day!" the plucky man said, with a bold toss of his head. "The prison walls are high, but a hawk soars higher. At all events, that chap of mine will soon step into my shoes," he said, pointing to his boy, who blushed.

Here their conversation was unexpectedly interrupted by a loud shouting of "Andrey! Andrey!" which filled all the room.

The cry awakened the two somnolent guards. All the visitors turned their heads in the direction of the voice, Andrey with wonder and curiosity, Varia with undisguised terror.

One of the prisoners opposite was beckoning with his hand energetically. Andrey crossed the room and approached the compartment.

"Mitia! Is it possible? you here!"

He had recognised a fellow-student and old friend of his,—the last person whom he expected to see in this place.

The guard intervened.

"Go to your place, sir," he said, rudely. "It is forbidden to visitors to speak to prisoners with whom no interview has been granted."

"Very well," Andrey said, politely. But he showed no hurry to withdraw.

"The third year! On suspicion!" the young man poured forth in the meantime. "Consumptive! Surgeon says I have only one-eighth of my lungs to breathe with!" he shouted at the top of his voice, triumphantly, as if he was quite delighted at communicating this extraordinary achievement.

A violent cough interrupted him. At the same time the signal for the closing of the interview was given, and the prisoners were led out. The visitors followed in their turn, Andrey and Varia keeping in the rear.

In the vestibule there was an unusual movement.

"What is the matter?" Varia asked, somewhat alarmed.

"A new political prisoner is being brought in!" Palizina told her.

In fact, two gendarmes were seen in the passage, one of them opening the gate, another keeping back the public.

Meeting the common guards, or being seen by them, was of no particular danger to Andrey, because none of them, except the one who was his friend, knew his face. With the gendarmes it was very different; he had the best reason in the world to keep out of their way as much as he could. But he was under the illusion that now the visit was over he was out of any danger, and he was so upset by what he had just seen, that he forgot common precaution in the anxiety to know who the new victim might be,—perhaps an acquaintance, perhaps a friend.

He pushed himself forward and stood on the footpath, his back to the railing, a few paces from the gate, waiting for the van to come. He did not wait in vain. When the van rolled in, the light falling full on its door, he saw through the small grated window the gaunt, ghastly pale face of the Stutterer! After having been kept for three days in a hospital, he was now considered sufficiently recovered from his wounds to be removed to the prison.

In the pain and absorption of that discovery, Andrey did

not notice that he was himself an object of rather attentive contemplation on the part of a red-whiskered gendarme, who was walking behind the van. Having looked at him several times, the man now squeezed himself between the railing and the van, anxious to share his startling surmises with somebody who was in the front.

In a minute he returned with another gendarme, who seemed his superior. But Andrey was nowhere to be seen. Without waiting for Varia, he had slipped out of the gate, and hastened alone to the guard's lodgings, where the precious letter was deposited. He was too much depressed to wish for anybody's company.

The sentinel, who had been staring at the van like all the rest, had not seen him pass. When the sergeant came to inquire if any one had left the vestibule, the man was ready to swear that nobody had gone out for the last five minutes.

CHAPTER VI.

LITTLE accustomed to the hard lot of a practical revolutionist, George spent two very unpleasant hours, whilst waiting for the return of his friend. He questioned Vatajko how matters stood with Andrey, in the secret hope that he would give him some encouragement. But the young man's answers, on the contrary, were such as to render George more and more uneasy.

"We were wrong in allowing him to go," George said, with tardy regret.

"Never mind," Vatajko observed calmly. "Andrey has been in worse predicaments than this."

The young man had already a little practical training, and was accustomed to regard all these dangers with a good deal of equanimity.

"What you say may be true," George replied. "But a man who has escaped great dangers may be lost in a small one."

Vatajko admitted it willingly, quoting, for better illustration, several striking examples from his own and his friends' experience.

He was not a very entertaining companion for a man uneasy in mind.

George felt himself hardly dealt with, and very unhappy. He was exceedingly dissatisfied at not having interfered, and began to reproach and torment himself bitterly for his lack of firmness—as was his wont on all similar occasions. He was prone to exaggerate his influence over Andrey, and now he persuaded himself that had he insisted energetically he would have induced him to leave the matter in David's hands, instead of wantonly risking himself in the wolf's den.

It was a happy moment for George when Andrey came back punctually at the time he had fixed.

The St Petersburg train started at half-past nine. There was no time to lose.

"We can go to the station at once," Andrey said. "The luggage is packed, I suppose?"

It was not. Absorbed in his brooding on what had been, and ought to have been, George had forgotten the immediate present. Fortunately, their preparations were not long in making. They had just sufficient luggage to have the appearance of ordinary travellers. They were soon ready, and on their way to the station. As Andrey was in a precarious position, precautions were taken. Vatajko went before them in a cab alone, carrying with him all their luggage—the two small trunks and a travelling bag. He had to take their tickets, secure places in the carriage, and then meet them in the street. They were to enter the station a few minutes before the train started, and go straight to the carriage, so that they might be exposed to view as little as possible.

Andrey and George followed Vatajko, at ten minutes' interval, alighting at a crossway not far from the station. Vatajko rejoined them much more quickly than they expected. He had taken no tickets,—for he deemed it absolutely impossible for Andrey to show himself at the station. The tracking had begun earlier than they expected—thanks to Andrey's recognition by the red-whiskered gendarme. A trap had been laid for him at the station. It was crowded with police. Two fellows in plain clothes—evidently spies who knew him—stood on either side of the entrance, looking impudently into the face of every one who came in. They would point him out to the police as soon as he entered, and he would be arrested on the spot.

Vatajko had therefore deposited the luggage in the cloak-room, and came to propose another plan for getting out of the town. They must drive to one of the nearest stations, and book there. David would go down to warn them if the coast was not clear.

"But why have you not taken a ticket for George?" Andrey asked. "He runs no risk, I presume. There's no reason why he should stop here."

This was quite true. Vatajko had not thought of that. The time was not gone, however, and George could easily catch the train if he chose.

This George peremptorily refused to do.

" We resolved to make the journey together," he said, " and I do not see why I could not book at the next station as well as you."

He was prepared to stand his ground firmly, and certainly would have, by way of compensation for his yielding on a former occasion. But Andrey did not show fight.

" Very well. Let us go together then," he said.

He was absent-minded and depressed, paying but little attention to what was going on around him. His visit to the prison and the letter had upset him, adding to the chaos which the recent reverses had brought upon him. He was still in the crisis of hesitation and uncertainty, unable to see his way clearly.

For some time the three walked along together, Vatajko explaining where they could get horses, and how they must manage to save time.

" If you don't object to making the journey on foot, that will be perhaps quicker and safer. The first station is about twenty miles off."

They approved of the idea—George especially.

" But how about our dress ? " he asked. " Gentlemen don't tramp, and to get peasants' dresses we must wait until to-morrow."

" Perhaps I can get dresses for both of you to-night," Vatajko said. " I can try the brothers Shigaev, two carpenter friends of mine."

The idea was very good, as it would permit them to leave early in the morning. Vatajko at once started on his errand.

He returned about midnight to his lodgings, where Andrey and George were spending the night, with a big bundle. He had arranged everything to mutual satisfaction.

The two brothers sent Andrey and his friend their greeting and God-speed. The bundle contained two complete peasant dresses, to which the brothers had added two linen sacks, with an assortment of various articles, such as travelling carpenters might be expected to carry. Finally, or rather above all, they had lent Andrey and George their own passports, a very effective protection against the police, in case their identity was suspected.

Andrey begged Vatajko to thank the brothers cordially for this great kindness, promising to send their passports back the day after they reached St Petersburg.

"You need not be in such a hurry," Vatajko said. "One passport, at least that of Philip, the elder brother, you can keep as long as you need. It suits you very well, and Philip does not mind getting into a bit of a scrape for your sake. He seems to have taken a fancy to you."

"How? Without ever having seen me? That sounds very romantic," Andrey said with a smile.

"No, he has seen you close, and spoken to you once. He was one of our fifty. Do you remember at one of your meetings a dark, young workman, who said that he did not want a revolver, but would come to the fight, his axe at his belt, which was much handier, and would do just as well. That was Philip Shigaev."

"Yes, I remember him well. I had only forgotten his name," Andrey said. "But we need not go on talking," he added, abruptly. "It is better for us to go to sleep at once. We have to rise early to-morrow."

He was afraid that if it went on, the conversation would turn upon the painful topics which he wished above all to avoid. What he wanted now was some rest, moral and physical, and he knew that there will be none for him once embarked upon these sad recollections.

"Until to-morrow!" he said to himself, mentally, closing his eyes with the firm resolution to sleep.

He had a vague presentiment that to-morrow everything would be clear and settled. This gave him a certain calm, and helped him to drive away his besetting thoughts.

He slept like a log. But on the morrow, whilst George was still asleep, Andrey was up wide awake. With the first gleams of consciousness, a strong conviction seized him that he had to perform some very urgent business, left unfinished the evening before. He remembered in a moment what he was thinking of before going to bed, the visit to the prison, the whole of what had happened yesterday, and all his sad experiences of the last few days.

What a mass of victims! Zina dead, Boris, Vasily, Botcharov dead also. The two Dudorovs and so many, many others buried alive, and as good as dead. He himself would be arrested one of these days, for he could not expect always to slip through the enemy's fingers, as he had until now. He too would be put to death, and who would be the better for all these hecatombs?

The vision of the crowd returning from the place of execution passed before him and sent a chill through his brain. But he shook it off.

No, that was not the upshot of his experiences and meditations! These people had not died in vain. They were the skirmishers who had perished in starting from its lair the great beast. For the survivors to grapple with it now!

The idea which, since the Uncle's tale, had been hovering over him at a distance, like a hawk making its circles above its prey, now swooped upon him, demanding immediate and final solution.

Half dressed and barefooted, he took to pacing up and down the room noiselessly, so as not to awaken George.

His idea was clearly formulated in his own mind. The struggle with the menial tools of the autocracy had had its day. An attempt against the Tzar himself must be made, and he was the man to make it.

"And Tania!" an inward voice of distress cried to him.

His heart sank, but echoed nothing in response. It received and returned the blow without bleeding, as if it had been a piece of india-rubber. In the face of the unmeasurable, unspeakable sufferings of their country from end to end, what were their own individual sufferings? It was a meanness even to weigh these against the others. Tania was his comrade, his fellow-worker in the struggle, as well as his wife. She would approve his resolution and bear courageously her share of sorrow, in an act done for the sake of their country's liberation.

It was not that which held him in suspense; if the thing was to be done, personal feelings would not for a moment stand in the way. The question which agitated him was, whether the thing itself was to be done or not.

Andrey knew that whatever his own conclusions were, they would not be final; the decision rested with the whole of the directing body of the party, who would certainly choose their course after mature deliberation. But there are cases in which the offer to do a thing is half the deed itself, and there are deeds in which the half seems as great as the whole. The gravity of the issue before him was such as would impose caution, even upon the rashest and most unscrupulous. And Andrey was neither unscrupulous nor rash.

Nothing was easier for him in his present state of mind than to answer the question in the affirmative. The failure of all his plans, the spirit of revenge, the deep and sweeping emotions of the last few days, all this was subdued for a time, but not destroyed. It lay there thundering in the depths of his heart, ready to burst forth at any moment on the surface. But he did not want to give way to these passionate impulses. He wanted to consider the matter on its own merits, without any reference to himself.

The moral justice and righteousness of the act he meditated was for him beyond all question. But would it be well timed? Would it be useful to the cause of their country's freedom? He discussed these questions again and again, laboriously, and as dispassionately as he could, with inner tremors, as those of a man walking upon an oscillating bridge, and fearing to make a false step.

The answers to which he could not help coming were— Yes, yes, and yes! The attempt would be a timely one, and useful. It would rest with the St Petersburg people to test his reasons and his arguments. As for himself, he resolved that he would make his offer.

Then came the personal question,—Why should it devolve on him, out of all the fellow-conspirators, to do that deed of retribution and self-sacrifice?

This question he was no longer able to discuss dispassionately, as if it were a geometrical problem.

That something which thundered and seethed in the depths of his soul now rushed upwards, not waiting for his decision. It flooded his whole being with fire. It made short work of hesitations, attachments, pity, as the irrupting lava burns to ashes fences, houses, smiling groves—everything in its path. He stopped short in the middle of the room. His face and eyes glowed,—gloomy, menacing, yet exalted,—as he threw both hands upwards with the same gesture he had made when he saw Zina on the day of her execution.

The decision was made, and was irrevocable. Now it could be talked about.

He awakened George, and told him on what errand he was now going to St Petersburg. George received the news with no particular enthusiasm. It seemed to sadden him rather than elate—on Tania's account more than on Andrey's, though he abstained from treading on such delicate ground. But he approved in the abstract of Andrey's arguments, and this was all that Andrey wanted from him for the moment.

They aroused Vatajko, who was sleeping in another room, and began to make their preparations for the journey. It was thought better not to leave the town earlier than eight o'clock, when the peasants would be going home after their marketing.

In the travelling sacks sent them by the brothers Shigaev, they found a provision of bread and salt, a measure, with some other light tools, and two good short-handled axes. It was Philip who sent them these favourite arms of his. Andrey and George put them in their belts. They completed their disguise, and, in case of need, might be advantageously used in self-defence. The only part of their costume not in harmony with their assumed calling was their boots. Vatajko had a pair of long shooting boots, which fitted George. As to Andrey, he had to go in his gentleman's boots, which did not quite agree with his attire. But this was too small a detail to be of any moment. They took leave of their host, and walked briskly out in the fresh morning, their sacks fastened to their shoulders.

On approaching the outer gates of the town, they saw two policemen standing at the entrance, in a lazy, expectant attitude. This was an uncommon sight. Since the abolition of the spirit monopoly, the living pillars of law and order had been removed from the gates. Two wooden pillars, painted in the official pie-bald colour, were alone left to represent authority. The presence of the two policemen had in all probability a special meaning.

As they approached nearer, this supposition became a certainty. A peasant woman, with an empty basket, in which she was now carrying her baby, passed through the gate unheeded. Two elderly men—a peasant and a citizen—were scanned from head to foot by the two policemen, but were also allowed to go their way unmolested, because the one was above fifty, and the other must have passed threescore. With a young artisan, who followed these, there was nearly a scuffle. Some question had been asked him, which he had evidently answered with impertinence, for one of the two policemen—a short-legged fellow, with a bulldog face—flew at him with raised fists. The young artisan parried the blow, and ran away, launching derisive taunts against the police, who are far from popular among our workmen.

It was not difficult for our travellers to guess on what business the two sentinels were standing there.

"We must get ready," George exclaimed, kindling with warlike spirit.

" By no means," Andrey replied.   " There will be always time for that.   Leave all to me.   We shall get through all right."

But he regretted inwardly that he had accepted George's company.   There was really no necessity to wantonly expose him to dangers, which might turn out serious after all.

They were now close to the gate.   The eyes of the two fellows were riveted upon them—upon Andrey in particular—with a mixed expression of impudence and perplexity.

" Stop ! " the short-legged policeman shouted, barring their way.

They stopped.

" Who are you, and where are you going ? " he asked.

" Carpenters, going home," was Andrey's quiet reply.

" Name ? address ? province ? time of stay in town ? " the policeman asked successively.

Andrey replied without hesitation.   He had studied his passport well.

" Why didn't you take the train ?   Everybody goes by the railway now."

" But the roads are free, I suppose," Andrey retorted sharply, thinking it good to resent this interference.

" Ah, well ! you'd better keep a civil tongue in your head. Have you a passport ? "

" Of course I have."

" Show me what is in your sack."

" Why ?   There is nothing of yours there," Andrey said, in a tone of annoyance.   " You are making us lose time to no purpose."

" Do what you are told, and look sharp," the policeman said, severely.

Andrey shrugged his shoulders, and opened the sack with a half-mocking, half-vexed air.   The policeman looked at its contents, and seemed himself to feel his stupidity in wasting thus his own time and that of other people.

" And you ? " he addressed George, in a much quieter tone.

" Semen Shigaev.   Going home also."

" Brothers ? " the policeman asked.

" Yes, half-brothers," George explained, remembering how little they resembled each other.

A batch of other people were approaching the gate in the meantime, to be examined in their turn.

"Go on," the policeman said, waving his hand helplessly.

Andrey shifted his sack on his shoulder, and was about to pass on, considering the incident well over, But here the other policeman, a lanky fellow, with a shrewd, pock-marked face, who had hitherto taken no part in the proceedings, leaned toward his choleric companion, who was evidently the chief, and whispered him a few words, pointing to Andrey's objectionable boots.

"Ha, stop!" the other shouted, stepping in front of Andrey. "You must go to the police station."

George stopped of his own accord. He did not doubt that everything was lost.

"Why to the police station?" Andrey said. "I am not drunk and my passport is all right."

"They will see that there! Our business is to stop you."

"But why?"

"That is our business."

The affair began to assume a very ugly aspect. To fight these two blockheads was easy, but it was difficult to escape on foot in broad daylight.

Whilst making a rapid survey of the place and thinking how to manage if the worst came to the worst, Andrey protested loudly against such treatment of a man with a passport, boasting of the many good employments he had had in his trade, and the number of masters who would give him the best references.

"Semen," he said to George, in the height of his virtuous indignation, "go and ask Mr Arkipov's manager to come here at once. It is not far," he explained to the policemen, and he named one of the neighbouring big streets.

His idea was to get George away. Alone he would feel much better, and would manage just as well.

The policemen seemed to offer no objection to George's going back to town ; they had no instructions for such a case. But George did not move. He understood Andrey's intention, which was very natural and correct from a "business" point of view. But he could not bring himself to go away, leaving him in such an evil plight.

"I would rather not," he said ; "Efim Gavrilich is so particular. He would not like to be disturbed for such a trifle."

It was impossible for Andrey to insist.

"Well, let us go to the police station at once then. We are in a hurry."

He wanted to leave the place before trying anything, for the gate was already crowded with passers-by, who stopped to hear the dispute.

"Wait for the patrol," the policeman curtly replied. "We cannot leave our posts for you."

"All right!"

They moved off a few paces, and sat on the ground, lighting their pipes to pass the time.

Finding nothing attractive in the spectacle, the crowd gradually dispersed. Even the policemen left off paying them much attention. But every minute the patrol might come. There was no time to lose.

Between two puffs of his pipe, George whispered,—

"Slip the blackguard a sovereign!"

Andrey nodded. He too was thinking of trying bribery first. Choosing a moment when there was nobody by, he said,—

"Listen, friend. How much will you take to let us go our way in peace?"

"How much will you give?" was the eager reply.

"I will give you this," Andrey said, impressively, showing a few coppers.

Offering, in these conditions, a big bribe would at once excite suspicions, and probably ruin everything.

"No; it is too little. We are two. Give us a rouble."

"Bah! I haven't so many roubles to throw away. Take a grivnik. I would not give so much if I was not in a hurry."

He had not, however, the necessary calmness to bargain as hard as he ought to. He increased his offer in an off-hand way, and they were free men again.

At the first village they hired a peasant's one-horse cart, and about dinner time arrived at the station. David was already there, hanging about the gates, to inform them that it was all right, no spy being visible anywhere. But this time Andrey insisted on their parting company. They entered the booking-office separately, and went to different carriages, agreeing to behave at all intermediate stations as if they were strangers. They would rejoin one another when they reached their journey's end.

CHAPTER VII.

TANIA was alone in her room, as miserable as three days' incessant mental torture could make her, when David came to tell her that Andrey had arrived safe and sound in St Petersburg, and would be with her in a couple of hours. Andrey had asked him to bring her that message, because he himself could not come straight to her on account of the disguise which he had to change.

David was surprised that Tania showed no pleasure on hearing this. The look she cast upon him was wondering, inquisitive, as if he was the bearer of a disagreeable piece of news that she tried her utmost to disbelieve.

"Who told you that?" she asked, incredulously.

"Nobody. We have travelled together all the way from Dubravnik and arrived together. I assure you that it was your Andrey in real flesh and blood, and not his ghost," David said, smiling.

It was only after this circumstantial statement that Tania awakened from a kind of torpor and gave vent to her exultation.

The fact was that she was persuaded Andrey had perished. This was merely an inference wanting positive confirmation. But she thought she had already made up her mind to it, and tried to keep off delusive hopes, so as not to break down altogether when the news of his arrest should arrive.

It is well known that the Tzar's subjects in general cannot enjoy much of the pleasure of free correspondence. As for the conspirators, they either abstain altogether from private letters, or at any rate restrict it as much as possible.

When she sent Andrey to Dubravnik, Tania could not hope to receive letters from him. But she exacted the promise that every evening he would post to her, in lieu of a letter, a copy of some newspaper, with her address written in his own hand.

This would not tell her much about him, but she would know at least that he was not arrested.

Andrey kept his promise scrupulously. Every morning at eleven Tania regularly received her copy of the *Dubravnik Leaflet*, the most stubbornly reactionary, and therefore the safest, paper Andrey could find. That paper probably gave greater joy to her than to all its few subscribers put together. The reception of this paper was the chief event of her day. She was agitated when the time for the postman's call drew near, and she was miserable if the precious parcel came in the afternoon instead of the morning.

But during the last four days she had received from Andrey nothing at all. The fatal accident at the Stutterer's house which ruined all their plans and prospects, the execution of their four friends, and all that followed, had so upset Andrey's mind, and had so completely engrossed his time, that he discontinued this mute correspondence. As he was in daily and hourly expectation of starting for St Petersburg, he did not attribute any importance to this trifling omission. Those who are in actual danger, especially if accustomed to it, have much difficulty in realising the hourly anxieties of those far away and in comparative security. Besides, Andrey knew that George intended writing to Tania, and he would certainly tell her that they were both safe.

George had, in fact, written. But his letter did not add much to Tania's peace of mind. It was written in hot haste, and George had no time to use either invisible ink or cipher. He wanted to say and explain so much,—the urgent nature of the affair which detained Andrey, their present hopes, the prospect of speedy return; and he had to do all this in the conventional roundabout language of allusions and allegories. The result was an epistle which seemed clear as daylight to himself, but was a maze of riddles to Tania, because she could not possibly know which phrase was to be taken in a direct and which in a figurative sense. After puzzling for hours over the enigmatical letter, she did not know whether something had happened which Andrey was attempting to set right before starting, or whether something had happened to Andrey himself, which his friends had fair hope of setting right,—a hope as to which she was free to hold her own opinion.

Andrey had written not a word himself, and his newspaper was wanting. She expected it with anxiety in the evening, that she might know which of the two interpretations of George's letter was the true one.   Nothing came in the evening, nor the next morning, nor in the two days that followed.   In the meantime the newspapers entered upon their hunt after sensational news from Dubravnik.   Andrey became the reporter's favourite topic.   His arrest was said to have taken place in this house and in that, in the street, and at the railway station.   The brief description of the persons arrested often coincided to a large extent with that of Andrey.   Fancy had been allowed free play, in order to supply dramatic details as to the manner of the arrest and the prisoner's conduct.   One paper announced, as from authentic sources, that the prisoner had already confessed his identity ; another, that he had been identified by overwhelming evidence ; a third, that he was already being sent under strong escort to St Petersburg.

The flood of arrests showed the fury of the chase after him. Andrey could not have multiplied himself so as to be arrested in different places at the same time.   But was it possible that he could be free and not give her a sign of his existence ? Every new telegram seemed to her more ill-omened than the former ones, and seemed of necessity true, though all the others were false.   The reading of the newspapers was real torture to her.   Yet she read them with avidity, all she could lay her hands upon.   The papers were scattered all over her room, which resembled the office of a journalist.

Three days of this anxiety told upon her as much as a serious illness.   Her face was paler and thinner, her eyes looked feverish.   At nights her fitful sleep was interrupted by frightful nightmares, inspired by her daily reading and thinking.

"It's almost a miracle that he's slipped out of that hell," she said to David, when he had told her Andrey's latest adventures.

"Yes, they made it very hot for him," David replied. "You must make it your special mission to keep him from mixing in similar affairs for six months at least.   He has spent all his chances for a long time to come.   Above all, don't permit him to leave St Petersburg on any account."

"I'll try my best," said Tania, smiling.   "But I fear there'll be little safety for him here now."

"It's the safest place anyhow," David said.

"By the way," she asked anxiously, "where have you left them ?   Not at the railway station, I suppose ?"

David explained that they separated after they had got through that dangerous place. He saw Andrey and George climb on a tramcar that would take them straight to head-quarters.

"Headquarters!" Tania exclaimed in a piteous tone. "They'll detain him talking there, I'm sure."

"No, they won't. George will remain there to tell them everything. Andrey said he would not stop a minute more than he could help."

"Did he?" Tania said, brightening up.

For that promise she forgave him in an instant all the anxieties he had caused her by discontinuing his daily messages.

"It was very good of you to come and forewarn me," she said to David.

Within herself the phrase had a different sound; it was very good of him to have asked David to do this!

David left, as the time for Andrey to come was within a measurable distance. On taking his leave he asked her to give Andrey some message. She had a vague recollection of having promised to give it. Certainly, she had nodded her head in sign of assent; but when David was gone, she forgot everything about him or his message, as she rushed behind the curtain of the window, from which the whole length of the street could be seen.

The idea that Tania might be uneasy about him dawned on Andrey's mind for the first time when the train was already running through the last few stations before St Petersburg. But he did not suspect for a moment that her fears could be of a serious nature. In requesting David, who had to go that way, to drop in at his place, he had simply in view the keeping Tania at home if she thought of leaving the house.

But as soon as he took a cab to the well-remembered street, the fever of expectation seized him, and grew upon him as he drew nearer and nearer. They passed the heart of the city rapidly; the wheels rolled over the soft, even wood of the long bridge. How gorgeous the river looked in that beautiful spring noontide! A black steamer, swift and shapely as a ling, was running down the stream and plunged beneath the bridge, its high black chimney breaking suddenly in two a couple of yards before it must have clashed against it, and then adjusting itself again with a jerk, as if by its own impulse. A large wooden barge was moving in the same direction, a tall handsome lad in a red shirt, open at the neck, propelling it with a long pole, whilst his companion at the helm leisurely hummed a song.

The wheels began to hammer sonorously again upon the projecting flint stones of the roadway. It was not far now. Here was the semicircular Cronversky. Every house, every shop, every tree, seemed to greet him like an old acquaintance in this quiet, peaceful place, where he had spent the happiest months of his life. The fresh smiling pictures of those days rushed upon him, driving away the grim and horrible recollections of the hell from which he had emerged. He wanted to believe, and he actually did believe at that moment, that his return to the old place, where Tania waited for him, would be a return to the old happiness, and to the quiet homely work in common, which made so much of that happiness. When he saw her at last at the window, motionless, her smile and eyes only giving evidence that she also had seen him; when he rushed in and clasped her in his arms, his plans and projects, the Tzar, the police, the conspiracies, all were forgotten, everything vanished in the sublime happiness of loving and being loved.

"Dearest!" she whispered, "I thought I should never see you again!"

"You were wrong to think that," he said, smiling. "I told you I would return safe and sound, and here I am."

Yes, here he was, her beloved, her hero, the most valiant of the valiant, returned from overwhelming perils that he had encountered for the sake of their common cause. She could hardly believe she had him with her again for a time whose limit she refused to see.

He was sitting in an armchair, and she upon his knees.

"And how have you got on here without me?" Andrey asked. "You look thin and pale, my child. Have you been well?"

"Not quite; but never mind. What does that matter now?"

She spoke lightly of her anxieties, and told him, laughing, the story of George's subtle epistle, which allowed such latitude of explanation.

But Andrey could easily infer from what she said, that for a time she had believed him lost, and he guessed the rest.

"Forgive me, my own, for my negligence!" he exclaimed. "Only now do I see how bad it was of me."

"Never mind!" she interrupted. "That might happen to anybody. You might have had to go out of town for a few days, or to hide somewhere, or you might have had no time at all to think of it. I was foolish to make so much fuss about a trifle like that. Next time I'll be more patient. . . ."

But her stoicism broke down at the thought that she might have again to pass through the ordeal of these sleepless nights, these horrible dreams, and these endless hours of waiting.

"No!" she exclaimed in another tone, clinging to him. "We'll not separate any more. Why should we? I can be with you and be helpful to you in so many ways. You don't think me a coward, do you?"

Putting both her hands on his shoulders, she drew herself playfully back, so that he might look her full in the face.

"No, I don't think you a coward," Andrey answered, kissing her face.

"It isn't danger that I fear," she proceeded. "Have I ever thought of that when you were here with me? But the uncertainty. . . . I can never tell you how I have suffered since you left. I lived only in waiting for your messages. I've worn out my eyes looking for them. But when they came it was no consolation, for I said to myself that you might have been arrested an hour after you had posted them. And the days and the nights when no message came! What did I not think! What did I not imagine about you! Ah, it's too bad of me to speak of it. I know you'll not remain quiet for long. But you must promise me now that whatever your next affair is, even if it's worse than that of Dubravnik, I shall go with you, and we shall share everything. Will you?"

She concluded with a charming mixture of affection and petulant self-confidence all her own, as if defying him to refuse such an offer.

But Andrey answered nothing, looking with blank dismay at her charming unsuspicious young face. She had herself, by her question, dispelled the incense of joy which had for a time clouded his mind. He remembered the last morning in Dubravnik, at Vatajko's house, and the great resolution which he came to. . . . He was a doomed man. Human happiness or companionship was not for him. The affair in which he was about to embark allowed of no companionship, and had no future but the grave.

To tell her now was the only share that he could give her in it. But he was silent. Trained as he was in the frightful experiences which steel the nerves of a conspirator—now that he had to lift the sacrificial knife over the breast of that beloved victim, he quailed, hesitated, and trembled.

"Andrey, dear! what's the matter? Why do you look like that?" Tania exclaimed. "You refuse? You are afraid that I shall unman you by my constant fears about you, if I'm by your side? Don't imagine that. I couldn't love you if you were not . . . what you are! When I heard of your dangers in that town, and the way you faced them, I trembled, but I was proud and happy as well. I thought it was all so like my Andrey! Believe me, I will never ask you to abstain from anything right and good."

"My darling, I know it," Andrey said, kissing her hands.

"Then why this hesitation and this troubled face? Why don't you promise me at once? Perhaps you don't love me enough to have me always by your side."

"I not love you enough!"

She smiled, and then she laughed outright.

"Well, it's some notion of yours, which you can keep secret if you like. When you have to start again on an expedition—we shall see how you'll get rid of me! Let us not speak of it any more. Now tell me all about Dubravnik. Omit nothing. I can hear everything you have seen."

She had persuaded herself that Andrey's sudden sadness was probably caused through her having revived the Dubravnik recollections. She knew that they were harrowing, but she wanted to show him that she was able to bear the worst.

Andrey was glad to have an immediate explanation thus staved off. There was no need to do it at once. He could very well give himself a respite, postponing the disclosure for a few days—until to-morrow at all events. Nobody could grudge him that last draught of unalloyed happiness.

He told her the story of the Dubravnik affair, though he gave her no opportunity to show the strength of her nerves. Whilst keeping in store for her that tremendous blow, he was most careful not to pain her by too crude a picture of what had actually happened.

He scarcely touched on the execution, saying that she must have read enough of that in the newspapers, and dwelling chiefly upon his personal adventures, which were only amusing now that all had ended well.

Tania was engrossed by his story, but her ear was not deceived by its easy tone.   When he finished, congratulating himself upon having cheered her, she leaned towards him, looking into his eyes.

"You are hiding from me," she said, "something very sad, that is weighing upon you, Andrey.   Tell me what it is.   I want to have my share in all you have to bear.   You will feel better yourself, I'm sure, when you have spoken it right out."

He was not sure that he would feel better, but certainly he could not feel worse than he did now behind the mask he had intended to present to her.

For a moment he was silent, collecting his strength.

"Tania!" he exclaimed.   "You have guessed aright.   I have resolved to attack the Tzar."

At first she did not understand.

"Have you not done it always?" she asked.

She took Andrey's words as referring to his opinion as to political action against the autocracy, which was being thrashed out just then in the revolutionary camp.

He corrected her in four words, clear and precise, that left no room for doubt, hope, or question.

This time the blow struck home, for her face changed colour.   Her mouth opened convulsively, ungracefully, as if she had been suddenly thrown from a height and had her breath knocked out of her.

"Oh, my God!" she gasped painfully, pressing her hands to her heart, and then dropping them helplessly on her lap.

Her dry glittering eyes moved from one point to another with a vacant, wondering expression.   "This is what I get for my waiting!" that bewildered look and sunken figure seemed to say.

Andrey rose from his seat and took her hand.   She yielded it mechanically, without looking at him.

"Tania," he said, bending over her.   "Will you listen to me?   I want to persuade you. . . .   I want to tell you, how and why I came to this decision. . . ."

His voice awakened her.   She turned quickly towards him. Her fingers clasped his hand nervously.

"Yes, yes! speak out.   I'm calm.   I'm ready to listen.   I want to know your reasons," she poured out the words hastily.

A hope crossed her mind that since it had to be reasoned out, it was not yet decided upon.

He told her how and why he had come to his resolution. This time he did not spare her the shocking details of the horrible execution, and no less horrible trial. He wanted to rouse in her the same indignation that he had felt on hearing and seeing all this himself.

But he failed signally. Tania listened cold, unmoved. Things which a moment ago would have pierced her heart, now rebounded from it as arrows from a steel breastplate.

"But this is all over, and can in no way be helped," her eyes and rigid face seemed to say. "What has this to do with that resolve?"

She was not a listener, but a fighter, struggling to protect that which was dear to her as the apple of her eye. He was fighting also—for the integrity of his soul, which was dearer to him than life and happiness.

Life is a struggle. The closest ties are no shield against this.

"And then I thought," Andrey proceeded, as if following Tania's inward replies, "that these horrors are but a faint image of what is being done everywhere, not with half-dozens, but with thousands and millions, and that there will be neither respite of, nor decrease in these sufferings unless we bring discredit, shame, and ruin upon the power that causes them."

He spoke much and forcibly in the same strain, warmed by the fire of deep conviction. He hoped to persuade her and stir her heart to a passion like his own. He succeeded only in slightly impressing her reason.

"Yes, but why of all men must you be called to do this?" she asked, in the same tone of obstinate wonder.

"Why should it not be I, Tania, dear? I came to that determination, and I must carry it out. If to-morrow somebody else comes forward to tell us that he had arrived at the same decision as I, I will gladly give him precedence. I have no ambition to die an illustrious death rather than to perish obscurely as most of us do. But such offers are not made every day, and not everybody would be accepted for an affair like this. They'll certainly entrust it to me."

Tania clasped her bowed head with her hands.

"They will, they will, they will!" hammered upon her brain. "All will be over if he only speaks."

The short happiness she had known within these very walls, before he had started to that terrible town, rose in her memory like a vision of paradise.   She could not renounce it voluntarily just when it was again within her reach.   The whole of her young nature rebelled against so great a sacrifice. She must dissuade him from this horrible thing at any price. It was her last chance to save him and herself.

She made a supreme effort to put her thoughts in order before making this new attempt.   It was difficult, because her mind was so confused.   But he would be good to her; he would not take advantage of her; he would try to look at the matter from her point of view.   She was sure that at bottom she must be right.

She took him by the hand and looked into his eyes pleadingly.

"Andrey, think it over again," she said.   "Are there not enough of murders and bloodshed!   What shall we get by it, but more horrors?   Gallows, gallows again! no end of them. I have thought much about it of late, and it has made me sick and rent my very heart, that the best and noblest should be slaughtered in this way.   Why should you not instead of this thing, try other means?   Why should we not do our work among the people, and let these horrid politics take care of themselves?   I don't put it well, but you understand what I mean. . . ."

"Yes, I understand," Andrey said, and then he asked, "Can you tell me when you thought of all this?   Was it perhaps on Wednesday last?"

"I can't tell exactly.   But why do you ask that?"

"Mere curiosity," Andrey began quietly.   "It was on that day, looking on the indifferent crowd returning from the execution that I asked myself the very same questions, and that many a bitter thought passed through my mind.   Our mission is a hard one, but we must fulfil it to the end.   What would the country have gained, had we abstained from returning blow for blow and gone on preaching and teaching in out-of-the-way corners, as Lena proposes?   They would not have hanged us, true.   But what's the good of that?   They would have arrested and sent us to Siberia, and let us rot in prisons all the same. We should not have one more day of life and work useful to the people than we have now.   They will not give us freedom, as a reward for good behaviour.   We must fight for it with what arms we can get.   If we have to suffer—so much the better!   Our sufferings will be a new weapon for us.   Let them hang us, let them shoot us, let them kill us in their underground cells! The more fiercely we are dealt with, the greater will be our following. I wish I could make them tear my body to pieces, or burn me alive on a slow fire in the market place," he concluded in a low fierce whisper, his face burning as he looked at her with fixed glowing eyes.

Instead of quenching she had fanned to flame the devouring fire smouldering beneath the ashes.

She felt with horror that the ground was slipping from under her feet. She did not know what to say, what to do. Yet it was too terrible to yield.

"Wait a moment . . . Andrey, dear!" she said, taking him by the arm as if he were going off there and then. "Only a moment. I have something more to say . . . very convincing. But I forget what it is. . . . All this is so terrible, that my head swims. . . . You must let me think. . . ."

She stood quite close to him, her eyes cast down, her head bent.

"I'll wait as long as you like, . . ." Andrey said, kissing the dear pale forehead. "Let us drop the matter altogether for to-day. . . ."

She shook her head energetically. No, she must and would find what she wanted to say at once.

"The peasants who believe in the Tzar—— No, that's not it! That part of society which now is neutral—— No, not that again!"

Suddenly she trembled in all her limbs and her very lips grew pale; she had discovered the great argument which was her bulwark, and she saw how weak it was, and yet how terrible.

"Oh, what will become of me when they kill you!" she gasped, covering her eyes with her hand and throwing back her head.

"My poor, darling child!" Andrey exclaimed, clasping her in his arms. "I know how heavy a cross yours is. It's so much harder to bear for those who have to remain than for those who have to perish. But, believe me, my own lot is not an easy one. Life is dear to me,—dearer than it ever was, since you loved me. It's hard to throw it away, to part with you, and die when I could be so happy! . . . I would have given anything to spare us that. But it cannot be. The blow must be struck. I cannot withdraw because I love you. I

T

should feel myself a coward, a liar, a traitor to my vows, to my cause, to my country if I did! It would be better to drown myself in the first dirty pool, than go on living with such a burden at my heart! How could I bear it? What would our love become then? . . . Forgive me, my darling, the pain that I cause you, not for my sake, but for the sake of our country. Think only, what is death, what are our sufferings, if we can bring nearer by one day the end of the horrors that are on all sides. . . ." .

Andrey spoke in a low voice, that sank sometimes to a faint whisper. He was exhausted by the unnatural struggle, and could fight no longer. His was a plea for peace, for respite. But these simple words of his melted Tania's heart and wrought in her a change when he least expected it.

However exalted, romantic, or youthful is a woman's love, if only she loves truly, there is always in it something of the pitying and protecting motherly element. It was that chord which Andrey had touched and stirred in Tania by that faint whisper of his. She was not convinced: at least she could not tell for certain whether she was or not, for she forgot all about his arguments. She surrendered. She pitied him so intensely, that she could not make his lot harder by her resistance.

Her face relented. The deep eyes once more shone upon him kindly and lovingly, as she caressed with trembling hand his hair and his face that lay upon her knees. She spoke to him in her soft soothing way, whilst inwardly she was pouring out upon him words of love and endearment even more tender than those she spoke aloud.

The future was all darkness to her; beyond the act upon which Andrey's mind was set she could see no more than beyond the grave. But she saw her way quite clearly in the present. She was his wife, his sister, his companion, and she resolved to pluck up all her courage to stand by him in this terrible trial, to support him, and to take upon her young shoulders as much of his burden as she could.

She was much calmer now. There was no trace of tears in her large sad eyes. But she was weeping tears of blood inwardly—not over her own fate now, for she had forgotten everything about herself to think only of him.

CHAPTER VIII.

ANDREY made his offer. It was accepted. The vast and complex conspiracy, of which he was to be the striking hand, had been set in motion, and was already making progress in its underground way.

One evening, about a fortnight after his return to St Petersburg, Andrey crossed the Tuchkov Bridge, directing his steps towards the Palace Square. He was still living at his old rooms, but by this time some signs of these being no longer safe had appeared, so that a speedy removal to other quarters was contemplated. This was the reason why Andrey made such a long circuit, for he could have greatly shortened his journey by taking the Gagarin ferry. He was going to see old Repin, and was naturally most anxious not to draw after him any spies who might be loitering about his house. Repin had sent word to him that he wanted to see him on important business. There was nothing unusual in such a summons, so that Andrey did not trouble himself to guess the purport of the invitation. Probably it was something referring to "business," general or private.

Repin was prepared for the visit, and was waiting in his study, having given orders that he was not to be disturbed by any one. The old man's face was pensive and preoccupied, as he sat before the table, lit by two candles in carved brass candlesticks, and looked absently over some of his briefs. He intended to make Andrey an offer, which he took very much to heart, and he had serious reason to think he must not lose time in urging it.

Whenever anything exceptionally grave is about to be done by the conspirators, even those who are not engaged in the actual work can occasionally guess that something is brewing. A vague atmosphere of danger and excitement spreads all around. The conspirators are seen to be more careful in observing precautions against the police. They exhort more urgently their sympathisers and occasional accomplices to be on their guard against domiciliary visits. They remove compromising papers from houses where at another time these are kept almost openly. Some of the members of the brotherhood, more nervous than others, show signs of mental preoccupation, when they ought to look cheerful and calm. Thus, even when the secret of what is to be done is kept most rigorously, those who know how to read the signs of the times can often foresee something.

Repin was one of that huge and diversified circle of friendly people which in Russia surrounds each and all of the conspirators. He had watched these ominous signs with keen and painful attention, and he was almost sure that a new outbreak was at hand. He had not for a long time seen any of the active conspirators, but a few days before he had met Tania at a small party at the house of a friend. They could not exchange more than a few words in private, but she looked so distraught and weary that his worst suspicions were confirmed. The anxieties of underground life must have become exceptionally severe, for he had never before seen her in such a state. He was powerless to tear her away altogether, but he might perhaps succeed in keeping both her and Andrey out of the turmoil for a time. He was resolved to try.

After his daughter, the person for whom he cared most was his extraordinary son-in-law. Had the choice of a husband for Tania rested with him, he would certainly have sought for her a companion not in the ranks of conspirators. But young people who take their own way in politics, are wont to ask for no guidance from their elders in other affairs of life. Besides, since Tania herself had joined the conspirators, the profession of her husband was a matter of small moment. So—the peculiar feeling of the best among the Liberals towards the revolutionists helping him—Repin at last came to accept and sincerely love this son-in-law of his. Had Andrey enrolled himself in some less desperate section of the revolutionary body, the old man would have been quite satisfied with him. They were on very good terms, Andrey visiting Repin as often as necessary caution and the great stress of his occupation permitted. Repin knew much of what concerned him, for Andrey was as frank and free with him as a conspirator can ever be with a trusted friend. Tania was indeed the more reserved of the two, being the younger and more open to the reproach of undue partiality.

The Dubravnik expedition, and the great dangers of Andrey's present position which resulted from it, were no secret to Repin. He considered that it was just the time for Andrey to get out of the way for a while. This was the foundation of his hope, that the plan he had in view would be acceptable both to him and to Tania.

He heartily welcomed Andrey, who had not been to see him since his return from Dubravnik, and asked him how Tania was.

Andrey answered that she was quite well.

"I think it's as unlikely for any of our people to fall ill as for a salamander to catch cold," he added. " It's so scorchingly hot in our underground region that I doubt if any microbes could stand it."

He smiled, but only with his lips; his eyes remained quite serious.

"It must be very hot indeed for you, Andrey. I am told that the police have had a severe reprimand on your account, and are now resolved to make amends. The chief said he would turn the town upside down till he got you alive or dead."

"Easier to say than to do," Andrey observed calmly. "They have boasted in the same fashion on many other occasions."

"Still, to begin with, they've got wind that you're here, which you probably did not expect. They may go a step further. Better not play with fire. Don't you think it is high time for you to get out of their way, and take an airing abroad? It is just on that point I intended to speak with you. . . ."

Andrey shook his head in sign of energetic denial.

"Don't be too hasty in refusing!" Repin exclaimed. "Let me have my say. . . . You will not be the worse for a few months' rest. To Tania the trip would be of particular use. She can read and study at leisure in any line she chooses. You don't deny, I presume, that knowledge is a thing which may be of some use for your revolution?"

"No, we don't," Andrey answered.

"Well then, you see that my plan has some good in it. She will store up something for the future, you will wear out something of your past, and you will both return at a better time.   The later the better, if you take my advice.   If you have any scruples to draw on your funds, I for my part undertake to provide you with as much as is needful.   What do you say to that ?"

Andrey was thinking—not exactly of the offer, as Repin supposed, for there was nothing in it to think about as far as he was concerned.   It crossed his mind that perhaps it would be acceptable for Tania. . . .   But no! it was out of the question for her also.   She would never consent to leave the country just now, even for a short time.

"You are very good indeed," he said; "but I am quite unable to accept your offer, and I doubt very much if Tania will.   But there is something else you can do for us.   May I ask you when you intend leaving the town for your summer villa ?"

"A month hence.   Perhaps a little earlier.   But how can this affect either of you ?"

"It would be well," said Andrey, "if you would go as early as possible, and if Tania could accompany you, and stay with you for three or four months."

This was a plan of Andrey's.   Knowing Tania to be so fond of her father, he had thought it would be easier for her to bear the parting if she was with him.   She had agreed to the suggestion—for Andrey's sake, because she did not see for herself that it would make any difference.

Repin said he should be always glad to have Tania with him as long as she chose.   It was something to get her out of the turmoil for a full four months.   But this was a poor makeshift.   He insisted upon his plan of their joint trip abroad, pointing out all the advantages of this over the temporary seclusion of the one of them who was by far the less exposed to danger.

"No," Andrey said in a decisive tone.   "I cannot leave town on any account.   It is useless to speak about it.   Let us drop the matter."

Repin's face darkened.   This tone, this obstinacy, and moreover the desire to keep Tania out of the way, showed clearly that the new outbreak he had foreseen must be something very tremendous indeed, and that Andrey himself had to play a conspicuous part in it.

"Some infernal affair of yours again ?" he asked in a low voice.

"Something of that kind," Andrey said, evasively.

For a moment both were silent.

" I really do think you need not be in such a hurry to break your head. You have risked it enough lately, and might take a short rest just now," Repin said at last.

" It can't be helped," Andrey answered. "Soldiers are not allowed to retire from service in time of war on account of their past dangers."

" But they are relieved now and then, to keep up your simile."

"Sometimes. . . . But sometimes they are not, and that is just the case with us now," Andrey answered.

This undaunted energy and courage were exactly what melted and conquered Repin's heart in respect to the revolutionists in general, and to Andrey in particular. He was so hopelessly sceptical himself, and he had seen so much cowardice and selfishness all round, that he could not help admiring such singleness of purpose. Unable to share the enthusiasm for their cause, he reserved his fellow-feeling for themselves as individuals.

But to-day irritation and disappointment at the frustration of his cherished plan outweighed everything else. He was angry with Andrey for what he considered needless obstinacy.

" Then you have quite made up your mind on that point ? " he asked.

"Yes, I have. It is useless to speak about it."

" Well I know by experience how intractable you all are. You have the rage of self-immolation, and you will go on breaking your heads as long as you have breath in you. Fanatics are inaccessible to arguments. They are incurable."

" *Et tu, Brute !* " Andrey exclaimed, with a sad smile. " I thought you knew us a little better. Fanatics you say ! I doubt if men answering that definition exist in flesh and blood. For my part, I confess that I have not met with any, though my experience has been tolerably long and varied. No, we are not fanatics, if you mean anything by that word. We are a sensible, hard-working set of people, perfectly willing to live, I assure you, and quite capable of appreciating all the pleasures of life, provided that we can do this without stifling our better selves."

" Yes," Repin drawled ; " but your better selves want so much that they may be at ease. And if you cannot get it, you grow wild as children who cry for the moon."

He went on in the same strain. Being angry with Andrey, he gave vent to his resentment, in attacking with especial bitterness the party to which Andrey belonged. He spoke of the futility of their efforts, of the reckless provocation which intensified the despotism against which they contended; of their rendering life utterly unbearable to the whole of educated Russia, for whom Repin also claimed a right to existence.

Andrey defended himself mildly and half jestingly at first. He was accustomed to such onslaughts from Repin. But the subject was too near his heart for him to remain calm, and the last accusation roused him.

"Your educated, free-minded Russia," he exclaimed, "is very careful, I know, about its right to existence, and about its comforts too. It would be much better for our common country if it were less so."

"Would you like us all to go into the street, throwing bombs at every policeman who passes?" Repin said ironically.

"What nonsense!" Andrey burst forth. "You need not throw bombs; you have your own weapons to fight with. But do fight, if you are men! Let us fight together. We shall be strong enough then to fight the autocracy once for all, and to overthrow it. But as long as you go on crouching and whimpering, you have no right to reproach us for not licking the hand that strikes us. If the blind fury of reprisals is extended to you, rend your garments and strew ashes on your heads, but bear it as your due. Make no complaints, undignified as useless, for you may make yourself hoarse with curses, reproaches, entreaties, but we shall not heed you."

"Who speaks of reproaches?" Repin said, waving his hand impatiently. "You may personally be right and justified in losing your reason under peculiar provocation. This would be an excuse for a common criminal before a common jury, but not for a political party before public opinion. If you pretend to serve your country, you must know how to restrain your passionate impulses, if nothing but defeat and calamity will be the result of them."

"Defeat and calamity!" Andrey exclaimed. "Are you so sure of that? Moscow was set on fire by a penny candle. We have thrust in the heart of Mother Russia a much bigger firebrand. Nobody can foretell the future, or be answerable for what it conceals. We do our best for the present; we have shown an example of manly rebellion, which is never lost upon

an enslaved country. With your permission, I will say that
we have brought back to Russians their self-respect, and have
saved the honour of the Russian name, which is no longer
synonymous with that of slave."

"By showing that they are incapable of anything but these
petty attempts against individuals? Is that it?"

"And whose is the fault?" Andrey retorted, firing up at
Repin's tone. "Not ours of course, but yours. That of great
Liberal Russia, that holds aloof from the struggle for freedom,
whilst we, your own children, are fighting and perishing by
thousands year after year! . . ."

Andrey did not in the least refer to Repin, who was rather
an exception to the rule. But for some reason or other Repin
felt the reproach very keenly. He kept silent for some time,
and when he spoke again, his tone and manner were changed.

"Let us grant what you say. We, the so-called society,
are cowards. But since you cannot change it, you must accept
it as any other fact of Russian actuality. The more reason
not to break your heads uselessly, trying to batter a hole in the
wall."

"No, we are not so hopeless as that," Andrey said, relenting. "We have something else to rely upon besides society,
and we are hopeful that even society will improve in time, when
new blood is infused into it. Has not a great philosopher said,
'The higher your estimation of the majority of men, the smaller
your chances of mistake?'"

Repin observed, that as far as his knowledge of great
philosophers went, none of them had said this, and one of
them had said the very reverse.

"Then they ought to have said it," Andrey answered. "If
they have not, I would not give a brass farthing for the lot."

He took his hat, and was putting on his gloves.

"Farewell, Grigory Alexandrovitch," he said. "I can't
say when I shall see you again."

He could not say more without betraying his secret.

They took leave of each other as heartily as they had met,
Repin repeating to Andrey that his house and connections
were at his service, whenever he might be in need of them.

Andrey nodded his head to say that he knew that and was
grateful. But his face wore a peculiar expression, which Repin
only understood later.

CHAPTER IX.

ANDREY did not go straight home. He had to pay a visit to headquarters, where he was detained by news of a very unpleasant nature. Repin's information proved correct with a vengeance. The police had resolved to hunt him down for good, and they had discovered that he had taken refuge somewhere on the other side of the Neva. This was very vexing. The friends advised him not to return home at all, but send word to Tania instead. It would be a great pity for him to fall into the hands of the police just now. Andrey understood it very well, but Tania could not leave the house alone and suddenly, he himself being absent. It would look suspicious. So he resolved rather to go home at once, so as to be able to leave early next morning. Danger seemed distant as yet, and he would take good precautions against the spies.

He took a cab to the Gagarin ferry, resolved to go the shortest way, not to keep Tania waiting. It was half-past eleven when he reached the embankment. The passengers were few at that hour. Andrey took a small ferry boat to himself, and could easily ascertain that he had reached the other side of the wide river before any other passenger had started from the embankment.

On the other bank he had to spend more time than he could have wished, so as to reach his house from the side where he would not be expected.

All this caused a considerable delay, and as he was usually very punctual, Tania had already had time to get alarmed about him, and she rejoiced at his safe return as if this meant something real and substantial to her.

"What was it that father wanted to see you for?" she asked him.

Andrey told her of the warning he had received from her father and from the friends at headquarters, which made it necessary for them to remove without delay. They immediately set to work to pack the little they intended to carry with them, and the next morning they successfully performed the double operation of disappearing quietly from the number of the living, and rising, Phœnix-like, from their ashes in another place.

Their new home was as secure from any danger as a series of the subtlest precautions dictated by long practice could make it. But even here Andrey's position was soon found not to be safe enough. The police suspected nothing as to the Tzaricide plot. The chase after him, undertaken on account of his past exploits, showed, however, no sign of abating. This was in itself quite bad enough. Numbers of spies knew him by sight. He ran the risk of being recognised and arrested in the street, whenever he left the house. On the other hand, to live secluded in a private apartment was very imprudent, because it would at once excite suspicion.

Headquarters were the best place for a man so precious to the conspirators as Andrey was. He was invited to settle down there accordingly. Here he was perfectly safe against the police, and could stay indoors for days and weeks unnoticed by any one.

This, of course, necessitated his immediate separation from Tania, which might have been postponed for a time, because the plot was far from being as yet complete. Tania was deeply grieved by this untimely separation; these last days they had to spend together were her treasure, which seemed to her the more precious the less of it was left. As to Andrey he was rather glad than otherwise.

Tania had fulfilled to the letter the pledge she had silently imposed on herself on that terrible morning when he first disclosed to her his secret. Her courage and self-denial never wavered all through that hard test. But she was so young, so little trained to grief, and Andrey saw too clearly what that silent heroism cost her. The sight of this gnawed at his heart, and he thought that it would be better for both of them if they ceased to see each other.

He, therefore, accepted readily the invitation to move to headquarters for the three weeks or so which still remained for him. The stern, bracing atmosphere of the place suited him. All was engrossed by "business" here. In his quality of permanent resident, Andrey transacted much of the current affairs, feeling as one on the field of an unceasing battle that raged all round him. He was at the very centre upon which all information converged from every part of Russia,—from prison cells, from fortresses, from Siberian mines and icy deserts,—every mail unfolding stories of wrecked lives, madnesses, suicides, deaths in every form, and family tragedies and bereavements, like their own, by scores.

This was not exactly consolation, but it reduced his own tragedy to its true proportions. With such sights constantly before his eyes, he could not make so much of his own and Tania's personal sorrows as he did when they were alone with each other. The spirit of the place had invigorated him. He grew much calmer. Of Tania he thought often but not with such pain as before. He came to be persuaded that she also was feeling as he was.

Once during Andrey's stay at headquarters a regular meeting of conspirators was held there, at which both himself and Tania were present. The meeting discussed the ordinary affairs, Andrey's special one having been entrusted to another body, which assembled at another place.

Tania took part in the proceedings in an ordinary businesslike way, listening with apparent calmness and giving her vote when the time came for it, like all the rest. Andrey was glad to see her so composed, but it did not surprise him. He thought it quite natural, that being a conspirator herself she should behave in that way.

When the meeting was over, the friends withdrawing one by one, Tania remained. She intended to spend the evening here, now that she was in. The flat was a spacious one. They easily found a room to themselves. But the permanent tenants, with a few guests, were in the adjacent room, talking so loudly, that their voices were audible through the closed door. This chilled and restrained the conversation. They talked on common topics, connected with to-day's meeting, as if nothing particular was abou to happen to them. Sometimes they sought for a subject for conversation, so as not to sit silent, as if they were strangers. This ended by becoming so insupportable to Tania, that after half-an-hour she rose as if she were suffocating, and said she must go home at once.

Andrey did not detain her.

"Will it be soon?" she asked, as she was on the point of leaving.

"Yes," Andrey said.

He needed no explanation to understand about what she was asking.

"When?" she asked again half audibly, casting her eyes down.

" A week hence," Andrey said briefly.

If it had not been already dark in the room he would have seen how her face changed colour at these words. She did not think it was so near! But she said nothing, and gave no sign of what she felt, standing motionless at the door, her hat on her head. Then she came close to him, and seizing him by the hand, said in a passionate, agitated whisper, her eyes glowing in the darkness,—

"I must see you before. . . . Not as to-day, not here, but there at our home. . . . Come! I cannot part with you thus. . . ."

He said he would come, and she went off hastily, without saying another word.

Andrey remained agitated and troubled in mind. That short passionate whisper and those glowing eyes had in a moment upset him, rekindling in him the thirst for life, love, happiness, he thought already blunted and subdued. He would see her! He could not go without seeing her, now less than ever. But he wished that this visit was over, or better still, that his act of self-immolation was to take place to-morrow, and not a week hence.

He was not born to be a martyr—he knew it only too well, and it pained him to hurt even a dumb creature. But frightful necessity over which he had no control compelled him to trample down his feelings as well as to throw away his life.

George had also remained at headquarters after the meeting, intending to pass the night there. When, an hour after Tania's departure, he came with a light into Andrey's room, to ask him to supper, he found him lying on the sofa, his hands clasped behind his neck, thinking.

In the night a strange dream visited him.

It must have been during his first sleep, for he went to bed very late. He remembered how his thoughts grew lighter and lighter, flying upward, as if they were birds, until he could no longer discern them clearly. For some time he saw their thin black tails, wound up in scrolls, waving slightly in the depths of a yellow mist above his head. Then these tails disappeared too, and he saw nothing but a vast expanse of empty yellow sky, stretching over an endless sandy plain, upon which he walked. He remembered at once how insidious is lying down to the peace of mind of a man who is in trouble, and he said to himself, that it was very lucky for him that he could sleep walking. People said it could not be, but that was evidently a mistake. He knew well that he was sleeping, yet he walked.

There was nothing around but grey sand, covered here and there with rocks and scattered boulders, which made it look still more désolate and wild.   Dark, low clouds swept across the sky very rapidly, though there was no wind below. Not a sign of life could be discerned anywhere, but the road that wound along the dreary desert bore traces of many footsteps.   Andrey wondered how he could be alone upon a road that seemed to be so much used, when he felt that he was not alone, but was walking in a crowd of companions.   They were strangers most of them, with blank shadow faces, like those of a crowd seen from a platform.   But among them he recognised at once Boris, Vasily, and also Botcharov.   The face of the latter could not be seen, for he was clad in a shroud, the long sleeves tied behind his back, and the hood lowered.   But Andrey knew that it was he.   The other two wore ordinary dresses, and looked at him sternly.

"We have met at last, old fellow," Boris said.   "You did not expect to see me, I suppose?" and he grinned ironically.

"He knows everything," Andrey thought in dismay. "No, I did not expect to see you," he answered aloud, "for I thought you were dead."

"So we are," said Boris.   "But we came to keep you company, and Zina sends you a letter.   Do you recognise Botcharov?   He has donned a shroud for fun.   But you can see him all the same."

With these words he lifted the hood of the shroud, and Andrey saw under it his own frightfully distorted face.   His blood ran cold, and his heart stopped beating, with unspeakable horror.   But whilst he was looking at that face, it changed into that of Botcharov, who said, winking merrily with one eye, "I did it for fun."

Andrey wanted to say that it was a poor sort of fun, but he dared not, for he was cowed by them all, remembering that the dead risen from their tombs are mischievous people.   He merely asked Boris, "Whither are we going?"

"To the rivers of milk, flowing in shores of pudding, that lie beyond the hills yonder," Boris answered.   "If you are doubtful, here is the old chap to explain to you how to do it in strict conformity with the laws of the Empire."

Andrey saw in fact old Repin, whom strangely enough he had not noticed before, dressed in a black mantle and large brimmed felt hat, like the torch-bearers at funerals, and holding under his arm something resembling a big portfolio.   He was walking straight before them all, never turning his head, as a man who has to show the way. But the next moment Andrey discovered that it was not old Repin, but the Tzar Alexander in person.

At the same time he remembered that he was bound to kill him, and without delay, though his time was not yet come, for this was a rare opportunity.

"I will have the merit of the deed, and no risk whatever," a voice insidiously urged him.

But his heart fainted, and his hands would not obey him. He tried again and again, with desperate efforts, but he could not move his hand, and he suffered greatly. Then he recollected that this was only a dream, and it was of no consequence whether he killed the Tzar now, for the thing would have to be done over again when he awoke. This put his mind at ease, and he said to the Tzar in a whisper so as not to be heard by the others,—

"You are lost if they know you. Why, being alive, have you come here?"

"I?" the other replied, also under the breath. "And why did you come yourself?"

"He is right," Andrey thought. "But we must slacken our pace, so that the others may pass us by."

He had hardly formulated his thoughts, when the whole crowd rushed fiercely upon him with outstretched arms, gnashing their teeth, and yelling "Traitor!" and the Tzar, who proved to be Taras Kostrov, seizing him fiercely by the shoulder.

"Ha!" cried Andrey, and awoke with a start.

In the dim light of the morning George was bending over him, looking him anxiously in the face, and shaking him by the shoulder.

"What is the matter? What do you want of me?" Andrey muttered, still under the influence of the dream.

"You were not well; groaning, gnashing your teeth, and shouting in your sleep. I thought you had better be awakened."

"I had a very bad dream," said Andrey, this time wide awake. "I saw Boris and Vasily, and they had called me a traitor. And the worse is, that I had deserved it."

"That was the word you shouted when I came to wake you up!" exclaimed George.

"Did I? Then it is not so offensive as it would have been otherwise," Andrey said, and he told him his vision.

thing occurred to him in any of his former enterprises. But now all his faculties were so completely engrossed by the great personal issue before him, that he had no attention left for anything else.

As the fatal moment approached this egotism of self-sacrifice became more exclusive and peremptory. The abhorrence of death is so strongly rooted in every man, that few can fully overcome it even in moments of great mental excitement. But no one can keep at such high pressure continuously. To cope victoriously with this powerful instinct in cold blood, to subdue and keep it down unflinchingly week after week under all sorts of moods and temptations, the flights of enthusiasm must have the support of an iron framework of reason.

Andrey, sober minded by nature and little inflammable, comparatively, was instinctively anxious to shun everything that was likely to divide and impair his energy and make it more difficult for him to keep himself well in hand. He foresaw what the leave taking with Tania would cost him, and at one time he had the idea of sending her word that he would not come at all. It would be better for them both that they should avoid the parting scene. He had no doubt she would understand and forgive him. But at the last moment he gave way. He realised too vividly the regret he would feel when there was no more chance of his seeing her. Had she not asked him to come? Why should he be so over-careful? He must and will look on that face and hear that voice once again. They knew very well, both of them, that there was no remedy for the unavoidable. They would not torment each other to no purpose. For his part he had resolved to be as calm as was possible.

This was probably the cause of a certain reserve and stiffness upon his face, when three days after his meeting with Tania at headquarters he came to see her.

It was morning.

The peculiar conditions of the new lodgings was such that he could go to see her either in the morning about twelve or in the evening at dark. He chose the morning.

Tania rushed to meet him and stopped, checked and frightened by the stony expression of his face, which she had never seen before. But why should she mind! The next moment she threw herself on his neck caressing him, looking

CHAPTER X.

THE conspiracy advanced rapidly to its completion, and the fatal day drew close. The body of conspirators charged with organising the attempt held daily sittings. As the chief actor in the coming drama, Andrey had to be consulted upon everything. He went to one of the meetings, but he sat buried in thought, hardly opening his mouth all the time, and he refused to go again. It bored him to listen and give his opinion upon the various contrivances, and he thought it not worth his while to risk himself in the streets for such a purpose.

He knew very well that he must, and would do his best, to make the attempt successful. The blow would be greater by far if the Tzar were killed, or at least wounded. But this was for the party. For the party the attempt was the essential matter, his own inevitable capture and execution were merely incidental. But in his individual brain the tables were turned. For him the essential was that he had to die. The attempt was a secondary affair, upon which he would have time to think when on the spot. In the meanwhile, he could not bring himself to take any interest in the matter. He had his own business to attend to—which was to die. The rest seemed not to concern him in the least.

The day after the general meeting at which he saw Tania a curious thing occurred. In cleaning and putting in order his revolver (with which the attempt was to be made), Andrey broke a spring. The time was rather short to get it repaired, for a holiday happened to intervene. Accordingly, a friend offered Andrey his own revolver, which he recommended as good in every respect and as never missing fire. Andrey accepted the exchange on trust, without so much as going once to a shooting gallery or into the fields to try his new weapon. He would never have been so careless had the same thing occurred to him in any of his former enterprises. But now all his faculties were so completely engrossed by the great personal issue before him, that he had no attention left for anything else.

As the fatal moment approached, this egotism of self-sacrifice became more exclusive and peremptory. The abhorrence of death is so strongly rooted in every man, that few can fully overcome it even in moments of great mental excitement. But no one can keep at such high pressure continuously. To cope victoriously with this powerful instinct in cold blood, to subdue and keep it down unflinchingly week after week under all sorts of moods and temptations, the flights of enthusiasm must have the support of an iron framework of reason.

Andrey, sober minded by nature and little inflammable, comparatively, was instinctively anxious to shun everything that was likely to divide and impair his energy and make it more difficult for him to keep himself well in hand. He foresaw what the leave-taking with Tania would cost him, and at one time he had the idea of sending her word that he would not come at all. It would be better for them both that they should avoid the parting scene. He had no doubt she would understand and forgive him. But at the last moment he gave way. He realised too vividly the regret he would feel when there was no more chance of his seeing her. Had she not asked him to come? Why should he be so over-careful? He must and will look on that face and hear that voice once again. They knew very well, both of them, that there was no remedy for the unavoidable. They would not torment each other to no purpose. For his part he had resolved to be as calm as was possible.

This was probably the cause of a certain reserve and stiffness upon his face, when three days after his meeting with Tania at headquarters he came to see her.

It was morning.

The peculiar conditions of their new lodgings was such that he could go to see her either in the morning about twelve or in the evening at dark. He chose the morning.

Tania rushed to meet him and stopped, checked and frightened by the stony expression of his face, which she had never seen before. But why should she mind! The next moment she threw herself on his neck, caressing him, looking into his eyes lovingly, resolved to dispel the gloom that hung upon his brow.

"Why did you not come yesterday or the day before," she said, gently. "I thought you would come You might have been not so very cautious for once, . . ." she added with a tinge of reproach.

She could not keep this back, though she hastened to lessen its sting with a smile. The words escaped her involuntarily. She was so disappointed at what she considered Andrey's carelessness of her last wish.

Andrey shook his head, and said curtly that it was not over-caution which had detained him.

It pained him to think that Tania could give such an interpretation to his behaviour. But why should he set her right? Why tell her of his struggles?

"It must be your affair," Tania guessed.

He nodded in silence.

Then she knew that the matter was progressing steadily, and that this was for certain their last interview. She dropped her head. But her short observation was to Andrey like a push which sets in motion a car standing on the rail. He began speaking of the attempt.

"Everything is already settled," he said, "and all is so well combined that we cannot fail."

He went on as if this was the most cheering topic for both of them. He entered into minute descriptions of the scheme, telling how they would contrive to break through the swarm of spies surrounding the Tzar on all sides during his morning walk around his palace; how he would keep out of the way until the very last moment, mentioning the small devices he would use so as to have more chance of escaping arrest before the Tzar came.

Tania drew herself a little away, looking at him with wide open eyes. She did not listen to his tale at all, she watched him wondering. As Andrey proceeded in his circumstantial narrative her wonder increased. Why was he telling it all to her? He seemed tired of the story himself, for his tone was dry and monotonous. His face wore the stony expression that had struck her when he first entered, only it was more marked. She did not recognise her Andrey. This man was a stranger to her.

"They have changed him there into another man!" she cried inwardly, as his words fell jarring upon her ears.

Not a word of love or affection, not one kind look! And this at their last interview, before they would part for ever, after such love as theirs had been!

"Yes, yes, they have changed him by stealth! This is not my Andrey. . . . Mine was a different man, . . ." she repeated, biting her parched lips and swallowing her tears lest she should entirely break down.

His narrative and explanations irritated her. When he began to talk about those skilful devices of theirs she could not contain herself any longer.

"Confound your Tzar and your devices and your sentinels!" she burst forth vehemently.

"Tania!" he exclaimed, with a look of pained surprise.

She clasped her head in despair. It was horrible she should treat him thus at such a moment.

"Forgive me!" she said, seizing his hand, and throwing her head down upon it. "I do not know what I'm saying."

She did not get up at once, but remained with her head leaning over the arm of his chair. Her hair fell over her cheeks and temples, hiding her face. Her lips were parted; she breathed heavily.

Andrey thought she was crying. The sight tore his heart. But what consolation could he offer? What could he tell her that would not sound flat and trivial, an insult to her great sorrow? He caressed her hair, gently trying to put it in order.

When she lifted up her face he saw that she had not been crying. Her eyes were feverish and dry. She looked hard at him, and turned her head away wringing her fingers.

She knew that he was on the point of going, and she might die here on the spot of a broken heart, or dash her head against the wall—that would not detain him, not even for these three days which he might well have given to her! A stone would be more pitiful than he was. He would feel nothing but contempt for her weakness if she said a word about it! . . . Why then had he come at all? . . .

Andrey rose in fact.

"Farewell, my darling!" he whispered, stretching out his hands to her.

She started as if he had said something quite unexpected.

"No, not yet!" she exclaimed, frightened. "Not yet!" she repeated in a loud voice, imploringly.

He drew her to him and pressed her in his arms.

"Farewell!" he repeated. "It is time. . . . Tania, my darling, my own," he exclaimed from the depths of his soul; "how happy we might have been together!"

She looked into his eyes and recognised at last her Andrey, her beloved, whom she had so wronged in her thoughts! She had recovered him, but only to feel more keenly that she had to lose him instantly, with no means of keeping him for another moment!

The pain almost distracted her. It was too horrible to be true. It could not be. To love as they did, and to let him go and be killed. . . . But she could not live without him! He was her life, the light of her soul! It was not her fault that he became all to her. . . .

"Listen, Andrey," she cried passionately. "You are mine. You told me that yourself, and I won't let you go. No, I won't! Do you hear?"

To her distracted mind it seemed strictly logical, unanswerably logical.

But the next moment her fingers clutching his arm slackened their hold. She bent her face down, and sank into the chair pale, exhausted, her eyes closed, waving her hand for him to go.

There was a something greater to which they had both pledged their all: lives, hearts, thoughts, happiness.

She gave him up, wishing that he would go quickly, and she not see it.

But it was harder for him to leave her now than if she had clung to his garments. He threw himself at her feet, kissing her hands, face, eyes, in a fit of vehement, wild passion.

"Go! I cannot bear it any longer. . . . I am better now. Go quickly."

He tore himself away by force, and ran downstairs as if all the furies pursued him. He could not see clearly for the mist in his eyes; his head was whirling, and the street swam as if he was drunk.

Tania did not hear him go away. But she heard the noise of the outer gate of the courtyard. As a man stunned by a blow on the head will revive at the touch of a red-hot iron, so Tania jumped up at this sound, and rushed to the window with the hope of catching a last glimpse of Andrey.

But he had already slammed the gate behind him and was gone. Gone, for ever gone! He was still alive, but for her he was lost, and everything seemed to have crumbled away for her in that frightful, unnatural, incomprehensible bereavement. She could not struggle against her grief any longer. Overpowered she covered her eyes with her hands, and fell upon the sofa, her face against the dirty chintz, and burst into burning, irrepressible tears. She thought that she would cry her very life out ! She could not have believed there were so many tears in her eyes. They streamed between her fingers—she had forgotten to use her handkerchief—wetting her hands through, covering with wet spots the cushion, whilst her body was shaken and her breast torn with convulsive, frantic sobs. Her love, her life, her youth, her all, seemed wrecked and submerged in that bleak emptiness which fell upon her. The cause ! The country ! They did not exist for her at that moment. She could think of herself alone, and her misery, which seemed to have no end, and no relief, but doomed to last as long as she had breath in her. . . .

Let us draw the curtain upon her sorrow. Her fit of despair will pass—not to-day and not to-morrow—but in time, and will leave her another woman. She would not have been so crushed had she to pass through the same trial a few years later. But it was her fate to begin at once with the hardest.

CHAPTER XI.

THE great and terrible day had come.

From early dawn Andrey only slumbered, awakened every quarter of an hour by his excessive dread of missing his time.

A strip of dazzling light, penetrating through a rent in the blind, played upon the wall opposite his couch, announcing a splendid day. When that strip reached the corner of the chest of drawers he knew that it would be time for him to rise. But he preferred to get up at once.

He pulled the bedclothes from the leather couch which had served him as bed during his stay at headquarters, and carefully folding them up he put them away in the yellow chest of drawers standing opposite.

"To-night I shall sleep in the cell of the Fortress, if I'm not killed on the spot," he said to himself.

He closed the drawers, and proceeded to pull up the blinds of the two windows.

The remark was made in the plainest matter-of-fact tone, just as if he had been merely stating that the weather promised to be fair that day.

He was in a peculiar state of mind this morning, as distant from despondent resignation as from exaltation or from passion of any kind. It was the cold, absolute inward peace of a man who had settled all accounts with life, and had nothing to expect or to fear or to give. True, there was yet that deed for him to do. But so much had been already overcome towards its completion, and the little which yet remained was now so certain to be carried out, that this great deed of his life he almost considered as accomplished. Whilst still a living man in full command of his mental and physical energy, he had the strange, but perfectly tangible sensation of being already dead, looking upon himself, all those connected with him, and the whole world, with the unruffled, somewhat pitying serenity of a stranger.

The whole of his life was clearly present to his mind, in the minutest details, very clear, the proportions well preserved. He thought of Tania, of the friends he was leaving behind him, of their party, of the country,—but in a calm dispassionate way, as if everything that held him to life had receded to an enormous distance. Of thrilling and ardent emotions, such as those which at one time had carried him almost out of himself in Dubravnik, there was no trace, and he was very glad of this. When all was well over with him, the work of his whole life fulfilled to the last without fear or guile, and he stood alone face to face with the great solemnity of death—these beautiful and elevating emotions would return to him, he knew, and uphold him in the last trial. But during these days of prepara-tion he had deliberately suppressed them as too fervid and vehement, whenever he had felt them stirring. He wanted to keep his head quite cool for the deed. The cold unbending will, planted on the granite foundations of necessity, would serve better for this occasion.

He was dressed and quite ready when the door opened noiselessly and Vatajko entered. He had come to St Peters-burg on " business," and whilst waiting for his own affair, had undertaken one of the accessory functions in connection with the coming attempt. As a temporary guest Vatajko also lodged at headquarters and slept in another room. He had been up long ago and waiting until it was time to come in to wake Andrey if he should be asleep.

" You are up already ! " he exclaimed by way of greeting.

Vatajko looked grave with a tint of bashfulness in his eyes. He was very glad of the opportunity of spending another half-hour with Andrey, yet he was nervous lest Andrey should be disturbed by his presence.

Andrey gave him a slight friendly nod, without saying anything. He was hardly conscious that the young man was there, looking at him wistfully. To him Vatajko was no more than a shadow.

" One of your sentinels," the young man began hesitatingly, " asked whether he might come to bid farewell to you here, as it can't be done when you are both on the spot. He says he knows you, and hopes it will not trouble you in any way."

" Not in the least. I shall be very glad to see him,"

Andrey answered out of a feeling of good-fellowship, though personally the matter interested him so little that he did not even ask who the man was. It was after a pause that he noticed his omission, and asked the sentinel's name.

"Sanepin," Vatajko answered. "You met him about a year ago when he was going abroad, and you were coming in."

"Oh, yes," Andrey said.

He remembered the crossing of the frontier, the German inn, the noisy debates; but how remote it all was now!

Sanepin came in fact shortly after Vatajko. At first he seemed somewhat subdued by the unusual circumstances under which the meeting took place. But he soon recovered his buoyancy, the loud talk and gestures of an old campaigner. In Andrey's appearance and speech there was nothing calling for special reserve or solemnity; he looked only a little more thoughtful and absent-minded than usual.

They recalled their meeting at the frontier,—Vulitch, David, even Ostrogorsky. Sanepin had returned to his fatherland three months before by way of the southern frontier. As he had spent most of his time in Odessa, Andrey asked after the revolutionists of that town,—Levshin, Klein, and the others. What did all this matter to him now?—he wondered mentally at his own curiosity. But he felt a strange pleasure in getting this useless information; it was something like throwing stones into a deep pit, which does not give back the noise of their fall.

They talked on various topics without once mentioning or alluding to the affair for which they had to start in a few minutes. The imminence of something unusual was revealed only by certain pauses and hitches in the conversation. Over the tea, which was served before they went, Sanepin told Vatajko how the porter downstairs mistook him for the police sub-inspector on account of his military appearance and imperative tone of voice. Both of them laughed. Andrey smiled faintly at the story. He drank his tea and ate his bread "on principle," remembering the relation between body and spirit, though he had but little appetite.

In return for Sanepin's story Vatajko began to relate somewhat incoherently how something similar had once happened to himself.

"It is time!" Andrey interrupted them in the middle of a sentence, looking at his watch. They broke up instantly, and rose to their feet, very serious.

The leave-taking was short and undemonstrative, none of the three wanting to waste time or words. The two young men embraced Andrey in turn in the Russian fashion.

"Fare thee well, brother!" Sazepin said, addressing him for the first and last time in the familiar second person singular.

Vatajko led his companion to the back stairs by which they could pass out unseen. Andrey remained behind, having to wait another twenty minutes. He had to appear last on the field, in order to diminish as much as possible the risk of being detected and ignominiously arrested before he had done anything.

Left alone Andrey felt much easier than under the eyes of his two companions. He was not sorry that nobody else came in. But he was still less able than before to concentrate his attention upon anything. Disjointed fragments of thoughts and broken recollections whirled through his brain with such feverish rapidity that the capacity for reckoning time forsook him entirely. Every two minutes he consulted his watch, fully persuaded that the time for him to wait had elapsed, and wondering exceedingly when he found that so little of it had actually gone. But for the movements of the second hand he would have thought his watch had stopped.

The minute hand having at last reached the right point, he put on his hat and went into the street for his last walk through the town: he would have to cross it once again on a solemn occasion. But that would be a ride not a walk. . . .

Rapidly he turned the corner of the Ekaterininskaia, where headquarters were to sever as quickly as possible his connection with the house he had lived in. Then he slackened his pace to his normal one, and looked upon the large strip of sky stretching over his head all along the street.

The placid eternal sun was shining brightly midway to the zenith, shedding floods of bountiful rays upon the busy town, the prolific earth, and foolish pugnacious men. Steadfast and spotless it looked down like a loving eye wide open with wonder upon the incapacity of its favourite children to make better use of the warmth, the joy, the life it poured into them.

Thin white clouds floated like carded wool in the depths of the azure vault. The air was very transparent and calm. It was one of the few fine spring days, so niggardly bestowed by nature upon the northern capital, but for that all the more appreciated by its inhabitants. Andrey also drew much pleasure from the contemplation of the beautiful, serene sky; it gave him the assurance that the Tzar's morning walk would not be put off on account of bad weather, as sometimes occurred.

This point was of the utmost importance. A few days ago the conspirators had been surprised by the announcement of a very untoward change in the projected movements of the court. The Tzar was to start on his summer journey before the usual time, and might leave town in a day or two. At such a juncture a day like this was a godsend.

The distance to the Palace Square, where the attempt had to take place, was considerable. But Andrey intended to traverse it all on foot: he would be more independent of chance in walking than in riding, and could easily regulate his pace so as to reach the spot in time, not one minute too soon or too late. Besides, as a foot passenger he would be much less noticeable on approaching the Tzar's promenade ground, which teemed with spies.

In his calm stoical mood Andrey walked along Lafonskaia Street, Transfiguration Square, and a part of Taurida Street, partly with, partly against the human stream, receiving upon his retina the images of faces—young, old, merry, serious; of horses, carriages, shops, policemen—all instantly forgotten as soon as he had passed them, attentive only to keep at his regular pace. Thus he reached the corner of the Taurida Garden, where a chance meeting with two perfect strangers upset his mental equilibrium, and brought disorder and tumult into the mental calm which he thought no longer subject to any disturbance.

These strangers, whose path came so unseasonably across his own, were two young folks,—a girl and a young man, looking like students, and to all appearances lovers. They came from the Greek Street, and were going arm-in-arm talking, along the outer railing of the Taurida Garden, smiling, caressing each other with their eyes. The young man was telling the girl in a low voice something very tender, judging from the radiant face of the girl. The pair went on slowly, almost reluctantly, as if burdened with their happiness, paying no attention to anything around.

But Andrey could not take his eyes off that girl; she was so remarkably like his own Tania. She was a little taller, and the lower part of her face was heavier, but the complexion, the quaint set of the head, the long eyebrows, resembling the outstretched wings of a bird, and that something which gives character to a face and to a figure, were exactly those of Tania. She was even dressed in dark blue, Tania's favourite colour. Andrey would have given much to see her eyes; he was sure they would be like those he was never to look into again. But the girl's face was turned in profile to him, and she never bestowed one glance in his direction.

She had melted and fascinated him all the same, awakening feelings and memories he thought lulled in eternal sleep. The stern mood of the man going to meet his gloomy destiny could not hold out against the charm of that vision. His benumbed heart beat again with the generous throb of human love, as he gave that beautiful child his unspoken blessing, mentally bidding her live and be happy, and be spared the bereavement her sister had to suffer.

The girl passed, smiling and blushing, little suspecting the emotions she had caused in the stranger against whom she had brushed. The couple turned the corner and disappeared. But Andrey could not at once recover his self-control. The layer of ice, with which by an effort of will he had succeeded in covering up all his feelings, was broken, and the sea of bitter sadness hidden beneath burst forth. He had no power to master and bind it fast again. The image of his Tania rose before him no longer as a distant shadow, but warm with life, suffering, love, and beauty, as close and real as the girl who had just passed him.

How was the poor child now? How will she be to-night, when the act anticipated has become an accomplished fact? How will she bear it, when all was over with him? . . . Thoughts each sadder than the other invaded his defenceless soul. Why had they loved each other? Why had they met at all? Had she never seen him, she would probably have loved George. They would have married and lived happy for who knows how many years! . . . Whilst now, only a few months of happiness to be paid for at so dreadful a price! . . . Pictures of the past rose in his mind one after another in the fulness of their charm or their painfulness. The scenes of their love: that face, those eyes glowing with a happiness that seemed eternal! And then the same dear face distorted by the anguish of that last farewell! . . .

Mechanically Andrey went on in the right direction, but his thoughts wandered far away. He did not notice in his absorption a dreadful sign ; the foot passengers whom he had hitherto passed by in his brisk though not exaggerated pace, were now passing him.   Unconsciously he had greatly slackened his pace.   He passed the Taurida Garden, the long Kirochnaia, a part of the Liteiny, and reached the Panteleimon church, and here it dawned upon him as a vague suspicion that he had walked somewhat more slowly than he should have done.   He looked at his watch, and his blood ran cold and his heart ceased beating in the blank horror of his discovery : he would be too late !   Only three minutes left and half a mile before him !   The Tzar might leave town, and not come out walking on the morrow. . . .

Love, pity, dreams, sorrows—all dashed away in an instant, vanishing in the twinkling of the eye, as a flight of sparrows in a stubble field vanish when a stone falls into their midst. His face pale, Andrey rushed forward, driven on and scourged by the awful thought that he had ruined everything by his foolish sentimentality !

He would have preferred running, if he could, but this would have singled him out for the attention of the police.   On, on ! he would walk and keep up appearances, and yet get on faster than cabs driving in the middle of the street.   He passed like an arrow the Panteleimon Street, the bridge, the summer garden, without feeling in the least tired.   Fear seemed to have doubled his strength ; but this was a delusion ; the overwhelming dread which tormented him, and set his heart hammering in his breast, had spurred him to extraordinary exertions only for a short time, and then were gnawing at the root of his strength.   As he hastened along the Field of Mars, his breath began to fail him. . . . But, on, on ! he might be in time yet ; the Tzar was some- times a few minutes late.   Again he dashed on, redoubling his efforts to keep at the same pace as before. . . .

He was suffocating.   His breast was aching as if pierced by hundreds of needles.   Every hundred yards cost him a greater effort.

The physical sensation he underwent in this mad race recalled to his mind in a flash another run of earlier days, when, pursued closely through woods and marshes, his horse falling under him, his salvation depended upon his reaching a large town before his pursuers.   But even then, in that race for life and freedom, he was not half so anxious to reach the goal as he was now in tha mad chase after death !—But he had no time to waste on parallels and contrasts. On, on! The drill-field is crossed as quickly as his failing strength permitted. He had not looked at his watch again in order not to waste one precious moment, but he knew only too well that he was hopelessly behind time. Yet he hastened on with furious energy. On, on! He had only two streets to get through. But already the ground swam under him, and his legs trembled. He must slacken his pace or run the risk of falling to the ground, and being picked up by the police as a drunkard. What was the use, moreover, of appearing in the sight of spies like a madman escaping from an asylum?

He went more slowly accordingly. When he issued upon a little bye-street near the Palace, where Vatajko stood waiting for him, he looked composed and presentable, but death and despair were in his soul. He could no longer doubt that the whole affair had miscarried owing to him ; he read that in the troubled face of his sentinel.

"What? I am too late?" he asked falteringly, only too sure of the answer.

"No ; you are not," Vatajko said, "but I thought you would be. The Tzar has taken a longer walk to-day on account of the fine weather."

Andrey gave a sigh of relief. Vatajko's words had refreshed and restored him, and almost taken away his fatigue, due more to mental than to physical strain.

"Nothing particular happened to detain you?" Vatajko inquired.

"Nothing whatever," said Andrey. "I will wait here on this bench," he added, pointing to a stone seat by the footpath. "Go and set the men in movement."

When alone Andrey lifted his right hand against the sky. He wanted to see whether it was sufficiently steady. Not quite! The fingers trembled, though not much. A few minutes after he lifted it again and found that it was all right.

He was quite ready now and waited calmly.

Another few minutes passed, and he saw Sazepin's tall figure advancing in his direction. Andrey rose to meet him half way ; Sazepin was the bearer of the final word which would bring him into the field.

Sazepin's face was solemn and even sad. When they were quite close he fixed upon Andrey a significant, reverential look, making a long affirmative nod, resembling a bow.

"Speak out!" said Andrey.

He understood that the message was a favourable one, but in a case of such gravity he wanted something positive.

"The Tzar is coming his usual way," Sazepin whispered.

Andrey nodded to say that it was all right, and moved forward, waving his hand slightly to Sazepin to bid him retire from the scene.

His turn was come now!

He was still some three hundred yards from the Palace Square, when he found himself in the very midst of the Tzar's spies and guardians, stationary and moving, watching every approach of the Tzar's way with the special purpose of keeping off, and at the slightest suspicion of arresting, all strangers male and female. One of them—a grey-haired respectable gentleman, whom Andrey would have never suspected of being a spy—approached him at once.

"Be good enough, sir," he said, politely, but impressively, "to take another road."

"Why?" Andrey asked ingenuously, moving at the same time forward so as to gain as much ground as possible.

"It is strictly prohibited for any one to go that way," the old gentleman said, following him closely. "Please return instantly, or you will get into trouble!"

Andrey shrugged his shoulders.

"But there is nothing in the street to prevent people crossing it!" he said, with assumed wonder, always going forward.

The old man waved his hand, and two tall figures in plain clothes, standing some thirty yards farther off, ran towards Andrey with the evident intention of laying hands on him. His position was a very critical one. He stopped, intending to enter if possible into some kind of altercation with the spies so as to gain a few minutes.

But the conspirators had calculated their movements well; at this very moment the Tzar's dog appeared at the mouth of the street, and the spies vanished; the Tzar would pass in a minute, and they were bound to have his way cleared before he came.

Andrey went slowly along and reached the corner of the street unmolested.

The Tzar was at this moment a few paces beyond the monument to Alexander I., facing the Palace.

From the window of a house opposite two young men

looked upon the scene of the coming encounter with beating hearts.

George was one of them.   He had seen Andrey's coming in collision with the three spies, and had already given him up for lost.   Now he saw the master of all the Russias turning the corner, and Andrey, calm, stern as fate, moving towards him. On seeing a stranger in his way the Tzar gave a momentary start, but still went on.

In breathless suspense George watched as the distance between the two diminished step by step until they seemed to him to have come within a few paces of each other and nothing had yet happened, and they were still advancing. . . . Why does he wait?   What could it mean? . . . But it was a delusion ; the distance which appeared in perspective so short was about fifteen yards.

Here according to regulations Andrey had to take off his hat and stand bareheaded until his master should pass.   But, instead of doing that act of obeisance, he plunged his hand into his pocket, drew a revolver, pointed and fired at the Tzar instantaneously.

The ball struck in the wall of the house at the Tzar's back some forty yards off, almost under the cornice.   The shot had missed ; the revolver kicked strongly, and had to be pointed at the feet for a fatal shot.   This Andrey discovered too late. For a moment he stood petrified with consternation, both hands hanging down.   The next moment he rushed onward, his brow knitted, his face pale, firing shot after shot.   The Tzar, pale likewise, the flaps of his long overcoat gathered up in his hands, ran from him as quickly as he could.   But he did not lose his presence of mind; instead of running straight, he ran in zigzags, thus offering a very difficult aim to the man running behind him.   That saved him ; only one of the shots pierced the cape of his overcoat, the rest missed altogether.

In less than a minute Andrey's six shots were spent.   The flock of spies, who at first had made themselves scarce, now appeared from all sides, their numbers growing every moment. George saw Andrey encompassed at all points by the crowd of them, wild at his having eluded their vigilance.   For a moment they stood at a distance, cautious, none daring to be the first to approach him.   Then seeing him disarmed and making no show of resistance, they rushed on him all at once.   But

George heard only their fierce shouts and cries, for he had covered his face with both his hands and saw nothing more.

Andrey was thrown into prison half dead. He recovered, and was in due time tried, condemned, and executed.

He had perished. But the work for which he died did not perish. It goes forward from defeat to defeat towards the final victory, which in this sad world of ours cannot be obtained save by the sufferings and the sacrifice of the chosen few.

THE END.

Printed by WALTER SCOTT, *Felling, Newcastle-on-Tyne*

List of Walter Scott's Publications.

CONTENTS.

Crown 8vo, about 350 pp. each, Cloth Cover, 2s. 6d. per Volume.

Half Polished Morocco, gilt top, 5s.

COUNT TOLSTOÏ'S COMPLETE WORKS.

MR. WALTER SCOTT has pleasure in calling attention to the series of translations of works by the eminent Russian novelist, Count Lyof N. Tolstoï, which he has published. These translations admirably reproduce the spirit and style of the original. The English reading public have been introduced to an entirely new series of works by one who is probably the greatest living master of fiction in Europe, and one upon whose personality and opinions, —social, ethical, and religious,—a unique attention is concentrated. To those unfamiliar with the charm of Russian fiction, and especially with the works of Count Tolstoï, these volumes will come as a new revelation of power.

The following volumes are already issued :—

VOL. I. A RUSSIAN PROPRIETOR.
VOL. II. THE COSSACKS.
VOL. III. IVAN ILYITCH, AND OTHER STORIES.
VOL. IV. THE INVADERS, AND OTHER STORIES.
VOL. V. MY RELIGION.
VOL. VI. LIFE.
VOL. VII. MY CONFESSION.
VOL. VIII. CHILDHOOD, BOYHOOD, AND YOUTH.
VOL. IX. THE PHYSIOLOGY OF WAR.
VOL. X. AND XI. ANNA KARÉNINA. (2 VOLS.)
VOL. XII. WHAT TO DO?
VOL. XIII. TO XVI. WAR AND PEACE. (4 VOLS.)
VOL. XVII. THE LONG EXILE, AND OTHER STORIES FOR CHILDREN.
VOL. XVIII. SEVASTOPOL.
VOL. XIX. THE KREUTZER SONATA, AND FAMILY HAPPINESS.

Uniform with the above.

IMPRESSIONS OF RUSSIA.
BY DR. GEORG BRANDES.

London: WALTER SCOTT, 24 Warwick Lane, Paternoster Row.

GREAT WRITERS.

A NEW SERIES OF CRITICAL BIOGRAPHIES.

Edited by Professor ERIC S. ROBERTSON, M.A.

MONTHLY SHILLING VOLUMES, CROWN 8vo.

Bindings:—Cloth, cut edges, 1s. ; cloth, uncut edges, 1s. ; half-morocco, gilt top antique (in a variety of new reproductions of old tints).

VOLUMES ALREADY ISSUED.

1 LIFE OF LONGFELLOW. By Prof. Eric S. Robertson.
"A most readable little work."—*Liverpool Mercury.*

2 LIFE OF COLERIDGE. By Hall Caine.
"Brief and vigorous, written throughout with spirit and great literary skill."—*Scotsman.*

3 LIFE OF DICKENS. By Frank T. Marzials.
"Notwithstanding the mass of matter that has been printed relating to Dickens and his works . . . we should, until we came across this volume, have been at a loss to recommend any popular life of England's most popular novelist as being really satisfactory. The difficulty is removed by Mr. Marzials's little book."—*Athenæum.*

4 LIFE OF DANTE GABRIEL ROSSETTI. By J. Knight.
"Mr. Knight's picture of the great poet and painter is the fullest and best yet presented to the public."—*The Graphic.*

5 LIFE OF SAMUEL JOHNSON. By Colonel F. Grant.
"Colonel Grant has performed his task with diligence, sound judgment, good taste, and accuracy."—*Illustrated London News.*

6 LIFE OF DARWIN. By G. T. Bettany.
"Mr. G. T. Bettany's *Life of Darwin* is a sound and conscientious work."—*Saturday Review.*

7 LIFE OF CHARLOTTE BRONTË. By A. Birrell.
"Those who know much of Charlotte Brontë will learn more, and those who know nothing about her will find all that is best worth learning in Mr. Birrell's pleasant book."—*St. James' Gazette.*

8 LIFE OF THOMAS CARLYLE. By R. Garnett, LL.D.
"This is an admirable book. Nothing could be more felicitous and fairer than the way in which he takes us through Carlyle's life and works."—*Pall Mall Gazette.*

9 LIFE OF ADAM SMITH. By R. B. Haldane, M.P.
"Written with a perspicuity seldom exemplified when dealing with economic science."—*Scotsman.*

10 LIFE OF KEATS. By W. M. Rossetti.
"Valuable for the ample information which it contains."—*Cambridge Independent.*

11 LIFE OF SHELLEY. By William Sharp.
"The criticisms . . . entitle this capital monograph to be ranked with the best biographies of Shelley."—*Westminster Review.*

12 LIFE OF SMOLLETT. By David Hannay.
"A capital record of a writer who still remains one of the great masters of the English novel."—*Saturday Review.*

13 LIFE OF GOLDSMITH. By Austin Dobson.
"The story of his literary and social life in London, with all its humorous and pathetic vicissitudes, is here retold, as none could tell it better."—*Daily News.*

14 LIFE OF SCOTT. By Professor Yonge.
"For readers and lovers of the poems and novels of Sir Walter Scott, this is a most enjoyable book."—*Aberdeen Free Press.*

GREAT WRITERS—(*Continued*).

15 **LIFE OF BURNS.** By Professor Blackie.
"The editor certainly made a hit when he persuaded Blackie to write about Burns."—*Pall Mall Gazette.*

16 **LIFE OF BUNYAN.** By Canon Venables.
"A most intelligent, appreciative, and valuable memoir."—*Scotsman.*

17 **LIFE OF VICTOR HUGO.** By Frank T. Marzials.
"Mr. Marzials's volume presents to us, in a more handy form than any English, or even French handbook gives, the summary of what, up to the moment in which we write, is known or conjectured about the life of the great poet."—*Saturday Review.*

18 **LIFE OF EMERSON.** By Richard Garnett, LL.D.
"As to the larger section of the public, to whom the series of Great Writers is addressed, no record of Emerson's life and work could be more desirable, both in breadth of treatment and lucidity of style, than Dr. Garnett's."—*Saturday Review.*

19 **LIFE OF GOETHE.** By James Sime.
"Mr. James Sime's competence as a biographer of Goethe, both in respect of knowledge of his special subject, and of German literature generally, is beyond question."—*Manchester Guardian.*

20 **LIFE OF CONGREVE.** By Edmund Gosse.
"Mr. Gosse has written an admirable and most interesting biography of a man of letters who is of particular interest to other men of letters."—*The Academy.*

21 **LIFE OF CRABBE.** By T. E. Kebbel.
"No English poet since Shakespeare has observed certain aspects of nature and of human life more closely; and in the qualities of manliness and of sincerity he is surpassed by none. . Mr. Kebbel's monograph is worthy of the subject."—*Athenæum.*

22 **LIFE OF HEINE.** By William Sharp.
"This is an admirable monograph . . . more fully written up to the level of recent knowledge and criticism of its theme than any other English work."—*Scotsman.*

23 **LIFE OF MILL.** By W. L. Courtney.
"A most sympathetic and discriminating memoir."—*Glasgow Herald.*

24 **LIFE OF SCHILLER.** By Henry W. Nevinson.
"This is a well-written little volume, which presents the leading facts of the poet's life in a neatly rounded picture."—*Scotsman.*

25 **LIFE OF MARRYAT.** By David Hannay.
"What Mr. Hannay had to do—give a craftsman-like account of a great craftsman who has been almost incomprehensibly undervalued—could hardly have been done better than in this little volume."—*Manchester Guardian.*

26 LIFE OF LESSING. By T. W. Rolleston.
27 LIFE OF MILTON. By Richard Garnett.
28 LIFE OF GEORGE ELIOT. By Oscar Browning.
29 LIFE OF BALZAC. By Frederick Wedmore.

The following Volumes will shortly be Issued :—

30 LIFE OF JANE AUSTEN. (Feb. 25th). By Goldwin Smith.
31 LIFE OF BROWNING. (March 25th). By William Sharp.

After this volume, the issue of this series will be bi-monthly.

32 LIFE OF BYRON. (May 25th). By Hon. Roden Noel.

Complete Bibliography to each volume, by J. P. ANDERSON, British Museum.

Volumes are in preparation by Goldwin Smith, Arthur Symons, W. E. Henley, Hermann Merivale, H. E. Watts, Cosmo Monkhouse, Frank T. Marzials, W. H. Pollock, John Addington Symonds, Stepniak, Moncure Conway, Prof. Wallace, etc.; etc.

LIBRARY EDITION OF "GREAT WRITERS."—Demy 8vo, price 2s. 6d.

London : WALTER SCOTT, 24 Warwick Lane, Paternoster Row.

THE CAMELOT SERIES.

EDITED BY ERNEST RHYS. IN SHILLING MONTHLY VOLUMES, CROWN 8vo.

1 ·ROMANCE OF KING ARTHUR. Edited by E. Rhys.
2 THOREAU'S WALDEN. Edited by Will H. Dircks.
3 ENGLISH OPIUM-EATER. Edited by William Sharp.
4 LANDOR'S CONVERSATIONS. Edited by Havelock Ellis.
5 PLUTARCH'S LIVES. Edited by B. J. Snell, M.A.
6 RELIGIO MEDICI, &c. Edited by J. A. Symonds.
7 SHELLEY'S LETTERS. Edited by Ernest Rhys.
8 PROSE WRITINGS OF SWIFT. Edited by W. Lewin.
9 MY STUDY WINDOWS. Edited by R. Garnett, LL.D.
10 GREAT ENGLISH PAINTERS. Edited by William Sharp.
11 LORD BYRON'S LETTERS. Edited by Mathilde Blind.
12 ESSAYS BY LEIGH HUNT. Edited by A. Symons.
13 LONGFELLOW'S PROSE. Edited by W. Tirebuck.
14 GREAT MUSICAL COMPOSERS. Edited by E. Sharp.
15 MARCUS AURELIUS. Edited by Alice Zimmern.
16 SPECIMEN DAYS IN AMERICA. By Walt Whitman.
17 WHITE'S SELBORNE. Edited by Richard Jefferies.
18 DEFOE'S SINGLETON. Edited by H.. Halliday Sparling.
19 MAZZINI'S ESSAYS. Edited by William Clarke.
20 PROSE WRITINGS OF HEINE. Edited by Havelock Ellis.
21 REYNOLDS' DISCOURSES. Edited by Helen Zimmern.
22 PAPERS OF STEELE AND ADDISON. Edited by W. Lewin.
23 BURNS'S LETTERS. Edited by J. Logie Robertson, M.A.
24 THE STORY OF THE VOLSUNGS. Edited by H. H. Sparling.
25 SARTOR RESARTUS. Edited by Ernest Rhys.
26 WRITINGS OF EMERSON. Edited by Percival Chubb.
27 SENECA'S MORALS. Edited by Walter Clode.
28 DEMOCRATIC VISTAS. By Walt Whitman.
29 LIFE OF LORD HERBERT. Edited by Will H. Dircks.
30 ENGLISH PROSE. Edited by Arthur Galton.
31 IBSEN'S PILLARS OF SOCIETY. Edited by Havelock Ellis.
32 FAIRY AND FOLK TALES. Edited by W. B. Yeats.
33 EPICTETUS. Edited by T. W. Rolleston.
34 THE ENGLISH POETS. By James Russell Lowell.
35 ESSAYS OF DR. JOHNSON. Edited by Stuart J. Reid.
36 ESSAYS OF WILLIAM HAZLITT. Edited by Frank Carr.
37 LANDOR'S PENTAMERON, &c. Edited by Havelock Ellis.
38 POE'S TALES AND ESSAYS. Edited by Ernest Rhys.
39 VICAR OF WAKEFIELD. By Oliver Goldsmith.
40 POLITICAL ORATIONS. Edited by William Clarke.
41 CHESTERFIELD'S LETTERS. Selected by Charles Sayle.
42 THOREAU'S WEEK. Edited by Will H. Dircks.
43 STORIES FROM CARLETON. Edited by W. B. Yeats
44 AUTOCRAT OF THE BREAKFAST TABLE. By O. W. Holmes.
45 JANE EYRE. By Charlotte Brontë.
46 ELIZABETHAN ENGLAND. Edited by Lothrop Withington.
47 WRITINGS OF THOMAS DAVIS. Edited by T. W. Rolleston.
48 SPENCE'S ANECDOTES. Edited by John Underhill.
49 MORE'S UTOPIA. Edited by Maurice Adams.

The CAMELOT SERIES may be had in the following Bindings:—Cloth, cut edges, 1s.; Cloth, uncut edges, 1s.; Half-Morocco, gilt top, antique (in a variety of new reproductions of old tints); Red Roan, gilt edges, 3s.

NEW PRESENTATION VOLUMES.

The "WINDSOR SERIES" of Poetical Anthologies.

Printed on Antique Paper. Crown 8vo. Bound in Blue Cloth, each with suitable Emblematic Design on Cover, Price 3s. 6d.

1 **Women's Voices.** An Anthology of the most Characteristic Poems by English, Scotch, and Irish Women. Edited by Mrs. William Sharp.

2 **Sonnets of this Century.** With an Exhaustive Critical Essay on the Sonnet. Edited by William Sharp.

3 **The Children of the Poets.** An Anthology from English and American Writers of Three Centuries. Edited by Professor Eric S. Robertson.

4 **Sacred Song.** A Volume of Religious Verse. Selected and arranged, with Notes, by Samuel Waddington.

5 **A Century of Australian Song.** Selected and Edited by Douglas B. W. Sladen, B.A., Oxon.

6 **Jacobite Songs and Ballads.** Selected and Edited, with Notes, by G. S. Macquoid.

7 **Irish Minstrelsy.** Edited, with Notes and Introduction, by H. Halliday Sparling.

8 **The Sonnets of Europe.** A Volume of Translations. Selected and arranged by Samuel Waddington.

9 **Early English and Scottish Poetry.** Selected and Edited, with Introduction, by H. Macaulay Fitzgibbon.

10 **Ballads of the North Countrie.** Edited, with Introduction, by Graham R. Tomson.

11 **Songs and Poems of the Sea.** An Anthology of Poems Descriptive of the Sea. Edited by Mrs. Sharp.

12 **Songs and Poems of Fairyland.** An Anthology of English Fairy Poetry. Selected by A. E. Waite.

13 **Songs and Poems of the Great Dominion.** Edited by W. D. Lighthall, of Montreal.

The above may also be had in various Calf and Morocco Bindings.

London : WALTER SCOTT, 24 Warwick Lane, Paternoster Row.

THE OXFORD · LIBRARY.

Handsomely Bound in Blue Cloth, Gilt Top, Uncut Edges,
Price 2s. each.

Comprises the most popular Novels of SCOTT, DICKENS, LYTTON,
MARRYAT, LEVER, etc., and original Stories by New Authors.

1 BARNABY RUDGE	27 VICAR OF WAKEFIELD
2 OLD CURIOSITY SHOP	28 PRINCE of the HOUSE OF DAVID
3 PICKWICK PAPERS	29 WIDE, WIDE WORLD
4 NICHOLAS NICKLEBY	30 VILLAGE TALES
5 OLIVER TWIST	31 BEN-HUR
6 MARTIN CHUZZLEWIT	32 UNCLE TOM'S CABIN
7 SKETCHES BY BOZ	33 ROBINSON CRUSOE
8 RODERICK RANDOM	34 THE WHITE SLAVE
9 PEREGRINE PICKLE	35 CHARLES O'MALLEY
10 IVANHOE	36 MIDSHIPMAN EASY
11 KENILWORTH	37 BRIDE OF LAMMERMOOR
12 JACOB FAITHFUL	38 HEART OF MIDLOTHIAN
13 PETER SIMPLE	39 LAST OF THE BARONS
14 PAUL CLIFFORD	40 OLD MORTALITY
15 EUGENE ARAM	41 TOM CRINGLE'S LOG
16 ERNEST MALTRAVERS	42 CRUISE OF THE MIDGE
17 ALICE; OR, THE MYSTERIES	43 COLLEEN BAWN
18 RIENZI	44 VALENTINE VOX
19 PELHAM	45 NIGHT AND MORNING
20 LAST DAYS OF POMPEII	46 BUNYAN
21 THE SCOTTISH CHIEFS	47 FOXE'S BOOK OF MARTYRS
22 WILSON'S TALES	48 MANSFIELD PARK
23 THE INHERITANCE	49 LAST OF THE MOHICANS
24 ETHEL LINTON	50 POOR JACK
25 A MOUNTAIN DAISY	51 THE LAMPLIGHTER
26 HAZEL; or, Perilpoint Lighthouse	52 JANE EYRE

The above may also be had in half morocco.

REWARD BOOKS.

2s. 6d. Plain Edges; 3s. Gilt Edges. Each Crown 8vo,
Cloth Gilt, Bevelled Boards.

1 LIVES GREAT AND SIMPLE
2 QUEENS OF LITERATURE
3 OUR AMERICAN COUSINS
4 LIFE OF GENERAL GORDON
5 OUR QUEEN
6 CONDUCT AND DUTY
7 NEW WORLD HEROES
8 LIFE OF GARIBALDI
9 LIFE OF DR. MOFFAT
10 LIFE OF W. E. GLADSTONE
11 LIFE AND WORK OF LORD BEACONSFIELD
12 LIFE OF RICHARD COBDEN
13 LIFE OF JOHN BRIGHT
14 LIFE OF H. W. BEECHER
15 LIFE OF DR. LIVINGSTONE
16 LIFE OF GRACE DARLING
17 FAMOUS ENGINEERS
18 THE VICAR OF WAKEFIELD
19 THE PRINCE OF THE HOUSE OF DAVID
20 THE BOOK OF MARTYRS
21 THE PILGRIM'S PROGRESS AND HOLY WAR
22 THE WIDE, WIDE WORLD
23 VILLAGE TALES
24 BEN-HUR
25 GOLDEN GLEAMS
26 MEMORABLE SHIPWRECKS
27 TALES AND SKETCHES OF THE COVENANTERS
28 UNCLE TOM'S CABIN
29 ROBINSON CRUSOE
30 ELIJAH, THE DESERT PROPHET
31 THE YOUNG WOMAN'S FRIEND
32 THE YOUNG MAN'S FRIEND
33 CHRISTIAN HEROINES
34 THE ANGELS' WHISPERS
35 A JOLLY FELLOWSHIP
36 IVANHOE
37 JACOB FAITHFUL
38 ETHEL LINTON
39 THE SCOTTISH CHIEFS
40 MOUNTAIN DAISY
41 HAZEL; OR, PERILPOINT LIGHTHOUSE
42 BARNABY RUDGE
43 OLD CURIOSITY SHOP
44 PICKWICK PAPERS
45 NICHOLAS NICKLEBY
46 OLIVER TWIST
47 MARTIN CHUZZLEWIT
48 SKETCHES BY BOZ
49 HEART OF MIDLOTHIAN
50 OLD MORTALITY
51 TALES OF THE BORDERS
52 VALENTINE VOX
53 CHARLES O'MALLEY
54 CRUISE OF THE MIDGE
55 UNA MONTGOMERY

The above can also be had bound in half morocco.

London : WALTER SCOTT, 24 Warwick Lane, Paternoster Row.

THE NOVOCASTRIAN SERIES.

POPULAR VOLUMES OF FICTION.

SQUARE 8vo. PRICE ONE SHILLING EACH.

Cashel Byron's Profession.   By G. Bernard Shaw.

The Ugly Story of Miss Wetherby.   By Richard
Pryce, Author of "An Evil Spirit," etc.

A Witness from the Dead.   (A Special Reporter's
Story.)   By Florence Layard.

Police Sergeant C 21 : The Story of a Crime.   By
Reginald Barnett.   (25th Thousand.)

The Devil's Whisper.   By the Author of " Police
Sergeant C 21."

The Kara Yerta Tragedy.   An Australian Romance.
By J. E. Harrison.   (15th Thousand.)

The Policeman's Lantern : Strange Stories of
London Life.   By James Greenwood, " The Amateur Casual."

Mysteries and Adventures.   By A. Conan Doyle.
Author of " Micah Clarke."

Oak - Bough and Wattle - Blossom : Stories and
Sketches by Australians in England.   Edited by A. Patchett Martin.
Mrs. Campbell Praed, C. Haddon Chambers, Douglas B. W. Sladen, Philip
Mennell, Edmund Stansfeld Rawson, S. Oldmixon.

Jack Dudley's Wife.   By E. M. Davy, Author of
" A Prince of Como," etc.

Vane's Invention : An Electrical Romance.   By
Walter Milbank.

London : WALTER SCOTT, 24 Warwick Lane, Paternoster Row.

BOOKS FOR THE YOUNG.

F'cap. 8vo, Cloth Elegant, Plain Edges, 1s. 6d.   Gilt Edges, 2s.

An Admirable Series for the Family or for School Libraries,
Splendidly Illustrated.

Miss Matty; or, Our Youngest Passenger. By Mrs. George Cupples. And other Tales. Illustrated.

Horace Hazelwood; or, Little Things. By R. Hope Moncrieff. And other Tales. Illustrated.

Found Afloat. By Mrs. George Cupples. And other Tales. Illustrated.

The White Roe of Glenmere. By Mrs. Bickerstaffe. And other Tales. Illustrated.

Jessie Oglethorpe: The Story of a Daughter's Devotion. By W. H. D. Adams. And other Tales. Illustrated.

Paul and Marie, the Orphans of Auvergne. And other Tales. Illustrated.

Archie Mason: An Irish Story. By Letitia M'Clintock. And other Tales. Illustrated.

The Woodfords: An Emigrant Story. By Mrs. Cupples. And other Tales. Illustrated.

Old Andy's Money: An Irish Story. By Letitia M'Clintock. And other Tales. Illustrated.

Marius Flaminius: A Story of the Days of Hadrian. By A. J. Buckland. And other Tales. Illustrated.

The Inundation of the Rhine. From the German. And other Tales. Illustrated.

The Little Orphans. From the German. And other Tales. Illustrated.

Select Christian Biographies. By Rev. James Gardner, A.M., M.D. Illustrated.

Leoline; or, Captured and Rescued. By Emily Grace Harding.

Life of David Livingstone. By J. Donald, F.R.G.S.

BOOKS FOR THE YOUNG—*(continued)*.

SHILLING REWARD BOOKS.   *Foolscap 8vo, Cloth Gilt.*

By E. STUART PHELPS.

GYPSY BREYNTON.
GYPSY'S COUSIN JOY.   In which Joy comes to Yorkbury.
GYPSY'S SOWING AND REAPING.   Which concerns Gypsy and Tom.
GYPSY'S YEAR AT THE GOLDEN CRESCENT.   In which Gypsy
goes to Boarding School.

Foolscap 8vo, Cloth Boards, price One Shilling each.

VERY SHORT STORIES AND VERSES
FOR CHILDREN.

By Mrs. W. K. CLIFFORD, Author of "Anyhow Stories," etc.

ILLUSTRATED BY EDITH CAMPBELL.

A NEW

NATURAL HISTORY OF BIRDS, BEASTS,
AND FISHES.

By JOHN K. LEYS, M.A.

LIFE STORIES OF FAMOUS CHILDREN.

Adapted from the French.   By the Author of "Spenser for Children."

Parchment Limp.   Price Sixpence.

PARENTAL COMMANDMENTS;

Or, Warnings to Parents on the Physical, Intellectual, and Moral
Training of their Children.

Square 8vo, Cloth Gilt, price One Shilling.

A CHRISTMAS CAROL:

Being a Ghost Story of Christmas.   By Charles Dickens.

Paper Cover, Price Sixpence.

HELEN'S BABIES.

With some account of their ways—Innocent, Crafty, Angelic, Impish,
Witching, and Repulsive; also a Partial Record of their Actions
during Ten Days of their Existence.

By THEIR LATEST VICTIM.

GUIDE AND HAND-BOOKS.

Fourth and Revised Edition. Illustrated. 3s. 6d. Cloth.

The Land of the Vikings; a Popular Guide to
Norway. By C. Jurgenson. Containing Maps, Skeleton Routes, Tables, and all information useful to Tourists.

Crown 8vo, Cloth Limp, Map and Illustrations, Price 3s. 6d.

Guide to Copenhagen and Its Environs. By Lucy
Andersen, author of "A Holiday in Italy."

Crown 8vo, Paper Cover, Price 6d. Numerous Illustrations.

Newcastle-on-Tyne of To-Day. A Descriptive
and Historical Guide. By W. W. Tomlinson.

Compact and Practical Phrase Books. Cloth Limp, 1s. each.

The European Conversation Books. No. 1—French;
No. 2—ITALIAN; No. 3—SPANISH (in preparation); No. 4—GERMAN (in preparation).

CONTENTS:—Hints to Travellers—Arriving and Leaving a Station—In a Railway Train—At a Restaurant—At an Hotel—Washing—Paying Hotel Bill—Telegrams and Letters—Enquiries—On Board Ship, etc., etc.

Just Published, Crown 8vo, Price 1s. 6d.

Guide to Emigration and Colonisation: An Appeal
to the Nation. By Waldemar Bannow, upwards of Eighteen Years a resident of Victoria, Australia.

Crown 8vo, Price One Shilling.

The Emigrant's Handbook to the British Colonies.
By Waldemar Bannow.

Price, Paper Boards, 2s. 6d., Cloth, 3s. 6d.

The Law of Compensation under the Agricultural
Holdings (England) Act, 1883. By Charles D. Forster, Solicitor, Newcastle-on-Tyne.

Price 2s. 6d.

Handy Guide to Conveyancing Costs under the
Solicitors' Remuneration Act, 1881. By J. Hough.

Crown 8vo, Cloth, Price One Shilling.

Elocution. (With Select Recitations.) By T. R.
Walton Pearson, M.A., of St. Catharine's College, Cambridge, and Frederic William Waithman, Lecturer on Elocution in the Leeds and Bradford Institutes.

Demy 16mo, Price Sixpence.

Lowes's Shorthand (Pitman Superseded: Taylor
Improved), for acquiring in half-an-hour the method of taking down Speeches, etc., without the aid of a master.

GUIDE AND HAND-BOOKS—*(continued)*.

Crown 8vo, Paper Cover, Price Sixpence.

The Turkish Bath: its History and Use. By Frederick C. Coley.

Crown 8vo, Price One Shilling.

Plain Facts about Infant Feeding and Management. Popular Treatise by C. Stennett Redmond, L.K.Q.C.P.L & L.R.C.S.L.

Demy 8vo, Price One Shilling.

Eye Diseases: What the Public should Know of Them. Two Lectures delivered at the Northumberland, Durham, and Newcastle Infirmary for Diseases of the Eye. By C. S. Jeaffreson, F.R.C.S.E., F.R.M.S.

Sixteenth Thousand, Demy 8vo, Price Sixpence.

The Ear: Its Structure, Mechanism, and connection with the Throat. By Richard Ellis, F.R.C.S.

Tenth Thousand, Royal 8vo, 62 pp., Price 6d.

The Doctor's Corner. By R. Clark Newton, M.S., L.M., M.R.C.S.L.

Price One Shilling.

Villa and Cottage Gardening. Specially adapted for Scotland, Northern England, and Ireland. By Alexander Sweet.

Square 8vo, Parchment Limp, Price Sixpence each.

Don't: Directions for avoiding Improprieties in Conduct and Common Errors of Speech.

Why Smoke and Drink? By James Parton.

THE EVERY-DAY HELP SERIES.

Demy 32mo, 126 pages, Price 6d. each.

How to do Business. A Pocket Manual of Practical Affairs and Guide to Success in Life.

How to Behave. A Pocket Manual of Etiquette.

How to Write. A Pocket Manual of Composition and Letter Writing.

Demy 32mo, Price Fourpence.

How to Debate. A Manual for Mutual Improvement Societies, with Hints on Public Speaking, and a list of subjects suitable for discussion.

Now Ready. Post Quarto, Price Sixpence.

The Ladies' National Housekeeper's Book, for any Year.

London: WALTER SCOTT, 24 Warwick Lane, Paternoster Row.

LOCAL PUBLICATIONS.

3 Vols. Royal 8vo.   Price 12s. 6d. each.

CHRONOLOGICAL HISTORY OF NEWCASTLE AND GATESHEAD, 15TH TO 17TH CENTURIES

By RICHARD WELFORD.

Cheaper Edition.   Crown 8vo, Cloth, 5s., 433 Pages.

NEWCASTLE TOWN.

By R. J. CHARLETON.   Illustrations by R. JOBLING.

With Four Maps, Crown 8vo, 574 Pages, Strongly Bound in Limp Cloth, Price 5s.

NEW COMPREHENSIVE GUIDE TO THE COUNTY OF NORTHUMBERLAND.

By W. W. TOMLINSON.

This Guide is an exhaustive repertory of the interesting facts—historical, antiquarian, and legendary—relating to the county.   Greater prominence has been given to the antiquities than in any previous work of the kind, and every care has been taken to describe them in the light of the most recent archæological research.

The Guide includes lists of the principal Hills, Crags, Loughs, Lakes, Denes; Pre-Reformation Churches ; Ancient British Camps, Castles, Pele-Towers, Roman Stations and Camps, Remains of Monastic Houses, as well as of the principal Hotels and Inns in the County, and is supplemented by a complete Index.

Crown 8vo, Paper Cover, Price 6d.   Numerous Illustrations.

NEWCASTLE-ON-TYNE OF TO-DAY.

A DESCRIPTIVE AND HISTORICAL GUIDE.

By W. W. TOMLINSON.

Just Published, Crown 8vo, Price 1s. 6d.

HEALTH RESORTS OF NORTHERN ENGLAND.

By RICHARD ELLIS, F.R.C.S., Edin., Senior Surgeon, Newcastle-on-Tyne Throat and Ear Hospital.

Crown Quarto, 48 Pages.   Monthly 6d.   Illustrated.

MONTHLY CHRONICLE OF NORTH-COUNTRY LORE AND LEGEND.

Established to preserve the wealth of Legend and Story of the North of England. ANNUAL SUBSCRIPTION, 7s. 6D., POST FREE.

Crown 4to, Price Threepence.

HISTORY OF THE DICKY BIRD SOCIETY.

By UNCLE TOBY.

With numerous Illustrations.   Cover designed by ROBERT JOBLING, and printed in eleven colours.

London : WALTER SCOTT, 24 Warwick Lane, Paternoster Row.

NEW BOOKLETS.

Bound in White Grained Boards, with Gilt Lettering.
Price One Shilling Each.

WHERE LOVE IS THERE GOD IS ALSO.

THE TWO PILGRIMS.

WHAT MEN LIVE BY.

By Count Leo Tolstoï.

These Booklets form three Stories by Count Leo Tolstoï, the eminent Russian writer, whose recent work, entitled "My Religion," has produced such an impression in Europe and America. These little stories, issued in Russia as tracts for the people, possess all the grace, naïveté, and power which characterise the writings of Count Tolstoï; and while inculcating in the most penetrating way the fundamental Christian principles of love, humility, and charity, are perfect in their art-form as stories pure and simple.

SQUARE 8vo, PRICE ONE SHILLING EACH.

Cover Printed in Twelve Colours.

MARY IN HEAVEN.

POEM BY ROBERT BURNS.

SEA POEMS.

BY VARIOUS AUTHORS.

WITH ILLUSTRATIONS BY ROBERT JOBLING.

London: Walter Scott, 24 Warwick Lane, Paternoster Row.

THE ELSWICK SCIENCE SERIES.

The Elswick Series is intended to supply Teachers and Students with good books, void of "cram." They will be issued as rapidly as is consistent with the caution necessary to secure accuracy. A great aim will be to adapt them to modern requirements and improvements, and to keep abreast with the latest discoveries in Science, and the most recent practice in Engineering.

Crown 8vo, Cloth, Price 3s. 6d. each.

PRACTICAL AND THEORETICAL TRIGONOMETRY.

By HENRY EVERS, LL.D., Author of "Steam," etc.

MANUAL OF STEAM AND PRIME MOVERS.

By HENRY EVERS, LL.D., Author of "Steam," "Navigation," etc.

In Preparation.

DESCRIPTIVE GEOMETRY.

By T. N. EAGLES, M.A., Author of "Constructive Geometry of Plane Curves."

SCIENCE LECTURES.

Crown 8vo, Cloth, Price 1s.   CONTENTS :—

The Natural History of Instinct.   By G. J. Romanes, F.R.S.
Animal Life on the Ocean Surface.   By Professor H. N. Moseley, M.A., F.R.S.
The Eye and Its Work.   By Litton Forbes, M.D., F.R.C.S.E., L.R.C.P.
The Movements of Plants.   By Ernest A Parkyn, M.A.
The Relations Between Natural Science and Literature.   By Professor H. Nettleship, M.A.
Facts and Fictions in Zoology.   By Dr. Andrew Wilson, F.R.S.E.
The Animals that Make Limestone.   By Dr. P. Herbert Carpenter, F.R.S.

PAMPHLETS.

THINK IT OUT! LECTURE ON HOME RULE.

By DR. THOMAS HODGKIN.   Price Threepence.

WEALTH AND WANT:

A Refutation of Henry George's "Progress and Poverty."   Price Sixpence.

CHRISTIAN SOCIALISM *v.* STATE SOCIALISM.

The Penny Dinner Problem.   Price Twopence.

STATE SOCIALISM: A LATTER-DAY TYRANNY.

By ELIJAH COPLAND.   Price One Penny.

THE SEVEN PILLARS OF SOCIALISM: AN INDICTMENT.

By REV. MARSDEN GIBSON, M.A.   Price Twopence.

A SCHEME FOR NATIONAL PENSIONS.

By REV. W. MOORE EDE, M.A.   Crown 8vo, Price One Penny.

THE GERMAN INSURANCE LAWS.

By REV. W. MOORE EDE, M.A.   Crown, 8vo, Price One Penny.

London : WALTER SCOTT, 24 Warwick Lane, Paternoster Row.

MISCELLANEOUS.

Complete in 24 Volumes, One Shilling each, strongly bound in Cloth.
Uniform in size and style with the "Camelot Series."

WILSON'S TALES OF THE BORDERS
AND OF SCOTLAND.
HISTORICAL, TRADITIONARY, AND IMAGINATIVE.
REVISED BY ALEXANDER LEIGHTON.

NUMEROUS ILLUSTRATIONS IN CHROMO-LITHOGRAPHY.

Imperial 8vo, Cloth, 10s. 6d. each.

LIFE AND EXPLORATIONS OF DR. LIVINGSTONE.

ENGLAND UNDER VICTORIA.

LIFE AND TIMES OF GARIBALDI.

Royal 8vo, Cloth, fully illustrated, Price 7s. 6d.

LIFE OF GENERAL GORDON.

Crown 8vo, 507 Pages, Cloth Gilt, Price 4s. 6d.

FOR A SONG'S SAKE, AND OTHER STORIES.
BY THE LATE PHILIP BOURKE MARSTON.

With a Memoir by William Sharp.

NEW AND COMPLETE EDITION OF

SCOTT'S BORDER ANTIQUITIES.

Royal Folio. Half Morocco Antique, £5 5s.

One Hundred Copper-plate Engravings of the Castles, Abbeys, Churches, Peles, and other Historical Remains of the Border Counties of Northumberland, Cumberland, Westmoreland, Roxburgh, Haddington, Fife, Selkirk, Stirling, mostly from paintings by Luke Clennell.

WITH INTRODUCTION, DESCRIPTIVE SKETCHES, AND VERSES, BY SIR WALTER SCOTT.

Demy 8vo, Cloth, Illustrated. Price 3s. 6d.

TO THE GOLDEN LAND.
SKETCHES OF A TRIP TO SOUTHERN CALIFORNIA.
BY SAMUEL STOREY, M.P.

London : WALTER SCOTT, 24 Warwick Lane, Paternoster Row.

NEW SERIES OF BIJOU BOOKS.

Crown 32mo. Price Sixpence each.

Printed on good Paper, with red line borders, and Bound in Cloth Limp, full Gilt Side, and in Parchment Limp.

---

1 Cheery Lays for Dreary Days.

2 Songs in the House of our Pilgrimage.

3 God's Greetings in Nature and Man's Responses.

4 Bijou Thoughts for Busy Moments.

5 Helpful Counsels for those who wish to make Progress in the Life of Holiness.

6 Suggestive Thoughts for Meditative Minds.

7 Sketches by Great Masters, of Scenes, Places, and Persons, taken from Standard Authors.

8 The Compliments of the Season ; or, Words for all Times.

9 On Business Only. Little Illustrations and Suggestions regarding Business Qualifications and Successes. A Book relating to Work.

10 Home, Sweet Home. Lyrics and Songs on Home and Family Life.

11 In Fun and in Earnest. Selections in Prose and Verse, chiefly humorous.

12 Golden Sands from the German Ocean of Thought. Selections from German Authors, Ancient and Modern.

13 The Land o' the Leal, and other Songs.

14 Bible Thoughts for all Times.

15 Golden Thoughts from the New Testament.

16 Gleanings from the Thoughts of General Gordon.

17 Sayings of 100 Great Men in Praise of Books. Edited by E. W. Cole.

18 The Funniest Book but One. 200 Gems of Fun. Edited by E. W. Cole.

Also in Sets of Six, Strong Cloth and Fancy Paper Boxes - 3s. 6d.

London : Walter Scott, 24 Warwick Lane, Paternoster Row.

ALPHABETICAL LIST OF BOOKS.

A Book of Blunders. By Rev. D. Macrae. Crown 8vo, Paper Cover, 1s.

A Christmas Carol. By Charles Dickens. Square 8vo, Cloth, 1s.

An Exile's Romance. By Arthur Keyser. Crown 8vo, Paper Cover, 1s.

Angels' Whispers. By Daniel C. Eddy, D.D. Crown 8vo, Cloth, 2s. 6d.

Australian Song, A Century of. *(See Windsor Series.)*

Ballads of the North Countrie. *(See Windsor Series.)*

Beaconsfield, Earl of. His Life and Work. By Lewis Apjohn Crown 8vo, Cloth, with Photograph, 2s. 6d. New Edition. 30th Thousand.

"A careful, and on the whole an impartial narrative of the facts in the career of the man it describes."—*Scotsman.*

Ben-Hur: A Tale of the Christ. By Lew. Wallace. Crown 8vo, Cloth Gilt, 2s. 6d.

Beresford, John Jervis, M.A. Last Year's Leaves. Poems. Cloth Gilt, 3s.

"Mr. Beresford's subjects are many and varied, and he displays a ready versatility in adapting his strains to the most opposite themes."—*The Morning Post.*

Blind, Mathilde. The Heather on Fire: A Tale, in Verse, of the Highland Clearances. Square 8vo, Paper Cover, 1s., Cloth, 1s. 6d.

"Remarkable for beauty of expression and pathos of incidents."—*Leeds Mercury.*

Bijou Books—

Bible Thoughts for all Times.

Bijou Thoughts for Busy Moments.

Cheery Lays for Dreary Days.

Gleanings from the Thoughts of General Gordon.

God's Greetings in Nature and Man's Responses.

Golden Sands from the German Ocean of Thought. Selections from German Authors, Ancient and Modern.

Golden Thoughts from the New Testament.

Helpful Counsels for those who wish to make Progress in a Life of Holiness.

Home, Sweet Home. Lyrics and Songs on Home and Family Life.

In Fun and in Earnest. Selections in Prose and Verse, chiefly humorous.

On Business Only. Little Illustrations and Suggestions regarding Business Qualifications and Successes. A Book relating to Work.

Sayings of 100 Great Men in Praise of Books. Edited by E. Cole.

Sketches by Great Masters, of Scenes, Places, and Persons, taken from Standard Authors.

Songs in the House of our Pilgrimage.

Suggestive Thoughts for Meditative Minds.

The Compliments of the Season; or, Words for all Times.

The Funniest Book but One. 200 Gems of Fun. Edited by E. Cole.

The Land o' the Leal, and other Songs

Crown 32mo, Cloth Limp, full gilt sides, 6d. ; also in Sets of Six, in strong cloth case, 3s. 6d. ; also in parchment.

Book of Martyrs. By John Foxe. Crown 8vo,
Cloth, Bevelled Boards, Illustrated, 2s. 6d.

Bright, John, and the Peace Party. By Lewis
Apjohn. Crown 8vo, Cloth, Bevelled Boards, with Photo, 2s. 6d. 25th Thousand.

" Is full of interest and instruction for all who desire to understand the political forces in operation about them."—*Liverpool Mercury*.

Camelot Series, The. Monthly Shilling Volumes.
Cloth, cut or uncut edges.

Autocrat at the Breakfast Table, The. By Oliver Wendell Holmes.

Browne, Sir Thomas, Religio Medici, Urn-Burial, Christian Morals, etc. With Introduction by J. Addington Symonds.

" The whole contents of this volume are delightful, and the excellent introduction by Mr. Symonds is all that could be desired."—*North British Daily Mail*.

Burns's Letters. Selected and arranged, with Introduction, by J. Logie Robertson, M.A.

" Should be read by all those who have hitherto derived their estimate of Burns's genius from his poems only."—*Literary World*.

Camelot Series—*continued.*

Byron's Letters and Journals. Selected, with Introduction, by Mathilde Blind.

"A charming volume, heralded by a vigorous and sensible introduction."—*Athenæum.*

Confessions of an English Opium-Eater, with Levana, the Rosicrucians and Freemasons, etc. By Thomas De Quincey. With Introductory Note by William Sharp.

"There has never previously been issued at the price so excellent an edition of De Quincey's *chef d'œuvre.*"

Defoe's Captain Singleton. Edited, with Introduction, by H. Halliday Sparling.

"The sketch of Defoe's life, indeed, is a model of what such work should be—succinct, businesslike, and entirely free from fine writing."—*Athenæum.*

Democratic Vistas, and other Papers. By Walt Whitman. (Published by arrangement with the author.)

"Next to the ' Preface ' to *Leaves of Grass, Democratic Vistas* is quite the best thing Whitman has produced in prose."—*Academy.*

Emerson, Select Writings of. With Introduction by Percival Chubb.

"In this volume we have most that is characteristic of the writings of Emerson. . . . Mr. Chubb gives a fair and candid estimate of his (Emerson's) undoubted worth."—*Daily Free Press.*

English Prose, from Maundeville to Thackeray. Chosen and edited by Arthur Galton.

"This is an admirable selection, made with good judgment, and a taste catholic enough to include specimens from all really representative masters of English prose."—*Scotsman.*

Epictetus (The Teaching of) : being the " Encheiridion of Epictetus," with Selections from the " Dissertations " and " Fragments." Translated from the Greek, with Introduction and Notes, by T. W. Rolleston.

"Mr. Rolleston has done his work in scholarly fashion. . . . We commend this little volume to all who care to acquaint themselves with the finest fruits of the natural theology of the ancient world."—*Manchester Guardian.*

Essays of Dr. Johnson, with Biographical Introduction and Notes by Stuart J. Reid.

"This is an excellent volume ; . . . it gives a very good idea of the immortal doctor's prose style."—*Cambridge Independent.*

Fairy and Folk Tales of the Irish Peasantry. Edited and Selected by W. B. Yeats.

"The reader has here a collection of Irish tales drawn from the best sources."—*Athenæum.*

Camelot Series—*continued.*

Great English Painters. Selected Biographies from Allan Cunningham's *Lives of Eminent British Painters.* Edited by William Sharp.

"The lives of Hogarth, Wilson, Reynolds, Gainsborough, and Blake form Mr. Sharp's choice, and nothing could be better."—*Saturday Review.*

Great Musical Composers. By G. F. Ferris. Edited, with Introduction, by Mrs. William Sharp.

"All lovers of music will hail the appearance of *Great Composers* in the 'Camelot Series.'"—*Dundee Advertiser.*

Hazlitt, William, Essays of. Selected and Edited, with Introduction and Notes, by Frank Carr.

"A delightful selection of William Hazlitt's essays."—*Literary World.*

Heine, Heinrich, the Prose Writings of. With Introduction by Havelock Ellis.

"Mr. Havelock Ellis has done his work earnestly and carefully, and gives us an excellent account of Heine's life and pursuits."—*Graphic.*

Hunt, Leigh, Essays by. With Introduction and Notes by Arthur Symons.

"No pleasanter book has been issued for a long while than this selection of Essays."—*Oxford Review.*

Jane Eyre. By Charlotte Brontë.

Landor's Imaginary Conversations. Selected, with Introduction, by Havelock Ellis.

"Those who may now read these charming talks for the first time will be glad of the opportunity of purchasing them in this cheap and accessible form."—*Oxford Times.*

Landor's Pentameron, and other Imaginary Conversations. Edited, with a Preface, by Havelock Ellis.

"Of all the series (of Imaginary Conversations) it is probable that a consensus of educated opinion would place the 'Pentameron' as the richest and best in many ways."—*Glasgow Herald.*

Lord Chesterfield's Letters to his Son. Selected, with Introduction, by Charles Sayle.

". . . The graces of life are not everything, but they are a very great deal, and Chesterfield is their most effective expounder."—*Literary World.*

Lord Herbert, Autobiography of. Edited, with an Introduction, by Will H. Dircks.

"In the 'Camelot Series' we have the Autobiography of Lord Herbert of Cherbury, edited by Mr. Will H. Dircks, whose prefatory essay contains all that is needed to introduce a popular edition of a famous book."—*Saturday Review.*

Camelot Series—*continued.*

Longfellow's " Hyperion," " Kavanah," and "The Trouveres." With Introduction by W. Tirebuck.

" The introductory notice is written with keen critical insight, and, though brief, presents a thoroughly appreciative and just estimate of Longfellow."—*Aberdeen Free Press.*

Malory's Romance of King Arthur and the Quest of the Holy Grail. (From the *Morte de Arthur.*) Edited by Ernest Rhys.

" An excellent selection for the opening volume of a cheap series of prose classics. Permanently valuable, well printed, and carefully edited, these classics are a marvel of cheapness."—*Cambridge Independent.*

Marcus Aurelius, The Meditations of. Edited by Alice Zimmern.

" On the whole, we should rank this first of the complete English translations of Aurelius."—*Classical Review.*

Mazzini's Essays: Literary, Political, and Religious. With Introduction by William Clarke.

" To say that this little volume forms one of the 'Camelot Series' is sufficient guarantee for the neatness of its binding and the clearness of its type. We have to thank the editor for the service he has done to English literature in bringing Mazzini within the reach of all."—*Oxford Review.*

My Study Windows. By James Russell Lowell. With Introduction by R. Garnett, LL.D.

" A charming edition of these essays."—*Yorkshire Post.*

Pillars of Society, The, and other Plays. By Henrik Ibsen. Edited, with an Introduction, by Havelock Ellis.

" Every competent reader of these dramas can see that Ibsen's dramatic grasp of character is very great, and his faculty of dramatising purely modern situations such as certainly no living English dramatists, and we think not even certain much-praised Frenchmen, possess."—*Manchester Guardian.*

Poe's Tales and Essays. Edited, with Introduction, by Ernest Rhys.

" . . . To those who are unacquainted with the writings of the gifted and eccentric American, it is almost impossible to describe their strange glamour of mystery and weird fascination."—*Dundee Advertiser.*

Political Orations, from Wentworth to Macaulay. Edited, with Introduction, by William Clarke.

" The volume may serve as a valuable hand-book of British parliamentary eloquence."—*Ruskin Reading Guild Journal.*

Camelot Series—*continued.*

Plutarch's Lives (Langhorne). With Introductory Note by B. J. Snell, M.A.

"Well selected; and very helpful introduction."

Reynolds's Discourses. With Introduction by Helen Zimmern.

"Miss Helen Zimmern edits the Discourses with a sensible and quite acceptable Introduction, in which the present value to artists of Reynolds's theory of art is fairly recognised."—*Saturday Review.*

Sartor Resartus. By Thomas Carlyle. With Introduction by Ernest Rhys.

"By far the best of the cheap editions now before the public."—*Newcastle Leader.*

Seneca, Selections from. With Introduction by Walter Clode.

"It is one of the most charming and interesting volumes of the 'Camelot Series.'"—*Pall Mall Gazette.*

Shelley's Essays and Letters. Edited, with Introductory Note, by Ernest Rhys.

"One of the most interesting of the set. . . . Mr. Rhys has done his work with care and intelligence."—*The Graphic.*

Specimen Days in America. By Walt Whitman. Newly revised by the Author, with fresh Preface and additional Note.

"We can praise Mr. Whitman when he writes prose. He did good service in the hospitals of the North, and he records his experience,—very strange and startling experience, too."—*Spectator.*

Stories from Carleton. Selected, with Introduction, by W. Yeats. [*September volume.*

Swift's Prose Writings. Chosen and arranged by W. Lewin.

"There is a serviceable introduction by Mr. Walter Lewin, who may be congratulated on the felicity of his selection and arrangement of the pieces printed. The book is a wonderful shilling's-worth."—*Scotsman.*

The Lover, and other Papers of Steele and Addison. Edited by Walter Lewin.

"A book which every lover of first-class literature will welcome."—*Sheffield Independent.*

Thoreau's Walden. With Introductory Note by Will H. Dircks.

"An introductory note by Mr. Will H. Dircks judiciously prepares the mind of the reader for the enjoyment of the American transcendentalist."—*London Daily Chronicle.*

Camelot Series—*continued.*

Thoreau's "Week." With Prefatory Note by Will H. Dircks.

" With both ' Walden ' and the ' Week ' published in an easily accessible form, the English reading public have now an excellent opportunity of making themselves acquainted with Thoreau's master-pieces, and estimating the value of his ethical creed."—*Pall Mall Gazette.*

Vicar of Wakefield. By Oliver Goldsmith. Edited, with Preface, by Ernest Rhys.

" This is a very neatly got-up edition of Goldsmith's classic story. We know of no other edition which is at once so cheap, so well printed, and of so convenient a size."—*Oxford Review.*

Volsunga Saga : the Story of the Volsungs and Niblungs. Translated from the Icelandic by Eirikr Magnusson and William Morris. With Introduction and Notes by H. Halliday Sparling.

" This unpretentious little volume is intended for the lover of poetry and nature rather than the student, that he may enjoy and wonder at this great work."—*Cambridge Chronicle.*

White's Natural History of Selborne. With a Naturalist's Calendar and additional Observations. With a Preface by Richard Jefferies.

" The last published writing of Richard Jefferies is, we believe, the preface which he contributed to the excellent edition of White's *Selborne* in the ' Camelot Series.' "—*Pall Mall Gazette.*

Canterbury Poets, The. Cloth, Red Edges, 1s.;
Cloth, Uncut Edges, 1s. ; Red Roan, Gilt Edges, 2s. 6d.

American Sonnets. Selected and edited by William Sharp.

" Mr. Sharp's critical and explanatory introduction is good read-ing, and he deserves all praise for the rich literary dish he has provided."—*Birmingham Daily Gazette.*

Australian Ballads and Rhymes. Poems inspired by Life and Scenery in Australia and New Zealand. Selected and edited by Douglas B. W. Sladen, B.A., Oxon.

" Mr. Douglas Sladen's pretty little volume is doubly welcome, not only as the first poetical anthology of the ' youngest born of Britain's great dominions,' but for its pleasant introduction of the singers whose songs have made it up, and for a valuable study of Henry Kendall as a bush poet."—*Academy.*

Ballades and Rondeaus, Chants Royal, Sestinas, Villan-elles, etc. Selected, with chapter on the various forms, by J. Gleeson White.

" Mr. Gleeson White's collection of *Ballades and Rondeaus* is a really delightful little book."—*Pall Mall Gazette.*

Canterbury Poets—*continued.*

Beaumont and Fletcher's Plays. Selected, with an Introduction, by John S. Fletcher.

"Any one who wishes to get some acquaintance of 'the sweets' of these dramatists without 'the bitters,' should give this little volume a place on their book-shelves."—*Oxford Review.*

Ben Jonson, Dramatic Works and Lyrics of. Selected, with Essay, Biographical and Critical, by John Addington Symonds.

"A selection discreetly compounded and introduced by an admirable biographical and critical preface."—*Saturday Review.*

Blake, Poems and Specimens from the Prose Writings of. Edited, with Introductory Notice, by Joseph Skipsey.

"It will delight every lover of Blake. The introductory sketch is one of the best we have read on the subject.—*Sheffield Independent.*

Border Ballads. Selected and edited by Graham R. Tomson.

"The best ballads are here given us out of a wide selection. The introductory note is scholarly and appreciative."—*Yorkshire Advertiser.*

Bowles, Lamb, and Hartley Coleridge. Selected, with Introduction, by William Tirebuck.

"The work has been well and sensibly done, and the little volume ought to be welcomed as giving us the works of three poets too little known nowadays; the preface is extremely good."—*The Graphic.*

Burns.—Poems. With Biographical Sketch by Joseph Skipsey.

Burns.—Songs. With Critical Estimate by Joseph Skipsey.

"The essays are valuable additions to Burns literature, and should be read by all who are admirers of the poet, and—for that matter—by all who are not."—*Derby Gazette.*

Byron. Vol. I.—Childe Harold and Don Juan. Selected, with Introduction, by Mathilde Blind.

Byron. Vol. II.—Miscellaneous.

"A felicitous selection, prefaced by an appreciative biography of the poet."—*Oxford Times.*

Campbell. With Introductory Notice by John Hogben.

"The introductory essay is all that such a notice should be. The little volume is a good one, and handy for the pocket."—*The Graphic.*

Chatterton. With Prefatory Notice, Biographical and Critical, by John Richmond.

"The editor has done his work with care and skill, and the biographical and critical notice with which the volume opens is a model of what such articles should be."—*Glasgow Herald.*

Canterbury Poets--*continued.*

Chaucer.   Selected and edited by Frederick Noël Paton.

"The introduction gives a readable sketch of Chaucer's life, and the old English is so edited that a modern reader will find no difficulty in understanding it."—*Scotsman.*

Children of the Poets.   An Anthology from English and American Writers of Three Centuries.   Compiled by Eric S. Robertson.

"A most delightful volume, the *best* of the series, which is saying a great deal."

Christian Year.   Thoughts in Verse for the Sundays and Holy Days throughout the Year.   By Rev. John Keble, M.A.

Coleridge.   With Introduction by Joseph Skipsey.

"The volume is edited with diligent care, and in the arrangement of the poems capital judgment and good taste are displayed."—*To-day.*

Cowper.   Selected, with Prefatory Notice, by Eva Hope.

"Miss Hope has done her work well and sympathetically, and the collection is welcome."—*Graphic.*

Crabbe.   With Prefatory Notice, Biographical and Critical, by Edward Lamplough.

"The selection has been carefully made, and we do not doubt that, under his new appearance, the old poet will be to many a most welcome guest."—*Wales Observer.*

Days of the Year.   A Poetic Calendar from the Works of Alfred Austin.   Selected by A. S.   With Introduction by William Sharp.

"To all who care for sweet thoughts sweetly expressed ; to all who find melody and harmony in Nature, this daily remembrancer of the things that we delight in cannot fail to be a welcome companion."—*Standard.*

Dobell, Sydney.   Selected, with Introductory Memoir, by Mrs. Dobell.

"The exuberant fancy, grace, and passion of the poet are well illustrated by the selections."—*Leeds Mercury.*

Early English Poetry.   Selected, with Critical Introduction and Notes, by H. Macaulay Fitzgibbon.

"The work has been well done, and should be in the hands of all students of Early English Poetry."

30

Canterbury Poets—*continued.*

Elfin Music. An Anthology of English Fairy Poetry. Selected and arranged, with an Introduction, by Arthur Edward Waite.

"This is a unique production, and abounds in gems of poetry, every great poet being placed under contribution. Mr. Waite's introduction is a careful historical treatment of the subject of fairy lore, which cannot fail to be of value to the student of literature."— *The Examiner.*

Emerson. With Prefatory Note by Walter Lewin.

"Readers may rest assured that no better, handier, or cheaper edition of the great essayist's poems—poems which, under all their rugged irregularities of form, are still brimful of deep and sincere thought—will ever be likely to come into market than that now lying before us in ' The Canterbury Poets.' "—*Dundee Advertiser.*

Goethe's "Faust," with some of the Minor Poems. Edited by Elizabeth Craigmyle.

"The essay by the editor is worthy of the subject ; and the little volume is a choice and handy edition of the great poem."—*Newcastle Daily Journal.*

Goldsmith, The Plays and Poems of. With Introduction by William Tirebuck.

"The introduction is a skilful piece of compressed biography, succinct, graphic, and faithful."—*Yorkshire Post.*

Greek Anthology, Selections from. Edited by Graham R. Tomson. [*September volume.*

Greenwell, Dora, Poems of. With a Biographical Introduction by William Dorling.

"The selection before us is excellent in every way, and includes some of the best of her poetical pieces."—*Oxford Times.*

Heine, Heinrich. Selected, with Introduction, by Mrs. Kroeker.

"Mrs. Freiligrath-Kroeker may be congratulated on her successful achievement, and we can heartily recommend her selections from Heine's poems to every English household where poetry is cherished." —*Literary World.*

Herbert's Poems, to which are added Selections from his Prose, and Walton's Life. With Introduction by Ernest Rhys.

"The volume is altogether a delightful, comprehensive, and important one, and Mr. Scott has done well to issue it in his very valuable, neat, and cheap series."—*Brechin Advertiser.*

Herrick—Hesperides. With Notes by Herbert P. Horne.

"A pretty edition, with some good notes."—*Athenæum.*

Canterbury Poets—*continued*.

Hogg, James, the Ettrick Shepherd. Selected. Edited, with Introduction, by the Poet's Daughter, Mrs. Garden.
" The reader may be assured that he has here the finest and most characteristic work of James Hogg."—*Oxford Times*.

Horace. Translations from Horace. With Notes. By Sir Stephen E. De Vere, Bart.
" This third edition is published in a cheap and handy form, and whatever verdict the public may pronounce on the translations themselves, no lover of Horace will refuse a grateful tribute of warm and well-merited praise to them, and to the admirable preface which sets them off so brilliantly."—*The Spectator*.

Hugo, Victor. Translated by Dean Carrington, with Introduction by Countess Martinengo-Cesaresco.
" The translation is good, and I am reading the poems with much interest. I have no copy of them in the original, but there is a source of much enjoyment in the translation."—JOHN BRIGHT.

Hunt and Hood, The Poetical Works of. Edited, with Introduction, by Julian Harwood.   [*November volume.*

Irish Minstrelsy. Being a selection of Irish Songs, Lyrics, and Ballads; Original and Translated. Edited, with Notes and Introduction, by H. Halliday Sparling.
" It is such an anthology of Irish poetry up to the most recent date as will be a revelation of hitherto hidden wealth to most readers, and to experts will seem a triumph of competent editing."—*Truth*.

Jacobite Songs and Ballads. Selected, with Notes and Introduction, by G. S. Macquoid.
" The selection is excellent, and the accompanying 'notes' exactly what is wanted in such a book."—*Arbroath Herald*.

Keats. With Introductory Sketch, by John Hogben.
" It is, like its fellows, a pleasant and convenient little volume; and Mr. Hogben's introductory sketch is fairly satisfactory."—*The Spectator*.

Landor. Selected and edited by Ernest Radford.
" Altogether, we cannot speak too highly of this beautiful little volume of selections from Landor."—*Volunteer Service Gazette*.

Longfellow. Selected, with Introduction, by Eva Hope.
" We have not seen yet so good a life of the poet as that which is included in this volume."—*Sunday School Times*.

Love-Letters of a Violinist, and other Poems. By Eric Mackay.
" He will probably be numbered with the choice few whose names are destined to live by the side of poets such as Keats, whom, as far as careful work, delicate feeling, and fiery tenderness go, he greatly resembles."—*Glasgow Herald*.

Canterbury Poets—*continued.*

Marlowe. Selections from the Dramatic Works of. With Introduction by Percy E. Pinkerton.

"It gives us all that is best and most worthy of preservation in the poet's works in a compact and handy form."—*Literary World.*

Marston, Philip Bourke.—Song-Tide : Poems and Lyrics of Love's Joy and Sorrow. Edited, with Introductory Memoir, by William Sharp.

"Altogether, this volume is one for which we cannot offer Mr. Sharp gratitude too warm."—*Academy.*

Milton's Paradise Lost. By J. Bradshaw, M.A., LL.D.

"All who desire to have the masterpiece of the great Puritan poet in a convenient and easily accessible form could not do better than become possessed of this issue."—*Dundee Advertiser.* .

Moore, Poems of. Selected, with Introduction, by John Dorrian.

"The selections are judiciously made, and are conveniently grouped in appropriate classes; and the volume as a whole contains most of what the general reader would care to see of Moore."—*Aberdeen Free Press.*

Ossian. Poems of Ossian. Translated by James Macpherson, with an Introduction, Historical and Critical, by George Eyre-Todd.

"The poems of Ossian, as all scholars know, deserve a high place in the world of poetry, and in this edition will be found all that is of value in a translation at once able and characteristic."—*Barrow News.*

Paradise Regained, and Minor Poems. Edited by J. Bradshaw, M.A., LL.D.

"Mr. Bradshaw's selection ought to gain new readers for our noble Puritan poet among a generation that knows him too little."—*Northern Daily Telegraph.*

Poe. Poems, with Selections from the Prose. With Biographical Sketch by Joseph Skipsey.

"A choice edition, with a very good preface."

Pope. With Introductory Sketch by John Hogben.

"Mr. Hogben's selection and sketch are alike to be commended."

Praed. With Introductory Notice by Frederick Cooper.

"The first to give in convenient and cheap form a substantive selection of the work of one of the most charming of English verse-writers. His introduction is good."—*Saturday Review.*

Canterbury Poets—*continued.*

Ramsay, Allan. With Biographical Sketch by J. Logie Robertson, M.A.

" The reading public have now what they had not before—a cheap and well-appointed edition of Ramsay, which gives all his best work and nothing but his best."—*Scotsman.*

Scott.—Marmion, etc. Edited, with Prefatory Notice, by William Sharp.

Scott.—Lady of the Lake, etc.

" A delightful prefatory notice."—*Derby Gazette.*

Sea Music. An Anthology of Poems and Passages descriptive of the Sea. Edited by Mrs. Sharp.

" A volume for all lovers of the sea, and who is not ? "

Shakespeare : Songs, Poems, and Sonnets. With Critical Introduction by William Sharp.

" The introductory note to this little volume of Shakespeare's Songs, Poems, and Sonnets is characterised by very sound common sense."—*Oxford Review.*

Shelley. Lyrics and Minor Poems. With Introduction by Joseph Skipsey.

" The very best and most characteristic of his work is represented."
—*Cambridge Undergraduates' Journal.*

Sonnets of this Century. Edited by William Sharp.

" The selection is very catholic and very complete, and we do not remember the name of any poet of the century whose work is worthy of consideration whom Mr. Sharp has failed to include."—*Spectator.*

Sonnets of Europe. A Volume of Translations. Selected and arranged, with Notes, by S. Waddington.

" The present selection is in all ways an admirable one."—*The Academy.*

Southey. Selections from the Poems of Robert Southey. Edited, with Biographical and Critical Introduction, by Sidney R. Thompson.

" The task of selection has been accomplished with insight and feeling. . . . Mr. Thompson also contributes a critical introduction, which is well written, shrewd, appreciative, and in every way competent."—*Notes and Queries.*

Spenser. Selected, with an Essay, Biographical and Critical, and Glossary, by Hon. Roden Noel.

" The introductory essay is well done, and altogether the volume is a valuable addition to the series of ' Canterbury Poets.' "—*Cambridge Independent Press.*

Canterbury Poets—*continued.*

> Whitman, Walt. Leaves of Grass. Edited, with Introduction, by Ernest Rhys.

> Whittier. Selected, with Introductory Notice, by Eva Hope.
> " Excellent, with a judicious memoir. It includes the poet's best work."—*Saturday Review.*

> Wild Life, Poems of. Selected and edited by Charles G. D. Roberts.
> " The editing of this little volume has been executed with enthusiasm and yet also with care."—*Spectator.*

> Wordsworth. Selected and edited, with Introduction, Biographical and Critical, by A. J. Symington.
> " Every student of Wordsworth will be glad to have the poems in so small a compass, and prefaced with such an intelligent critical notice."—*Civil Service Gazette.*

Cashel Byron's Profession. *(See Novocastrian Series.)*

Cheap Food and Cheap Cooking. To which is
added Hints for the Management of Penny Dinners for School Children. Illustrated by Coloured Diagrams. By the Rev. W. Moore-Ede, Rector of Gateshead-on-Tyne. Twentieth Thousand. Crown 8vo, price One Penny.

Child's First Steps in Learning. A Series of
Graduated Lessons for School and Home use, in Large Bold Type. Crown 4to, price Sixpence.

Children of the Poets : An Anthology from English
and American Writers of Three Centuries. Edited, with Introduction, by Professor E. R. Robertson, M.A. This Volume contains contributions by Lord Tennyson, William Bell Scott, Robert Browning, James Russell Lowell, George Macdonald, Algernon Charles Swinburne, Theodore Watts, Austin Dobson, Hon. Roden Noel, Edmund Gosse, Robert Louis Stevenson, etc. Printed on Antique Paper, Crown 8vo, 440 pages, price 3s. 6d.

Christian Heroines ; or, Lives of Female
Missionaries in Heathen Lands. By Daniel D. C. Eddy, D.D. Crown 8vo, Bevelled Boards, price 2s. 6d.

Christian Socialism *v.* State Socialism. The Penny
Dinner Problem : How may hungry children be fed without pauperising parents ? By a North-Country Woman. Crown 8vo, price Twopence.
" Is written in a bright, clever, and attractive style. It reveals a most intimate knowledge of the ways and peculiarities of the very poor, and great powers of observation and much skilful analysis of character."—*Newcastle Daily Chronicle.*

Cobden, Richard, and the Free Traders. By
Lewis Apjohn. Crown 8vo, with Photo Portrait, price 2s. 6d.

"To those members of the working and trading classes who have fallen under the influence of the reciprocity craze we recommend, as a corrective, the perusal of this cheap volume."—*Liverpool Mercury.*

"I find it very interesting."—Rt. Hon. JOHN BRIGHT.

Colleen Bawn; or, The Collegians. A Tale of
Garryowen. By Gerald Griffin. Crown 8vo, Cloth, Bevelled Boards, price 2s. 6d.

Compensation, the Law of, under the Agricultural
Holdings (England) Act, 1883. By Charles D. Forster, Solicitor, Newcastle-on-Tyne. Price, Paper Boards, 2s. 6d., Cloth, 3s. 6d.

"Several text-books have already been written on this very important Act, but for fulness of information, for clearness of arrangements, for lucidity of style, and for general helpfulness to all who desire to grasp the scope and the contents of the Act, this volume has as yet no superior."—*The Oldham Chronicle.*

Conduct and Duty. A Treasure Book of Intel-
lectual, Physical, Social, and Moral Advice. Selected from the Teachings of Thinkers and Writers of all Times and Countries. By William Thomas Pyke. Crown 8vo, Cloth Gilt, price 2s. 6d.

"A real treasure book. It contains a wealth of intellectual, physical, and moral advice."—*Melbourne Daily Telegraph.*

Copenhagen, Guide to. By Lucy Andersen.
Crown 8vo, Cloth, price 3s. 6d.

Count Tolstoï's Works. In Monthly Volumes.
Crown 8vo, 2s. 6d. per vol.; Half-Polished Morocco, gilt top, 5s.

Anna Karénina. (2 vols.)

"As you read on you say, not, 'This is like life, but, 'This is life.' It has not only the complexion, the very hue, of life, but its movement, its advances, its strange pauses, its seeming reversions to former conditions, and its perpetual change, its apparent isolations, its essential solidarity. It is a world, and you live in it while you read, and long afterward."—*W. D. Howells.*

A Russian Proprietor, and other Stories.

"For the issue of this series of the great Russian novelist's romances Mr. Walter Scott deserves the thanks of all who are interested in high literature; and the influence of such widespread perusal as must follow cannot but be to the welfare both of English fiction and of the readers thereof."—*Academy.*

Count Tolstoï's Works—*continued.*

Childhood, Boyhood, Youth.

"The quality pre-eminent in 'Childhood, Boyhood, Youth' is charm—charm of manner, magic of comprehension. It is a study of childhood and adolescence conceived in a vein at once 'fictional' (to quote the new jargon) and real. That the most baffling of all literary secrets—the secret how to present youth and the complex and evanescent emotions of youth—is Tolstoï's own is known to every one who knows his 'Katia.' But the present work is his most shining triumph in this way."—*Scots Observer.*

Ivan Ilyitch, and other Stories.

"'The Death of Ivan Ilyitch,' which is the leading tale of the present volume, is a superb realistic study both of a disease and of a man, and there are several other very impressive sketches. This edition will certainly give Tolstoï a great reputation in Britain."—*British Weekly.*

Life.

"The new volume of the English version of Count Tolstoï's works contains his ethical and religious treatise on 'Life.' It is well rendered by Miss Isabel F. Hapgood, and will be eagerly read by all who have been attracted by that powerful book 'My Religion.' . . . It need not be said that this work shows power, acuteness of thought, and a fruitful simplicity of idea. . . . The translation cannot but serve the highest interests of literature and philosophy if it serves to spread wide a knowledge of Count Tolstoï's original and impressive teaching."—*Scotsman.*

My Confession.

"By the translation of 'My Confession,' English readers are put in possession of the third and last of the series of works through which Tolstoï has set forth the fundamentals of his creed and the mental history by which he has reached it. The essence of his doctrine is simple, and can be gathered from any one of these volumes. . . . If any of the three is to be passed by, it must by no means be this concluding volume, which possesses the deep and pathetic interest which attaches to the spiritual struggles of a lofty soul."—*Manchester Guardian.*

My Religion.

"It is the spiritual autobiography of a remarkable man and a remarkable writer, upon whose life the progress of religious belief has had extraordinary practical effects, and whose eminence as an artist and a thinker has given something like a new promulgation to the fundamental doctrines of Christianity. . . . The moral force of the work lies in the earnestness with which it teaches a return to the Christianity of Christ. . . . The English translation will be welcome to a large number of readers to whom accounts of the original are familiar."—*Scotsman.*

Sevastopol.

[December volume.

Count Tolstoï's Works—*continued.*

The Cossacks: A Tale of the Caucasus in the Year 1852.

"It is almost full of the exceedingly convincing descriptions of Russian people and places, in which Count Tolstoï has certainly no living rival."—*Saturday Review.*

The Invaders, and other Stories.

"Readers who have not yet learned what 'realism' in fiction means in the hands of the Russian author who is the greatest of living novelists will find it in Mr. N. H. Dole's English translation of Tolstoï's 'Invaders, and other Stories,' just published by Mr. Walter Scott, of Paternoster Row. The descriptions of scenery with which these tales abound are as exquisite as any in the same author's novel of 'The Cossacks.'"—*Echo.*

The Long Exile, and other Stories for Children.

[November volume.

The Physiology of War, and Power and Liberty.

"Napoleon's glory was never more plainly shown to be an empty thing than in Tolstoï's powerful examination of his career. It is rather to those who are interested in Tolstoï, however, than to those who are interested in Napoleon that the books appeal. They have a rapidly growing audience in this country, and to them Mr. Huntingdon's clear version will be heartily welcome."—*Scotsman.*

War and Peace.   (4 vols.)   ·   *[October volume.*

"As you advance in the book, curiosity changes into astonishment, and astonishment into admiration, before this impassive judge, who calls before his tribunal all human actions, and makes the soul render to itself an account of all its secrets. You feel yourself swept away on the current of a tranquil river, the depth of which you cannot fathom; it is life itself which is passing, agitating the hearts of men, which are suddenly made bare in the truth and complexity of their movements."—Vte. E. M. de Vogüé, in *Le Roman Russe.*

What to Do?

"We have arranged for ourselves," says Count Tolstoï, "a life which is against the moral and physical nature of man, and we use all the powers of our mind to assure men that this life is a real one." As showing the result of Tolstoï's consideration of the present state of things, and as an exposition of his ideas as to how the social question is to be solved, this volume forms one of the most interesting of the many books which Count Tolstoï has written.

Covenanters, Tales and Sketches of the : Being a
choice Selection of Narratives in connection with the Persecution of the Scottish Covenanters. Crown 8vo, Cloth Gilt, with numerous full-page Illustrations, price 2s. 6d.

Death's Disguises, and other Sonnets.   By Frank
T. Marzials.   Crown 8vo, Parchment Limp, 3s.

"A charming and finely-wrought little book of poems."—*Scotsman.*

Democracy. Crown 8vo, Cloth, 2s.

Devil's Whisper. *(See Novocastrian Series.)*

Dickens, Charles. Crown 8vo, Cloth, 2s.

Barnaby Rudge.	Oliver Twist.
Martin Chuzzlewit.	Pickwick Papers.
Nicholas Nickleby.	Sketches by Boz.
Old Curiosity Shop.	

A Christmas Carol: Being a Ghost Story of Christmas.
Square 8vo, Cloth Gilt, price 1s.

Dicky Bird Society, History of the. By Uncle
Toby. With numerous Illustrations, Crown 4to, price 3d.

"Little children, and big ones too, may well read with pleasure Uncle Toby's *History of the Dicky Bird Society.*"—*National Reformer.*

Doctor's Corner. By R. Clark Newton, M.S., L.M.,
M.R.C.S.L. Tenth Thousand, Royal 8vo, 62 pp., price 6d.

CONTENTS :—Digestion and Indigestion—Headaches—Consumption, is it Curable?—Is it Contagious?—Breakfast—Dinner—Diet of the Sick—Corpulence—Scarlet Fever—Use of Fruit—Water as a Summer Beverage—Feeding of Children—RECIPES: Beef-tea; Cold Essence of Beef; Jelly; Rice; Milk; Baked Calves' Feet; Digested Milk and Soluble Meat; Demulcent Drink; Soyer's Tapioca and Cod Liver; Tamarind Whey, etc.

Don't. Directions for Avoiding Improprieties in
Conduct and Common Errors of Speech. Square 8vo, Parchment Limp, 1s.

Early English Poetry. *(See Windsor Series.)*

Elijah, the Desert Prophet. By the Rev. H. T.
Howat. Crown 8vo, Cloth, Bevelled Boards, price 2s. 6d.

Elocution. (With Select Recitations.) By T. R.
Walton Pearson, M.A., of St. Catharine's College, Cambridge, and Frederic William Waithman, Lecturer on Elocution in the Leeds and Bradford Institutes. Crown 8vo, Cloth, price 1s.

"This concise and well-arranged treatise is exactly one of the useful little handbooks which we should like to see distributed by the School Board throughout the length and breadth of their Young England, wherein so much in the matter of speech has been wilfully neglected and therefore remains to be repaired."—*The Stage.*

Elswick Science Series. Crown 8vo, Cloth, price 3s. 6d.

> Practical and Theoretical Trigonometry. By Henry Evers, LL.D., Author of "Steam," "Navigation," etc.
>
> "In following the line of practical usefulness he has succeeded in writing a book for students such as was really needed, and will, we are inclined to think, gain considerable popularity."—*Athenæum.*
>
> Manual of Steam and Prime Movers. By Henry Evers, LL.D., Author of "Steam," "Navigation," etc.

Emigrant's Handbook to the British Colonies. By Waldemar Bannow. Crown 8vo, price 1s.

"His advice to emigrants is written in a kindly and friendly spirit, and is brimful of useful information. . . . To all who have any thoughts of emigration we strongly advise a careful reading of Mr. Bannow's excellent book."—*Newcastle Daily Journal.*

England under Victoria. Imperial 8vo, Cloth, 10s. 6d.

Ethel Linton; or, The Feversham Temper. By E. A. W. Crown 8vo, Cloth, Bevelled Boards, price 2s. 6d.

European Conversation Books. Cloth Limp, 1s. each. No. I. FRENCH. No. II. ITALIAN. No. III. SPANISH. No. IV. GERMAN.

Every-Day Help Series, for Young Men and Young Women.

> How to do Business. A Pocket Manual of Practical Affairs and Guide to Success in Life. Demy 32mo, 126 pages, Cloth Limp, price 6d.
>
> How to Behave. A Pocket Manual of Etiquette. Demy 32mo, 126 pages, Cloth Limp, price 6d.
>
> How to Write. A Pocket Manual of Composition and Letter-Writing. Demy 32mo, Cloth Limp, price 6d.
>
> How to Debate. A Manual for Mutual Improvement Societies, with Hints on Public Speaking, and a list of subjects suitable for discussion. Cloth Limp, price 4d.
>
> Ladies' National Housekeeper's Book, for any year. Post 4to, price 6d.

Eye Diseases: What the Public should know of them. Two Lectures delivered at the Northumberland, Durham, and Newcastle Infirmary for Diseases of the Eye. By C. S. Jeaffreson, F.R.C.S.E., F.R.M.S. Demy 8vo, price 1s.

" Dr. Jeaffreson has few equals either in knowledge and skill, or in his power of clear and interesting exposition, of the subject treated in this pamphlet."—*Newcastle Daily Leader.*

Famous Engineers. J. F. Layson. Crown 8vo, Cloth, Illustrated, price 2s. 6d.

Garibaldi, Life of General. By Howard Blackett. Imperial 8vo, Cloth, Gilt Edges, 10s. 6d.; also Crown 8vo, Cloth, Illustrated, price 2s. 6d.

General Gordon, Life of. With Photographic Portrait taken at Khartoum. By the Authors of " Our Queen," "Grace Darling," etc. 90th Thousand. Crown 8vo, Cloth Gilt, price 2s. 6d.

" The book before us is thoroughly well done. The story of Gordon's eventful and romantic life is told clearly, graphically, and without unnecessary *padding.*"—*The Literary Churchman.*

Gladstone, W. E. His Life and Works. By Lewis Apjohn. 45th Thousand. Crown 8vo, Cloth Gilt, Illustrated, price 2s. 6d.

" A straightforward and pleasantly-written narrative of the career of the Premier, embracing also brief summaries of the condition of the country, political and social, at the most memorable epoch of his life. The book will be found especially valuable to students of current politics."—*Scotsman.*

Goldsmith's Vicar of Wakefield. Crown 8vo, Cloth, Illustrated, price 2s. 6d.

Golden Gleams: Being Choice Selections from the Words and Works of the Rev. Henry Ward Beecher. Crown 8vo, Cloth Gilt, price 2s. 6d.

Grace Darling, Heroine of the Farne Isles. By the Author of "Our Queen." 80th Thousand. Crown 8vo, Cloth, Bevelled Boards, price 2s. 6d.

Woman's Work—Ancient Northumbria—The Childhood of a Heroine—Lighthouse Homes—Lighthouse Guests—Christmas at the Longstone Lighthouse—A Wedding in the Family—" Prevention Better than Cure "—August Pic-Nic Pleasures—The Perils of the Ocean—The Wreck of the *Forfarshire*—Grace to the Rescue—After the Event—A Visit to the Duke and Duchess of Northumberland at Alnwick Castle—The Darling Family at Home—An Early Death—" Being Dead, yet speaketh "—Conclusion.

Great Writers. Monthly Shilling Volumes. Cut or Uncut Edges. A New Series of Critical Biographies. Edited by Professor Eric S. Robertson.

Brontë, Charlotte. By Augustine Birrell.

"Those who know much of Charlotte Brontë will learn more, and those who know nothing about her will find all that is best worth learning in Mr. Birrell's pleasant book."—*St. James's Gazette.*

Bunyan. By Canon Venables.

"A most intelligent, appreciative, and valuable memoir."—*Scotsman.*

Burns. By Professor Blackie.

"Unless we are much mistaken, his monograph will take rank with the best essays that have been written on Scotland's best-loved bard."—*Pall Mall Gazette.*

Carlyle, Thomas. By Richard Garnett, LL.D.

"This is an admirable book. Nothing could be more felicitous and fairer than the way in which he takes us through Carlyle's life and works."—*Pall Mall Gazette.*

Coleridge. By Hall Caine.

"Brief and vigorous, written throughout with spirit and great literary skill, often rising into eloquence."—*Scotsman.*

Congreve. By Edmund Gosse.

"Mr. Gosse has written an admirable and most interesting biography of a man of letters who is of particular interest to other men of letters."—*The Academy.*

Crabbe. By T. E. Kebbel.

"No English poet since Shakespeare has observed certain aspects of nature and of human life more closely; and in the qualities of manliness and of sincerity he is surpassed by none. . . . Mr. Kebbel's monograph is worthy of the subject."—*Athenæum.*

Darwin. By G. T. Bettany.

"Mr. G. T. Bettany's *Life of Darwin* is a sound and conscientious work."—*Saturday Review.*

Dickens. By Frank T. Marzials.

"Notwithstanding the mass of matter that has been printed relating to Dickens and his works . . . we should, until we came across this volume, have been at a loss to recommend any popular life of England's most popular novelist as being really satisfactory. The difficulty is removed by Mr. Marzials's little book."—*Athenæum.*

Emerson. By Richard Garnett, LL.D.

"As to the larger section of the public, to whom the series of Great Writers is addressed, no record of Emerson's life and work could be more desirable, both in breadth of treatment and lucidity of style, than Dr. Garnett's."—*Saturday Review.*

Great Writers—*continued.*

Goethe.   By James Sime.

" Mr. James Sime's competence as a biographer of Goethe, both in respect of knowledge of his special subject, and of German literature generally, is beyond question."—*Manchester Guardian.*

Goldsmith.   By Austin Dobson.

" Mr. Dobson's narrative is clear and well arranged, and his remarks on Goldsmith's literary work are full of common sense.   In many respects a model of short biography."—*Athenæum.*

Heine.   By William Sharp.

" This is an admirable monograph . . . more fully written up to the level of recent knowledge and criticism of its theme than any other English work."—*Scotsman.*

Hugo, Victor.   By F. T. Marzials.

" Mr. Marzials's volume presents to us, in a more handy form than any English or even French handbook gives, the summary of what, up to the moment in which we write, is known or conjectured about the life of the great poet."—*Saturday Review.*

Johnson, Samuel.   By Colonel F. Grant.

" Colonel Grant has performed his task with diligence, sound judgment, good taste, and accuracy."—*Illustrated London News.*

Keats.   By W. M. Rossetti.

" Valuable for the ample information which it contains, and the sympathetic and authoritative criticism which it furnishes."—*Cambridge Independent.*

Longfellow.   By Professor Eric S. Robertson.

" A most readable little work, brightened by fancy, and enriched by poetic feeling."—*Liverpool Mercury.*

Marryat.   By David Hannay.

" What Mr. Hannay had to do—give a craftsman-like account of a great craftsman who has been almost incomprehensibly undervalued—could hardly have been done better than in this little volume, and though fortunately there is no fear of Marryat's ceasing for many a long day to be popular with boys, it is to be hoped that this book may help to restore his popularity with other than boys."—*Manchester Guardian.*

Mill.   By W. L. Courtney.

" A most sympathetic and discriminating memoir." — *Glasgow Herald.*

Rossetti, Dante Gabriel.   By Joseph Knight.

" Mr. Knight's picture of the great poet and painter is the fullest and best yet presented to the public."—*The Graphic.*

Great Writers—*continued.*

Schiller.   By Henry W. Nevinson.
"This is a well-written little volume, which presents the leading facts of the poet's life in a neatly rounded picture."—*Scotsman.*

Scott.   By Professor Yonge.
"For readers and lovers of the poems and novels of Sir Walter Scott this is a most enjoyable book."—*Aberdeen Free Press.*

Shelley.   By William Sharp.
"Another fit memorial of a beautiful soul. . . . it is a worthy addition, to be cherished for its own sake, to our already rich collection of Shelley literature."—*The Academy.*

Smith, Adam.   By R. B. Haldane, M.P.
"Written throughout with a perspicuity seldom exemplified when dealing with economic science."—*Scotsman.*

Smollett.   By David Hannay.
"A capable record of a writer who still remains one of the great masters of the English novel."—*Saturday Review.*

Library edition of Great Writers, printed on large paper of extra quality, in handsome binding, Demy 8vo, price 2s. 6d. per volume.

Guide to Emigration and Colonisation : An Appeal
to the Nation.   By Waldemar Bannow, upwards of Eighteen years a resident of Victoria, Australia.   Crown 8vo, price 1s. 6d.
"Mr. Bannow writes in a practical, terse fashion ; and the information and advice he furnishes render his book a valuable help to persons who are thinking of emigrating."—*Sheffield Daily Telegraph.*

Gypsy Series of 1s. Reward Books.   F'cp. 8vo,
Cloth Gilt.   By G. Stuart Phelps.

Gypsy Breynton.

Gypsy's Cousin Joy.   In which Joy comes to Yorkbury.

Gypsy's Sowing and Reaping.   Which concerns Gypsy and Tom.

Gypsy's Year at the Golden Crescent.   In which Gypsy goes to Boarding School.

Handy Guide to Conveyancing Costs under the
Solicitors' Remuneration Act, 1881.   By J. Hough.   Price 2s. 6d.

Hazel; or, Perilpoint Lighthouse.   By Emily Grace
Harding.   Crown 8vo, Cloth, Bevelled Boards, price 2s. 6d.

Health Resorts of Northern England. By Richard Ellis, F.R.C.S. Edin., Senior Surgeon, Newcastle-on-Tyne Throat and Ear Hospital. With New Chapters on Whitby, Scarborough, Redcar, Saltburn, Harrogate, etc. Where to go, and why, with Hints on Sea Bathing, etc.

"Dr. Ellis has done very good service in classifying for his professional brethren the 'Health Resorts of the North of England,' and has placed in the hands of the laity a little work which all may read with interest and profit. It is rich in facts of history, and is replete with points of geographical and geological worth."—*Liverpool Medico-Chirurgical Journal,* Jan. 1884.

Hedley, George Roberts. Ballads and other Poems. Crown 8vo, price 3s. 6d.

"There are some verses which have all the ring in them of some of the work of the old dramatists. The book is a melodious collection of good things."—*Newcastle Courant.*

Helen's Babies. With some Account of their Ways. Royal 16mo, in Cloth Gilt, with numerous full-page Engravings. Price 1s. ; Bevelled Boards, Gilt Edges, 1s. 6d.

Hume and Smollett's History of England. Imperial 8vo, 1420 pages, Cloth, price 7s. 6d.

Ingraham, Rev. J. Prince of the House of David. Crown 8vo, Cloth, Bevelled Boards, price 2s. 6d.

Infant Feeding and Management, Plain Facts about. Popular Treatise by C. Stennett Redmond, L.K.Q.C.P.I. & L.R.C.S.I. Crown 8vo, Cloth, price 2s.

"An exceedingly useful treatise on a most important, yet much neglected study, for those having care of the young."—*Irish Tribune.*

Irish Minstrelsy. (*See Windsor Series.*)

Jack Dudley's Wife. (*See Novocastrian Series.*)

Jane Eyre. By Charlotte Brontë. Crown 8vo, Cloth, price 2s.

Last of the Mohicans. By Fenimore Cooper. Crown 8vo, Cloth, 2s.

Lays of the Highlands. By J. S. Blackie. Square 8vo, Cloth, price 2s. 6d.

Kara Yerta Tragedy. (*See Novocastrian Series.*)

Lever, Charles. Charles O'Malley, Crown 8vo, Cloth, price 2s.

Life Stories of Famous Children. Adapted from the French. By the Author of "Spenser for Children." Foolscap 8vo, Cloth, price 1s.

Lincoln and Garfield: New World Heroes. The Life Story of two self-made Men whom the People made Presidents. Crown 8vo, Cloth, Bevelled Boards, Illustrated, price 2s. 6d.

"We know no better book for the encouragement of young men to rise to be worthy of the endowments of mankind, the blessings of a birthplace in a free country, than the *Lives of Lincoln and Garfield."—Warrington Guardian.*

Lives Great and Simple. By S. A. Tooley.

The Volume contains Lives of General Gordon, Princess Alice, Henry Irving, Alexander Macdonald, Lord Wolseley, Dr. William Chambers, Lord Lawrence, Robert Dick, Anthony Trollope, Sir William Fairbairn, Robert Tannahill, James Garfield, Janet Hamilton, Charles Dickens, Thomas Edward, Thomas Carlyle, Henry Scott Riddell, William Leighton Leitch, Henry M. Stanley, Edward Irving. Crown 8vo, Cloth, Bevelled Boards, price 2s. 6d.

Livingstone, Life of David. By J. S. Robertson. Imperial 8vo, Cloth, Gilt Edges, 10s. 6d.; also Crown 8vo, Cloth, 2s. 6d.

"No one can read Livingstone's life without admiring and loving the man. Above his greatness as an explorer rises the massiveness of his character; and his large-hearted love for the poor negro, his deep hatred of the accursed slave trade, his sturdy independence, strong iron will, stern tenacity of purpose, and calm fortitude under trouble or disaster, stamps him a truly great man."

Livingston's Poems and Songs. Crown 8vo, Cloth, 3s. 6d.

Lytton, Bulwer. Crown 8vo, Cloth, 2s. 6d.

Alice; or, the Mysteries.	Night and Morning.
Ernest Maltravers.	Paul Clifford.
Eugene Aram.	Pelham.
Last Days of Pompeii.	Rienzi.
Last of the Barons.	

Mansfield Park. By Jane Austen. Crown 8vo, Cloth, 2s.

Marston, Philip Bourke. For a Song's Sake. And other Stories. By the late Philip Bourke Marston. Crown 8vo, 507 pages, Cloth Gilt, price 4s. 6d.

"A brief memoir by Mr. William Sharp, ably and sympathetically written, introduces the stories, and makes the volume one which the author's many admirers will be eager to possess. . . . Powerful studies, romantic in sentiment."—*The Scotsman.*

Marryat, Captain. Crown 8vo, Cloth, price 2s. 6d.

Jacob Faithful.	Peter Simple.
Midshipman Easy.	Poor Jack.

Mary in Heaven. Poem by Robert Burns. Illustrated. Square 8vo, 1s.

Memorable Shipwrecks and Seafaring Adventures of the Nineteenth Century. Crown 8vo, Cloth Gilt, with Illustrations, price 2s. 6d.

Moffat, Robert, Life of. By Rev. W. Walters. Crown 8vo, Cloth, Bevelled Boards, price 2s. 6d.

Christian Foreign Missions are characteristic of the nineteenth century. Robert Moffat's life was a marvellous illustration of the grandeur and power of goodness, and his labours were full of proof of the saving efficacy and civilising effects of the Gospel.

Monthly Chronicle of North-Country Lore and Legend. Crown 4to, 48 pages, price Sixpence.

The *Monthly Chronicle* has been established to preserve the great wealth of legend and story that abounds in the North of England. Every number contains a variety of articles of great popular interest. Most of the articles are illustrated with engravings of the persons or scenes described.

Mountain Daisy, A. By Emily Grace Harding. Crown 8vo, Cloth, Bevelled Boards, price 2s. 6d.

"It is entitled to the first place in the order of merit."—*Academy.*

Mr. Barnes of New York. By A. C. Gunter. Crown 8vo, 1s.

New Booklets. By Count Tolstoï. White Grained Boards, Gilt Lettering, price 1s.

Where Love is, there God is also.

The Two Pilgrims.

What Men Live by.

"They are very beautiful and impressive stories, and deserve to be widely circulated in this form."—*Scotsman.*

Newcastle and Gateshead, History of. Fourteenth
to Sixteenth Centuries. Edited by Richard Welford. In three
volumes, Royal 8vo, Cloth, price 12s. 6d. each ; Half Morocco,
15s. ; Full Morocco, 21s.

" Its plan is admirable. . . . The style is excellent, being marked with
a scholarly refinement. For a record of local annals the book strikes us
as coming very nearly up to the standard of perfection."—*Antiquarian
Magazine.*

Newcastle-on-Tyne of To-day. By W. W. Tom-
linson. Crown 8vo, Paper Cover, price 6d.

Newcastle Town. An Account of its Rise and
Progress : Its Struggles and Triumphs : and its Ending. By
R. J. Charleton, with Illustrations by R. Jobling. Crown 8vo,
Cloth gilt, price 5s.

New Natural History of Birds, Beasts, and Fishes.
By John K. Leys, M.A. Foolscap 8vo, Cloth, price 1s.

"Mr. Leys has not only a talent for diverting story-telling, but also for
instilling into youthful minds happy thoughts, the echo of which will linger
long in childish memories."—*Methodist Times.*

Nine Months on the Nile. By the Rev. Hampson
S. Eckersley. Crown 8vo, Cloth, price 2s. 6d.

" Cannot fail to delight the home reader, and be of great service to all
future travellers in the same regions who may have the opportunity of
perusing its instructive pages."—*Methodist Times.*

Northumberland, Guide to. By W. W. Tomlinson.
Crown 8vo, Limp Cloth, with Maps, price 5s.

" Mr. Tomlinson's work is very readable ; and we feel he has done the
county some service in accumulating so many facts, and arraying them in
such a pleasant manner."—*Berwick Gazette.*

Norway, Popular Guide to. By C. Jurgenson.
Containing full description of that wonderful Country, Maps of
the Routes, and every other information useful to the Traveller.
Revised edition, Cloth, price 3s. 6d.

" Evidently he knows the country, its fiords, its roads, its people, and its
customs, and he has the faculty of planning and writing in such wise as to
make his book a really useful, handy, popular guide."—*Leeds Mercury.*

Novocastrian Series, The. Popular Volumes of
Fiction. Square 8vo, Paper Covers, price 1s.

A Witness from the Dead. (A Special Reporter's Story.)
By Florence Layard.

" Well told."—*Manchester Guardian.* " Ingenious and interesting."—*Scotsman.*

Novocastrian Series—*continued.*

Cashel Byron's Profession.   By G. Bernard Shaw.

"Cashel Byron ran away from school, and adopted the 'profession' of pugilism.   He also falls in love with a beautiful and wealthy lady. The story is powerfully written, and the interest never flags from beginning to end."—*North Wales Observer.*

"Hidden Money in London."   By James Greenwood, "The Amateur Casual."

Jack Dudley's Wife.   By E. M. Davy, author of "A Prince of Como," etc.

"Written with excellent skill, and succeeds in holding the interest well up from first to last."—*Scotsman.*

Oak-Bough and Wattle-Blossom : Stories and Sketches by Australians in England—Mrs. Campbell Praed, C. Haddon Chambers, Douglas B. W. Sladen, Philip Mennell, Edmund Stansfeld Rawson, S. Oldmixon.   Edited by A. Patchett Martin.

"Two of the stories are particularly good—Mr. Haddon Chambers's 'Pipe of Peace,' and Mrs. Campbell Praed's curiously suggestive episode, entitled 'Miss Pallavant.'   It is one of the cleverest short stories which Mrs. Campbell Praed has written."—*Academy.*

Police Sergeant C 21 : The Story of a Crime.   By Reginald Barnett.   (25th Thousand.)

"It must suffice to call attention to its absorbing and exciting interest."—*Globe.*

The Devil's Whisper.   By the author of "Police Sergeant C 21."

The Kara Yerta Tragedy : An Australian Romance.   By J. E. Harrison.

The Policeman's Lantern : Strange Stories of London Life. By James Greenwood, "The Amateur Casual."

"Touches of the bizarre aspects of life on the city streets, or among the 'shady' members of a city population."—*The Scots Observer.*

The Ugly Story of Miss Wetherby.   By Richard Pryce, author of "An Evil Spirit," etc.

"A bright tale of clever imposture."—*Pall Mall Gazette.*
"Clever."—The *Academy.*

Vane's Invention : An Electrical Romance.   By Walter Milbank.

"Told with much realistic effect."—*Academy.*

Oak-Bough and Wattle-Blossom.   *(See Novocastrian Series.)*

Our American Cousins. By W. E. Adams. Crown 8vo, Cloth, 2s. 6d. ; or cheap edition, Paper Covers, 1s.

"We can heartily recommend Mr. Adams's book to those Englishmen who want to know something about America."—*Saturday Review.*

"Altogether, it is a sober, sensible book, by a level-headed observer of men and things."—*Pall Mall Gazette.*

Our Queen: A Sketch of the Life and Times of Victoria. By the Author of "Grace Darling." 70th Thousand. Crown 8vo, Illustrated, Cloth, Bevelled Boards, 2s. 6d. ; Gilt Edges, 3s.

In sending forth these sketches of the life and times of our Queen, we feel that no apology is needed. It is impossible for any nation not to feel interested in its Sovereign, and we are so happy as to have a monarch whose character and actions have so endeared her to the hearts of her people that any information respecting her is eagerly welcomed.

Parental Commandments ; or, Warnings to Parents on the Physical, Intellectual, and Moral Training of Children. Square 8vo, price 6d.

"Very sensible advice—agreeably readable—terse, interesting, instructive, well considered, and accurate ; readers will doubtless learn some points which they don't know."—*The Lancet.*

Pilgrim's Progress and Holy War. By John Bunyan. Crown 8vo, Cloth, Illustrated, 2s. 6d.

Police Sergeant C 21. (*See Novocastrian Series.*)

Policeman's Lantern. (*See Novocastrian Series.*)

Queens of Literature of the Victorian Era. By the Authors of "Our Queen," "Grace Darling," etc. Containing Lives of Mary Somerville, Harriet Martineau, Elizabeth Barrett-Browning, Charlotte Brontë, George Eliot, Felicia Hemans. Crown 8vo, Cloth, Bevelled Boards, 2s. 6d.

Raffalovich, Mark Andre. Crown 8vo, Cloth, Bevelled Boards, price 3s. 6d each.

In Fancy Dress.

"These sonnets and songs abound in pretty conceits, quaint similitudes, fantastic touches, and antithetical smartness."—*Saturday Review.*

"Careful in construction, and accurate in finish."—*The Academy.*

"It is Thyself."

"'It is Thyself' is a book that should not be overlooked, for it is full of fine things of slight but dexterous fashion."—*Scottish Leader.*

Religious Sentiments of Charles Dickens. By
Charles H. McKenzie.

"The book may be safely recommended to all students of Dickens desirous of studying a not unimportant aspect of his many-sided mind and character, as entirely free from religious or theological cant and the fulsome and nauseous jargon of the sects."—*Society*.

Revolution, Tales of. By Jane Cowen. Crown
8vo, Cloth, 2s. 6d.

"The tales are well and simply told; adapted to implant in the mind of the reader, and especially of the young, an admiration of patriotic self-sacrifice, and a strong sympathy with freedom."—*Cambridge Independent*.

Robinson Crusoe. By Daniel Defoe. Crown 8vo,
Cloth, 2s.

Romantic Ballads and Poems of Phantasy. By
William Sharp. Parchment Limp, 3s.

"Mr. Sharp is a genuine and very delightful poet." — *Manchester Examiner*.

Sacred Song. (*See Windsor Series.*)

Science Lectures delivered before the Tyneside
Sunday Lecture Society. 1s.

> Animal Life on the Ocean Surface. By Professor H. N. Moseley, M.A., F.R.S.
>
> Animals that make Limestone. By Dr. P. Herbert Carpenter, F.R.S.
>
> Eye and its Work. By Litton Forbes, M.D., F.R.C.S.E., L.R.C.P.
>
> Facts and Fictions in Zoology. By Dr. Andrew Wilson, F.R.S.E.
>
> Movements of Plants. By Ernest A. Parkyn, M.A.
>
> Natural History of Instinct. By G. J. Romanes, F.R.S.
>
> Relations between Natural Science and Literature. By Professor H. Nettleship, M.A.
>
> The Seven Lectures may be had in one volume, price 1s. 6d.

Scott, Sir Walter. Crown 8vo, Cloth, price 2s.

Bride of Lammermoor.	Kenilworth.
Heart of Midlothian.	Old Mortality.
Ivanhoe.	

Scott, Michael. Crown 8vo, Cloth, price 2s.

Tom Cringle's Log.	Cruise of the Midge.

Scottish Chiefs.   By Jane Porter.   Crown 8vo,
Cloth, 2s. 6d.

Sea Poems.   By various Authors.   Illustrated.
Square 8vo, 1s.

Seven Pillars of Socialism.   An Indictment.   By
Rev. Marsden Gibson, M.A.   Crown 8vo, 2d.

Shorthand, J. D. Lowes's (Pitman Superseded :
Taylor Improved), for acquiring in half-an-hour the Method of
taking down Sermons, Speeches, etc., without the aid of a master.
Demy 16mo, price 6d.

"Mr. Lowes has long been considered, and justly so, one of the best
shorthand writers in the country; and has often been urged to place in
the hands of the public the system which he practises, and which he has,
by years of careful study, brought to a state of perfection.   The system is
noteworthy for its simplicity; and that it can be efficiently practised is
proved by the successful career which Mr. Lowes has had as a reporter."—
Newcastle Daily Journal.

Skipsey, Joseph.   Carols, Songs, and Ballads.
Crown 8vo, Bevelled Boards, price 3s. 6d.

"The whole book deserves to be read, and much of it deserves to be
loved.   Mr. Skipsey can find music for every mood, whether he is dealing
with the real experiences of the pitman, or with the imaginative experiences of the poet, and his verse has a rich vitality about it.   In those
latter days of shallow rhymers it is pleasant to come across some one to
whom poetry is a passion, not a profession."—*Pall Mall Gazette.*

Smollett, Tobias.   Crown 8vo, Cloth, price 2s. 6d.

Roderick Random. | Peregrine Pickle.

Sonnets of this Century.   *(See Windsor Series.)*

Sonnets of Europe.   *(See Windsor Series.)*

Sonnets of this Century.   With an Exhaustive and
Critical Essay on the Sonnet, by William Sharp.   Edition de
Luxe.   In Crown 4to, printed on Antique Paper, price 12s. 6d.,
and in Demy 4to, printed on Whatman's Hand-made Paper,
price 42s.   50 copies printed and numbered.   Only a few copies
now left.   The volume contains Sonnets by Lord Tennyson,
Robert Browning, A. C. Swinburne, Matthew Arnold, Theodore
Watts, Archbishop Trench, J. Addington Symonds, W. Bell
Scott, Christina Rossetti, Edward Dowden, Edmund Gosse,
Andrew Lang, George Meredith, Cardinal Newman, by the late
Dante Gabriel Rossetti, Mrs. Barrett-Browning, C. Tennyson-
Turner, etc., and all the Best Writers of this Century.

Songs and Poems of Fairyland. *(See Windsor Series.)*

Songs and Poems of the Great Dominion.
(See Windsor Series.)

Songs and Poems of the Sea. *(See Windsor Series.)*

State Socialism: a Latter-day Tyranny. By Elijah
Copland. Crown 8vo, 1d.

Stockton, Frank R. A Jolly Fellowship. Crown
8vo, Cloth, Illustrated, 2s. 6d.

Summer Legends. By Rudolph Baumbach. Translated by Helen B. Dole. Crown 8vo, 2s. 6d.

**The Ear: Its Structure, Mechanism, and Connec-
tion** with the Throat. A Popular Lecture. Hints on the
Domestic Treatment of Throat and Ear Diseases, including
Affections of the Mouth and Nose, with Prescriptions. By
Richard Ellis, F.R.C.S., etc. Sixteenth Thousand. Demy 8vo,
price 6d.

The Lamplighter. By Miss Cummins. Crown
8vo, Cloth, 2s.

The Best Way to Get on: a Practical Guide to
Money Making and Money Spending. Crown 8vo, Paper
Cover, 1s.

The Refugees of Martinique. By Eugene Sue.
Crown 8vo, Paper Cover, 1s.

The Turkish Bath: Its History and Use. By
Frederic C. Coley, M.D. Contents:—The History of the
Turkish Bath—How to take a Turkish Bath—Rules for the
Turkish Bath—The Theory of the Turkish Bath. Crown 8vo,
Paper Cover, price 6d.

"In fact the little book is a complete *vade mecum* of the Turkish bath,
brightly written, and bristling with scientific information popularly conveyed."—*Oxford Times*.

The Inheritance. By Miss Ferrier. Crown 8vo,
Cloth, price 2s.

The White Slave. By R. Hildreth. Crown 8vo,
Cloth, price 2s.

Think It Out. Lecture on Home Rule. By
Thomas Hodgkin, LL.D., Author of "Italy and her Invaders,"
etc. Crown 8vo, price 3d.

"A very readable contribution to a well-thrashed-out subject, and is
particularly valuable, as coming from a well-known and advanced Liberal
of the North of England, who is respected as being a clear thinker and a
somewhat advanced politician."—*Gainsboro' Times.*

Trigonometry. (*See Elswick Science Series.*)

Ugly Story of Miss Wetherby. (*See Novocastrian Series.*)

Uncle Tom's Cabin. By Harriet Beecher Stowe.
Crown 8vo, price 2s.

Valentine Vox. By H. Cockton. Crown 8vo,
Cloth, price 2s.

Vane's Invention. (*See Novocastrian Series.*)

Very Short Stories and Verses for Children. By
Mrs. W. K. Clifford, Author of "Anyhow Stories," etc. Illustrated by Edith Campbell.

"Mrs. W. K. Clifford's *Very Short Stories* form a dainty little volume of
the tiniest tales ever printed, with happy verses interspersed. She has the
rare knack of entering into the fantastic thoughts and queer fancies of childhood, and her little poems seem to sing themselves; the words are almost
music."—*Daily Telegraph.*

Village Tales. By Miss Mitford. Crown 8vo,
Cloth, price 2s. 6d.

Villa and Cottage Gardening. Specially adapted
for Scotland, Northern England, and Ireland. By Alexander
Sweet. Crown 8vo, price 1s.

"This is an excellent little book. . . . It is evident that the writer is a
man who has practised what he teaches, and knows how to give all the
needful directions for doing the work in an amateur's garden."—*Gardeners'
Chronicle.*

Wealth and Want: a Social Experiment made and
described by Henry Broadbent, Esq. Being a refutation of
Henry George's "Progress and Poverty." Crown 8vo, price 6d.

"A cleverly written *brochure.* Some of the sketches of character are
decidedly clever."—*Cambridge Press.*

"The author is not without a sense of humour, and can sketch a
character."—*Saturday Review.*

Why Smoke and Drink? By James Parton.
Square 8vo, Parchment Limp, 1s.

Wide, Wide World. By Miss Wetherell. Crown
8vo, Cloth, price 2s. 6d.

Wilson's Tales of the Borders. Crown 8vo, Cloth.
Now issuing in 1s. monthly volumes.

The *Scotsman* says :—"Those who have read the tales in the unwieldy
tomes in which they are to be found in the libraries will welcome the
publication of this neat, handy, and well-printed edition."

The *Dundee Advertiser* says :—"Considering how attractive are these
tales, whether regarded as illustrating Scottish life, or as entertaining items
of romance, there can be no doubt of their continued popularity. We last
read them in volumes the size of a family Bible, and we are glad to have an
opportunity to renew our acquaintance with them in a form so much more
handy and elegant."

Windsor Series of Poetical Anthologies. Printed
on Antique Paper. Crown 8vo. Bound in Blue Cloth, each with
suitable Emblematic Design on Cover, price 3s. 6d.

Australian Song, a Century of. Selected and Edited by
Douglas B. W. Sladen, B.A., Oxon.

"'A Century of Australian Song' is one of the pleasantest fruits
of this centenary season."—*Adelaide Observer*, 27th October 1888.

Ballads of the North Countrie. Edited, with Introduction,
by Graham R. Tomson.

"Mr. Tomson has provided an interesting introduction, and a
brief helpful commentary. The choice is representative of the best
in the larger minstrelsies, and the book is externally attractive."—
Scotsman.

Children of the Poets. An Anthology from English and
American Writers of Three Centuries. Edited by Eric S.
Robertson, M.A.

"The selection has been made with much judgment and good
taste."—*Spectator.*

Early English and Scottish Poetry. Selected and Edited,
with Introduction and Notes, by H. Macaulay Fitzgibbon.

"Mr. Fitzgibbon gives some interesting information in his introduction, which furnishes a good, practical, and serviceable account of
the subject."—*Spectator.*

Irish Minstrelsy. Edited, with Notes and Introduction, by
H. H. Sparling.

"'Irish Minstrelsy' gives us the works which resound in the brain
of every young Irishman, and which constitute his political gospel.
They cannot be too attentively studied by all Englishmen who desire
to understand the real character of Ireland's demand for Home
Rule."—*Manchester Guardian.*

Windsor Series—*continued.*

Jacobite Songs and Ballads. Selected and Edited, with Notes, by G. S. Macquoid.

"A book which has narrowly escaped being perfect is 'Jacobite Songs and Ballads,' edited by Gilbert Macquoid."—*Graphic.*

Sacred Song. A Volume of Religious Verse. Selected and arranged, with Notes, by Samuel Waddington.

"It is almost needless to say that the volume contains many poems of great beauty. . . . We may add that the editor's notes are brief and pertinent, and that the contents, as well as the attractive appearance of the volume, make it suitable for a present."—*Spectator.*

Sonnets of this Century. With an Exhaustive and Critical Essay on the Sonnet. Edited by William Sharp.

"The selection is very catholic and very complete, and we do not remember the name of any poet of the century whose work is worthy of consideration whom Mr. Sharp has failed to include."—*Spectator.*

Sonnets of Europe. A Volume of Translations. Selected and arranged, with Notes, by Samuel Waddington.

"Mr. Waddington has been now for so many years engaged upon the Sonnet that he has practically acquired the right to say what he likes about it."—*Manchester Guardian.*

Songs and Poems of the Sea. An Anthology of Poems and Passages descriptive of the Sea. Edited by Mrs. William Sharp.

"It was a happy thought of Mrs. William Sharp to collect so many well-said things by singers, past and present, about the ocean in 'Songs and Poems of the Sea.' Almost everything notable is here."—*Graphic.*

Songs and Poems of Fairyland. An Anthology of English Fairy Poetry. Selected and arranged, with an Introduction, by Arthur Edward Waite.

"It provides a representative selection of the best fairy poetry in British literature, and an appreciative essay on Elfin lore."—*Scotsman.*

Songs and Poems of the Great Dominion. (New Anthology of Canadian Verse.) Edited by W. D. Lighthall, M.A., of Montreal. Pieces and Passages descriptive of Canada, its Scenery, Life, Races, History; the Canoe, the Forest, the Toboggan; the Settlements, the North-West.

"We are well pleased with the volume from cover to cover."—*Morning Chronicle* (Montreal).

"The volume is interesting as well as charming, and deserves to be widely read."—*Scotsman.*

Windsor Series—*continued.*

Women's Voices. An Anthology of the most Characteristic Poems by English, Scotch, and Irish Women. Edited by Mrs. William Sharp.

"Mrs. Sharp's volume is well arranged, and is really representative of what is excellent in women's poetry."—*Saturday Review.*

Witness from the Dead, A. (*See Novocastrian Series.*)

Women and Men of the Day. By Lillie Harris. Crown 8vo, price 1s.

World of Cant, The. 120th Thousand. Crown 8vo, price 1s.

The *Daily Telegraph* says—"Decidedly a book with a purpose."

The *Scotsman* says—"A vigorous, clever, and almost ferocious exposure, in the form of a story, of the numerous shams and injustices."

Young Folk's Library. F'cap 8vo, Cloth Elegant, Plain Edges, 1s. 6d. Gilt Edges, 2s. An admirable Series for the Family or for School Libraries. Splendidly Illustrated.

Archie Mason: An Irish Story. By Letitia M'Clintock. And other Tales. Illustrated.

Found Afloat. By Mrs. George Cupples. And other Tales. Illustrated.

Horace Hazlewood; or, Little Things. By Robert Hope Moncrieff. And other Tales. Illustrated.

Jessie Oglethorpe: The Story of a Daughter's Devotion. By W. H. Davenport Adams. And other Tales. Illustrated.

Leoline; or, Captured and Rescued. By Emily Grace Harding.

Life of David Livingstone. By J. Donald, F.R.G.S.

Marius Flaminius: A Story of the Days of Hadrian. By Anna J. Buckland. And other Tales. Illustrated.

Miss Matty; or, Our Youngest Passenger. By Mrs. George Cupples. And other Tales. Illustrated.

Old Andy's Money: An Irish Story. By Letitia M'Clintock. And other Tales. Illustrated.

Paul and Marie, the Orphans of Auvergne. And other Tales. Illustrated.

Young Folk's Library—*continued.*

Select Christian Biographies. By Rev. James Gardner, A.M., M.D. Illustrated.

The White Roe of Glenmere. By Mrs. Bickerstaffe. And other Tales. Illustrated.

The Woodfords: An Emigrant Story. By Mrs. Cupples. And other Tales. Illustrated.

The Inundation of the Rhine. From the German. And other Tales. Illustrated.

The Little Orphans. From the German. And other Tales. Illustrated.

Young Man's Friend, containing Admonitions for the Erring, Counsel for the Tempted, Hope for the Fallen. Designed for the Young Man, the Husband, and the Father. By Daniel C. Eddy, D.D. Crown 8vo, Cloth, Bevelled Boards, price 2s. 6d.

Young Woman's Friend; or, the Duties, Trials, Loves, and Hopes of Woman. Designed for the Young Woman, the Young Wife, and the Mother. By Daniel C. Eddy, D.D. Crown 8vo, Cloth, Bevelled Boards, price 2s. 6d.

ADDENDA TO ALPHABETICAL LIST OF BOOKS.

A Scheme for National Pensions. By Rev. W.
Moore Ede, M.A. Crown 8vo. Price One Penny.

Bogatzky's Golden Treasury. Square 8vo, Cloth, 1s.

Camelot Series, The. Monthly Shilling Volumes.
Cloth, cut or uncut edges.

    Aristotle, The Ethics of. Chase's Translation (newly
revised), with Introductory Essay by George Henry Lewes.

    Davis, Thomas, The Prose Writings of. Edited, with an
Introduction, by T. W. Rolleston.

    " So far as Irishmen are concerned, among ' the voices which can
affect our lives so greatly to ends of wisdom and happiness,' there is
none more potent than that of Thomas Davis ; and no one has more
often or more eloquently reminded us of this than Mr. T. W.
Rolleston."—*Freeman's Journal.*

    Early Reviews of Great Writers. Selected and edited, with
an Introduction, by E. Stevenson.

    " The selection has the double attraction of a literary curiosity,
and of a carefully chosen set of examples of the principles of criticism
that had sway in the beginning of this century."—*Scotsman.*

    Elizabethan England : from " A Description of England," by
William Harrison (in " Holinshed's Chronicles "). Edited
by Lothrop Withington, with Introduction by F. J.
Furnivall, LL.D.

    " Skillfully selected, and introduced by Dr. Furnivall with char-
acteristic energy, Holinshed ought to prove not the least popular of
the neat and well-varied Camelot books."—*Saturday Review.*

    English Fairy and other Folk Tales. Edited by E. Sidney
Hartland.

    " Mr. Hartland has succeeded in bringing together an excellent
collection."—*Scotsman.*

    Landor's Pericles and Aspasia. With an Introductory Note
by Havelock Ellis.

Camelot Series—*continued.*

More's Utopia, and Life of Edward V. (including Roper's Life of More). Edited, with an Introduction, by Maurice Adams.

"Mr. Maurice Adams deserves special thanks for the appreciative and deeply interesting article on Sir Thomas More and his writings which forms the introduction to this charming little book."— *Glasgow Herald.*

Northern Studies. By Edmund Gosse. With a Note by Ernest Rhys.

"The essays, taken together, form the best account of modern Scandinavian literature that is available to an English reader."— *Scotsman.*

Sadi: Gulistan, or Flower Garden. Translated, with an Essay, by James Ross; and a Note upon the translator by Charles Sayle.

"The book is one of interest, and owes its chief charm to the numerous anecdotes, aphorisms, and *bon mots* with which Sadi illustrates and enforces his ·didactic instructions." — *Manchester Guardian.*

Spence's "Anecdotes, Observations, and Characters of Books and Men." A Selection, Edited, with an Introduction and Notes, by John Underhill.

"Mr. Underhill has given, in convenient form and with much good taste, a useful and compact selection of the most interesting portion of one of the most famous gatherings of eighteenth-century *ana.*"— *Saturday Review.*

Canterbury Poets, The. Cloth, Red Edges, 1s.;
Cloth, Uncut Edges, 1s. ; Red Roan, Gilt Edges, 2s. 6d.

Great Odes: English and American. Selected and edited, with Introduction, by William Sharp.

"The selection is a judicious one, and gives a good idea of the Great Odes of the English-speaking races."—*Oxford Review.*

Humorous Poems of the Century. Edited by Ralph H. Caine.

"Mr. Ralph H. Caine has got together a really amusing collection of humorous poems of the century to add to the Canterbury Poets." —*Manchester Guardian.*

Lady of Lyons, The, and other Plays. By Lord Lytton. Edited, with an Introduction, by Farquharson Sharp.

"Many people will be glad to have the text of all three pieces in the neat and handy form in which they are here presented."—*Scottish Leader.*

Canterbury Poets—*continued.*

Owen Meredith (the Earl of Lytton), Poems of. Selected, with an Introduction, by M. Betham-Edwards.

"The selection is well made, and the selector's brief criticisms are adequate and to the point."—*Scotsman.*

Painter-Poets, The. Selected and edited, with an Introduction and Notes, by Kineton Parkes.

Career of a Nihilist, The. A Novel. By Stepniak.

Crown 8vo, Cloth, price 5s.

"One expects a Nihilist romance by Stepniak to be full of the actualities of the situation, to display the genuine and intimate sentiments of revolutionary society in Russia, and to correct not a few of the impressions formerly gathered from novelists who only know that society by hearsay and at second-hand. The reader will not be disappointed in this expectation. No one can read this story . . . without deep interest."—*Athenæum.*

Contemporary Science Series, The. Crown 8vo,

Cloth, 3s. 6d. per vol.; Half Morocco, 6s. 6d.

Aryans, The Origin of the. By Dr. Isaac Taylor. With numerous Illustrations.

"The author has accomplished his purpose with a lucidity, carefulness, and comprehensiveness that leave nothing to be desired. No better book on the subject, indeed, is likely to be accessible to the English reader wishing to become informed of the extraordinary changes of doctrine that have taken place during the last nine or ten years in regard to the subject of which it treats."—*Newcastle Leader.*

Criminal, The. Numerous Illustrations. By Havelock Ellis.

"The value of Mr. Ellis's book is that it brings together for the first time in our language, and within brief compass, the result of the scientific investigations that have been made into the characteristics of the criminal, viewed both on the physical and on the moral or intellectual side."—*Scotsman.*

Electricity in Modern Life. By G. W. de Tunzelmann. With 88 Illustrations.

"It is with much pleasure that we call attention to this volume, for the author has very successfully grappled with the difficulty of placing so intricate a subject in a form simple and plain enough to be understood by the ordinary reader. . . . The volume is illustrated by numerous carefully-drawn pictures and diagrams."—*Guardian.*

Evolution and Disease. (135 Illustrations.) By J. Bland Sutton.

"The work is of special value to professional men, yet educated persons generally will find much in it which it is both interesting and important to know."—*The Scottish Weekly.*

Contemporary Science Series—*continued.*

Hypnotism. By Albert Moll.

" The book is a valuable contribution to the science of which it treats."—*Volunteer Service Gazette.*

Manual Training. By Dr. C. M. Woodward, Director of the Manual Training School, Washington University, St. Louis, Mo. Illustrated. [*September.*

Physiognomy and Expression. (Illustrated.) By P. Mantegazza.

" A good, popular treatment of the subject of physiognomy, which should embody the results of recent scientific inquiry, was decidedly a desideratum, and in the volume before us we have the want very adequately met."—*Sheffield Independent.*

Sanity and Insanity. By Charles Mercier, M.B. With Illustrations.

" The author's treatment of his whole subject is masterly, and no reader can glance at it, even superficially, without gaining much information which will certainly be of interest, and may quite possibly be of practical value to him in the relations of life."—*Bradford Observer.*

Sex, The Evolution of. By Professor Patrick Geddes and J. Arthur Thomson. With 90 Illustrations, and about 300 pages.

" A work which, for range and grace, mastery of material, originality, and incisiveness of style and treatment, is not readily to be matched in the long list of books designed more or less to popularise science. . . . The series will be, if it goes on as it has begun, one of the most valuable now current."—*Scottish Leader.*

Village Community, The, in Britain. By G. L. Gomme. Numerous Illustrations.

" His book will probably remain for some time the best work of reference for facts bearing on those traces of the village community which have not been effaced by conquest, encroachment, and the heavy hand of Roman law."—*Scottish Leader.*

Dombey and Son. By Charles Dickens. Crown
8vo, Cloth, 2s.

Descriptive Geometry. By T. H. Eagles, M.A.
Crown 8vo, Cloth, price 3s. 6d.

Fabian Essays in Socialism. Demy 8vo, Paper
Cover, 1s.

German Insurance Laws; or, How they Manage
National Insurance in Germany. By the Rev. W. Moore Ede, M.A. (formerly Lecturer on Political Economy in the University of Cambridge). Crown 8vo. Price One Penny.

Golden Land, The. By Samuel Storey, M.P. Cloth,
Demy 8vo. With numerous Illustrations. Price 3s. 6d.

"If all the literary productions of globe-trotters were like this, we should have no cause for complaint."—*Glasgow Herald.*

Gordon, Life of General. Royal 8vo. Illustrated.
Price 7s. 6d.

Great Writers. Bi-Monthly Shilling Volumes.
Cut or Uncut Edges. A New Series of Critical Biographies. Edited by Professor Eric S. Robertson.

Austen, Jane. By Goldwin Smith.

"Mr. Goldwin Smith has told the simple story of Jane Austen's life and work in a genially appreciative manner that makes it a valuable contribution to our literature."—*Table.*

Balzac. By Frederick Wedmore.

"A finished study, a concentrated summary, a succinct analysis of Balzac's successes and failures, and the causes of these successes and failures, and of the scope of his genius."—*Scottish Leader.*

Browning. By William Sharp.

"This little volume is a model of excellent English, and in every respect it seems to us what a biography should be."—*Public Opinion.*

Byron. By Hon. Roden Noel.

"This is one of the best monographs we have seen concerning the life and works of Byron."—*Volunteer Service Gazette.*

Eliot, George. By Oscar Browning.

"Mr. Browning's book is well written and easily read, whilst the information supplied in it cannot fail to prove attractive to all who take an interest in literature."—*Brechin Advertiser.*

Hawthorne, Nathaniel. By Moncure Conway.

Lessing. By T. W. Rolleston.

"Mr. Rolleston's life of Lessing is a most instructive book, and shows a mastery of his subject."—*Cambridge Independent.*

Milton. By Richard Garnett, LL.D.

"Within equal compass the life-story of the great poet of Puritanism has never been more charmingly or adequately told."—*Scottish Leader.*

Schopenhauer, Arthur. By William Wallace.

Holmes, Oliver Wendell. Crown 8vo, Cloth, gilt
top, 1s. 6d. each.

The Autocrat of the Breakfast-Table.
The Poet at the Breakfast-Table.
The Professor at the Breakfast-Table.

Ibsen's Prose Dramas, in 4 vols. Edited by William Archer. Crown 8vo, Cloth, 3s. 6d. each.

Vol. I.—"A Doll's House," "The League of Youth," and "The Pillars of Society."

Vol. II.—"Ghosts," "An Enemy of the People," and "The Wild Duck."

Vol. III.—"Lady Inger of Östråt," "The Vikings at Helgeland," and "The Pretenders."

"Mr. Archer's translations are in every way admirable."—*Graphic.*

Ingraham, Rev. J. Crown 8vo, Cloth, 2s.

The Throne of David.
The Pillar of Fire.

Imitation of Christ, The. Square 8vo, Cloth, 1s.

Uniform with Canterbury Poets.

Impressions of Russia. By Dr. Georg Brandes. (With Portrait of the Author.) 353 pages, Crown 8vo, price 2s. 6d. Uniform with Count Tolstoi's works.

"Dr. Brandes has had exceptionable advantages for studying the land and the people, and his book supplies much interesting information about a country of which less is known than of most European nations."—*Brechin Advertiser.*

Kreutzer Sonata, and Family Happiness. By Count Tolstoi. Crown 8vo, 2s. 6d. Half Polished Morocco, gilt top, 5s.

Music of the Poets, The : A Musicians' Birthday Book. Edited by Eleonore D'Esterre-Keeling. Quarto, Cloth Elegant; Emblematic Design on Cover; Gilt edges, 6s. May be had in a variety of Fancy Bindings.

"A Musicians' Birthday Book is one of those happy ideas that seem to have been yearning for fulfilment; now that it is realised every one asks why we should have had to wait so long for it. Certainly not for lack of conscious straining after novelty. Season after season there have appeared too manifest efforts to depart from the formal diary with poetic quotations of more or less appositeness; yet it was left for Eleonore D'Esterre Keeling to draw upon the great storehouse of personal interest and romance in music. The birthday book she publishes is a really beautiful production. Against a certain number of the days there are set only lines from the poets, these being chosen for their relation to musical subjects; but against others we find bars of music enclosing a suggestive theme. The music quotations are rendered doubly interesting by being, in a number of instances, fac-simile productions of the composers' manuscript. . . . The book ought to have a place in every music stand."—*Scottish Leader.*

Mysteries and Adventures. By A. Conan Doyle.
Square 8vo, Paper Cover, 1s. *(In the Novocastrian Series.*

"The collection can be most cordially recommended to all who like sensational stories when told with skill."—*Yorkshire Post.*

Scott's Border Antiquities of Scotland and England.
Royal Folio. Half Morocco antique, £5, 5s.

Sevastopol. By Count Tolstoï. Crown 8vo, 2s. 6d.
Half Polished Morocco, gilt top, 5s.

"The pictures are as vivid and interesting as anything to be found in 'War and Peace,' and they are like nothing else in literature."—*Scotsman.*

Stanley and Africa. By author of "Life of General Gordon." Illustrated. Crown 8vo, Cloth gilt, 2s. 6d.; also imperial 8vo, Cloth gilt, 10s. 6d.

"The book is distinctly interesting all through. It should be in every town and village library."—*Derbyshire Gazette.*

The Elixir of Long Life, and other Stories. By Honoré Balzac. Paper Cover, 1s.

The Land of Sunshine and Gold. By E. Towers.
Crown 8vo, Cloth, price 3s. 6d. Illustrated.

Uncle Toby's Birthday Book. Cloth, 16mo, 1s.

Vanity Fair. By W. M. Thackeray. Crown 8vo, Cloth, 2s.

BY OLIVER WENDELL HOLMES.

The Autocrat of
the Breakfast-Table.

The Poet at
the Breakfast-Table.

The Professor at
the Breakfast-Table.

Reduced fac simile of HOLMES and LANDOR.

3 *Vols., Crown 8vo, Cloth, Gilt Top, in Shell Case.   Price 4s. 6d.*

3 *Vols., Crown 8vo, Cloth, Gilt Top, in Cloth Pedestal Case, 5s.*

The Vols. may be had separately at 1s. 6d. each.

Also in Half Polished Morocco, Gilt Top, Antique.

UNIFORM WITH ABOVE.

SELECTIONS FROM LANDOR (in 3 Vols.):—

1 IMAGINARY CONVERSATIONS.

2 PENTAMERON.

3 PERICLES AND ASPASIA.

London : WALTER SCOTT, 24 Warwick Lane, Paternoster Row.